OWNED

Blood Ties Series

A.K ROSE

ATLAS ROSE

For the defiant woman in all of us...who secretly yearns for a basement of our own.

Warning

The Bloodties Series is part of the Cosa Nostra, mafia world which contains several interconnected series. The tone is **dark**, involves a number of romantic interests for our female main characters and reader discretion is advised.

More information on the content warnings can be found here.

Please be aware of your own triggers and limitations. This is a Mafia/Gang related world and are not heroes or heroines, they are hungry, ruthless and they do bad things to themselves and to others.

If you're okay with this, please read on. I hope you enjoy this darkly rich, forbidden series. I can't wait to bring you *so much more....*

Listen along to the playlist here on Spotify

ONE

Vivienne

I STARED AT THE CONTRACT...AND THE WORDS TYPED IN bold font.

Interim right to possess/use:

1. *No physical part of the party may interfere with the subject. These acts include, but are not limited to:*

1.1. The insertion of extremities into any part of the subject, including party/ies' penis/es, fingers, or tongues for the party/ies' personal use and enjoyment, until such time as the party/ies have been awarded full ownership of the subject by The Order.

Until that time, the subject shall remain the property of The Order and will be subjected to random physical examinations to ensure compliance by all parties involved.

Failure to comply with this shall terminate this preliminary contract between London St. James and The Order and will result in immediate action against the party/ies and the removal of the subject. This shall remain solely at The Order's discretion and removal of the subject and termination of this contract may be initiated at any time by The Order.

He couldn't touch me.

The words swam.

*The subject...*me. My body, my soul...my entire being reduced to being the *'vessel'* they'd created. One to be used by anyone they saw fit, to be probed, fucked, or used in the most degrading, possessive ways by the *'party/parties'*. The words blurred in front of me—just not by London St. James, by the looks of it.

The thud of footsteps grew louder, making me jerk my gaze to the study door. I hurried, shoved the contract under the leatherbound journal, and stepped backwards as the door of the study opened and London St. James walked in. Heat licked between my thighs at the sight of him, heat and fear that gripped me tightly.

I hated him.

How he controlled me.

How he *consumed me.*

How he looked so fucking perfect in his tailored slacks and open-collared white shirt. He moved, sounded, and felt just like a man. But London St. James was no man, not one with a soul, at least. That cold, callous gaze found me instantly, before he shifted his focus to the desk and closed the door.

"You bastard."

He said nothing, just moved closer.

"Did you hear me?" I snapped, hating how he was so fucking controlled, while I...I felt like I was coming apart on the inside. *"I said—"*

"I heard you the first time, Vivienne."

I licked my lips, still feeling the bruise his mouth had left behind. But the bruise was *nothing* compared to the terror he'd put me through...the terror of releasing the one person who could save me from this hell.

Ryth consumed my mind, from the first time I'd seen her when she was dragged into The Order, held down, and branded just like me, to the moment we'd both tried to escape.

Only, she had escaped, hadn't she? Helped by the devil in front of me and his men, men he called *sons*. And he made sure I knew Ryth's survival depended on my obedience...and that of her father, Jack Castlemaine.

He'd let Ryth and her brothers run, given them a car with money and guns, and had his men watch them until they'd reached the city limits. Then they'd taken Jack who knows where to be locked up and guarded, while he'd dragged me back here. To this...*this...this fucking house.* His house.

I wanted to burn it down, to destroy his home in the most brutal fucking way while he stood there and watched. I wanted to decimate his world. My focus moved to his mouth, to those unforgiving lips, and that ache between my legs pulsed harder. Just as long as he kissed me while I was doing it. He stepped closer, then stopped at the edge of the desk, his gaze fixed on the white corner of the contract peeking out from under the journal where I'd frantically tried to shove it back.

He pushed the corner of the journal, exposing more of the contract until his signature was revealed. "I see you've found something to occupy your time."

"Fuck you."

He met my stare, those dark eyes glinting.

"Fuck you all the way to hell." I stepped closer. "You can't touch me, can't fuck me...can't do a damn thing."

The tight curl of his lips made me tremble.

"Take me to Jack," I demanded, jutting my chin in the air. "Take me, or..."

"*Or?*" he repeated, only when he said the word, it made me stop, my thoughts racing. "Go on, *or what?*"

"Or...or I'll make your life a living fucking hell."

Something moved in those dark eyes. He moved fast, closing the distance between us and striking out to grab me softly around the throat. "And what makes you think you don't already?"

My breath caught.

My pulse raced.

There was a second where there was a flicker of torture, one carefully hidden behind the mask, before it was gone once more, leaving the heartless stare of the monster behind. His grip shifted, his thumb slowly stroking the vein in my neck. Was he thinking of choking me, or biting me like a goddamn vampire?

I couldn't stop my racing heart, feeling it kick with his touch. He knew it...he *felt it*. A twitch came at the corner of his mouth, and all of a sudden, I was burning up, fevered by the feel of his hand. *Oh, Jesus...no.*

A hard knock came on the study door, shattering the moment. When he dropped his hand, I reached out and grasped the corner of the desk to steady myself. Deep breaths consumed me as he turned and strode away. *Snap the fuck out of it...there is no way this can—*

He opened the door and I caught a flash of platinum blond hair before the low growl of his son slipped in. "He's here."

A nod. "Show him in."

Show who in? I tried to gather myself, tried to find that burning rage that seemed to be so goddamn fleeting whenever the motherfucker touched me. Footsteps echoed and I tracked the sound as it came closer and a man I'd never seen before stepped in...carrying a small black doctor's bag.

London closed the door behind the guy, not once meeting my gaze.

"Who the fuck is this?" I demanded. "What's going on?"

"Something I should've done the moment I brought you here," London replied...*but that was all he offered.*

Fucking nothing.

I stared at the stranger, at the same unflinching goddamn stare, and I knew instantly he was *one of them*, the kind of man who called me a *'vessel'*. I wasn't a person to them. I wasn't real.

"Sit," London commanded, motioning to his chair.

But I didn't move, not until he turned to meet my gaze. Clasps snapped open before the doctor pulled items out of his bag.

"Vivienne..." London urged, those eyes sparking. "We can either drug you and knock you out to do this, or you can cooperate. It's up to you."

My heart was thudding, the sound loud in my ears. I knew this scenario, I'd been here before. I lowered my gaze to the sterile dressings the stranger had pulled out and placed on London's desk. "Are you going to mark me?" I met my captor's stare.

"No," he answered, stepping closer. "You've been fitted with a tracking device from The Order. I want it out of you."

That heavy booming in my chest sped. "You do?"

He gave a slow nod, then turned to sink into the chair like a dog slinking back to its cruel master.

I understood now who the stranger was...a doctor.

"Those things are usually just under the skin on the underside of the arm." The doctor's cheeks reddened as he tried not to meet my gaze. But no doctor from The Order I'd known was embarrassed about anything they did.

So, this wasn't one of their men...

"You'll need to remove your blouse," he urged.

I held London's stare. "I got it the first time," I muttered, my fingers moving to my buttons, opening them before I shrugged the garment free and placed it on the desk in front of me. The awkward doctor's eyes widened at the caramel lace bra. The lace left gaps, enough for a glimpse of my nipple to peek through. The doctor glanced away, embarrassed again.

"Where the fuck did you find this kid, London?" I asked. "What kind of game are you playing here?"

The monster in front of me said nothing as the awkward idiot beside me gripped my wrist and lifted my arm. I stretched high, giving the hesitant doctor all the access he wanted. But I saw the twitch in London's steely stare. He liked my questioning, almost as much as he liked watching this guy run his fingers down the underside of my arm.

"Maybe it's in the other one," the doctor muttered.

I stretched my other arm up as London watched from behind the desk. The doctor's fingers skimmed, pressing and probing.

"Hmm," he murmured, drawing my focus back to him as he ran his hand along my arm for the fourth time. "I can't seem to find it."

My stomach clenched. "Maybe I don't have one?"

"Impossible," London answered as he stood and stepped closer. His icy resolve was thawing right before my eyes. Deep creases furrowed his brow and those hard lips tightened. "It has to be there."

The young idiot just shook his head, panic flaring as he frantically searched my other arm. I tried to remember the moments after my robot foster parents dragged me to The Order and left me behind. I'd kicked and fought, screaming until my voice was hoarse, and even now I could still feel the burn.

But my battle had been short-lived as they covered my mouth with a rag, knocking me out.

When I came to, I was different, tied down on a table, my head swimming with whatever they'd given me, and a burning below my navel where they'd tattooed me. I'd hurt everywhere in the days and weeks that followed. I still hurt, only this pain was different. This pain I used for rage. I couldn't remember a cut under my arm, but that didn't mean there wasn't one.

"It's not here." The doctor shook his head.

"It *is.*" London leaned over the desk, glaring. "Find it."

I winced at the idiot's bruising grip as he probed and dug, grinding muscle against bone. I clenched my jaw and looked away, refusing to allow him to see my pain.

"Maybe it's somewhere else on her body?"

I flinched and jerked my gaze back. "What?"

But the doctor didn't speak to me. It was like I wasn't in the room at all. He just shifted his stare from London to my breasts.

"Can you work around her bra?" London growled.

"It'd be easier..."

There was a flare of London's jaw. "Take it off, Vivienne."

I flinched. He wasn't serious...*fuck you...*

Asshole.

I held his stare, lowered my arms, and reached around my back. He didn't like this. He didn't like this at all. I took at least a little comfort in that as I unhooked my bra and let it fall.

"If she could stand."

I jerked my gaze to the asshole beside me. "*She* is right fucking here," I snapped, then shoved upwards, turned, and lifted my arms until I pushed my breasts toward his face. "Is this better? Does this give you *everything you need, doctor?*"

My rage was more for London than this idiot just following orders. But I couldn't stop it from spilling out. I narrowed in on the doctor as he glanced at my breasts then looked away, and London's icy stare burned hotter on the side of my face, like his own personal brand. The bastard may as well tattoo me too and be done with it.

He didn't like this, didn't like another man touching me, even if it was at his own insistence.

The doctor paled as he cupped my breast, his thumb grazing my nipple before it pressed against the underside. "Is this what you need?" I asked again, softening my tone until the tension in the room *seethed*.

Good.

I wanted London as volatile as I could get him as the young, good-looking doctor cupped my breast. "You're cute," I murmured. "Do you live around here?"

"Vivienne..."

The warning was savage. I turned and met his gaze. "Yes?"

London's jaw clenched, flaring the muscles as the doctor felt along the underside of my breast and stopped. Pain followed as he pushed, sharp, piercing. "Ouch."

"Sorry," the kid muttered, glancing at London. "I think I found it."

"Then get it out," my captor forced through clenched teeth.

The young doctor almost looked excited as he motioned. "You'll need to lie down."

"Fine." I turned and sat on the end of London's desk, then lay down, stretching my hands high over my head.

Heat moved between us as London stared down at me splayed out across his paperwork. I lifted my foot, searching for purchase, and kicked out, driving the mouse of his Mac across the room to clatter against the wall. "*Oops.*"

His eye twitched and his bloodless lips pressed together as cold splashed the underside of my breast.

"This is going to sting," the kid cautioned.

"When doesn't it?" I answered, holding London's stare.

I didn't cry out when the needle entered, biting down as the pinch roared through my breast. Still the monster above me didn't look away. Not even when the dull pressure came and a tiny *tink* hit the desk beside me.

"It's out," the doctor said, pleased.

"Good." London met his stare, then gave a nod.

Euphoria filled me at the loss of The Order's control. Until the pressure came once more, only this time sharper, deeper. I jerked my gaze to the doctor, who had his head bent, focused on what he was doing. Then I made a mistake and looked down.

He was pushing in something else...something that looked an awful lot like what he'd just pulled out of me. "What the fuck are you doing?"

He didn't answer.

I jerked my focus to London. "What the fuck is he doing, London?"

Those bloodless lips curled and that possessive glimmer shone once more.

"You *piece of fucking shit*," I growled as a tug came under my breast.

Once.

Twice.

"It's done," the kid declared as he lifted his gaze, proud of himself. Until he met my savage glare.

"Get the fuck *off* me." I shoved his hand away and scurried from London's desk, stumbling backwards.

"Thank you, Leon," London murmured, his focus fixed on me. "You may leave."

The kid just nodded. "Okay, sure."

He moved fast as he bundled his scalpel and swabs back into their container and shoved it back into his bag before heading to the door. Then stopped, his hand on the door handle. "My payment."

"Carven will see to it on your way out."

A nod and the kid just left, fumbling his way out of the study and slamming the door behind him with a *bang*.

I just glared at London.

Hating him.

Craving him.

"This was your plan all along, wasn't it?"

He held my hate and didn't once look away.

I made no move to cover myself, just stood there inhaling the sharp scent of the alcohol used to clean the wound, while my breast throbbed and ached. One he lowered his gaze to. "Vivienne..."

"Save it," I snarled. "Or you know what? How about you *ram it instead, London? Right up your fucking ass.*"

I snatched my blouse and bra from the desk, then marched for the door. I refused to allow the tears to come, refused to acknowledge the blur as I yanked the door open and strode along the hallway.

He followed, just like I'd known he would, making sure his property didn't do anything rash like throw herself off the fucking stairs. God knows *that* would be an inconvenience for him. The hallway was a blur as I headed toward the low drone of voices before a thud and a click came from the front door.

Carven turned and watched me as I cut across the foyer. His gaze fixed to my breasts that jiggled as I moved. "Nice," he muttered, then licked his lips.

"Fuck you, too." I snapped as I strode past then up the stairs. "*Fuck all of you.*"

Movement came from the top of the stairs as I climbed. The other twin watched as I gripped the banister and took the stairs two at a time until I strode past to my bedroom. He said nothing as I shoved open my cell door and spun.

London climbed the last stair and headed for my bedroom before he stopped.

Tears shimmered in my eyes.

But they weren't tears of pain or sadness.

They were of uncontrollable rage.

I clenched my fists, refusing him entry.

The sting of betrayal mingled with the dull ache of my breast that felt like the controlling grip of a hand—*his hand.*

But London St. James just stood there, staring, then lowered his gaze to my breast. "I'll be back later to dress your wound."

I curled my lips, baring my teeth, and growled. "Touch me and I'll claw your fucking eyes out."

He gave a careful nod. "You can try," he murmured. "But I think you'll find—"

I didn't wait for him to finish, just took a step backwards, grabbed the door...and slammed it in his face.

TWO

London

Bang!

She slammed the door.

My own goddamn door...

In my own *fucking* house.

Right in my face.

That nerve jumped at the edge of my eye. I swung my gaze to the sons' room, then remembered they'd just left. That's right. Jesus, get it together. Just leave and let her fucking seethe. I headed for the stairs. My jaw was clenched, biting down on the anger.

Defiant. Fucking. Brat.

I should go back in there.

I should go back in there and—

I stopped three stairs down and turned to glare at her doorway. *Force her back to that bed and underneath me where she belongs.*

Her breasts jiggled in my mind, those tight, dusty pink nipples puckering as she raged. But that would only hurt her more. I'd open up that incision under the swell of her breast from where the young med student had implanted *my* tracker chip. Still, I wanted to...*touch her.*

Harsh breaths moved through me. My body and mind were at war, fighting the urge to both take care of her and throttle the ever-loving fuck out of her. The woman was a goddamn menace. A pain in my ass....*so why the hell was I so goddamn addicted?*

My cock kicked at the memory of her lying spread out on my desk, arms raised over her head, that challenge in her eyes. My lips turned dry. I licked them, staring at the glossy gray paint of her door, rage rippling behind it. I knew she was standing there, hating me. My pulse sped at the thought. Was she waiting to be taught a lesson? Was she waiting for me to take her downstairs and show her exactly how far her goddamn antics were going to get her here?

My balls clenched and that delicious ache spread along my shaft, tingling at the head. A pulse, and I knew a drop eased from the aching eye, wetting my fucking boxers. Christ, she made me want to fist myself like a goddamn teenager to relieve the tension. She made me want to take it all out on her body.

I'd never wanted to fuck so bad.

Still, I forced myself to turn and keep moving, making my way downstairs. Vivienne Evans was a piece of this game, nothing more, nothing less. I provided safety, a roof over her head, food for her to eat, and clothes for her to wear. I provide all those things to maintain her compliance. If I couldn't obtain that with the protection I gave her—then I'd take it by fear.

She was starting to understand that. If not now, then she would soon enough. I grabbed my phone and typed out a message to my security detail:

> Make sure she doesn't leave, under any circumstances.

I made my way to the garage. *Fuck, these last few days had been a goddamn mess.* A pang cut across my chest, making me massage the hard knot of muscles at the back of my neck. I was too old for this shit. I'd give myself a goddamn heart attack if I wasn't careful. I grabbed the keys inside the door, pressed the button on the sleek gunmetal gray Audi, and climbed in, fighting the urge to pull up her bedroom camera on my phone and watch her.

She was probably still standing there, glaring at the door. Or was she crying?

No.

A woman like Vivienne didn't allow herself to break down. She swallowed her rage, unleashing it the moment you weren't prepared. I needed to be careful around her. The woman was unpredictable, vengeful even. A curl came at the corner of my mouth. I was playing with fire when it came to her, and Christ, I smelled smoke everywhere. All it'd take would be a breath of air to ignite her, but I wouldn't allow her that, would I?

No, I'd tighten my control. I had put my own goddamn tracker in her.

I'd watch her day and night.

I'd make sure she knew she was *owned.*

I hit the button on the garage door, shoved the car into gear, and pulled out of the garage, accelerating past the two guards I had patrolling the grounds. They weren't the sons, but they'd do until Colt and Carven returned, they couldn't be too far away. I wanted to get to the storage yard and back before they returned. I couldn't take the risk of having her alone when they were there. Not after the meet and greet the other night in my study.

They were trigger happy at the best of times. One confrontational remark from her and they'd probably snap. Jesus, is this what it was like to live with a house of teenagers? Always belligerent, ungrateful, and highly-fucking-strung.

Ryth and her goddamn brothers had been a close call. If I'd allowed her to be taken, or worse...*killed*, I'd never get close to the real player here...I'd never get close to *King*. That was what drove me, the need to find him.

I pulled out onto the street and turned my attention to the phone beside me. A nagging feeling worked its way under my skin...*her*. She was fast becoming a problem for me. Consuming my focus...making me react in ways I couldn't afford.

My hands clenched around the wheel. What I really wanted was them around her throat. One at least, while I explored her body with the other. The memory of the other night came roaring back, her on the bed, the towel wrapped around her, gaping at her thighs.

"Christ," I snarled, my pulse thrumming. I jerked the wheel, pulling the car over to the side of the road.

I didn't have time for this. I didn't have time for *her*.

But I couldn't stop myself as I reached for my phone, opened my apps, and pulled up the feed on the camera in her room. I watched her pace the floor of her bedroom with a look of pure rage on her face. She was dressed again, her blouse anyway, her full breasts swaying as she moved, making me goddamn stare. In an instant, I was mesmerized, watching her. Just like I always watched her.

At first, I'd told myself it was to ensure her safety...

Weeks later, I was still here...torturing myself. She stopped pacing and lifted her gaze to the camera. But it wasn't the dummy one I had installed in the corner of her room. It was the real one, discreetly tucked away at the head of her bed. I didn't know how she'd found it. The damn thing was almost impossible to see. But she saw it now, coming closer until her face filled the screen of my phone, her deep brown eyes commanding, her wild fucking hair unleashed, the kind I wanted to fist and pull taut.

There was an intense look of concentration on her face before the camera blurred with her fingers. Then the image shook, zooming right into those eyes as she pulled the damn thing out. I let out a snarl. Fucking thing cost me over five thousand dollars...that she now threw to the floor.

"Don't you *fucking dare*—" I snarled as the darkness drove down...

Then there was nothing.

I stared at the dead feed.

"*Goddamnit,*" I yelled as I switched feeds and watched her from another as she straightened, flicked her hair back indignantly, and turned away.

"Pain in my goddamn ass," I growled as I lowered my phone.

But I couldn't end the view, not yet. I just shifted my gaze to the flow of traffic in front of me, then looked again, hating how I still fucking wanted her. More now than ever.

I shoved the car into gear and pulled out, heading to the on-ramp that'd take me clear across the city and past the seedy clubs Killion and his chumps frequented. The news of the attorney's death had caused a shockwave through the elite. There were a lot of federal court judges and high-end attorneys very nervous right now.

Of course, they had no idea who'd committed the heinous act.

The police assumed it'd been a former client and right now they were scouring the thousands of sick assholes he'd locked up over the years, never once considering *he* was the sick asshole that'd been the cause of it all. There'd been no camera feed to investigate, no fingerprints of Ryth or her brothers left behind. For all Intents and purposes, there'd been nothing for the police to go on.

The sons made sure of that, sending in a very discreet cleaning crew, one I'd paid handsomely.

The killing had been brutal.

And expected.

I pushed the Audi harder, moving through the traffic on the highway, my mind returning to the last moments with Ryth and her brothers. One bargaining chip was crucial to gain access to King, but two? Two would shift the power to me. If I couldn't have Ryth, then I'd have her father.

As long as he gave me what I wanted.

Because I wouldn't give him a choice.

I drove to the discreet white storage facility nestled in a quiet commercial area, and pulled up in front of the entrance. *Precision Storage* said the signage out front. *No Vacancy*, it had underneath. I opened my window, leaned out and punched in the code, then waited for the heavy steel gate to roll open. The sign said no vacancy because it wasn't built for business, not the normal kind anyway.

Rolls of razor wire ran along the top of the surrounding fenceline. CCTV cameras were fitted throughout the grounds, watching every inch of the facility. It kept *my* business...

I drove through the gate, pulled up in the empty parking lot, and parked. The steel gate rolled closed as I climbed out. I checked the streets, making sure no one drove past, then turned and made my way toward the main building, nodding at one of my men as he stepped into view around the corner.

Armed security.

Razor wire.

State-of-the-art security.

Still it wasn't enough.

I reached up and massaged the tight muscles at the back of my neck. It wasn't anywhere near secure enough, not when it came to the kind of men I was making a move against. Haelstrom Hale wasn't just ruthlessly powerful, he was also unpredictable as fuck.

I pressed my thumb against the sensor, waited for the heavy steel door to unlock, glanced at the small window of bullet-proof glass they spied through then pushed it open and stepped into the cool, air-conditioned foyer.

"Mr. St. James." The guard rose from behind the desk.

"How is he?"

"Quiet," the mercenary answered. "A little too quiet."

He was surprised at that, but I wasn't. "Good."

I made my way along the hallway, past the other locked doors, to a room further in the back of the building. I pressed my thumb against the sensor and waited for the *thunk* of the lock before I opened the door and pushed through.

He was waiting for me, just like I knew he would be. I scanned the open space. It was big, almost as big as any apartment. A microwave and a jug sat in a small kitchenette and a bathroom showed off the open-area bedroom. There were no walls in this space, no privacy either. But after being in prison, I was sure Jack Castlemaine was used to that.

He didn't move, sitting at the small round table with last week's newspaper open in front of him. He was given limited access to the outside world. A man like Jack was resourceful, to say the least...which was the only reason he was still alive.

I glanced at the white bandage peeking out from the collar of his shirt. He'd suffered a number of injuries, the worst was a bullet wound, but after the shootout at the abandoned warehouses, it was lucky any of us were still alive, least of all him.

"I see you're making use of your time." I motioned to the spread-out clippings beside him.

He didn't answer, just kept busy with the task at hand.

I didn't like that...

"I hope your accommodations are—"

"Where is my daughter?" he asked, not bothering to lift his head.

I stopped at the edge of the table and looked down at the man. "Safe."

Only then did he meet my gaze. "I don't believe you."

I gave a chuff and searched his gaze, picking the man apart before I reached into my pocket, drew out my phone, and pressed the programmed number. He didn't look away, not even when the sound of ringing came through the speaker as I placed the phone on the table. It took a long time for her to answer... puffing and panting when she barked. "Yes...*yes, I'm here.*"

"It took a while," I murmured. "I hope we weren't disturbing you?"

A flush broke out on her father's cheeks.

He didn't like the idea of his daughter fucking three men, least of all her stepbrothers. Oh, the scandal. But Jack Castlemaine should know that isn't the worst thing that could happen to a daughter...least of all his.

"No," Ryth gasped, swallowing her breaths.

I opened my mouth to speak, but her father leaned forward and cut me off. "Are you safe?"

"Dad?" Surprised delight filled her voice. "Yeah, we're safe."

He closed his eyes, breathing hard. "Good...where are—"

I reached out, pressed the icon, and ended the call. Anger flared as he opened his eyes, meeting mine. "You bastard."

I just smiled, plucked my phone from the table, and slid it back into my pocket. "Tell me where he is?"

Jack stilled, his eyes narrowing. "You know this is not going to work, right?"

I leaned forward, bracing my hand on the edge of the table. "*Never,* isn't a word in my vocabulary, Jack. Not when it comes to me getting what I want. Now, I'm going to ask you again...*where is he?*"

Jack inhaled, then released his breath. "Benjamin will come. He'll be looking for me. What will you do then, London? Are you going to play The Order on one side and battle the Mafia on the other?"

That fucking nerve beside my eye came back with a vengeance, twitching and pulsing. "If I have to. Now, where is King?" I leaned over him. "Tell me how to get to him."

But the bastard didn't flinch. "You and I know that's not going to happen. If he wanted any kind of contact with you, he would've already reached out. You won't get near him." His voice softened. "No matter how many of his daughters you control."

I slowly straightened. "He will if he wants them back." I glanced at the newspaper clippings, seeing what interested the man. I'd spent a lifetime finding out what makes people tick. One look at Jack and I knew he was going to be a hard nut to crack.

But I would... I had time.

And his goddamn daughter.

A slow nod, and I headed for the door. My hand was on the handle when he spoke.

"She'll hate you, you know that, right?" I stilled. "It won't matter what you do, or why...she'll hate you regardless."

That nerve just...wouldn't...fucking...quit. "It doesn't matter what she thinks." My mind returned to Vivienne. "She means nothing."

"You just keep telling yourself that," he sneered.

I yanked the door open and strode out, checking that it locked securely, leaving Jack's words dying in the room behind me. My pulse sped as I made my way back to the front door. He was wrong. So very fucking wrong—

Pulse.

Pulse.

Pulse...

I pressed my finger against the twitch, then shoved the door open, leaving it to slam hard behind me.

22

Vivienne meant nothing to me. Nothing more than a chess piece to play...nothing more than a pawn in my goddamn game...and I was going to prove it.

THREE

Vivienne

"Oww." I STOPPED PACING THE LENGTH OF MY BEDROOM and looked down, gently pulling out my blouse to see the crimson stain. "*Sonofabitch.*"

I tenderly cupped my breast, wincing. The pain was a dull, aching throb. But that was nothing compared to the sting of his betrayal. I should've known...should've *not* expected anything different from him. "Stupid...*stupid goddamn idiot.*"

I did feel like an idiot.

He made me feel like that.

Like I was so fucking weak and gullible.

And for a second I was, wasn't I?

Carried away by the fantasy of London being anything other than a cruel, controlling piece of shit. I glanced at the shattered camera ground into the plush carpet. Obsessive, *lying* bastard. I clenched my fists. Destroying the camera wasn't enough. It wasn't *anywhere* near enough. I wanted to tear his goddamn house apart and ruin his life until he made the decision to let me go.

Just like he'd let Ryth go.

I carefully pressed my hand against the wound, then looked at the smear. Burning anger crackled inside me. I'd make him want to get rid of me. I could do it, too. I'd had a lifetime of being shut down, locked away, smothered, and not wanted. I flinched. That hurt more than any goddamn cut under my breast. I lowered my hand to the tattoo on my abdomen.

Not wanted.

Just *used*.

But I wasn't going to be used anymore. I wasn't going to wear red. Not anymore. I was done allowing others to control me. I strode to the door and yanked it open. Fear trembled through me as I stepped out into the hallway.

I searched the foyer, finding silence. It wasn't too late for me to run. I'd find Ryth and her brothers. Or, hell, I'd be on my own if it came to that. No one to *not want me* anymore.

London could keep his tracker in me for all I cared. He could watch me on the cameras day and night as well, as long as I was far away from The Order. As I headed for the stairs, that fear turned back to anger. Silence filled the air, but I knew I wasn't alone. I knew there were men out there watching me, making sure I didn't do anything stupid, like try to run.

I made my way to the kitchen. The thought of cutting that *thing* out of myself and leaving his *pathetic* ass behind rose until I pushed it away. I wouldn't get a foot outside the house before the guards got me. Besides, I had Ryth to think about.

Her safety, and her freedom were at the sacrifice of mine, and London made sure I knew that, even if she wasn't aware. If she'd known, there was no way she would've run without me. I knew that.

We had a connection, one I'd felt the moment I stepped into her room that night at The Order. I knew we'd be friends. I *knew* we'd be allies. I needed that now more than ever.

I made my way around the dark stone kitchen counter, dragging my fingers along the surface, leaving a smear behind, then headed back to his study. Now that I was alone, I wanted to see what other secrets London St. James held.

The fact he'd been watching me for years was goddamn creepy, but it was the *why* that plagued me. Why me? What could I possibly give him? I was no one. Just a pain in everyone's ass, shoved from a controlling girls' home to foster parents who hated me. I walked back along the hallway, stopped at the study door, and pushed the handle.

But it was locked, the tiny sensor light glowing red. "Figures." I turned and scanned the walls, then lifted my gaze to search for the cameras I now knew were planted all through this house, just like he'd planted them in that bastard Killion's house.

God, this shit was crazy.

Kidnapping.

Murder.

Trafficking.

So much trafficking.

These men weren't just dangerous—they were filthy rich, too. I gave up trying to understand any of it. Now, I was just trying to survive. "And find a goddamn way out of this."

I left the study behind, made my way past the kitchen, and turned, making my way into the most stunning formal dining room I'd ever seen. A massive branch hung suspended over the long, elegant table. One made of the most sensational array of small white lights I'd ever seen. It sparkled, even without being switched on. Black, red, and gray consumed the space from the plush leather seats, gleaming glass table top, and gorgeous red flowers. The colors were muted and murky behind dark, closed blinds.

I left the room behind and headed back to the kitchen, stopping at the one door that made me catch my breath. The lock glowed red. I didn't need to reach out to know that the way downstairs to the basement was barred. Still, I felt myself reach out and test the handle, fighting an acute surge of desire.

Thump.

The lock held. Part of me was thankful, the other part...*the dangerous part,* wasn't. I turned away, fighting that battle inside and headed for the stairs, glancing at the door to the garage before I climbed the stairs. Locked doors, rules and control. I felt like I was going crazy here...I *would* go crazy here if I didn't get out, and soon.

I stopped at the landing on the second floor, my focus turning to his bedroom. I half expected an electric lock on his door, just like the one he had on mine. But there wasn't any. I moved without thinking, making my way closer, excitement thrumming in my veins.

I swallowed hard as I glanced over my shoulder. I hated how I felt like a damn child, then I turned back, twisted the handle of his bedroom door, and stepped in. His scent hit me like a rag pressed against my face. I froze, hard breaths sawing, which only seemed to make it worse.

I stared into the gloom. Even in the middle of the day, the room was pitch black. Closed off from the world with electronic blackout shutters, it spoke a lot of the man. "Cold and callous, that's what."

My steps were soundless as I moved toward his bed. But I stopped at the edge and stared down. I couldn't move, couldn't bring myself to touch, couldn't do a damn thing. Looking at the soft gray velvet covering invoked the same reaction as that leather bench in that room in the basement.

Fear gripped me.

Fear like I'd never felt before.

My pulse was booming, breaths panting.

The room started to spin. I turned and raced for the door, leaving the heady scent of him behind. *Bang!* I slammed the bedroom door behind me. My hand trembled gripping the handle as I stared at the landing before I forced myself to move. My knees shook, making me grip the banister for strength. *Jesus,* I thought I was going to pass out.

How the hell can a damn bedroom affect me like that?

How the hell can *he* affect me like that?

My mind spun.

And my pussy throbbed.

I needed to get a handle on this.

I needed to get some *control.*

I needed—I ground my teeth—my anger. That's what I needed, my rage. That throb at my breast invaded, making me lift my hand and cup the swell. Hissing at the sting, I climbed until I came to my floor once more. But I wasn't done with my vengeance. I wasn't anywhere *near* done.

A memory invaded. A sound outside my bedroom door, followed by the shuffle of steps.

The sons...

I know you're there. I can hear you breathing. My own voice echoed back to me, followed by the quiet, husky response of a man. *Can you?*

Can you?

Can...you?

"Yes, I could, motherfucker," I snarled and headed along the hallway past my room until it sank into the gloom. "I could."

There were three doors. Two opposite and one at the end. I chose that one, pushing the handle and shoving it open. The door hit against the wall with a *boom*. I stepped in and scanned the sparse bedroom. The king-sized bed was unmade, the mattress brand new. The bedroom had been lived in. The walk-in closet door was open, showing the faint outline of clothes hanging inside.

I made my way over, flicked on the light, and stared at the space. A black leather jacket, a motorcycle helmet. Expensive shoes were still in the box and it looked like three brand new black tuxedos still wrapped in plastic were pushed to the back.

The room looked like one that was supposed to be lived in, but it wasn't. The things here were forgotten, or stowed away like they weren't important. There was nothing here for me. I walked out, closed the door behind me, and turned to the door on the right.

A turn of the handle and I stepped into the bathroom. Porcelain gleamed when I switched on the light and glass sparkled. Two plush black towels hung from the towel rack and an array of expensive men's cologne and skin care bottles sat between two basins. Body wash and shampoo waited in the shower stall, but I turned and left, leaving the door open this time, as I faced the last unexplored room.

This had to be one of their rooms. Where the other one lived, I wasn't sure. I stepped up, turned the handle, and pushed open the door. Darkness and the heady scent of pain and sweat swallowed me in an instant, rocking me.

"Oh," I groaned as I breathed deep, then bowed my head.

My body clenched and tightened, warming, making me fucking hate them even more. I forced myself into the room, then reached and flicked on the light. But the light wasn't brilliant, the low glow filled the room just enough to spill across the two single beds against the wall on either side.

But it wasn't just the beds that made me stop and stare. "What the fuck?" I moved toward the one hugging the wall on the far side of the room. The black comforter was pulled up neat as a pin, the pillow indented in the middle. Steel gleamed, lying across the middle of the bed.

What the hell was this?

I leaned down and fingered the thick straps and steel shackles. They were almost the same as the ones downstairs in the basement, the ones London had threatened me with before. But these were wider and thicker, stitched in Velcro as well as the metal clasps. My mind raced, imagining the twins here. Was it the cruel blond asshole? Or the quiet one...

My mind raced as I turned and took in the rest of the room. There was a desk against the wall. Gold gleamed from a very expensive looking gaming console. The sight of it gripped me. I glanced back to the beds against the walls. If there was any way to piss them off, it was to trash their plaything.

The thought grew fangs and bit deep.

I was moving before I knew it as I touched the pristine desk and shoved the wide desk chair aside. "I'll show you what happens when you cage me."

My voice trembled. Fear gripped me tightly as I clasped my hands around the gleaming PlayStation console. There was a second when I thought twice about this, about the shackles on the pathetic single bed and the perfect console in my hands. But I forced that voice aside, sucking in hard breaths. *Just do it...just do it...just—*

I yanked *hard*, tearing the cords free as movement came from the doorway.

Shadows moved in against the door.

Two of them.

I jerked my gaze toward piercing blue eyes as the blond stepped inside. Rage sparked in his stare as he looked from my face to the console in my hands as I lifted it over my head. "Don't," he growled.

The one behind him didn't move.

He didn't say a *goddamn thing*.

But it was the asshole with the peroxided hair I fixed on, the one who liked to threaten...let's see how he threatens me now. I heaved the machine down, using all the force I had.

"NO!" the asshole screamed as he flung himself through the air until he slammed into me.

I was lifted and driven backwards as the room tilted.

"You fucking BITCH!" he roared.

I slammed backwards, bouncing on the mattress until the hard metal shackles dug into my back. *"FUCK YOU!"* I screamed, bucking and fighting.

"You *goddamn selfish bitch!*" he shouted, looming above me. "Do you have *any idea what you've done?*"

All I saw were those eyes. All I felt was his hands. His body...*his scent* was overwhelming. I lifted my head from the bed, lips curled, spitting the word in his face. *"Yes!"*

He froze, his eyes wide as he jerked a panicked look over his shoulder to his brother, who still stood in the doorway. "It's okay." He lowered his tone. "Colt, it's okay."

I didn't understand why he was so scared for his brother, nor at that moment did I care. I lashed out, driving my hand to his face, until he struck and grasped my wrist, moving faster than I'd ever seen anyone move before.

That rage glinted in his stare as he turned back to me.

"You like to slap," he snarled, his gaze narrowing. "But I'm not London, little girl." He drove my wrist back and slammed it against the buckle on the bed. "You don't get to hit me."

"Get the fuck off me, *NOW!*" I roared, fighting as hard as I could.

But I was pathetically weak against his cruel hands and savage ways. He unleashed a snarl as he tore his gaze from mine to my hand over my head. He moved, and stood up. The clink of steel sounded before leather closed around my wrist. It happened so fast. One minute I was thrashing and struggling, the next one wrist was tethered above me and he moved to the other, closing the Velcro around me.

"Stop!" I kicked, driving my hips from the bed. *"Let me go, NOW!"*

The blue-eyed bastard just slowly rose, staring down at me. I knew instantly when that cold, controlled rage shifted to something else. He looked down, his gaze fixed on my breasts. Cold air slipped in through the gaps of my blouse. I sucked in a breath and looked down, to see buttons missing.

"Colt," the bastard called his brother and inhaled. "How are you doing, buddy?"

How was *he* doing? I was the one strapped to a fucking bed with a goddamn murderer standing above me. If *this asshole* thought I didn't remember what he'd done in that warehouse, then he was *fucking delusional.* "I saw you!" I snarled, baring my teeth. "I saw you kill all those men."

He froze, his brow pinching. "You saw me, huh?"

God, he was so calm. So fucking calm...

An icy lick of terror passed through me as the mute twin stepped in from the doorway, bits of his shattered console crunching under his boots.

"So you know what I'm capable of," his brother added above me, drawing my gaze. "That's good. I don't have to pretend. I hate pretending."

He sank to the edge of the bed, sitting beside me. "We're going to get you a new one, Colt," he reassured, staring down at me. "Just as soon as I..."

His big hand closed over my breast, his fingers sliding between the gaps of my blouse.

"*Stop!*" I barked. "Get your *murderous* hands off me!"

"Murder isn't all these hands have done," he growled, then yanked my blouse, widening the gap.

His fingers found my nipple, thumbing it as he rose and leaned over me. He braced one hand against the bed as the other gently massaged my breast. I winced with the instant flare of pain.

I froze, feeling the heat of his breath against my ear. "No part of the party, slash, parties, right?" he murmured. "That's what the contract says. But we're not a party, *daughter*. No, we're not a fucking party at all."

His hand left my breast and moved lower, pushing under the waistband of my slacks, forcing his way.

"CARVEN!"

I jolted with London's roar as it filled the bedroom.

"Get off her, now!"

The bastard just smirked, then leaned closer, whispering, "Looks like *daddy* saves you again, wildcat. But it's only a matter of time...only a matter of time, then he'll be too late."

I held my breath, waiting, as he slowly rose.

There was a twitch in the corner of his mouth...

Before London strode into the room, looking at the shattered remains of the console, then placed his hand on the mute twin's shoulder. "We will deal with this. Don't worry."

Then he turned that savage, icy glare my way.

FOUR

London

I CROSSED THE ROOM, FEELING SAVAGE AT THE SIGHT OF HER strapped down like that, Carven's hand all over her breast, smearing blood across her nipple. I fought the urge to tear him off her. But still, I was fucking panicked, searching that volatile blue stare for a glimpse of the madness inside.

The muscles of his jaw flexed. That icy stare was chilling. Only, he didn't react, not the way I expected him to. Instead, he seemed almost...*tortured* as he pulled away from her.

"Carven..." I spoke carefully, trying my best to find a way to unfuck this situation. "You can step away from her now."

Metal clanked from the straps' buckles as Vivienne grunted and yanked at the bindings around her wrists. *Be still, for Christ's sake!* I cut her a glare.

But the defiant pain in my goddamn ass just bared her teeth, her eyes wild and feral like the damn wildcat they'd called her. She didn't know what she'd just done, how bad this situation was. Bits of plastic crunched under my boot as I slowly stepped forward. And she had no idea how volatile they were.

The sons were unpredictable at best, and downright terrifying at worst. I should know...it's how I'd found them. Beaten, starved...*murderous at the age of ten.*

Colt was the one who stepped forward and grabbed his brother's arm, drawing his attention, and that icy stare shifted from me to him. Life came back into Carven's stare. It was a glimmer at first, like he'd been lured back from the edge of the abyss and from killing us all. His brother was the only one who could ever do that, not even I commanded that kind of respect, even after all these years.

"Get her out of my room, London," Carven murmured, turning that chilling stare my way. "Now."

I strode forward, clenched my jaw, and tried to ignore the rage in her eyes as I reached for the straps. *Fuck. Fuck!* I pulled the shackles free, one then the other. Her bare breasts jiggled as I grabbed her arm and hauled her up from the bed. *"Move."*

I left her no time to snarl or hiss, just dragged her belligerent ass through the sons' room and out the door. She stumbled as she went, her ankle buckling as she stepped on the console, but then she was out.

I wasted no time, glancing over my shoulder before I drove her through the open door of her bedroom. A kick, and the door closed with a *bang.* Then I was on her in an instant, crowding her, driving her backwards to the bed as I roared. *"Do you have ANY idea what you've done?"*

She tripped and windmilled her arms, catching herself before she fell. Savagery darkened those gorgeous brown eyes. "What *I've* done?" She clenched her fists and strode forward, pushing against me. *"I'm* the one locked up like a goddamn animal here. I'm the one fucking *tracked."*

Tracked...

Didn't she see what I was doing here?

Didn't she see I was trying to...

She'll hate you, you know that, right?

Jack Castlemaine's words rose in my head.

"Why!" She threw her hands in the air. "Why am I here...what could you *possibly* want with me? You can't fuck me, right? That's what the contract says. Although I have no fucking idea why they'd even give a shit. But it's there. I read it in black and white. You can't use me, so then *why am I still here, London? Why. Am. I. Here?"*

Why was she here?

Why...

She was a plan fifteen years in the making. A plan B that went sideways in the most spectacular way possible and I was still trying to get it back on track. Because Vivienne Evans haunted me in ways I couldn't understand and I loathed her for it.

She'll hate you...

Those words stuck as I looked down, finding the bright crimson smear on her blouse. The sight hit me harder than her hand ever could. *She'll hate you...it won't matter what you do, she'll hate you regardless.* I swallowed that sting and narrowed in on her. "You want to leave?"

She flinched, expecting a fight. "Yes." Her voice was softer, like she was a little wary now. "I want to leave. Let me go. I'll find Ryth, you can keep track of the both of us if you have to, but I won't be here...with you."

"And what makes you think she wants you?" I hated my callous tone. "She's with her brothers, running for their lives. It'll be hard enough staying under The Order's radar. With you it'd be impossible. You'd get them killed, Vivienne. You'd get them all killed."

I didn't like the way she swallowed and looked away, hiding her pain from me...

I was the monster in her eyes. The one keeping her locked away like a criminal. Only, I was trying to save her damn life. I looked at that smear, and the soft sweep of her breasts as her blouse gaped when she turned back to me. "Do not move." I met her stare. "I mean it."

I headed for the door and yanked it open. The sons' bedroom was quiet, the killing rage eased—for now. Until the next time she decided to do something stupid, like poke the damn bear. I made my way downstairs and headed for my bedroom.

Jesus, if I'd been just a few minutes later in getting there...

I'd be cleaning her blood alright, just a lot more of it.

Carven would've killed her. There was no doubt about that and there wouldn't have been a damn thing I could've done to stop him. I opened the door to my bedroom and headed for the bathroom, remembering the way Carven flinched.

The son was acting strangely around her, the looks, the remarks.

Maybe it'd been a bad move bringing her here after all.

Maybe I should've kept her locked up, hidden in another compound far away from Jack Castlemaine and every other asshole who wanted to put thoughts in her head, especially about running. He sure as hell worked a number on the child that wasn't his. Look where that almost got Ryth...*killed.*

But it wasn't too late to pack her up and shove her somewhere apart from under my goddamn nose. Because the woman was well and truly under my skin.

I opened the cupboard, pulled out the Betadine, swabs, and gauze dressings, and left the bathroom behind, unable to shake the way Carven had reacted. He should have been terrifying. He should have been covered in her damn blood. The goddamn game was the only thing that soothed Colt, staving off the nightmares and the terror. It was the way he coped after what he'd endured.

But the way Carven froze when faced with the machine's destruction unnerved me. I'd never seen him hesitate like that before, never seen him so much as flinch when it came to reacting. The son was ruthless, a pitbull when it came to his brother, so the fact Vivienne was still alive, or even upright to still be a mouthy pain in the ass spoke volumes.

I headed out of my room and climbed the stairs, glancing at the sons' bedroom door that was now closed. Low murmurs slipped out, but I couldn't hear what Carven was saying.

The console was easily replaceable, but the fact it had taken us six weeks of endless night terrors and murderous bouts of rage after the last one crashed and stopped working was something we didn't want to go through again...*ever*.

I opened her bedroom door, expecting her to lunge at me, hissing and spitting, the moment I stepped inside. But she didn't...she was right where I'd left her, glaring at me from the side of her bed. A surge of excitement rose. Maybe she was trainable after all...maybe Vivienne would do exactly as I told her.

"Blouse off," I commanded, glancing at the gaping front of the ruined garment before I headed for her bathroom and busied myself by spreading out the dressings.

Movement came from the bedroom, but I didn't look, just scrubbed my hands, then squeezed Betadine into a cotton swab before heading back to her. "The placement was unavoidable,

I'm afraid. So you'll need to wear something soft that won't rub the wound, until it heals, at least."

She said nothing as I neared, fighting the urge to meet that rage. The walls closed in as I stared at her perfect breasts. "This will be easier if you lie down."

She didn't move for a second, then slowly sank to the side of the bed and lay backwards. I placed the sterile packet on the nightstand, gripped the swab as well as a clean one, and leaned over.

"Move as little as possible," I murmured, my pulse racing as I swallowed the rest of my words. *I don't want to hurt you.*

Her chest rose hard as I fixed on that perfect swell and gently swiped the two stitches under her breast. She flinched, making me freeze. "Are you in pain?"

I couldn't stop from meeting her stare as she shook her head. "No."

"Good." I nodded, turned back to the task and cleaned her wound, then dabbed it dry carefully. The wound wasn't opened, which was a damn miracle. I made sure my touch was careful as I placed the dressing in place, making sure it didn't pull.

Then I moved to her walk-in closet, headed to the drawers I'd filled with lingerie, and pulled out a soft, lavender lace bralette before grabbing a cashmere top in the same color and strode back to her. "Get dressed." I held out the clothes. "We're leaving."

She pushed up from the bed, staring at the clothes in my hand. "Leaving, to go where?"

"Somewhere I should've taken you days ago. I'll be downstairs waiting."

I left then, grabbing the plastic packets and used swabs before making my way downstairs. It wasn't until I was in the kitchen stowing the rubbish away that I allowed myself to breathe. I gripped the counter, closed my eyes, and bowed my head. "What a goddamn mess."

I allowed myself a second before I opened my eyes and straightened. Lo and behold, the wildcat slunk down the stairs. I tracked the sound of her steps, then turned around and froze, scowling. "Where is the cashmere I gave you?"

"On the bed, where I left it."

Twitch...

That nerve at the corner of my eye ticced. I ground my teeth, met the challenge in her stare, and swallowed the bite of my words. "Fine."

"Fine," she snarled back.

I lifted my hand, motioned the way to the garage, and swallowed my anger once more. Living with this woman, I was starting to despise the taste. I followed her, snatched the keys from inside the door, and unlocked the car. She climbed in before I could get to her damn door and slammed it with a *bang*, leaving me to stand there like a goddamn schmuck before I watched her turn her head and meet my gaze.

She knew...

She fucking knew what she was damn well doing.

I clenched my fists as I fought the urge to drag her out of the damn thing and slam the door closed before opening it once more, just to prove a fucking point. But I didn't, just turned from her stare and climbed in behind the wheel, ignoring her goddamn smirk as I stabbed the button and started the engine.

I tore out of the garage, accelerating hard the moment I hit the asphalt, throwing her back against the seat and wiping that smile from her face.

She said nothing as I made my way to the highway, heading out of the city to a place I didn't think I'd ever step foot in again. The silence as we drove was deafening. More than once I was forced to bite down on my words and instead let her sit in the quiet.

She shifted on the seat, casting sideways glances as I worked the gears. More than once I caught her staring at my hands wrapped around the wheel before she looked away, forcing herself to stare out her window. "Are you cold?" I asked, making sure I drew her focus as I adjusted the temperature and pressed my hand against the vent near her leg.

I splayed my fingers, following the stream of cool air to her thigh. The touch was careful, still she swallowed hard, staring at the contact. "No."

But there was a huskiness in her tone. This time it was my turn to smirk. Seemed like the little hellcat liked my hands...

Which was a good fucking thing.

Because I wanted them all over her.

"Where are we headed?"

I cut her a glance. "She speaks."

"Funny."

"Why, are you nervous to be with me?"

"No," she snapped a little too quickly. "*Justwantedknow.*"

I gave her a quick look. "Don't mumble your words, Vivienne."

The corner of her lip curled into a sneer. "So how much longer are you going to treat me like a child?"

"For as long as you keep acting like one," I replied as I pulled out around a car and accelerated.

"Fucshitsjugh."

Annoyance flared as I turned to her. "What?"

That anger roared to life in her glare, her cheeks reddening. "Nothing."

"That's what I thought."

She remained quiet the rest of the hour drive, pouting the entire way. But the moment that towering, ominous building peeked through the thick tree line, my attention was pulled away from her hurt feelings. My stomach rolled, driving that familiar, aching pain through my chest. My pulse fluttered, like a crow trapped in my belly, clawing and fighting to get free. *Private Property, keep out.* The faded sign still sat sideways, now riddled with bullet holes, some of them fresh.

Had the sons been here?

If not them, then someone had, someone just as tormented.

I slowed the car, took the tight corner on the winding road, and slowly pulled into the driveway past the remnants of the burned down guard hut which sat at the front, then stopped at the cracked open gate.

She stared across the expansive grounds, her focus on the dark, mottled brown mansion towering in the near distance.

"I'll be right back." I turned to her and waited until she met my stare and slowly nodded.

I climbed out, leaving the driver's door open, and strode toward the gate. The hinges squealed, seizing on one side, making me stride forward to push it. But the damn thing wouldn't budge. I glanced over my shoulder and saw her staring wide-eyed at the building before she shifted her terrified gaze to me.

I hated the distance between us...hated even more that we were here.

I gripped the rusted steel and my tendons corded as I drove my strength against the damn thing until it gave, opening all the way. Then I was shoving the other side open, dusting the filth off my hands against my pants. I'd carry a lot more stains by the time we were through.

A quick glance her way, and I made sure she wasn't coming apart, then I shoved the car into gear and eased us through and along the driveway to the ugly, gothic brown brick mansion left behind to rot. I felt stretched thin when I climbed out, as though the air echoed here, piercing and shrill with chilling screams.

"What is this place?" she asked quietly, her gaze drawn to the darkened windows up high.

"Hell," I answered as I closed the driver's door and stepped around the front of the car. "This...is hell."

She followed me, staying a few steps behind as I headed for the front door. Gravel crunched under my boots, the sound resurrecting memories I absolutely didn't want to relive. But here I was.

I climbed the stairs and reached for the handle, bearing down before I shoved it inwards. Long wooden boards had been yanked from barring the entrance, leaving gruesome rusted nails behind. "Careful." I glanced over my shoulder and reached for her hand. "You don't want to cut yourself on that."

I expected her to fight the connection.

I expected her to rage.

But she didn't. Instead, she gripped my hand and followed me inside.

Our steps resounded as I led her forward. But in my head, there weren't the rotting floorboards and peeling painted doors of this carcass. No, terror lived blinding bright in my head, so piercing it was painful. I led her past the front foyer, where faint sunlight fought through filthy windows to illuminate the space. Still, I didn't speak, letting her take it all in.

Past the foyer was the library, the door open, letting the foul stench of decaying books spill out.

"Ugh." She covered her nose, staring into the room.

I tugged her hand, pulling her forward past the large open room which was meant to be joyful, but I doubted this place knew what joy was. "The first thing I noticed about this place when I walked through those doors was the smell." My voice sounded caustic. "It's faded now, of course. But once you breathed it, once you let it inside, that kind of foulness stays with you. It stains you. It infects you."

She turned to me. Those words were cruel...but necessary.

"Despair and torture have a certain...flavor to them, as you well know, Vivienne."

She whimpered, and in that moment, I knew...

She was starting to remember.

"The ammonia stuck on my palate for days, and what I saw in the eyes of all those children told me the rest. It was so quiet for a house," I said as I stared into that shell of a playroom. "So quiet for a house filled with children. Their footsteps were silent, their breaths shallow, like just existing made too much noise, and they feared the consequences."

I turned to her, made sure she saw me, then I glanced at the large red open door. The one fixed with four heavy bolts on the outside, and tiny little scratches on the inside. Ones which were barely two feet tall.

A whimper tore free from her.

She released my hand and clenched her fists. Her olive skin turned a sickening shade of yellow. "What happened to them? To all the children..." She looked at me. "Tell me, London. Tell me what happened."

I didn't answer her just hold her stare...waiting for the pieces of the puzzle to fall into place.

Until she rocked back on her heels, her brow furrowing in agony as she answered her own question.

FIVE

Vivienne
_____

"The Order." That room swayed, blurred, and darkened as it all hit home. "The Order happened, didn't it?"

He gave a slow nod, his jaw tightening as he looked around. "But as bad as this place was...the home for the sons was far worse. The atrocities they endured there, the discipline, the training. It was enough to break someone..."

Sons.

Sons...

A low, tortured sound ripped from the back of my throat. I closed my eyes and doubled over, bracing my hands on my knees. But with each breath, I dragged that filth into my soul. "Daughter," I moaned. "They called me *daughter*." I forced myself up, to meet his stare. "They called me *daughter* and you call them...*the sons*." I stepped closer, desperation screaming inside me. "But they're not *your* sons, are they, London? They aren't *your*..."

"No," he answered.

That biting answer took more than its share of flesh.

47

"But Carven and Colt are still part of my family. I carried them from that place when they were just boys. They are mine to protect, mine to care for. They know all my secrets, every single one, and they know all of yours."

"My secrets?" I shook my head. "I have no secrets."

He took a step closer. "Vivienne...you *are* the secret."

My stomach clenched as he turned back to me, those knowing eyes fixed on mine. "You were taken from this place before they could do too much damage and placed with the couple who raised you. They didn't hurt you." He turned to me, staring into my soul. "I made sure of that."

He made sure...

He made...sure...

I froze, my thoughts colliding as pieces of the puzzle slipped into place. The book I'd found in his study with pictures of me, pictures he should *never* have had. As I met his stare, I finally understood how helpless I was. It was all him, every step of every way. He had all the power...all the control. "Who the fuck *are* you?"

"A man that's trying to undo the damage he's done." He stepped closer. "I couldn't get you away from The Order, that would've drawn far too much attention. But I paid your foster parents not to hurt you. That was the best I could do."

With every step, this monster became all too real. My past... those *nightmares*. The cold. The dark. The screaming. *"Oh, God."* I stumbled backwards, away from those scratches on the door and the fetid stench of terror, and turned.

I was running before I knew it, hurling myself through that rotting corpse of a house and lunging for the front door. My heels clattered as I stumbled down the stairs toward his car and slammed my hand on the hood, feeling the warmth of the engine before my knees buckled.

"Easy." Strong arms wrapped around my waist, keeping me from hitting the ground. "Easy now, I have you."

I moaned and shook my head, trying to push him away. But I may as well battle the night. London St. James was the night, cold, empty, endless. He turned me around, placing his hand at my back, pulling me against him. "Hold on to me, Vivienne."

In that moment it was all I could do to stay upright. I found myself gripping his arms, clinging to him. Hating that I needed him as I lowered my head to his chest. "What the fuck, London...*what the fuck!*"

"I understand." He was so calm...so controlled. *So cold.*

I lifted my head, meeting that empty stare, then punched against his chest, pushing him away, stumbling backwards. "You *understand?* You stay the fuck away from me. *Do you understand that, asshole? Stay...the...fuck...away from me, you sick fuck!"*

My heels sank through the rocks and into dirt, making me twist and stumble. I was going to be sick...I was going to—*run.* I slammed my hand against the side of the car and pushed off. All I saw was the darkening sky and the murky shrouded trees in the distance.

I needed to get out of here. I needed to—

I lunged, driving myself forward.

"Vivienne!" London screamed.

Daughter.

Daughter.

Daughter.

And the sons...

A wounded sound tore free as I ran for the darkness.

"FUCK!" His steps crunched against the stones behind me.

But in my head, all I could hear were his words. *What makes you think she wants you...what makes you think. She. Wants. You?*

"Vivienne, *stop running!*"

The heavy thud of his steps grew louder, until his cruel grip closed around my arm and he yanked me backwards. *"STOP!"* he bellowed, those dark eyes wild and wide. *"Stop, for Christ's sake!"*

"Get off me!" I thrashed, lashing out, fighting with all I had. Tears stung my eyes as that ache in my chest grew claws. *"Get the fuck off me!"*

But this time he was grabbing my wrists as I aimed for his face. *"STOP!"* He roared. *"I said...STOP, Vivienne!"*

"I don't belong!" The words tore open the festering wound I held inside. *"I don't belong anywhere!"*

He froze, his hands clasped around my wrists.

As much as I fucking *loathed it,* my tears flowed. "I don't belong," I blubbered. "Not with Ryth, not with *anyone.*"

"What?" His brow furrowed.

"That's what you said, right?" I yanked my hands, trying to pull out of his hold. "But it's not like I need you pointing it out to me. It's been obvious *my entire goddamn life!*"

Still, he didn't let go.

The sting of pain ebbed, leaving me feeling emptier than I'd ever felt before. Still I fought him, desperate to get away, to hide my shame. "Let me go, London...*just let me go*. I don't belong. Not here, not with my parents, not with Ryth...not *anywhere*."

His brow furrowed and hard breaths made his chest rise and fall. "You think no one wants you?"

"Think?" I barked laughter as the pain in my chest turned into a wall of fire. "I don't need to *think*. I *know* no one wants me."

With a snarl of anger, he wrenched me close and grabbed the back of my neck so I couldn't get away. *"Well, I want you, Vivienne!"* he growled as those bottomless eyes stared into my soul. *"I...fucking...want...you!"*

I froze, tears stinging, unable to catch my breath. I couldn't think...only *feel*. Feel the weight of his stare boring into mine and the strength of his grip. Surprise widened his eyes, as though he realized exactly what he'd said. Then in an instant, his hold eased.

"Just remember that the next time you forget where you belong." His tone softened as he looked away. "Now..." he breathed hard, trying to collect himself. "Get back in the goddamn car, Vivienne, and let's get the fuck out of here."

I didn't stop him when he lowered his hand, captured mine, and pulled me with him. My gaze shifted to that terrifying, hulking house as I let him lead me back to the car and open the door. I let him guide me inside before he leaned down, tugged the seatbelt into place, and closed the door with a soft *thud*.

Still my tears came, slow and burning. I swiped them with the backs of my hands, watching him as he strode around the front of the car. But I couldn't stop them, no matter how hard I tried. I said nothing as he climbed in behind the wheel and started the engine.

He glanced my way, his face caressed by the dashboard lights before he turned back. Night closed in, darkening the sky, making the gruesome house even more terrifying than it was before. London reached around, grasped the back of my seat, and backed the car up.

My pulse spiked, thrumming in my veins with his attention. There was an awkwardness now, one that hadn't been there before. He cast sideways glances as we drove toward the gate, slowed enough to crawl through, then turned back onto the winding road. The headlights cut through the gloom before we plunged into the darkness that spilled from the thick trees.

Beep.

I glanced at his phone sitting in the console between us, then to the message that cut across the display.

H: You're needed.

H? Who was that? Helene...Harmony? What other names of women could I conjure that started with the letter H...*and why the fuck did I care?* I looked away, my cheeks burning, as London leaned forward and swiped the screen, ending my view.

"Sorry for occupying your time," I muttered.

"You didn't *occupy* my time, Vivienne," He threw a glare my way.

I didn't know if his annoyance was in response to me or the damn message. But he turned colder as he drove, sinking back onto that stony focus once more. It looked like tonight's lessons and confessions were well and truly over and I couldn't be more excited at the prospect of getting as far away from that godforsaken place and London St. James as possible.

A shudder tore through me and my teeth gnashed. My breath caught before it tore free like razor blades with a moan. I leaned forward, grasped my knees, and felt like I was about to throw up.

He reached over, adjusted the temperature, and aimed the warmth onto me. "It's that place. It does the same to me. You'll be okay, you just need warmth."

I gripped my knees, shivering as the blast of warm air washed over me. We drove in silence, with not even the radio to distract the panicked thoughts in my head. All I had was the whoosh of the warm air until finally I stopped shivering.

Something had changed between us. Something I didn't like. I searched for that bite of anger as I slowly straightened, watching him out of the corner of my eye. But as hard as I tried to find that outrage toward him, it was gone. Instead of fury, I felt an *aching* need to look at this man...to do more than look, if I was honest. Questions filled my head as I watched those sure hands work the gears and turn the wheel, too many for me to prioritize with any sense.

The muddled mess in my head was still overshadowed by his desperate revelation. *You think you're not wanted? Well, I want you, Vivienne!*

My pulse raced. I couldn't think of anything else but the anguish in his eyes. Anguish he so carefully hid under that emotionless, stony exterior. By the time we turned into the driveway, I was already reaching for the door handle, desperate to be away from him. Pity I couldn't outrun my own torment.

He said nothing as he killed the engine and I climbed out. Still, I could feel that stare all the way to the door to the house. I had to get out of there, find some distance...regain some control.

My steps were a blur as I raced up the stairs. I glanced at his bedroom door as I kept climbing. This panic was the same one I'd felt before, the one that had hit me as I stood by his bed. Heat moved through me as I reached the top of the stairs and raced for my room.

There were no heavy steps following, no chase this time around. I hurried inside, closed the door, and leaned against it, sucking in sawing breaths. "No...just no."

I was so heavy. So very heavy.

Tortured and strained, I closed my eyes. But all I could see were those hands. Those strong goddamn hands as they gripped the wheel, and that careful, dark stare. I don't know how long I stayed like that, paralyzed by the terror that I now knew the truth of how he felt.

I didn't like it. I wanted to undo this entire evening, starting with me smashing that fucking gaming console. Steps resounded, heading toward my room. I turned at the soft rap of knuckles.

"Vivienne," London murmured. "I have your meal."

"I don't want it," I snapped, then eased my tone. "I don't think I can."

"I'll leave it outside your door."

Relief hit me. I couldn't look at him, not now. Maybe not ever.

The clatter of plates came. Shadows moved under the door as I stepped backwards until I neared the bed. The soft lavender cashmere top still lay thrown to the bottom of the bed, discarded out of hate. That moment felt like a lifetime ago, before I knew the truth. The truth of my past. I turned away and headed for the bathroom as wracking shudders came once more.

Memories hit me.

Ones that were faded and old.

I'd always thought I imagined it.

The screams. The terror.

The *boom...boom...boom...*that came with the flashing lights.

Storms had always terrified me beyond anything I'd ever experienced.

They didn't hurt you. Those words haunted me as I undressed and went into the bathroom. I turned on the water as hot as I could stand it and stepped into the spray, desperate to wash the evil from that place off me.

Two seconds was all it took before I sank to the floor of the shower, tears pouring from me.

They didn't hurt you.

His words were all I heard...

I made sure of that.

SIX

London

_____

I *FUCKING WANT YOU, VIVIENNE!* THE WORDS RESOUNDED AS I placed the tray on the floor outside her room and rose. *Fucking idiot.* I stared at her bedroom door. *Stupid, goddamn idiot. You've ruined—*

Beep.

I grabbed my phone and looked at the message.

> H: Where the fuck are you?

"Shit."

I glanced at her door. The last thing I wanted to do was leave her right now. God knows I'd opened a door to hell and all the demons were about to come pouring out with the scent of her blood in their noses. But when the Devil himself demanded my presence, I had no choice but to obey...

For now...

But not forever.

I glanced at the food and winced. It was rushed...*messy*. I hadn't had time to prepare it properly, my damn fingers still shaking as I'd pulled it all together for her and put the rest of the ingredients away. Smoked salmon, warmed potato au Gratin with a side of steamed asparagus and cracked pepper butter. There was something missing. I scowled, thinking...

Beep.

That nerve in the corner of my eye twitched. My lips curled as I lifted my phone.

> H: If you don't answer me…

"Fuck you," I snarled and typed out a message.

> On my way. Don't do a damn thing until I get there.

Send.

I glanced back to the tray, then forced myself to leave, heading for the stairs and the garage once more. The engine of the Audi roared back to life. The garage door lifted and I drove out. I glanced back in the rear-view mirror at the empty space which Carven's black Explorer usually occupied. The sons were out, tracking down a lead we had on King. I needed that lead to pan out, to give me *something*.

I needed it like my life depended on it.

Because it did.

I focused on the road, pushing everything else out of my mind. I needed to be careful, to be cold. I needed to be fucking *ruthless* walking in here. I sank down into that darkness...shutting everything down, until—

The dark chocolate mousse...

"*Shit!*" I roared, and punched the steering wheel.

I'd forgotten her fucking mousse. The one I'd made this morning especially for her, with the flecks of white chocolate through it—the one I knew she'd love. The fucking mousse...the goddamn mousse. My pulse spiked and that twitch came back with a vengeance, making the headlights of the oncoming cars flare and glint. "Goddamn *idiot*. What else are you going to fuck up here?"

First the damn outburst...*I fucking want you!* The words rang like a damn bell inside my head. I might as well have fucking fallen at her damn feet. I might as well have told her everything. But that would only drive her away, wouldn't it? That would only ruin everything.

"Goddamn Banks...goddamn *Castlemaine!*"

I needed to get Jack to talk, needed to push him harder. I'd thought having Ryth's life in my grasp might make him give me all the information I wanted about King. But it seemed I was wrong. I pushed the Audi harder, turning onto the on-ramp before heading northwest.

Maybe when Carven found Creed Banks, I might be able to use him to make Jack talk. Banks was a corrupt motherfucker, but not nearly as bad as I needed. He was more a weak fuck than anything. But weak men were easy to use. And I'd use him. I'd use them all to get what I wanted.

Even her?

Vivienne's face filled my mind. Those brown eyes had shimmered with unshed tears, tears she'd refused to let fall until she was in the damn car. She was stubborn and strong. Not a person who'd easily bend...or break. One look at her past and you knew that. But I didn't need to bend her, did I?

Only over the damn table with my hand between her thighs...

Jesus.

Whatever we had between us was getting out of hand. She was a mark. That's all. Nothing more than a tool for me to use. *Christ, I wanted to use her.* I shifted gears, taking the hard bend in the road and accelerating now that the road had opened up.

My pulse thudded louder in my ears, drawing me back to the fact the woman was under my skin. I was the one who was supposed to be in control here, the one who had her in my control. Only, I was coming undone around her, revealing things that gave her the upper hand.

I needed to change that.

Need to undo what I'd done.

But all I could think about was her.

Her pain.

Her goddamn body.

"Shit," I muttered as I turned onto the long, winding road and, as the towering fence of The Order came into view, I realized I was far too fucking vulnerable to survive this damn night.

I slowed the car, pulled up outside the guard hut, and pulled out my ID. But the guard barely looked at it. Instead, he nodded. "Parking is to the left, Mr. St. James."

I tore my gaze to the building in the distance. "To the left?"

"Due to the explosion, sir."

I gave a slow nod, hiding my surprise, and eased the car through the gate as it opened. Lights blazed bright on the front of the concrete building. This place wasn't just a jail for the women they brought here, it was Haelstrom Hale's own sick, fucking playground. Anything he wanted he had here. Sex trafficking. Murder. Blackmail...and most of all, breeding.

The degrading things he did here were endless...and with two Supreme Court Justices and three fucking Senators in his pocket, no one would dare look his way. Except King...*and me...*

High visibility yellow tape shone neon in the dark. "Jesus," I muttered, as I nosed the car against a bank of trees instead of where I normally parked and killed the engine before climbing out. My gaze was riveted on the damage. Half of the damn wall was missing, and blown out sections of it littered the ground. No doubt that was how Jack Castlemaine had escaped. To do that kind of damage would require a squad of men.

The sheer fact they were able to get inside and past the guards that patrolled every inch of this building intrigued the hell out of me. His team was good, but mine was better.

No matter what King wanted to throw at the Hale Order to get his buddy free, I'd still beaten him. I was the one who had Jack... and his daughters.

I fought a smirk and reached into my pocket as I headed for the side door. How many fucking times had I been in this place? Too goddamn many. At first it had been because I'd wanted to, then as things changed...it was because I couldn't escape, and as I tried to undo the damage I'd done, it became out of desperation. I pressed my card against the scanner and yanked open the door. "And here we are."

Stark white walls and brilliant, blinding lights. I blinked, looking away for a second until my eyes adjusted to the glare. But I didn't need to look where I was going. I knew this place like the back of my hand—*because I built it, right?*

Almost.

I'd almost built it.

I exhaled hard, nodding as a guard passed.

"Mr. St. James," he murmured.

I turned, lifted my hand, and pressed the card to the scanner. The moment I stepped through the doors, I could hear the roar.

"You don't get to think, DO I MAKE MYSELF CLEAR? Your job is to DO!" The savage bellow bounced against the walls. "You fucking *do* and you do it *my way.* You should've killed your fucking conscience when you had the chance, Riven, now get the fuck out!"

Fuck, this was going to be a goddamn minefield.

I slowed at the entrance to the large office at the end of the hall. But I didn't have to wait long. The door jerked open and Riven strode out, his lips curled, his teeth bared. He cast a savage glare my way as he left the door open and strode past without saying a word.

Movement came from inside. I inhaled deep and buried every goddamn emotion I ever had way down deep. You don't flinch in the face of a Great White with its jaws open wide. No, you stand your ground...*and lie like a bastard.*

I moved quietly, made my way inside and closed the door softly behind me. Haelstrom jerked a savage glare my way. Soulless eyes narrowed in on me before he ran his fingers through his hair. He said nothing. Just let the seething silence speak for him.

I made my way to the dark row of bookshelves that ran along the wall and leaned back against them.

"Where the fuck were you?" he snarled.

"Busy," I muttered.

"Too busy to answer my goddamn texts?"

"Yes."

There was a twitch at the corner of his mouth. He was riled...as riled as I'd ever seen him. You don't poke a man like Haelstrom when he was at the edge...unless you were me. "Please don't confuse me with your steward. I'm not Riven. My time is my own."

He stilled. "Even when I need you?"

I kept my voice low. "Even then." He inhaled hard, his chest rising. "But I'm here now."

"Yes," he answered carefully, then rounded his desk and went to the small bar at the corner of his office, pouring himself a drink before swallowing the contents in one gulp. He didn't turn around, just spoke to the wall. "Do you know anything about this?"

Careful.

I didn't miss a beat. "How can you ask me that? I'm your oldest ally."

He turned around, his eyes fixed on mine. He was ruthless. A viper raised to strike. "It's King. I know it is." He poured again, not once offering. He never did. A man like Haelstom Hale didn't care about you or your wants. In fact, you didn't even exist outside his bounds. You occupied space in his world to serve his own selfish needs and nothing more.

The moment you stopped being useful to him...

Well, that's when you stopped existing.

His fists clenched and a vein bulged in the corner of his eye. "I *hate* being blind when it comes to him."

"I know."

"Do you?" He stepped closer. "I feel like my eyes have been gouged out and I'm stumbling around fucking bleeding out all over the place. They even blew up the goddamn control room, did you know that?"

My brow rose. "No, I didn't."

He swung a hand through the air. "All my fucking cameras, all my goddamn hard drives. They took it all out."

"How many were there?"

He wrenched that hostile stare my way. "I have no idea. No *fucking idea*. Everything was fine, then the bombs detonated. Six of my men were dead...and Castlemaine was gone."

Six men...

Had to be at least four...four highly trained men. Were they sons? My mind went back to the fresh bullet holes in the fence of the Hale orphanage and raced, trying to fit the pieces together.

"I want that sonofabitch found, London."

I lifted my gaze to his. "I know."

"So why the fuck haven't you found him?" He stepped closer, narrowing in on me. "If there is anyone who could track this bastard down, it's you. So why the fuck haven't you found him."

"You know why."

Another step...until he stood right in front of me. "Tell me again how this guy is nothing more than a ghost. Tell me how after all these fucking years we haven't got one image, not one glimpse of what the man looks like, and yet...he can walk his fucking team into my house and destroy it, leaving not a trace of him behind— taking the one fucking man who's ever made contact with him. Tell me...because I'm starting to doubt your loyalty."

My stomach clenched.

"My loyalty has not wavered, not once...you forget, I was the one who set all this in motion. I was the one who told you to obtain something King wanted."

"But you wanted no part of me taking the bastard's sperm, did you? You wanted no part in us tearing that cryo facility apart to get it, either."

My pulse kicked in my chest.

Hammering, just like it always did.

"No," I answered. "I might've suggested you lure him out into the open with bait...but I didn't think that bait would turn out to be—"

"Daughters." Christ, my pulse was booming. My breaths turned shallow. Haelstrom looked down, his gaze fixed on that rapid motion. "Daughters I could use."

But he didn't know...he didn't know.

Because if he did, I'd be dead.

Haelstrom turned away. "But you didn't once waver, did you? You didn't once betray me. You stayed strong."

My heart was still hammering when he drained his glass and refilled it once more. "It's the only reason you're still here. So get me that information, London. Get me King. Get me Castlemaine...Hell, get me the Banks bastard, for all I care. Just get me *someone*."

"I will," I murmured.

Silence filled the room. It seemed the conversation was over and I was dismissed. "The contract..." I started.

"What about it?"

"Don't you think we can do without the preliminary bullshit?"

He turned, his gaze searching mine. "You want her that much, London?"

I tried to slow my breath, but it was like slowing a locomotive that'd gone off the rails. I licked my lips. "I want what I paid for."

He gave a soft chuff, then drank and lowered the glass. "And pay you did. Get me what I want and I'll sign her over to you."

I clenched my jaw, desperation howling inside. But I could see Haelstrom was done talking about this. Pushing him right now would draw the kind of attention I didn't want. I wanted Haelstrom far away from Vivienne...and I wanted him away from me. "Fine."

He gave a nod. I turned, jaw bulging and hate burning inside me, and headed for the door.

"Before you go, there's a dinner I need you to attend."

My stomach dropped and my balls clenched. "When?"

"Friday evening. I expect you at my side, *ally*. Ophelia will be there and she's specifically requested your attendance."

That nauseous feeling just grew stronger. I gave a nod, not that he needed it or cared, before I opened the door and left the room. I didn't slow, timing my steps carefully, even though I wanted to run from the place. Before I could press my card against the scanner, the double doors flew open and Macoy Daniels strode through, looking absolutely bereft.

He flinched and jerked his gaze to mine, his eyes wide with panic. "St. James."

"Daniels."

He jerked that panicked stare to the hall behind me, then back. "Have you heard about Killion?"

Idiot. "I have. My deepest condolences. I know how close you were."

There was a flinch, then a nod. "Do you know any—"

"I do not." There was a flicker of annoyance. Pain and fear were a dangerous mix in weaker men. It made them lash out. I didn't give him an opportunity. "If you'll excuse me."

He didn't move, just stood there while I stepped around him and strode through the door. It was only when I was in my car that I allowed the terror and the fear to escape. My hands shook until I clenched them around the wheel, forcing myself to not unravel as I slowed at the gates of the compound, then turned out onto the road.

But two seconds later, that terror turned into something I could use.

Something I knew well...

Determination.

Get me King. Get me Castlemaine. Hell, get me Banks, for all I care.

I glanced at the man in the rear-view mirror, to the stony determination in his eyes...then fixed my stare on the road ahead...and drove to the storage facility. It was time to get a little more aggressive with the questioning. It was time to find King before Haelstrom did—*once and for all.*

SEVEN

Vivienne

THE SCRATCHES ON THE GODDAMN DOOR...

I tossed in the bed, shifted my ass and closed my eyes. Screams echoed in my head. Children's screams. Screams I'd heard my entire life. But I'd forced them down, hadn't I? I'd told myself they were the result of an overactive imagination. They weren't real, *they were never real.* Because if they had been...

The home for the sons was far worse...far worse—I clenched my eyes closed—*far worse.*

Jesus.

I opened my eyes and stared at the ceiling. Those words echoed in my head. The glimpse of sleep I'd had was now long gone. After what I'd seen tonight, I doubted I'd ever sleep again. I shoved against the thick comforter and pushed upwards, my gaze moving to the faint moonlight that spilled in through the window.

I fucking want you, Vivienne!

My breath caught at the words. Goddamn him. Goddamn him to hell. I kicked the bedding aside and rose as cold instantly wrapped around me. I shivered and reached out, searching. My fingers brushed softness. I grabbed the lavender sweater from the end of the bed and pulled it on.

It was cold tonight...and getting colder.

I moved toward the window and looked out of my cell. Fall was here, snatching away the leaves and bringing a brand new ache inside me. Winter had always been my favorite time of the year. Not that it had ever brought the kind of joy the other kids possessed. Still, you could always dream...

I wrapped my arms around my middle and turned away, glimpsing the empty tray on the desk. But it wasn't the remnants of my meal that occupied my thoughts, it was the desk. Not this desk...*his desk*. I gave a soft chuff. London's words might ring in my head, but if he thought he'd rocked me with his lies and manipulation, then he was wrong.

Unless it's not a lie.

I shook my head, and slowly went to the door. It was a lie, because that's all he did. Lie. Manipulate. Control. But he couldn't control me, not anymore. I knew what kind of bastard he was now. He wouldn't play me, not ever again.

I tested the handle, found it unlocked, and quietly opened it. My gaze went to the hallway and the sons' room, and a pang of guilt washed over me. I kicked myself for smashing the damn console now. I shouldn't have done that. I wasn't sure what had come over me. Actually, I was. It was this place, and that...*asshole*. "I want you, my ass," I muttered. "Let's see if I can change that, shall we?"

I tore my gaze away and moved to the stairs. Thoughts of how to make amends were quickly shoved away. *No part of the party, slash parties, right? But we're not a party*...the savage bastard's growl pushed in. I swallowed as a shudder tore through me. Yeah, there was no way I was going near that psycho bastard.

I made my way downstairs and stopped at London's floor. Darkness beckoned me forward, enticing me to try to invade his space one more damn time. I stared at his door in the dark. My mind shifted to the electronic lock outside his study door. Still, there was a mechanical lock. If there was a lock, then there had to be an override key somewhere.

What better place to hide it than where the bastard slept?

I stepped around the banister and moved to his door. It'd be locked, it had to be. But the moment I bore down, the handle gave way. "Well, well, well." I shoved it open and stared into that murky gloom.

The scent of him washed over me, making my pulse race and my body come alive. I crossed my arms over my chest once more and stepped in. "Nope," I whispered. "Not gonna freak out this time." I moved to the bed, half expecting him to sit up and stare at me.

Jesus...what would happen if he did that?

I'd die. No...I wouldn't. I licked my lips, staring at the sheets. Unable to help myself, I grabbed the top of the dark gray comforter and pushed it down. Clean sheets, tucked in neatly. Everything about the guy was precise. I yanked and shoved, wrenching his sheets free and tore them back. Then I grabbed his pillow, ready to toss it across the room, and stopped.

The scent of him grew bolder as I pulled it close. I closed my eyes, inhaling deeply. Jesus, he smelled good. He smelled so fucking good. Too good. I opened my eyes, my body warming. "Oh, Jesus."

In my head, his hand was around my throat, his eyes fixed on the towel I wore. One that parted between my thighs. He wanted to part it more. I knew that. I lowered my head and pressed my face deeper into the pillow. Fuck, I wanted him, too. I wanted him to touch me. I closed my eyes and unleashed a moan, then pulled back. Instead of tossing it across the room like I wanted to, I put it down, then grabbed the sheets and the comforter, trying my best to fix the mess I'd made.

When I was done, I straightened. Even in the gloom, I saw it was still a damn train wreck. I reached over, flicked on the lamp on the nightstand beside his bed, and stared at the destruction. Panic found me as I took in the now crumpled bedding. I leaned over and smoothed it out as best I could, then pulled away.

He'd know.

And he'd be pissed.

But before that happened, I wanted to do as much damage as I could, and there was no better ammunition than information. I glanced at the drawer of his nightstand and tugged it open. Heat flushed in my cheeks as I leaned closer. I was stepping over the line here. Messing up the guy's bed was one thing, but rifling through his bedside drawers was a whole other thing.

I reached inside, brushed something hard, and pulled it out. Pink. The damn notebook that I'd found in the study downstairs. He had it here, beside his bed...*why?*

I sat on the edge of the bed, opened it, and rifled through the pages once more. The photos were missing. I scowled. "What the fuck?" And I flicked through the rest of the book.

They were all gone...*except*...

For one.

Only that one wasn't taken in the past. No, that was one recent. It was me, lying on the bed dressed in that damn towel, with my hand between my legs. "So you *were* watching." A surge of satisfaction moved through me.

I didn't know why I liked him looking at me like that. Maybe I was heady with the thought of having just a little bit of control here. My focus went to the dull throb under my breast and the tracker he'd had implanted inside me, the control he allowed me.

I pushed the photo into the journal and tucked it back inside the drawer. I wasn't after information I already knew. The guy wanted to fuck me, that was easy to see. My hand stopped as it slid the book inside. I could use that...like my own weapon.

My pulse spiked, punching against my chest. I tried to push that thought away and knelt down, forcing myself to focus on searching the drawer for the override key instead. But apart from two other journals and a wide velvet box, there was nothing.

I couldn't stop myself from touching the box again, from entertaining the thought—*don't do it. It's none of your business. You're getting far too wrapped up in this*—still, I pulled it out, my fingers sliding over the joint before I opened it. The light from the lamp spilled over the fine chain and massive teardrop diamond.

It was stunning.

The most beautiful piece of jewelry I'd ever seen up close like this.

I pulled it closer and touched the jewel and, for a fleeting second, entertained the idea he'd bought it for me. But that was stupid. That was stupid and I wouldn't wear it anyway. I closed it and it almost hurt to put it back. Anger moved through me, anger at myself and at him as I pushed my hand in deeper, searching the back of the drawer, trying to find *something*.

But there was nothing. I searched the drawer underneath it, then moved to the nightstand on the other side of the bed. It wasn't until I went to shove the bottom drawer closed that I felt it...*a scrape.*

One that was out of place.

I pulled the drawer open and closed it again, this time more slowly. There it was...the scrape as it closed. I glanced over my shoulder to the open bedroom door, then turned back. My pulse was booming as I lifted the drawer, yanking it hard until it popped open, and on the underside was a key taped to the bottom.

I dug my nail underneath and yanked it free. Glue came with it, sticking to my fingers as I stared at the key. But it was what I wanted, it had to be. Why else would a snake like London St. James hide it like that? I moved faster, pushed the drawer back and rose. I switched off the lamp, left the bedroom and the stunning necklace behind, and made my way downstairs to his study.

The red light of the electronic lock blinked. I tried to ignore the fact he was probably watching me. If he wasn't already, he soon would be. I hurried, pushed the sticky key into the lock, and twisted. The mechanism gave a *clunk* before I pushed down on the handle and opened the door.

I flicked on the light, ignored the rows of books this time, and headed for the desk. I didn't care if I had to find a sledgehammer to open the damn thing. I wanted answers to the burning question in my head. *What the hell did he want with me?*

It was the only question that mattered. The only one that drowned out all the others. If I could figure that out, then maybe I'd be able to bargain for my freedom. Part of me understood how stupid that sounded, and the other part just wanted to survive.

I rounded the desk and started yanking on the drawers. But instead of them being locked, they wrenched open. He hadn't locked them...*he hadn't locked them?*

I glanced toward the door, then back to the thick folders sitting on top of the desk. One yank and I dragged his chair close before I sat down and started unraveling the guy once and for all. I searched folder after folder. But there wasn't anything new, just a whole lot of shit I didn't understand.

"More DNA reports," I muttered, staring at the names listed on the forms.

Names that meant absolutely nothing to me.

"This is bullshit." I sat back and stared at the mess of pages spread across his desk.

There had to be more. There had to be *something*.

I straightened, dug underneath the mess, and pulled out another folder labeled *Contract*.

Contract? Goosebumps raced along my arms as I opened it and picked up the first report. The right to use contract I'd seen before, but this was different. This wasn't about what he could and couldn't do to me. This was...how much he'd paid.

"Holy shit." I stared at the amount listed. A number that was mind blowing. *"Three million dollars?"*

For a blinding second, surprise filled me, and, if I was honest, a satisfaction as well...

Until I remembered what it was for.

For me.

To possess, use, own.

That's what my life was worth to them? Three pathetic million dollars. Anger pushed in, grabbed the flicker of satisfaction around the throat and beat the living shit out of it. It was for me...for fucking—

A slight roar came from somewhere close and the faint rumble of a car's engine followed.

"Shit." I stared at the mess in front of me. "*Shit!*"

I shoved upwards and swept the files together as that guttural howl came again, only this time it was louder. The sons...it had to be. Fuck, they'd kill me if they found me. I slid the folders into the drawer, trying desperately to remember which way they went in. But it didn't matter. No doubt Mr. Three Million Fucking Dollars would figure out I was crawling through his things soon enough.

I shoved the drawer closed and something dropped from under the top. It was a business card, steel gray with white block letters on the front. *Precision Storage, we protect what's valuable to you.* I picked it up and stared at it. *We protect what's val...*

"Goddamn it, Colt!"

The deep howl was filled with desperation that made me shove the drawer closed. *Colt...the quiet one must be hurt.* Carven's wretched howl blended with those terrifying cries still stuck in my head. I stumbled for the door and flicked off the light, which plunged the study into darkness once more.

I waited for the sound of grunting and moaning to move away, then cracked open the study door and slipped out. They didn't see me as I stopped at the end of the hallway, peeking out as Carven carried Colt toward the stairs and up, leaving drops of bright red blood in their wake.

Lots of blood...

Jesus. I flinched and jerked my gaze upwards, following them as they disappeared from view, then I stepped forward. The splatter wasn't just tiny flecks that littered the tiled floor, they were big, round drops, a lot of them.

I flinched at the terrifying cry that rang out. My heart thundered as I took a step without realizing. The guttural groans that followed were sickening. As much as I was scared, I felt for him, and it was that anguish that pulled me up the stairs, following them.

"You need to stop fucking protecting me!" Carven snarled. *"How many fucking times do I have to tell you, you stubborn sonofabitch!"*

I climbed to the second floor and kept moving.

I forgot all about the contract and the money.

I forgot about everything.

All I heard was the torment in that guttural plea, and that hit me hard. I stepped out on my floor, glanced at my bedroom door, and contemplated hiding. But I'd broken his console...hadn't I? I'd broken his fucking console and I was a goddamn bitch for doing it.

I owed him.

I owed him to at least try.

My damn knees shook as I made my way to their bedroom. The door was open, and shadows moved in the dull light inside.

"Fuck, this is a mess. We're gonna have to call the doctor."

There was no answer, not one I heard anyway.

I stepped inside, staring at Carven's back as he leaned over his brother sitting on the end of the bed I'd been strapped to. Their heads snapped my way. A savage glare from Carven nailed me to the spot before he barked. "What the fuck do you want?"

But there was the blood...and a lot of it. I stared at the mess that soaked through Colt's shirt, catching the glint of... "Is that glass?"

He didn't answer, just glared as he pushed past me heading for the bathroom. It was the wretched agony in his brother's eyes that pulled me forward. I slowly knelt in front of him, looking at the blood that was soaking through his shirt. Blood that cloyingly clung to my nose. I didn't see the murderer anymore. I didn't see my abductor. I saw the son. The one who'd protected his brother with his life, and by what Carven had said, not for the first time.

His skin was washed out, paling in front of me, making his wide topaz-blue eyes even more noticeable than they had been before. Hard shudders gnashed his teeth. Whatever had happened tonight was bad...and I didn't need an explanation that it was most likely highly illegal and dangerous for all of us. But he was hurt. Right now, that's all I cared about.

"It's going to be okay." I turned from the glass shards embedded in his side to that wide-blue stare. "You hear me? It's going to be okay."

"Get the fuck out," Carven snarled behind me. "We don't need you sticking your fucking nose where it doesn't belong."

He knelt, dropped a small plastic basin on the floor in front of him, unscrewed the lid of a brown bottle, and poured a big splash into the basin. The bitter stench of Betadine rose up to slap me cold for the second time today. I winced, unable to look away from Carven as he set to work, grabbing a set of tweezers and a fistful of cotton swabs before tossing them in the antiseptic, then looked up at his brother. "This is gonna hurt, okay?"

His dark-haired twin just held his stare, giving a slow, careful nod. Then he reached out, grabbed my hand, and clung tight. Carven froze at the contact, glancing from my hand to Colt's. There was a scowl and a tiny shake of his head. "Colt, no."

"She stays." That same deep, husky tone I'd heard outside my door came as he held my hand. "She stays right here. Promise me..."

But it wasn't his brother he spoke to...it was me.

My heart thudded as I glanced at the gaping gashes in his side, then I met that piercing stare, finally finding purpose. "I promise," I answered. "I'm not going anywhere."

EIGHT

London
_____

HEADLIGHTS BLURRED FROM THE CARS ON THE HIGHWAY behind me as I headed for the storage yard on the other side of the city. One by one they turned off or sped past when I slowed to a crawl. I had to be careful now. Maybe now more than ever. There was far too much at stake. Too many knives were up in the air...and all I needed was to slip just once and I'd kill us all.

I slowed the car and pulled onto the off-ramp, headed the long way around to the yard, and stopped outside the gates. Darkness consumed the view behind me as I pressed in the code, waited for the gates to open, and drove through.

Do you want her that much, London?

Hale's words filled me as I parked the car around the back and killed the engine. The bastard knew I did and he dangled the goddamn contract like a piece of meat in front of me, knowing full well I was starving.

Three million dollars.

It was more than Killion had paid for Ryth, I knew that.

I climbed out of the car and closed the door behind me. *I would've paid more for Vivienne.* I adjusted my jacket and glanced around the open area of the yard—*I would've paid a lot more.*

Seething fury filled me as I headed for the external door, pressed my card against the lock, and stepped through. I *was* desperate, more than desperate. I was cornered with my back to the wall and I didn't like it. No, I didn't like it at all. I headed past the other rooms and the other visitors and made my way to the one room I cared about. The room where Jack Castlemaine waited, holding his daughter's life in his hands.

Humm.

My phone vibrated as his door came into view. I lifted my hand and stared at the screen, scowling before I answered. "Did you get the information I wanted?"

"No."

Shit.

"There was a problem..." Carven added carefully, his blunt tone a little more caustic than normal.

"Tell me."

"We were fucking ambushed. It wasn't just any damn biker bar we walked into, was it? It was one who was an ally of King himself."

"A fucking ally? How the hell does King have alliances with the goddamn HellFire Rebels?"

"I don't know. But he does."

I dragged my fingers through my hair. "How bad?"

"Colt was glassed. Stupid fuck stepped in when I had a handle on the situation."

That was a lie. Because there was only one way Colt would ever put himself in danger, that was to save his brother. Memories hit me. The sons were ten years old when I'd found them the first time. Colt was beaten bloody, slipping in and out of consciousness after protecting his younger brother.

He took all the beatings.

Drawing their wrath and fury by lashing out at the wardens of the Hale Orphanage time and time again. He was a savage when I found him, bruised, broken...and mute.

It took me a fucking year to get them out. A whole fucking year in that place. That kind of damage was irreparable. I turned around and headed back for the door. "Where are you now, at the hospital?"

"No. He refused to go. We're at home."

I stopped walking. "At home?"

"Yeah, he's fine. I patched him up and dressed the wounds. He's sleeping..."

Sleeping? Carven wouldn't interrupt me to tell me his brother had been hurt but was now fine without a reason. "And..." I urged.

"He held her hand, London. He held her damn hand and refused to let her leave. He spoke, and you know he rarely speaks. But he spoke for her. *He...spoke...for...her.*"

He spoke for her?

My heart thudded. I swallowed the flare of jealousy, picturing him holding onto her. She'd let him, too. She'd let him because she'd felt bad after what she did. I knew her, better than she knew herself. "That's good," I answered, turning back to Jack Castlemaine's door. "I'll be done as soon as I can."

"I need to go out, tie up some loose ends. He's asleep now, the weather is clear, only stars in the sky, so we should be good."

No storms...

Not tonight.

"Good. See you soon."

I hung up the call and placed my phone back into my pocket before I pressed my card against the scanner and opened the door. Shadows clung to the corners of the room, the chairs were empty, and the bed was pushed against the far wall, as well. One careful scan and I found him standing against the wall, facing away from me.

I had no doubt he'd heard my conversation, but what little information he gleaned from that would be minimal. Jack wasn't a player in this game...he was a pawn—one who stood between me and King.

I closed the door, drawing his gaze.

Jack turned to me, his dark eyes looking even more haunted in the gloom.

"We're running out of time, Castlemaine," I murmured as I unbuttoned my jacket and slipped it off. "Any moment now, Haelstrom is going to track Ryth and her brothers down and there won't be a damn thing I can do to stop it."

I dropped my jacket across the back of the armchair and kept walking. That merciless side of me pushed to the surface. "I can only keep her safe for so long, Jack. You understand that, right? My men are there watching her, ready to move in on my word, but still..."

He didn't flinch at the threat, just watched me carefully as I stopped in front of him. I glanced at the dressing taped across his shoulder. He looked a little pathetic standing there against the wall. Small...insignificant.

"All it takes is one call," I pushed him. "One call, and her life is forfeit." Those dark eyes held mine as I continued. "Give me the information I want and I promise she won't be harmed."

Something passed through his stare. A flicker of *rage* before it passed. He was angry...good.

"You think King gives a shit about you? You think he gives you a second thought? He's ruthless...and dangerous and he's going to get your daughter killed, Jack. You raised her as your own. You protected her...and you need to protect her now. Give me King and I'll make sure no one touches a hair on her head."

"You won't hurt her."

I stopped with the quiet words, then answered carefully. "No? How can you be sure?"

Jack just searched my gaze.

I clenched my fists. "Tell me where you meet him." They were the same goddamn questions, questions he evaded out of some sense of loyalty. "Tell me how he contacts you. Tell me what he looks like."

His brow furrowed.

I lashed out, grabbed him around his throat, and unleashed a snarl as I swung my fist. *Crack!* The blow collided with the side of his mouth and he stumbled sideways, slamming against the wall.

But not once did he move to defend himself.

No.

Jack Castlemaine was weak...

Weaker than anyone I'd ever known.

Agony tore through me as I stared at what I'd done. My knuckles burned as he straightened, blood smeared at the corner of his lips. I couldn't catch my breath, couldn't think. My stomach was a hard knot in my belly. *You have to do this...you have to do this. YOU HAVE TO DO THIS!*

I grabbed him around the throat, driving him back against the wall. "You will tell me what I want to know, Castlemaine. You *will* tell me..."

Jack held my stare before he turned his head and spat. Flecks of blood and spittle flew through the air to smack against the cold concrete floor.

"You will tell me," I snarled, shoving him away. "You'll fucking tell me."

But he just held my stare with blood running down his fucking face.

That stare unnerved me.

Maybe it was the smear of his blood across my knuckles.

Or my own goddamn guilt for doing this.

I reached into my pocket, pulled a handkerchief free, and wiped his blood from my knuckles before shoving it back. "For both our sakes," I muttered as I turned and strode for the door, grabbing my jacket from the chair as I went.

The door closed behind me with a *thud,* and the sound echoed with my footsteps. Guilt weighed me down as I made my way outside. I didn't want to be this version of myself. I didn't like it. But I would become it. I'd channel that hate and desperation and rage into Jack Castlemaine's face if it meant I'd get what I wanted.

I pushed through the door and headed for my car, hit the remote, and climbed in behind the wheel.

My knuckles throbbed. I clenched my fist and stared at the smear Jack left behind.

Hard breaths moved through me. I was reaching for my phone before I knew it, then I opened the apps and pulled up the camera feed. I flicked through to the sons' room, finding Colt's hulking shape under the dark comforter. The shackles hung under the mattress, unused for tonight. He shifted as I watched, pressing his hand against his side.

He held her hand, London, and refused to let her leave. He spoke for her...*he...spoke...for...her.*

"He spoke for her..." I repeated aloud.

I pressed the button, flicked to her room, and narrowed in the camera. The room was dark...but the expensive camera still picked up everything—including her empty bed. I scowled and pressed the button for her bathroom.

Nothing.

I pressed again, cycling through the kitchen, the dining room, and the living room.

Nothing...

"What the fuck," I snarled as my cheeks burned, and shifted the view to my study.

But the room was empty, the door still locked. Panic filled me and made my hands tremble and my chest burn. Frantically, I flicked through the entire house, stopping on my bedroom before I moved on...

Until something caught my attention.

A sliver of darkness that wasn't usually there.

I'd stared at the camera feeds of my house so many times I knew every angle and every shadow...but this—this was different. I narrowed in, letting the focus adjust before I froze. "No...no, you fucking did not."

Anger gave way to excitement, then torment as I stared at the cracked open door.

I stabbed the button and the engine of the Audi roared to life before I tossed the phone aside, leaving it to bounce against the passenger's seat as I shoved the car into reverse. I left all thoughts of Jack Castlemaine and King behind as I punched the accelerator and raced for home. All I could think about was that cracked open door...And the basement that she was no doubt exploring...

On her fucking own.

NINE

Vivienne
_____

Soft white lights barely illuminated the room in the basement. But they were bright enough to cling to that shrouded thing at the end of the leather bench. It was that *thing* that had called me down here. That *thing* I couldn't get out of my head.

That *thing* that made my pulse race and my core quiver.

Just like it was quivering now as I stared at the hulking outline. I clenched my grip, and the teeth from the master key bit into the soft flesh of my palm. The pain pulled me back to reality. I eased my hold, took a deep breath, and looked over my shoulder.

I shouldn't be here...

Not with Colt asleep, badly wounded upstairs.

He could wake any moment. Would he come looking for me?

Maybe...I wasn't sure.

So I had to hurry.

I moved through the doorway and made my way closer, then skirted the machine and reached out, touching the cloth.

"Why the fuck do you want me?" I yanked, revealing a black, brushed steel casing. "What could I possibly have that you want this much?"

My heart kicked at the sight. The device was discreet, and terrifying all at the same time. A thick pink dildo with bulging veins was attached to a piston arm. I froze, my pussy clenching at the sight. Hard breaths consumed me. I dragged my teeth across my lips and reached out, touching the soft silicone, imagining what it might feel like to be impaled by this toy.

But it was more than that, wasn't it? My pulse skipped as I neared the truth of it. The real trigger was how it would feel to be *controlled by him*. Bits of clear plastic sheeting were still embedded in the bolt holes, as though they'd been torn free in a frenzy. Because it was brand new.

Something to be used on me.

"No part of the party-slash-parties," I whispered, still hearing Carven's threat ringing in my ears. "*Sonofabitch*," I moaned, closing my eyes as a wave of desire washed through me.

"Does it interest you?"

I wrenched my gaze to the doorway. London stood there, cloaked in shadows, that predatory stare fixed on me. He sucked in hard breaths as he stepped inside, glancing at the exposed machine beside me. My mind raced, my gaze fixed on the way his chest expanded and fell. Had he been running?

In the corner of my eye, the tiny blinking red light drew my attention. I didn't need to look away to know the reason for his urgency. "You saw me on the camera...you watched me."

He didn't answer, just stalked closer, his baritone voice hitting me in all the wrong places. "Would you like me to use it on you?"

*Oh, Jesus...*I swallowed hard, watching him as he came closer, one achingly slow step at a time.

"Well?" He stopped on the other side of the machine. "Would you like me to use it on you?"

Yes. "No." The tremble in my voice made me a liar. "You like it so much, how about I use it on you?" There was a twitch at the corner of his mouth. Still, those bottomless eyes picked me apart. "Take the tracker out of me."

"Take it out? Why?"

"Why?" Annoyance flared. "Why? Because I'm not—"

"Mine?"

I froze, giving him all the time he needed to step around the machine. I stumbled backwards until I hit the bench, trapped between him...and getting nailed by a goddamn machine.

"Where are you going to run to, Vivienne?" He grabbed the back of my neck, spearing his fingers through my hair and stared into my soul. "Where are you going to go?"

Panic filled me. Inside my head, the screams from The Order mingled with Colt's cries of pain. I still felt the son's big hand clasped around mine, still felt every catch of his breath as his brother picked shard after shard of glass from his side.

"You're not going anywhere," London answered for me. "It's about time you understood that. You're one of us now. You're family."

My face heated. *"Family?* We're no fucking family, London. If we are, then we're one sick version of one."

His hold tightened and dragged me closer. I bucked, fighting. But it was pointless against his strength and I slammed against his hard chest. His body was so goddamn warm, so strong, so—

Christ, he smelled good—forceful as he leaned down and murmured against my ear. "We *are* family, Vivienne. You want to call me daddy? Will that make you feel better about this?"

The heat from my face plunged to my core.

I bit down on my lip and closed my eyes.

I couldn't speak, only shake my head.

"I bet if I reached into your panties, I'd make you out to be a liar."

A whimper tore free.

One hand slowly trailed down, while the other around the back of my neck pressed against me. "I bet you're practically *dripping.*" The back of a curled finger skimmed the outline of my breast before brushing my waist and moving lower. "I could take care of that. Right here. Right now. I'd control the machine. I'd control you."

He was going to make good on his promise, going to sink his fingers inside me. He was going to—*break the contract.*

No...no, this isn't happening. I jerked backwards, tore out of his grasp, and pushed away as I stared up into those dark eyes. "Fuck you."

His smirk only grew bolder. "I want to fuck you, Vivienne. I think I've made my intentions clear. I want to lose myself inside you and find out just how tight you are. I want you to remind myself exactly what I'm fighting for."

"You don't need to fuck me to know that," I snapped. "Greed, pure and fucking simple."

He stilled, and a crease furrowed his brow.

"Tell me, London, am I worth it?"

"Worth...what?" He scowled.

"The three million dollars you paid for me."

He stepped closer, pushing me hard against the bench so I overbalanced, falling for a second, before he grabbed my arm to answer. "To me you are."

"*Why?*" I barked. "*Why? Tell me...tell me why any of this?*"

His lips curled, flattening as he drew in a deep breath. "You wouldn't understand."

"Wouldn't I?" I met his glare with one of my own. "Try me."

For a second, I thought he was going to tell me. That he was going to own being the fucking snake he was, until in an instant, he closed down. The mask slipped into place. Gone was the man who seethed with desire and in his place was the player. The mastermind who moved the pieces behind the scenes— who'd made me stand there and watch as my best friend and her brothers were gunned down before lifting a finger to help them.

"You're playing a very dangerous game here, wildcat."

"So are you," I answered. "When you play with me." He gave a soft chuff, causing me to jut my chin higher and lift my hand. "I suppose you'll beat me senseless just to take this from me."

His nostrils flared and a glint of rage sparked as he slowly looked down to the key as I unfurled my fingers. "Keep it," he said, slowly sliding his hand down my arm, and stepped away.

Keep it? I shook my head, confused, then looked down and froze. "You're bleeding."

"What?"

I grabbed his hand, hating it felt so fucking good. "There's blood on your hand, London. You're bleeding."

He slowly pulled back, sliding from my grasp, a look of exhaustion weighing him down. "That's not my blood, Vivienne," he said carefully. "Besides, I'll bleed for better reasons this year."

He took a step backwards, giving me space. "It's late, you should be in bed."

The fighter rose inside me. I opened my mouth to tell him to go to hell, but stopped. There was exhaustion in his stare, a weariness. I glanced again at the crimson smear on his hand. Whatever had happened tonight weighed him down...

As much as I hated it, he was right. My body was heavy, my soul just fucking sad after the things I'd endured today. Christ, it felt like I'd lived an entire lifetime in one day. I stepped sideways, keeping him in the corner of my eye, and clenched my hand around the key once more before hurrying from that room and the basement.

I moved fast, my bare feet soundless as I made my way up the stairs, glanced at the sons' closed bedroom door, and slipped through my own, then closed it behind me. Heavy, sawing breaths filled me as I pressed against the door, staring at the murky outline of my waiting bed.

I stumbled toward it, collapsed, and lay down, then pulled the comforter up high. *You want to call me daddy? Will that make you feel better about this?* My nerves were raw. My body was plump, swollen and *aching*. I didn't want to feel that desire for him. But I did...*Jesus, I did.*

I closed my eyes and reached down.

Would you like me to use it on you?

"Yes," I whispered as I plunged my hand under the waistband of my bottoms and drove my fingers inside myself. "Yes, I want you to use it on me. I want you to use it. I want you to fucking use it,

London." I was so wet, squelching and slick, coating all the way along my fingers.

I'd barely brushed my clit before I was clamping, releasing...and coming *hard*.

I wanted it again and again.

I wanted to beg him. Because I would beg, I'd crawl on my hands and knees when it came to that. I'd be anything he wanted. I rolled, slid my fingers free, and curled my knees to my chest.

Sleep...

I closed my eyes and waited for darkness to come.

I didn't have to wait long, plunging headlong into the emptiness. And into the hell of that place once more. Screams filled me, terrifying, shrill screams. Screams of children and *them...*

YOU'RE NOTHING! DO YOU HEAR ME! YOU MEAN NOTHING! YOU EXIST BECAUSE OF The Order!

I bucked and wrenched free from the nightmare with my heart booming in my ears and the shrill sound of my own scream bouncing off the walls. I tried to catch my breath as I opened my eyes to stare at the ceiling. Tears welled, tickling the corners of my eyes. I sensed movement before I saw the shadow shift next to my bed.

I lurched backwards, staring at the large, looming figure beside me, until I realized who it was. Fear moved through me as Colt stared down at me. Then he turned and slowly stepped away. But he didn't leave. No. He walked to the wall and turned. With his hand pressed against his side, he slowly slid down to sit on the floor.

I didn't understand what he wanted. My tears blurred his face as he drew his knees up to his chest. He didn't speak a word, just watched me, and it took me a second before I understood what he was doing.

He was watching over me...

I caught the movement of his head as he slowly nodded. The gesture said it all...

No one will hurt you, not while I'm here.

Warmth slid down my temple and leaked through my hair as I rolled on my side, faced him, and closed my eyes. I'd never had anyone do that for me before, never had anyone look out for me. I was the one who'd protected, the one who'd fought. I was the one who'd dragged the ones I cared about out of hell as we ran for our lives.

But as I stared at Colt, sitting with his back against the wall, I realized I didn't have to do that here.

I didn't have to do that for them.

Family. London's voice echoed as I closed my eyes once more.

Sleep came for me again. Only this time it wasn't cruel or brutal. This time, it slid around me, pulling me in close. I let myself succumb and slipped away, knowing I was safe here. Because I had a guardian...

One who was as soundless as the night.

TEN

London
___

I GLANCED AT THE STUDY DOOR FOR THE MILLIONTH TIME, then gave a snarl and pushed my chair backwards. Who the fuck was I kidding? I couldn't concentrate worth a damn this morning. Not when I knew she was in her room above me...

I dragged my fingers through my hair and rose.

Christ, I didn't need this. Not now, not when the goddamn wolves were circling. Hale was getting impatient—*actually, no. He'd passed impatient a bombing ago*—now he was hunting for a target, one he could take his frustration out on. He'd make an example of them. If there was one thing Haelstrom was good at doing, it was that—gutting someone he once trusted and hanging them out to dry.

I couldn't be that person.

Not now...not ever.

I glanced at the door, my attention drawn to the memory of her standing in that room in the basement staring up at me with so much lust and torment. No, I had to keep my focus until Hale felt the honed edge of my own blade pressing down on his

94

neck. Then he'd know...he'd know it had been me the entire time.

My phone vibrated on the desk in front of me. I snatched it up, glanced at the display, and answered. "Anything?"

"Yeah," Carven muttered. "But you're not going to like it."

A sinking feeling swept through me. "Tell me."

"So, I found where they were staying and it's right in the middle of the Rossi stronghold."

I clenched my jaw. That much I'd figured out for myself. Still, the confirmation was all I needed. "Did you track it down?"

"Yeah, and Creed Banks, as well."

My stomach clenched as my heart pounded. "Is he still there?"

"No."

I scowled. "Go on."

"According to the satellite footage, he was dragged in there by his two sons...and carried out—in a fucking body bag."

"*Shit!*" I paced, thinking...

"That's not the only thing." He made me stop cold. "The car he was hauled into belongs to a doctor at Sacred Heart. Looks like he rocked up not long before they carried him out."

"Rossi's man?"

"By the looks of it."

"Fuck." I closed my eyes, as if this could get any worse. "I needed him. I *fucking* needed him." Carven said nothing. Because what was there to say? "Do you have the details on this doctor?"

"Sending them now."

"If Banks is out, then it'll only be a matter of time before they link the warehouse to us," I muttered, spilling my fears out loud. "They'll come for Castlemaine and they'll wipe us out to do it. They'll tear him apart to get to King and there won't be a damn thing I can do to stop them."

"Do we move him?"

Thinking...thinking...thinking. "No," I muttered as pieces started to fall into place. "We just give them a new trail to follow. One that will lead them back to the Rossis."

"Are you sure about that?"

"Am I sure if it's him or us?" I answered. "Yeah, I am."

My phone beeped in my hand. "Then it's all there, and London?"

"Yeah?"

"Check in on my brother before you leave?"

As if he had to ask. "Of course."

I hung up the call and pulled up the doctor's details. Lucas DeLuca, Emergency Medicine, Sacred Heart. The photo that filled the screen was a nice-looking guy. A stand-up guy, by the looks of it. So how in the fuck did he get mixed up with the Rossis?

There was only one way to find out. I grabbed my jacket from the back of my chair and rolled my sleeves down as I pocketed my phone. I only hoped I didn't need to hurt him. But I would... and I wouldn't think twice about it, either.

I made my way out of the study, not bothering to close the door this time. It made no difference, did it? The tightness at the corner of my mouth tugged higher. No, it didn't matter a damn, not when you had the most infuriating woman that God ever put breath into living under your roof, eating your food, and messing up your goddamn bed.

My gaze narrowed as I made for the kitchen. The low hiss of something searing filled my ears before the smell of steak wafted through the air. Instantly, my mouth watered.

"Frances," I murmured, catching the chef's attention as he gently turned the Wagyu strip and placed it carefully on a plate. "Everything set for tonight?"

His crisp, white double-breasted jacket was spotless, not even a smear, as the four-star Michelin chef gave a nod and answered in a thick French accent. "Yes, Mr. St. James. Everything will be prepared exactly as you instructed."

"Good." I gave a smile. "Colt will enjoy the tasting."

"Oh, don't worry," he waved the tongs in the air like a weapon. "He's already had a ten-egg omelet and a massive fruit platter this morning. I'm surprised I haven't received another text already. For someone who's just had surgery, he's doing surprisingly well."

"Surgery."

"On his appendix, sir."

"Oh." I nodded. "Of course."

The chef gave a scowl for a second before turning back to the stove and busying himself with the rest of the trial for tonight's dinner. I left him muttering in French. I could only expect it had something to do with the fact I'd apparently had no idea my own son had even had surgery. But if the chef had an opinion, he kept it to himself.

Because he understood the assignment.

And the penalties for divulging anything that went on within these walls.

All of my staff did.

I passed the dining room and caught sight of my main steward as he set out the dining table. Black. Red. Understated, and no barrier against the glass. Those were the instructions and by the looks of it, he was delivering. "Guild."

"Mr. St. James." He gave a nod.

I left them behind and headed for the stairs. Christ, my damn heart was fluttering. Thoughts of tomorrow night's dinner pushed in, filling me with fear, disgust, and self-loathing. So I focused on the meal tonight, one set for two. I glanced at her closed door and went along to the twins' room. If she didn't want to be a prisoner, then she would eat with me.

No more meals delivered to her room...

No matter how much I'd enjoyed making them for her.

It was time to test that defiance, stretch her until she reached her limit...*then stretch her a little more.*

My breaths deepened with the thought. The hunger plunged all the way down to my cock. Fuck, I wanted to stretch her. I wanted her dripping, aching, and filled to the fucking brim.

But that would come.

As soon as Hale signed the goddamn contract.

I lifted my hand, knocked gently on the door, then pushed it open. Colt was sitting at the desk, head down, quiet as he busied himself.

"New console, huh?" I crossed my arms and leaned against the wall.

The son was bare-chested, apart from the white bandage taped around his middle, holding the padded dressing on his side in place. Hard muscles bunched as he moved, leaning over to attach cords into the back of the console, giving me a view of his back.

Surgery on his appendix...Frances's words filled me as I stared at the mess that was Colt's back. Thick silver scars slashed across the middle, peppered with small cigarette burns. But they were nothing compared to the criss-crossed jagged lines that marred his front. There were neat ones too, made by a surgeon's steady hand as he'd tried to undo the damage done to the boy.

So many fucking surgeries.

And so many goddamn beatings.

It was a miracle he'd survived.

He didn't glance my way, nor did he stop what he was doing. Only once did he turn away...to adjust the view on his phone toward where he worked. The screen drew my gaze and I stiffened at the sight.

His phone sat on its side, braced in a holder to allow him to watch the CCTV footage on the screen. Vivienne was in her bedroom, a towel wrapped around her middle. Her long hair was wet, fresh from the shower. I scowled, then turned back to this son who spied on her...just like I did.

He held her hand, London. Carven's voice echoed in my head as I watched Colt glance at the camera feed, watching her before he switched on the curved monitor in front of him and pulled over the console. The console bought to replace the one she'd smashed. The *only* thing that brought Colt any peace.

But as I watched the male work, sneaking glances at her as she rubbed lotion along her bare legs all the way to the juncture of the towel, I realized he didn't care about the game anymore. He had something else to occupy his time. And for the first time in his entire life, I watched my twenty-one-year-old, brutally damaged son become infatuated.

"You feel it, too, don't you?"

He glanced my way, those ocean-blue eyes darker than I'd ever seen them. But it wasn't with jealousy, or rage. They were dark with desire. Because that is what she invoked in us, wasn't it? Her bloodline be damned, this madness was deeper than hunger, crueler than greed.

She thought that's all she was to us.

I looked at the phone angled just where he wanted.

She was wrong.

I turned back to Colt as he gave one slow nod.

A flare of jealousy ignited, until it was snuffed out by that need to protect her. Because now she would be protected by the most dangerous of us all. I gave him a smile, then turned away. "Watch her, son. Watch her, and protect her with your life."

Those words carried me all the way to the garage. I left the smells and the bustle of the house staff behind and climbed into the Audi. I could trust my sons to do more than hunt and kill for me now. I could trust them with *her*.

I drove across the city, pulling into the parking lot outside the tired looking city hospital. Mottled gray walls divided the rows upon rows of glinting windows that reached sky high. Patients spilled out of the automatic double doors at the emergency entrance. I climbed out, locked the car, and crossed the street, heading for them.

They stared as I walked past, adjusted my jacket into place, and stepped through the doors into the seventh level of Hell. Crying children, yelling men. People sat huddled against the walls, cramming every inch of the waiting room and front desk area.

"I told you once before. No insurance, no doctor." A large, tired-looking triage nurse shook her head at a young mother with a screaming baby on her hip.

I didn't wait, didn't see them. I couldn't *afford* to see them. Instead, I stepped around her, stopped at the desk, and drew the triage nurse's stare. "Oh, no way did I just see you cut the line here, Mr.—" she scanned me up and down, her stare slowing. "Fine-ass specimen of a man. Tell me, gorgeous, what can I do for you?" she beamed.

I gave her a smirk and leaned closer. "I'm looking for a Lucas DeLuca, is there any chance..." I searched her chest for a name badge. "Rochelle, that you might direct me to him?"

"Doctor DeLuca?" Her eyes widened, sparkling. "Why yes, he's in his office." She lifted her hand and pointed along the hallway. "Straight down there on the right."

I gave her a wink, then watched as she flushed, and grinned. But the smile slipped as I glanced at the young mother and her crying baby. She saw it, the act, the pretense. I gave her a nod before I turned around and walked away.

The sounds. The smells.

They hit me almost harder than I could bear.

I swallowed hard, then reached into my pocket, pulled out black leather gloves, and slipped them on. I didn't want to see the children in pain, or their frantic parents pacing the hallways, desperate to ease their child's pain. I wasn't a man of emotions, nor was I kind.

But the sight of those small, helpless infants did something to me. Something I allow. It made me question...

I tore my gaze away, tugged the gloves into place, and clipped the strap around my wrist as I glimpsed a closed door toward the end of the hallway. Nurses shuffled in and out of the break room on the opposite side. The women stared, the men scanned me up and down. But I paid them no mind. I turned my focus to the darkened office before I bore down on the handle and slipped inside.

It was quiet, *too quiet,* before soft snores came from the floor toward the back of the room. I moved quietly around the desk, one that was stacked with folders that towered over everything else. Why on earth anyone would subject themselves to this, I had no idea.

The snores were deep and steady and muffled the sound of my steps as I neared the small cot shoved into the corner of the room. I reached into my pocket and pulled out my gun and silencer as I stood over the...Rossi fool. A kick at the end of the bunk, and I waited for the snores to stop. But they didn't. The man slept like the dead, but I supposed he kept enough of them for company. I kicked again, only harder this time.

His eyes snapped open, his gaze shifting instantly to me as I stepped closer and kneeled down.

I'd expected confusion.

I'd expected fear.

I'd expected the man to start fumbling and blubbering or at least scream for security.

But the doctor didn't do any of those things, not even when I lifted my hand, glanced at the glove wrapped around my gun, and spoke. "I assumed the hours here at the hospital were insurmountable, doctor. On top of the house calls you make."

"Wait, I—"

I didn't give him a chance to finish, just slapped my hand against his mouth, lifted the gun, and pressed the silencer to his head. "You won't talk, do you understand me? You won't say a word until I tell you to. You'll be quiet and patient, and when I ask you the questions I'm here for, you'll answer. Because if you don't, I'll splatter your brains all over your office wall. Do I make myself clear?"

My palm warmed with the heat of his heavy breaths, then he slowly nodded.

"Good. Now, the safehouse you attended for Benjamin Rossi. You met with three men, correct?"

His eyes widened. The bloodshot whites were almost neon in the dark as he shook his head.

"No?" I slid my hand from his mouth, my finger ready around the trigger.

"No," he answered. "I met with two, the third was already dead when I got there."

"He was already dead?" My mind raced as it conjured up various scenarios, trying to find one that'd fit.

The last we knew of Creed Banks was him leaving The Order after he'd tried to get Elle Castlemaine to leave. The video footage of that night still played out inside my head. I'd watched it over and over again in the hours after Ryth's capture, trying to get a step ahead of Riven.

But I'd been too late.

I still kicked myself at the missed opportunity to get to King.

Or capture one of his men as they stormed The Order.

"They killed him?" I focused, meeting his stare.

"They didn't say and I don't assume."

"Huh," I muttered as my finger moved from the trigger. Still, I didn't lower the gun. "The body, where is it?"

"Somewhere safe."

Anger flared, sending a chill through me. "That wasn't what I asked. Where is the body?"

"No." He shook his head. "You're not getting it, I promised..."

I pressed the gun harder against his skull. "Right now, I'm the only thing that stands between them and those who seek to take Ryth and kill her brothers. So believe me when I tell you, I'll do whatever it takes to prevent that from happening. But only because it serves my interests. Now, you don't want my interests to change, do you, doctor?"

He held my stare for a second before he slowly shook his head.

"There are far worse men out there than me, believe me. I need to keep those men occupied, I *need* to keep them looking somewhere else. So, I'm going to ask one more time...*where is the body?*"

"It's at a holding facility off Beauchamp Place."

"A holding facility?"

"Where we burn the bodies of those who have no insurance. But it's safe. I have it stowed away so they won't destroy it without my approval."

That twitch came at the corner of my eye. I knew about places like that where they piled the dead in the refrigerated units and had the furnace running twenty-four hours a day. I pulled the gun away and slowly rose. "I'm going to need that address, Doc. Now, I'm going to trust that you'll keep quiet about this little meeting. I can trust you, right?"

He swallowed hard and slowly pushed up. The guy looked fit and strong. But he also looked exhausted. He rose from the cot and slowly made his way to the smothered desk, then fumbled for a pen and a notepad. The sound of his scrawl was punctured by the tearing of paper.

He turned and held it out, meeting my stare. "Ryth and the guys..."

"Are safe." I took the paper. "For now. How long that lasts is a mixture of variables. Some I can control, others I can't." I held up the paper. "Now, you won't be calling the Rossis about this, will you?"

He flinched and his voice deepened. "No. I won't."

I just gave a nod, unscrewed the silencer from the gun, and slipped it back into my pocket as I made my way around his desk. His hard exhale reached me as I grabbed the handle of his door and stopped. "Oh, and one more thing, doctor. Get some sleep, you look like hell."

Then I left, kept my eyes down, and slowly worked my gloves off before tucking them back into my pocket. Rochelle was busy when I slipped past, fighting with another faceless person in need.

But I didn't see them.

I didn't see anyone.

Just made my way back to the Audi, that slip of paper clenched in my hand. Could I trust the good doctor to hold up his end of the bargain and keep his mouth shut? I didn't know, and I sure as hell wasn't about to find out.

I started the engine and pressed the contact on the screen, waiting for it to answer. Carven was still out, still hunting. I gave him the details as I drove. He was suspicious, but eager. If there was anything that the sons had on their side, it was speed and accuracy. They were the weapon you didn't see coming.

By the time I drove to the exclusive boutique store on the upper side of the city, Carven had all the information he needed. I pulled in and switched off the ignition before I leaned forward and hit the button for the glove compartment. With the gun and the silencer stowed away, I climbed out.

Cars swept past as I buttoned my jacket, then stepped out, closed the door, and locked it behind me. For these perfect moments, I wasn't the ruthless bastard, nor was I the hunter. I stepped up to the door and pressed the doorbell, then waited.

It was answered quickly by a stunning brunette. Her eyes brightened and her red lips stretched wide in a smile. "Mr. St. James, please, come in."

I gave her a curt nod and stepped in. The delicate scent of flowers washed over me as I made my way into the store. The place was empty, just how I liked it. "Did it arrive?"

"Oh, yes, it most certainly did. Would you like to see it?"

"Please."

She left and returned seconds later with a large rectangular box she placed on top of a glass display case. I waited while the top was removed and she plunged her hands under the black tissue paper to draw the dress free.

Black.

Floor length.

Exquisite.

She stepped around the counter as she swept the garment across her arm. "Your wife is sure lucky."

All I saw was the thigh-high split.

And that soft fabric against her tanned skin.

All I saw was black. *Black* she'd wear for me.

"If you'd like, I could try the dress on for you..." she murmured carefully. "So you can see it against skin."

I knew what she wanted. It wasn't the first time the attendant had made her intentions perfectly known. I'd been polite before, discreetly feigning ignorance. But the woman just wouldn't take the hint. I met her gaze. "No, and if you act inappropriately toward me again, I'll have you fired."

The smile on her face faltered, then plunged headlong into terror.

"Now, the shoes," I murmured as I held her stare and watched the fear in her eyes like it was a blood sport.

Anger seethed inside me. As hard as I tried to push Haelstrom's words away, they slithered back...

Friday evening. I expect you at my side, ally. Ophelia will be there, she's specifically requested your attendance.

A shiver passed through me. But instead of fear, I tasted rage.

The kind that pushed me closer to that dangerous edge.

I narrowed in on the attendant in front of me and kept my voice utterly controlled. "Now, the shoes..."

ELEVEN

Vivienne

I screwed on the top of the La Mer body oil as I glanced once more at the spot where Colt had sat the entire night without saying a word. It was weird that he'd sat there...no, more than weird. It was...*fiercely protective* and I wasn't used to it. Not with the way he'd leaned his head against the wall, balanced his arms on the tops of his bent knees and watched me, or the damn silence that came with him.

But somehow, I'd slept...maybe better than I had in forever.

There were no terrifying houses and sickening screams waiting for me when I'd fallen into the emptiness that time. There was *nothing*. Just a dreamless slumber that felt so damn good. Now my body felt lazy and...*lush*.

I smoothed the cream onto the top of my foot and rubbed it in until it shimmered, then slipped from the bed and rose. The silence was one thing. Now I was left with four damn walls that felt like a cage again.

I didn't like it.

Not one damn bit.

With a sigh, I strode back into the bathroom. Smokey dark eyes looked back at me as I neared the mirror. I looked a little haunted after yesterday and last night. That place. That goddamn man...*take the tracker out of me*...my gaze shifted to the swell of my breast and the dull throb as the memory of that basement came roaring back. *Why?* A goddamn, *godawful* deep growl followed. That calculating stare filled me. He was there, always there. *Because I'm not*—still he cut me off with that possessive word. *Mine?*

Mine...

The word lingered.

"No. I'm not yours, asshole," I whispered, staring at myself in the mirror. "No matter how much money you paid for me."

I brushed my hair off my shoulders. It was scrunched and wild, not straightened and blown out like I'd been wearing it. I lowered my gaze to the off-the-shoulder black top with a plunging neckline that went perfectly with the wide-legged pale pink slacks split to mid-thigh. *Mine,* the bastard's voice still echoed. London St. James might be a heartless sonofabitch, but his personal assistant had beautiful taste in clothes.

Pity her boss was an asshole.

I placed the body oil back on the counter and strode from the bathroom. There was no sense in shoes, it's not like I was going anywhere, so I padded barefoot to the door and opened it. But instead of silence, there was a clatter that came from downstairs. I glanced at the sons' closed door, then turned back. Colt must be in the kitchen.

There was only one way to find out.

If I had to stay another day confined in my room, I was going to start redecorating...with a chair through the damn wall. The smell of food hit me as I made my way down to the foyer. Steak...garlic, some kind of—

A man walked around the end of the kitchen counter, and I froze. *Butter...some kind of butter.* There was a stranger...in London's house. I glanced around, then slowly walked toward him. A stranger that wore a chef's uniform. "Ah, hi," I murmured.

But the guy didn't speak, just looked at me, nodded, and went back to cooking whatever he was cooking. Which smelled fucking delicious. I stepped nearer and peered over the stove until he glared at me, forcing me backwards. "Damn, okay."

I stepped away, watching from the corner of my eye as a buff guy dressed in black stepped around the corner from the dining room.

"Hi," I offered.

"Ms. Evans," he answered, then went about his business.

I knew the house was immaculate and my room was always clean. But I hadn't seen any staff until now. I scowled, did they know about me, exactly? Like that I was here against my will? I stepped forward and opened my mouth to tell them—

What, Vivienne? London's voice echoed inside my head. *What are you going to tell them, and where are you going to go?* I winced, hating how even now I knew exactly what he'd say. As I stood there, feeling trapped, the chef kept cooking and the guy dressed in black stepped around me before disappearing.

I thought about going upstairs to Colt, but the idea of sitting there in silence was too much to bear. So I went to the only place I could think of and the only place that didn't scare me. I headed for his study. The master key was tucked in my pocket. I pulled it out, but before I could insert it in the lock, I tried the handle.

It was open.

"Huh." I pushed the door open and stepped inside. Sunlight spilled through sheer curtains, but the light in the room was darker and more masculine during the day.

I glanced along the shelves of books then made my way to the desk. A desk that had a neat stack of folders with a sticky note attached. The closer I came, the more suspicious I was, until I stood over them.

If you're going to make yourself at home, Vivienne, you'd better start here.
L.

"L." I muttered, flicking the corner of the note. "Fuck you, L. How about that?"

He always had to sound so goddamn condescending, so damn proper. I looked around the study. I wondered where his personal assistant worked? Probably remote. I wouldn't be able to stand staring at that obnoxious sonofabitch all fucking day either.

I bet if I reached into your panties, I'd make you out to be a liar.

My body trembled with the words. Heat followed, only now it was bolder, hotter, hitting me right between my legs. I closed my eyes and rocked forward as I gripped the edge of the desk. "Fuck you, London St. James. Fuck you..."

I opened my eyes. I just needed something to focus on, anything to distract me from the faint scent of cigar, leather...and that dangerously seductive cologne. I dragged a deeper breath into my lungs. "Christ, that smells nice," I muttered, testing the locks on his drawers. What did you know, they were unlocked...

All of them...

Like he was letting me in, allowing me to see all his dark, hidden secrets.

I froze and scowled at the implications of that. He was trusting me, knowing I could expose him if I wanted to.

We're family.

Those words rose. *Family.* Like they were the sons and I was the daughter. *You want to call me daddy? Will that make you feel better about this?*

I swallowed and sat in his chair as I ran my hand along his desk. I was slipping, losing that edge of hate I'd carried with me since he'd dragged me into this house kicking and screaming, and I didn't like it. No, I didn't like it at all. I plucked off the note he'd left me and pulled the file close.

The moment I opened it, I froze. There was a photo of the house of horrors, only it wasn't in ruins like it was now. It was alive, seething and cruel. A man stood outside along with three women and a group of children. They were all girls, every single one of them.

The boys' home was far worse...

Those words hit me as I stared at the women in the photo, then him...the man standing next to them. The one who held the plaque that read *Hale Home.*

"Hale," I muttered. I knew the name...*only too well.*

I'd heard it whispered and wielded like a weapon. I knew who owned The Order and I was looking at the sick sonofabitch himself. The only question was, why was London making moves against him?

He had Jack Castlemaine.

He'd protected Ryth.

Even if he'd done it to serve his own selfish needs. The only question was, what were those needs...*and where on Earth did I fit in?* That question above all nagged me. As I flicked through the printed information on the history of the house, I didn't find an answer. What I did find under the first file was another sticky note, this one with some kind of IP address.

I turned to the Mac, bumped the mouse, and watch the screen come to life. Vivienne. I was set up with my own login...only it was locked with a password. I glanced back at the note, but all it had was the address. "Nice one, dickhead. You forgot to leave me the password."

Only he didn't forget, did he?

Because a man like London didn't forget a damn thing.

He was testing me.

I clenched my jaw and started typing...*Vivienne, incorrect. Viv, incorrect. Vivienne Evans...incorrect.*

The damn thing was going to freeze me out.

You can call me daddy...

Call him daddy.

"No," I shook my head. "No fucking way."

But that nagging cursor just blinked and blinked and *blinked.* "Goddammit." *Daddy,* I typed, and the screen came alive, opening up to a screen just for me. There was a folder with my name on it. As much as I wanted to explore it, I left it to open up the browser and typed in the address from the note.

It took me to a prompt.

I scowled, staring at the black background and the tiny cursor waiting. Then intrigue got the better of me:

> Hello?

I hit send and waited...

> Who is this?

"Who is this?" I muttered and typed in.

> Who is this?

> Viv, is that you?

My heart lunged. No, it couldn't be. My breaths were racing, my fingers trembled as I typed.

> Ryth, is that you?

> Yes! OMG. Is it you?

I let out a cry, my throat thickening.

> Yes, it's me. God, I didn't think I'd ever talk to you again. Are you okay? Where are you?

I waited.

> Caleb says it's not safe to say. But I'm okay.
> Are you okay?

I lifted my head and stared at the study door. I wanted to say no, that I was terrified and desperate to get out of here, but those words didn't come. Instead, I hated myself more than anything for telling her the truth as I typed.

> Strangely, yeah. I…I'm okay and I'm safe. Protected even, which is super fucking distressing.

> I don't know whether to laugh or be even more concerned. Have you seen my dad?

Her dad? Shit. My thoughts turned to him. I'd invaded London's study to find him, hadn't I? Somehow, I'd been sidetracked.

> No, but I will.

> Good. When you do, will you tell him I love him? I have to go now, we're just about to leave. We're heading to a place that might be safe. We'll talk soon. I love you, Viv. Stay safe.

My throat tightened at the words as I typed.

> I love you, too, Ryth.

Then I hit send and sat back and watched the screen. She was safe…and able to talk to me…and that hit me harder than anything he'd ever done. Tears welled in my eyes. I swallowed hard, but I couldn't budge the lump in the back of my throat.

Then the study door opened, making me jump. London strode in and closed the door behind him, but didn't once look my way. I closed the chat down in a hurry, then realized I didn't need to. Because he wanted me to talk to her. He'd orchestrated this all.

I glanced at the open file as he casually unbuttoned his jacket, removed it, and placed it over the end of the desk before he reached into the pocket of his pants, which drew my gaze to how they hugged his tight ass, before he drew something out and dropped them on the desk in front of me.

They were black leather gloves.

The kind you strapped on...

And in an instant, the image rose in my mind.

The feel of those gloves running over my breast. His thumb circling my nipple. Blood hummed in my veins as I swallowed once more. Still, he didn't speak to me, didn't meet my stare, and for that I was thankful. Heat rushed to my cheeks as he rolled up the sleeves of his shirt, exposing the corded muscles of his strong forearms, and rounded the desk.

"Vivienne," he murmured as he gripped the back of the chair and leaned over me. "I hope your day was productive."

He was too close...

Too damn close.

My panting breaths only drew his scent in deeper. That rich, seductive, erotic-as-hell scent. I bit down on a moan as he leaned harder against me and entered his login code to change the screen on the Mac before he turned his head and stared at me.

Abort...

ABORT!

I tried to push away, but I was wedged in, unable to do anything but meet that dark carnal stare and try my best not to come in front of him. "Fine."

There was a twitch in the corner of his mouth as he held my stare. "Good."

He turned back to glance at his messages, then hit keys to send information to somewhere else before he logged off and opened up my login screen once more. "I take it you found the log in details easily enough."

"Yes."

"Yes?" He glanced my way and straightened, towering over me, waiting...

"Yes, *London.*"

That vile, soul-destroying stare pinned me to the spot before he gave a small chuff and turned away and made his way around the desk to open the door and stride out, leaving it ajar. I tried to focus on the files in front of me, my damn cheeks hot and blazing, but I couldn't focus on a damn word. Instead, I tracked those heavy steps as he left and returned, carrying a pear.

He casually strode across the office and grabbed his iPad and opened it up, oblivious to me once more. I forced myself to stare at the words that made no sense and flicked open the page. But I watched him in the corner of my eye as he reached in his pocket, pulled out a survival knife, and opened it up. Steel shone, making my pulse stutter as I fixed on the honed blade as he sliced a piece of pear and neared the desk.

And placed it casually on the desk in front of me.

The order was simple: eat.

He turned back, skimmed his finger across the screen of his device, and scanned email after email. I reached out, grabbed the piece of fruit, and bit down. God, that was delicious. Somehow, I settled enough to read the words on the page in front of me as we lapsed into an easy silence, one where he divided his focus between carving slices and placing them on the desk in front of me, all while he pretended I wasn't there, until there was no pear left and I held the last slice in my hand.

The slice that should've been his.

But it wasn't, and above all, that disturbed me.

Not only did he share his food.

He made sure I was fed more than he was.

I slipped the last bite in my mouth and chased the dribble of juice that ran down my thumb before I slowly pushed upwards and gathered the file in front of me. "I'll just leave you to it, then."

He glanced up, but didn't once answer. The hunger in his stare was answer enough. I grabbed the paperwork and hurried to leave the study and his damn possessive gaze behind.

I didn't even glance at the chef, just strode for the stairs and climbed, with the sweet taste of my crumbling resistance on my tongue. I all but slammed my bedroom door as I closed it with a *thud* behind me, leaned my back against it, and tried desperately to contain myself.

Until I noticed it...

A large black box on the end of my bed.

"What the fuck," I whispered, and stepped forward.

The box was huge. Matte black. Enticing. I dropped my file on the bed beside it, grabbed the envelope placed on the top, and pulled out a small white card.

Dinner will be at 8pm sharp.
This time, Vivienne, please wear the damn clothes.
L.

My hands were shaking as I put the card down, grabbed the top of the box, and lifted. Black tissue paper covered the garment. I swept it aside and reached in, pulling out the most stunning dress I'd ever seen.

A dress that was *black*.

TWELVE

Vivienne

This time, Vivienne, please wear the damn clothes...

HE'D SAID PLEASE. I STARED AT MYSELF IN THE BATHROOM mirror with those words ringing in my head, *he'd said please...*

Heat rushed to my cheeks as I stared at the stranger in front of me. I'd set out to do the bare minimum just to spite him, but this...this was so not that. Instead of smoky and black, I was... understated. Blushed. Gold shimmering highlights against my cheeks made my skin look sun-kissed. I brushed the glimmer along the line of my shoulders with the thick brush before I put it back down and glanced at the clock.

It was almost eight and the captive was about to go...where? I had no idea. But it was somewhere. A thought pushed in, cold and slippery like an eel. One that made me feel sick. Was it to one of those parties the men from The Order took the other girls to? The ones where they came back traumatized and used by too many men to count? Was London St. James about to break me?

My stomach clenched. The glaring white overhead lights made the bathroom sway. He wanted me to wear black, right? And not just the dress either. The lingerie he'd placed next to the garment was black too. Soft black velvet matching panties and bra—if you could call them that.

The bra cups were nothing more than a cage around my breasts, leaving my nipples exposed under the dress, and the panties were no better. The soft velvet straps plunged between my thighs and wrapped around my waist, crisscrossing over the flesh of my ass. There was only one reason he wanted me to wear this. I reached out and grabbed the vanity as I tried to steady myself on the dangerously high stilettos. Because he wanted to expose me to others.

Owned, right?

Three million dollars owned.

He needed to get his money's worth somehow.

Run...the thought gripped me. *Run...where?* My mind turned to Ryth and the messages I'd shared with her. Ones that London had set up for me.

I met my own gaze in the mirror. He wouldn't do that if he was going to hurt me, right?

He wouldn't do all of—I stared at the stunning black dress in the mirror—*this.*

Everything about him screamed the opposite of what those men did. He wasn't a man who shared anything, not that I'd seen, unless it came to his sons...and now me. I inhaled deep and straightened as I fought the stab of fear inside me. I had to trust he wouldn't do that, but if there was anything I'd learned with the man, it was trusting London would only get you in trouble. Or worse...*killed.*

I made my way out of the bathroom.

If I couldn't trust, then I'd fight and run if it came to that. I'd cut his goddamn tracker out myself, with my nails if I had to. Until then, I'd play his games. I smoothed the dress down, fluffed the strands of my hair nervously, then went to the door.

And I'd make sure I was the one in control.

The house was quiet when I stepped out of my room. Quiet and...*eerie*. I gripped the banister and made my way downstairs, the elegant dress skimming the stairs behind me until I hit the foyer. Then I saw him standing with his back to me at the entrance to the kitchen.

My gaze moved down his body, taking in his immaculate black shirt and tight trousers that hugged the hard curve of his ass and every inch of his thick, masculine thighs. I couldn't stop staring, even as he sensed me and turned, then I was fixed on the swell of his cock. Fuck, he was big, wasn't he? *Jesus...*

Heat flushed my cheeks. I forced myself to look away, to meet those intense dark eyes instead. He said nothing as I walked toward him, not a *'you're late'*, or *'you look beautiful'*. No, he just stared.

But as I neared the entrance to the kitchen, I realized he wasn't heading for the door. The waiter from earlier was there, though, moving around in the kitchen behind London as he poured two glasses of champagne. Then it hit me. We weren't going anywhere, were we? The dinner was...here.

Then, if it was here, who else was coming?

I tried to keep my panicked thoughts from conjuring vile scenarios as London lowered his gaze, taking in the damn dress he'd so desperately wanted me to wear. A dress I both hated and wanted to wear forever. I knew I looked different, but the asshole could at least try not to gawk.

Well, say something! I unclenched my jaw, ready to snap, until there was a twitch at the corner of his mouth and it inched higher. That devilish smirk hit me right between my thighs. My pulse surged and heat rushed to my cheeks, forcing me to look toward the dining room behind him.

He grabbed the two glasses of champagne from the waiter and motioned me to the table. I followed, scanning the empty chairs. "This was for us?"

"No, Vivienne." He placed my drink on the table and pulled out my chair. "This was for you."

For me?

There were no other place settings laid out. Still, I was nervous as I sank into the chair. "Is it just us then?"

"The sons are out," he answered as he took his own seat at the head of the table opposite me. "They'll return later, if that's what you're asking."

My face burned as I nodded. Still, he saw the reaction as I looked at the empty seats.

"Tell me," he commanded, his focus narrowing in on me.

In that moment, I understood just how dangerous it was to be the sole object of his attention. I flinched, then shook my head. "Nothing."

"You looked almost terrified," he murmured carefully. "So it must be something."

The heat in my cheeks burned hotter as I met that stare. "I thought you might...have guests."

"Guests?"

"Yeah, *guests.*" I tried to hide my shame by grabbing the champagne. "I've seen what happens to the girls they take out from The Order, and I've seen them what they look like when they came back, too."

He knew...I saw it in the flinch as he asked carefully. "And you think I'd do that to you?"

I held his stare. "I don't know, do I?"

When he spoke, his voice was etched with disdain. "I might be many things, Vivienne. But I'm never like that. You are..."

Mine...

That unspoken word roared between us as the waiter neared and placed a plate down in front of me.

That's what he wanted to say, wasn't it? That I belonged to him. *Three million dollars, remember?* Heat burned in my cheeks again as the waiter straightened.

"Pan-seared sea scallops in brine butter sauce," he announced softly.

I didn't look away from London, just answered, "Thank you."

Tension built between us as the waiter placed London's plate down and left without another word. I watched London out of the corner of my eye, and each careful movement goaded me as he slowly picked up his utensils and ate in goddamn silence.

Everything about him was silent.

Moody.

Volatile.

Quiet.

I did the same, stabbing the scallop before I hacked it with my knife and shoved it into my mouth. I didn't taste the goddamn brine butter sauce, I was too busy choking on the bitter tang of rage. I chewed and swallowed, chasing the food down with the champagne until I'd drained the glass. Then the waiter was there, appearing out of nowhere to pour me another.

Still, I was fixed on the flare of his chiseled jaw as London savored each bite, then glanced at my plate. "You're not eating. Aren't you hungry?" He lowered his gaze to the dress, and to my breasts. "Because I know you are."

That fire ignited. "You seem to know a lot about me."

"I do."

So. Fucking. Smug. I just wanted to smack that knowing twinkle out of his eyes. I clenched my jaw and forced the words out. "Then you also know I'll figure out what you want with me."

A brow rose. "You will?"

You will? He goaded me until I just wanted to... "Yeah." I grabbed my champagne again. "I will."

I lifted the glass to my lips, but this time, I didn't drink. Instead, I licked the drop that collected on the outside of the glass, chasing it with my tongue. That slowly wiped the smirk from his face. That hunger burned between us once more as if it hadn't ever really left.

"Take it out, London." I held his stare. "Take it out of me now."

He shifted his gaze from my lips to my breasts as I slowly rose from the seat. "Take it out or I'll claw it out."

Those infernal eyes didn't leave mine as I stalked along the table toward him. Suddenly, I realized what this was. It was payback from when he'd dragged me to that roof and made me watch as Ryth and her brothers were hunted down. Anger spurred me on until I was heady with the rush.

London carefully placed his napkin down next to his plate and slowly rose. "I'd rather put something else *in* you." He turned to me. "How about that?"

I froze as fear punched through me. "What?"

"You heard me." He grabbed me around the waist and lifted.

I bucked for a second, pushing against him before he plonked me hard on the table. My hands flew backwards, my fingers skidding against the glass top. In an instant, I was back outside that house of horrors with his hands everywhere. Only this was different. He didn't flinch, just grabbed my waist and yanked me hard against him.

He looked down, his stare taking in every inch of me. "Fuck me, you are *annihilating.*"

I tried to shove him away as he reached down, slid his hand into the slit of the dress, and captured the back of my thigh. My legs were parted by the force of his body. I could feel every hard inch of him bulging against his trousers.

"So fucking perfect, aren't you, wildcat?" He swept my dress aside, exposing my entire lower body.

That ravenous stare raked every inch of what he'd paid for as his thumb skimmed the black strap of my panties that ran around my waist. *Get out of this...get out—* "But you can't, can you?" I snarled.

Movement came in the corner of my eye. The waiter slipped into the room, not once glancing our way as London manhandled me.

That only made the rage in me burn hotter. I fixed that rage on the man who ran his hands along my bare thighs. "You can't do a damn thing, or they'll take me."

I enjoyed the dangerous glint in his eyes, maybe a little too much. "But I'm sure I could find someone who could ease the ache in me." I glanced at the waiter, and licked my lips. "If you're not able."

A savage sound slipped from London. He grabbed my face, fingers cruelly digging into my jaw as he tilted my gaze to his. "And his blood would be on your hands. Just remember that."

There was no trace of the man I'd seen a second ago.

The man who'd been dangerously calm and controlled...

Someone else stood in his place now. Someone ruthless...and desperate. A shiver of fear coursed through me as he lifted my calf, placing my heel on the edge of the table, the movement forcing me backwards. "I'd gut him, Vivienne...I'd spill his blood all over this fucking table if he even looked at you."

The memory of the pear came roaring back to me. The way he'd wielded the knife, slicing pieces to place on the desk in front of me. Panic stole my breath as he skimmed his thumb down my crease and gently massaged the swollen flesh around my clit as the waiter poured champagne into London's glass, then left.

I bit down on a moan, hating his hands on me. "Let's see if I can do something about that ache, shall I?" he murmured.

I shook my head, slowly thrashing it from side to side. "No," I moaned as he grabbed my other heel and lifted it to the table until I lay on my back, my knees bent, my pussy on display. "I fucking hate you," I whimpered.

"I know you do," he answered in that cold, sinister tone. "I can feel how much you hate me right now. Such a pretty little cunt." He rubbed and rubbed, stoking that fire.

"No." I slammed my thighs closed, catching his hand against me.

"No?" he murmured, tugging his hand out from my body to yank a chair out before he sat. My pussy may as well be served on a fucking plate for him. But he didn't stop rubbing with his other hand wedged in tight. "Even if I can't *fuck you*, Vivienne, I'm sure I can do something to ease your need."

He ran his thumb along the lips of my pussy, and pushed my flesh into my core. "How's that?"

I clenched my fists, thrashing my head to the side as heat bloomed through me.

"No?"

"*No!*" I groaned, hanging onto a thin thread of hope. "Jesus, no...*no...*"

Every stroke, every caress made me desperate to part my thighs. I needed him to look at me, needed his tongue, needed his fingers. *Fuck, I needed his cock.*

"You going to come for me, wildcat?" he whispered, that low, careful tone tipping me over the edge.

My knees trembled, inching apart.

"That's the way...show daddy what he paid for."

I whimpered and bit down on my lip, but it was too late. A trembling, throaty sound tore free as he pushed deeper, running his fingers along the edges of my pussy. "Please..." I whimpered.

"Now that's a word I could get used to hearing." He rubbed the outside of my clit. "Show me," he demanded. "Show me how you *please* yourself."

I was already unclenching my fist and reaching down.

"But I want you to look at me when you do it."

I stopped, my heart hammering, my core dripping. It wouldn't take much...not if I—

I swallowed hard and pushed upwards, glaring into that infernal stare as my hand continued down. He held my stare, then followed my fingers as they sank deep and slid out. "Jesus Christ, you're so fucking wet." His fingers trembled as he tugged, opening my slit to watch. "That's the girl...get all the way in there."

Heat bloomed with the words. My body clenched as he rubbed, grinding my lips against my clit. "You like that, don't you? You like being my brat? My good little fucking brat. I paid good money for you."

"Three...million...*dollars,*" I moaned.

He jerked his gaze up, those dark eyes burning with hunger. "Yes, three million dollars...and I would've paid more."

A moan ripped free. *He would've paid more.* I thrust my fingers in and worked my body before I slid out and circled my clit. He would've paid more. "How much?"

He leaned down, parted my slit around the trail of my fingers, and licked my clit. *"Everything."*

I came under the touch of his tongue. My hips bucked and drove me against his mouth. He grabbed my thighs and forced my body back against the table. "That's one, wildcat. I'm sure you have a few more in you." He licked again, and the warmth of his tongue danced around the sensitive flesh.

He pushed my legs wider apart, all the way.

"Fuck me," he moaned as he sucked gently. "I want inside this cunt. I want you writhing. I want you coming, I don't care how. My tongue, my cock...*my control.* You're going to be my destruction, aren't you, Vivienne? You're going to fucking ruin me." He sucked and drew me into his mouth.

My core clenched and spasmed as I came again...

"And I'll love every fucking second of it."

THIRTEEN

London

She didn't act like a child now, not splayed out on the table in front of me. Nor did she sound like one with the guttural moans that resounded in the back of her throat. I stared down at her weeping pussy. One slow slide of my thumb caught her come before it fell and I slipped it onto my mouth. Jesus, she tasted perfect. Too fucking perfect.

Easy...

Stay the fuck in control. Remember the contract.

Fuck the contract.

I clenched my jaw and focused as I softly ground the plump flesh against her clit until she dragged her hands high and gently thrashed her head. Give me a man to murder...fuck, give me a thousand, and I'd do it in a heartbeat, as long as I could claim her. But I couldn't. I couldn't, and it was fucking torture. My cock strained my pants, rubbing against the growing wet spot. I wanted to take her to the basement and strap her down. I wanted to fuck her how she needed to be fucked.

I wanted to make her mine...

I lowered my head and licked, catching her come as it trickled, and I fought every cell in my body as it screamed *fuck her now!* My balls clenched and my cock pulsed. I was about to goddamn explode just at the taste of her.

"Tell me how much you want me, Vivienne." I trailed my mouth along the lips of her slit and worked my way higher until I kissed that quivering nub and drew it into my mouth.

"Fuck you."

I smiled as I lifted my gaze to hers and sucked harder, watching as she arched her spine. Inch by dangerous inch, I drew her into me and she fought me every step of the way. Strands of her hair fell to her shoulders. But it wasn't enough. I wanted her wild. I wanted her *free*. As free as I could manage, anyway. I reached up, slid my hand along the nape of her neck, and captured the clip in her hair.

Thick, gorgeous hair drifted out as I opened the clip and let it fall around her before I tossed the ornament aside. "You're to wear your hair down for me, do you understand that?"

She lifted her head and bared her teeth. "Then I'll cut it off."

My cock pulsed at the savage glare of defiance, then I felt the air shift behind me, turning colder, harder, and *more dangerous,* and it wasn't Guild. Carven and Colt had stopped in the doorway to watch her. But our little wildcat was oblivious as I kept up the massage and lowered my head once more. "You going to hiss at me, wildcat? Going to claw and howl? Come on, kitten, show me those fangs."

She shoved upwards and her eyes were wild. Her hair was a tousled mane. She opened her mouth to unleash a tirade of obscenities even mid-orgasm, and froze. Her eyes widened, fixed on the twins behind me, before she grabbed for her dress and tried her best to cover herself.

I lashed out, grasped her around the wrist, and stopped her. "Stop. Let them see how beautiful you are."

She jerked those spectacular brown eyes to me.

My lips twitched and inched upwards. "After all...*we are family.*"

Colt stepped forward and cast a shadow along the table. He was bigger than his brother, older by a whole three minutes. The protector...the defender...*the virgin.* He didn't say a word, just placed his hand on her shoulder and gently pushed her back down.

He stared at my thumbs as I resumed rubbing her pussy, and I gently parted her slit, exposing her body to his gaze. His breaths deepened and his brow furrowed. It was Carven's words that came back to me. *He spoke for her. He fucking spoke for her.*

She had no idea of the implications of that.

Because the male didn't speak...

He just killed.

The motion of my fingers stoked her fire, easing, driving, and rubbing that tiny nub now plump and swollen. Her breaths deepened and her brow furrowed as she was desperate and dangerously close once more. "That's my girl," I murmured, my focus divided by the quivering of her body as I rubbed around and around and around. "That's my good girl. You need to be fucked, wildcat."

"*Yes.*" She bucked her hips off the table. "*Please...oh God.*"

I met Colt's stare and eased back just a little. "I can't help her."

Captured by her desperate sounds, he reached down. He didn't touch her anywhere else, just stared into her eyes and slid his finger all the way inside.

"Oh, *Jesus*." She grasped his wrist and drove him even deeper inside her, then slowly thrust. "Just like that. Fuck, just like that."

I'd never seen him like this. Tortured. Consumed. But still utterly in control, just like I'd trained him.

He opened her legs wider with his other hand as he looked down. His thick fingers slid inside and came away slick. That look of hunger was dangerous as she rode his fingers harder. His eyes widened and his breaths were faster than I'd ever seen before, and I'd seen him take on four skilled men at once. But this wasn't a blood sport. This was all *her*. "I'm going to—fuck, I'm going to—" She bucked once, then unleashed a low moan and climaxed.

Behind me, Carven watched his twin. But not once did he come closer...not once did he look at her. As Vivienne held his twin's fingers inside her, he turned around and left.

"How's that, wildcat?" I turned back to watch as she opened her eyes.

She said nothing, just slowly released Colt's hand. Her breaths were deep and consuming while she watched Colt as he slowly slid his fingers out of her body.

Slick trails were left behind as he brushed her thigh and stepped away. Something passed between them, a kind of longing. One I'd never seen in Colt before. He didn't look at me, just clenched those damp, sticky fingers into a fist, then turned and followed his brother up the stairs.

"Oh, fuck," she hissed, closing her legs.

But the magic was gone now, grown cold, just like our discarded meal. I slid my hands down, letting her slowly sit up. "You may go, Vivienne."

She didn't need to be told twice as she slid from the table and hurried from the dining room. She left, just like they always left...and the clattering of her heels hit me harder this time. I closed my eyes, still feeling the ache of my cock.

I gave her a second before I headed for my bedroom. My steps slowed at the landing to my floor as I fought the need to go to her, to do the one thing I'd promised myself I wouldn't do...tell her the truth.

That she wasn't the only one owned here. I was just as trapped as she was...and she was the one well and truly in control.

But as I glanced up to her bedroom door, I caught movement. Colt stepped out of his room and instantly glanced down at me. His fingers were still curled, holding onto the feel of her as he stopped outside her bedroom door.

I wasn't the only one smitten by the woman.

And by the tortured look on his face, I knew he shared my pain.

But his brother was a very dangerous problem altogether.

I headed for my bedroom, stepped inside, and reached for the buttons of my shirt. Tonight's dinner hadn't gone to plan, but I was starting to learn a lot went that way when it came to her...

I worked the buttons of my shirt and kicked off my shoes as I glanced at the gun on the nightstand next to the bed, then my gaze found the freshly cleaned tuxedo hanging in the closet near the door, which reminded me of the hell I would have to endure tomorrow night.

Ophelia pushed into my mind, turning the desire I'd felt a second ago to barely controlled rage. I shoved her away and forced myself to focus on the only one who mattered, then tugged my belt free and unbuttoned my pants before I looked down.

The small darkened patch was obvious. "Jesus, the woman makes me come like a prepubescent fucking kid." I looked again. I was still hard as fuck. With a groan, I stepped into the shower and turned the faucets.

She was upstairs.

She was upstairs and I was having to—I braced my hand against the shower wall and fisted my cock. Fucking Hale. Fucking contract. I closed my eyes and thrust within my fingers. In my head, I was buried in her pussy, feeling her kick and moan underneath me. I licked my lips and I could still taste her. My pulse boomed harder than it had in a long damn time. I wanted more. I wanted her...*Christ, I wanted her.*

I wanted that short-lived disobedience even as she opened her legs wider for me. That spark of anger...that rage. That fucking pussy...

I froze, my breaths hard and heavy. *No...no, this—* "Jesus..."

My balls clenched as the pulsing vein kicked and I came hard, with barely more than one fucking pull. Warm slick pulsed from my cock and splashed against the tiles. I released a moan, sucked in a hard breath, and pushed upwards.

Thoughts of Colt pushed in. Was the son still standing outside her door? Or had he finally beaten the demons of his past and taken comfort in Vivienne's arms? There was something between them. Something that made the savage part of my nature lift its head and loose a savage snarl.

But I couldn't afford to keep her to myself. If he was smitten, there wouldn't be a damn thing I could do to stop it. All I knew was that no one had better come between him and her, and that included his blood.

There was no telling what he'd do...

And I would be helpless to stop any of it. I washed and rinsed and stepped out of the shower even more desperate than I was when I'd stepped in. I felt strung out, exposed like I'd been rubbed raw on the inside. I climbed into bed, my hair still damp. I'd wanted tonight to be perfect, but it hadn't turned out that way. I'd let my emotions get away from me.

That never happened.

Not to me.

It wasn't who I was.

I closed my eyes.

But instead of sleep came memories. Fragments of a life I'd once had. The cold steel of a silencer. The soft *pfft* of a muffled shot. Eyes that stared back at me, wide, terrified eyes that looked at a monster. Just like the doctor had looked at me. But I wasn't that man, not anymore. I was a new breed of savage. A new ghost.

One who'd spent far too long alone.

———

"THIS IS A GODDAMN MESS, you realize that, don't you?" I shook my head and stared at Carven. "You should've moved the body when you had the goddamn chance. It was the whole fucking reason we acted when we did."

The son just stared at me. Those cold ice-blue eyes looked right through me.

He said nothing. Just waited as I turned away and paced the goddamn study. The vein at my temple throbbed. I could feel my blood pressure climbing with every damn thing that didn't go to plan.

First, it was dinner last night.

And now the fuckup with the one thing I'd needed Carven to take care of.

If I couldn't trust him, then I couldn't trust anyone...

I released a heavy breath and tried to keep the bite out of my tone. "You'll move it from the warehouse tonight."

"You know I will. I'll be at the meeting point after your dinner tonight. I had no choice but to hide it. We were fast, but so were Rossi's men, and you didn't want me taking them out, remember? So we're here," he answered, his tone careful. "But this has nothing to do with a dead body, London. And everything to do with *her*. You're always like this when you have to see her. Caged, desperate. I don't like it."

I closed my eyes.

Her...

Ophelia.

I sensed him move. Soundless steps brought him closer. "Let me take care of her. No one has to know."

I turned and met that icy stare, and the throb at the slide of my head drilled deeper. Just the thought of him anywhere near Ophelia made my stomach churn. Never again...I'd promised him when I carried him and his broken brother from that orphanage and away from her clutches, and this was me determined to keep that promise.

I swallowed the tang of acid down and forced my breaths to slow...for him. "No." I shook my head. "Not yet."

"Not yet?" he repeated. "When, London? Answer me that. How much longer do we have to play this goddamn game?"

"Until I find King." It wasn't the answer he wanted, but it was the only one I had. "We make one wrong move and they all go to ground and we'll never find them."

"So we let the spiders play their games." He held my gaze. "And we search for the lighter fluid and the matches."

I gave a slow nod. "And when the time comes...we burn their nest to the ground."

"And everyone along with it," he answered.

My focus turned to Vivienne. "I'll make sure no one touches our family...ever again."

"All you have to do is get through tonight."

A shiver passed through me as I took a step toward the door, and stopped. "Just be ready. The moment I'm done with the party, we need the body. I want that contract signed...and I want her out of their clutches once and for all."

"I'll be waiting," Carven assured. "For whatever you need."

I gave a nod, then left. Night was almost here...and I had a party to attend.

FOURTEEN

London

I ADJUSTED MY NECKTIE AS I MET MY GAZE IN THE MIRROR. But there was no flicker of life in my eyes. No fear. No hate. Just an emptiness that shimmered in the depths of my stare. One I was getting far too used to seeing. I headed out of the bathroom and grabbed the black velvet box from the nightstand drawer before heading for the bedroom door.

The house was quiet as I stepped out...until the crack of a door sounded from the floor above. Vivienne stopped at the top of the stairs above me as she saw me. Her eyes widened as they fixed on mine. Images rose of her splayed out on the table in front of me. My breaths deepened and my pulse fluttered. The woman hit me like a drug. My vein tapped and the blowback in the syringe bloomed as she rushed through my bloodstream, until I quickly pushed the memory aside.

I couldn't afford to think about her. Not tonight.

Someone so perfect had no place in the fucking filth I was about to touch.

Her gaze shifted to the box in my hand and for a second, there was a flicker of confusion before the tiny flinch of pain. I forced myself to head downstairs. Each step was a pounding fist inside my chest. Guild opened the front door as I neared. One nod was all he gave, and even that was almost too much.

"Protect her at all costs," I murmured, low enough so she didn't hear.

I knew he would. The man was highly trained.

All of them were. I only employed the best of the best, especially when it came to her.

Then I was gone. I left the house and Vivienne behind and made my way to where my driver waited. I didn't look back, just slipped into the back seat before he closed the door. It wasn't until we were far enough away from the house that I released the breath I was holding and tried to find some control. My stomach was hard and my pulse was racing. I licked my lips and pulled out my phone.

My fucking fingers shook when I punched in the code and opened the app. It was fucking habit to track her through the house. I shouldn't be watching her. Tonight, of all nights, I needed to keep a clear head. Still, I narrowed in, finding her standing outside my bedroom. There were no doors barred to her now, all locks were off and that included the basement.

She had everything...*including me.*

But she didn't go into my bedroom. Instead, she turned and walked away with her fists clenched at her sides and a look of pain on her face. Was she upset? Angry after last night? I dragged my teeth across my lip and rubbed my jaw as I remembered Colt's fingers sinking into her pussy. So fucking wet...so fucking insubordinate, spitting hateful words even as she came all over his fingers.

Fuck, I shouldn't be thinking about her.

Not here, not now.

As much as I hated it, I closed the app down and tucked my phone back in my jacket, removing temptation. Instead, I focused on the drive as we made our way through the city to the discreet, sprawling estate to the south. Our headlights carved through the night when we passed other cars as they headed back out after dropping off their guests.

The vilest of the vile, right?

And here I was amongst them.

What did that say about me?

The car pulled around the circular driveway and pulled up in front of the massive house. Doormen were waiting to open my door. "I'll message you, Gabriel."

"I'll be nearby, sir."

I gave a nod and climbed out. I gripped the expensive teardrop diamond necklace and adjusted my jacket, then lifted my gaze to Ophelia's mansion. The bitch was going to be dangerous tonight, high on her own importance and her taste for pain. It'd be too easy for her to have new prey. I needed to be careful, locked down and emotionless. This was no place for my real feelings to get in the way. That would get my family hurt, or worse...back there in The Order.

I inhaled hard and opened the lead-lined vault inside my head. The vault where I tucked anything good in my life. Because they had no room here in hell. Carven was first. Savage. Cold. Loyal to a goddamn fault. I tucked him away, followed by his sullen, silent brother. Then came the feisty breath of fresh air... my little wildcat, Vivienne. Only she didn't go quietly, did she? She kicked and screamed. Blazing too goddamn bright and like a moth to a flame, I was drawn to her. Her feel, *her taste, her fucking innocence.* As I climbed the stairs and inhaled the fetid tang of cigar and cruelty, I shoved her into the safety of my mind-vault and slammed the door.

I'd pay for that, I was sure of it.

Even the fantasy of her was volatile.

And I fucking loved it.

In there, she was protected and safe.

I grabbed a glass of champagne from a waiter as I stepped inside the door and walked along the entrance. My gaze moved to the brand new mammoth art piece hanging on the left. Charcoal and something else...something that made me stop and look. The medium darkened brown, mottled...looking almost like...

Blood.

That's what it looked like.

I lowered my gaze and read the title underneath.

Brand new exhibit here at Ophelia Master's this fall. The piece was haunting, two children with their backs turned, hands clasping each other's in a moment of comfort and solidarity. If it hung in any other foyer, then it might be touching. But not here...*no...not here.* A shiver raced along my spine. If there was anything Ophelia loved more than power and control, it was her goddamn art.

Art that was displayed somewhere in this house.

Art I wanted to stay the Hell away from. So I kept walking.

Macoy Daniels was standing amongst a group of vile, pretentious fucks. He glanced my way as I entered and fixed on me.

Look away, motherfucker.

I kept moving but I still felt the heat of his gaze follow me as I headed for the main reason I was here—Haelstrom Hale. Everything else was just a blur. Paper crinkled in the breast pocket of my jacket as I left the chatter behind and headed deeper into the house. The overhead lights grew duller as I moved through the rooms, heading to the sitting area in the back. I'd been here three times before...and that was three times too many.

I found him sitting amongst the select few, legs crossed, a tumbler of top-shelf Scotch in his hand. He turned his head toward me, not missing a word in his conversation with the others until he gave a slow smile. "London, good to see you."

I gave a nod. *Not like a had a fucking choice, did I?* "Wouldn't have missed it."

"You know Devlin and Zander?" Hale motioned to the others who just stared at me like I was a threat.

I was. Just not in the way they thought. "Sure. Gentlemen." I gave a nod.

"Why don't you take a seat?" Hale motioned to the rest of the group. But there were no seats left. He knew that. "I'm sure we can make room."

I gave a smile, one that made me reel inside, and gave a chuckle. "Maybe later." I lifted the velvet box in my hand. "I have a prior engagement."

I knew the effect that would have on Hale. Anyone else and any other time, he'd take the refusal as an insult, but not for his Ophelia. The vile fucking cunt. Instead, he gave a nod and glanced behind me to the other guests. "I'm sure she'll be too excited to see you."

"I'm sure she will," I murmured and nodded again to the others.

They just stared as I left. But not one would say a word in my absence. They all knew better.

I had a reputation, one I carefully honed with blood. You didn't get this close to Haelstrom Hale otherwise, even if I'd tried to leave that reason long behind. I scanned the others and found Macoy still watching me. I met his stare until the fucker looked away.

But it was that stare I didn't like.

It was too sly, too...*knowing.*

I didn't like it. I headed toward him until the throaty sound of feminine laughter stopped me in my tracks. My stomach clenched. All thoughts of doing anything other than fucking running left my mind. I narrowed in on the gleeful sound and felt sick. Champagne wasn't strong enough, not for this. I drained my glass and headed for the bar. "Scotch, the good stuff," I demanded, watching the waiter as he turned, grabbed a tumbler, and lifted the twenty-six-year-old single malt from behind the bar.

But it wasn't him I focused on. Movement came from the corner of my eye. I tried to steel myself as a hand slid along my arm and the cloying drone of the most hateful bitch God ever put breath into followed. "There you are. I was starting to worry."

I met her gaze and forced a smile. "Wild horses couldn't keep me away."

Ophelia Masters was a stunning woman...on the surface. Wide, dark brown eyes and full, plump lips, with high cheekbones that made her face angular and harsh. She lowered her gaze to watch the red talons of her fingers trail along my arm. But I knew it was an excuse to look at the black velvet box on the bar in front of me. "I thought you might be too involved with your new pet to come...but then again, you can't fuck her yet. Can you?"

I stared into those sinister eyes and caught the glimmer of amusement.

The interim contract Hale had given me had her stench all over it.

Getting to King was only one part of the equation.

She was the other.

"She's a pet, Ophelia. Nothing more."

"Oh?" She glanced at the box. "A three-million-dollar pet, I heard."

I captured her chin, tilting her gaze to mine. "Still, I'm here."

There was a twitch in the corner of my mouth as she moved close, grasped my balls, and squeezed, then murmured against my ear. "Good, because I'd gut the bitch."

Agony punched through my body and my stomach rolled. It was more than the pain, more than the threats. I closed my eyes as she turned her head and kissed the corner of my mouth. Disgust burned inside me as she pulled away. "Tell me, how are the sons? Their screams were quite delicious. Is the mute one talking yet?"

Kill her...

Kill the fucking bitch.

Somewhere in the room, a waiter clinked a glass and announced dinner was served. But I was too busy swallowing the hateful fucking stare she branded me with. I didn't flinch, didn't let her see the panic that roared inside. "*My* sons are fine, thank you."

"You're mine, London." She searched my eyes, staking her claim. "You don't fuck unless it's me. Do you understand that? You owe me, remember?"

"How can I forget it?" I answered as her grip eased and slid along my flaccid cock as she tried to find life.

But there was none to be found.

My ass tightened as the rest of the guests left us behind when they headed for the dining area in the room next to us as she reached for the black velvet box on the bar and opened it. Gold shimmered and the five-carat diamond glinted.

There was a hint of a smile as she pulled away, but instead of leaving with the other guests, she grabbed the bottom of her dress and hiked it up. "Get on your knees, London. I need that delicious tongue of yours."

I wanted to be sick...*no,* I was going to be sick.

I swallowed hard as my pulse boomed. "Here?"

Inside that vault inside my head, a woman's shrill screams echoed as the bitch in front of me smiled and answered. "Here."

FIFTEEN

Carven
_____

HE WAS ACTING STRANGE. QUIET, AND NOT JUST NOT speaking quiet. He was quiet to me...and I didn't like it. I pulled the Explorer into the driveway of the warehouse, punched in the code, and waited for the gate to open. "What the fuck is going on with you?"

He turned his head and met my stare, but said nothing, as he clenched his fist. But I knew my brother, maybe better than he knew himself. I tore my gaze from the clenched movement, knowing full well it wasn't an action of violence.

It was about her...

Because it was the hand he'd used to fuck her, right?

His fingers up in her cunt.

In her fucking cunt.

I didn't like him touching her.

Or the way he was now.

Different.

I didn't like different.

Not when it came to him.

Fuck.

This had nothing to do with her, did it? Not really...not when I got to the root of my rage.

I'll make sure no one touches our family...ever again. London's words shanked me.

Jesus. Jesus, I was going to be fucking sick.

I let out a snarl, shoved the four-wheel drive into gear, and punched the accelerator, driving my brother hard against the seat as I tore into the warehouse parking lot and pulled up hard. Darkness surrounded us. There were no buildings out here, nothing but open spaces all around. A rumble came in the clouds overhead as I killed the engine and climbed out.

A storm was coming.

Just one more fucking thing to deal with.

"Are you coming?" I snarled through the open door.

He scowled, glanced at the sky through his window, then climbed out. I made my way to the steel door, punched in the code, and yanked it open before I hit the lights and strode inside. Boots echoed inside the open area. I glanced at the temporary cold room at the rear of the building then turned around and watched him stride toward me.

"Hey." He kept walking, heading for the cold room, until I stepped in his way, giving him a punch in the shoulder. *"I said, hey!"*

His jaw clenched, and anger burned in his stare.

"You don't walk past me when I'm fucking talking to you, you got it?"

Anger flared in his eyes. His jaw clenched, but he didn't push me back, just stepped around me and kept heading for the cold room. I turned away from him, staring at the guns set out on the rack. No, he didn't push me back. Didn't hit me. Didn't so much as raise his goddamn voice, did he?

Because his voice had been taken from him...*by her.*

"Fuck, this is a mess." I lifted my gaze to the hunting ground, the wall of names, faces, and information we'd captured throughout the years.

This place wasn't just a home away from home. Nor was it just a storage facility for weapons, cars, and everything else we couldn't keep at home. It was also a place where we planned. I shifted my stare to 'the nest' and narrowed in on one face alone.

The one we hated above all others.

Her...

Ophelia Masters.

"He's going to her, you know that, don't you?" I stared at the *bitch.*

The howl of the door hinges stopped instantly. I glanced his way, watching my brother freeze with his back to me.

"He'll do whatever that vile cunt wants to get the daughter signed over to him...just like he did for us."

Colt swung around, those blue eyes wide and fixed on me before he looked at the nest.

I saw the terror.

The fear.

I saw it all in the way his chest rose hard and fell. Inside his head, he was running. Inside his head, he was fighting, just like he'd fought when he was a goddamn kid. Then in an instant, he strode toward me, his face filled with rage. A tremble of fear cut through me as he grabbed me around the throat.

His big hands clenched, then released. My brother had been slashed in the side last night, then badly patched up, and was probably still bleeding internally, but none of that mattered to him, did it? He'd still fight, and he'd still bleed. Because he was just like London.

He knew then. Fuck, I didn't want to tell him, but it was eating me up. "I don't know how to stop it," I whispered around his fists, my hands at my sides. "I don't know how to get him away from her."

There was a furrow in my brother's brow. He liked that as much as I did. London wasn't a fucking father to us. He was a *savior*.

"Now," Colt snarled.

I searched his eyes, looking for what he was trying to say. All I saw was panic and rage. "Now? Now what?" I growled. Frustration roared inside me. He'd spoken for the daughter, but now, when I needed him...when *London needed him*, he just said, *now?*

He released my throat, leaving a throb behind, then turned and walked away.

Rage flashed deep inside me. I took a step, ready to charge the motherfucker and take him to the floor, until he stopped at the open door of the cold room and met my stare. *Now. Now. Now...*

My gaze moved to the cooler behind him and to the body of Creed Banks. We had our instructions, ones which London was very clear on. We'd meet him after the party, give him the body, and he'd *'discreetly'* have it delivered to that sick motherfucker Haelstrom.

*Discreetly...*that was the word he'd used, right?

I shifted my gaze to my brother. That knowing fucking stare said it all. *Now.*

"Now?"

He gave a slow nod.

Fuck me...

He didn't wait, just disappeared inside. The muted crinkle of heavy plastic echoed before a heavy *thud.* Then he strode out with the body over his goddamn shoulder. Panic filled me, the thunderous thrum worsened by the *bang* of the cold room door.

Then my brother was gone, leaving his deafening scream in his wake.

I had no choice but to follow as he dropped the body in the back of the Explorer and climbed into the passenger seat. I slipped in behind the wheel and cut him a glare. "You sure you want to do this?"

He slowly turned his head and that steely stare said it all...*yes.*

SIXTEEN

Vivienne

THUD. THE FRONT DOOR CLOSED AS LONDON LEFT, TAKING the black velvet box with him.

The necklace wasn't for me? Of course it wasn't for me. Stupid. Goddamn. Idiot. I stared down the stairs at the goddamn waiter as the flash of anger hit me out of nowhere.

My heart thundered, feeling like it'd been ripped out of my chest, stomped on, and set alight.

What did you expect, you moron? That he actually gave a shit about you? That last night was anything more than getting his fucking money's worth? I flinched and looked away as I waited for the waiter to leave. *Idiot...idiot...idiot...*still, I couldn't stop the pain, not when it slammed into me like a goddamn bus. You hate him, remember? You. Fucking. Hate. Him.

I cupped my breast and still felt the small throb, which reminded me exactly what this was.

An abduction.

And he was my captor.

"Goddamn you," I whispered as I stared at that closed front door.

But my body betrayed me as it still ached for his fucking touch. The memory of that roared to the surface and my pussy clenched. Fuck, I couldn't get him out of my head. Those merciless eyes and that fucking mouth. Even now, I'd get on my knees for him. I closed my eyes, feeling Colt's thick fingers as they slid inside, and grew wet. I'd get on my knees for all of them if they demanded it.

And I hated knowing that.

I made my way downstairs, haunted by that panicked feeling. I had to change this, had to create some distance between us. I *had to* remind myself of the plan. *Find a way to get to Ryth's dad...*

If there was one person who'd know how to get me out of this, it was him. I lifted my head as I realized I'd stopped walking. But I wasn't in the kitchen, or the study, where I wanted to be. Instead, I stood outside his bedroom door, drawing in the rich, seductive scent he'd left behind.

Christ, I wanted him.

I entertained the idea of invading his room once more. I'd climb into his bed, fuck myself on his nice clean sheets, and leave. Maybe he'd even watch, and yet what would that do? He'd still be gone, right? Still enjoying his dinner with another woman.

Would he fuck her?

Of course he would.

I was betting a man like London had women frantic to sleep with him. Now it seemed like he had one more...me. I winced and turned away as the heat of that knowledge burned in my cheeks. I couldn't believe I was so goddamn stupid. I made my way downstairs, desperate to hide my shame from the waiter who was obviously more than a fucking waiter.

No asshole saw what he had last night and carried on today polishing the silverware. "You want to play like that? Fine," I muttered as I headed for the study, thoughts of trashing the fucking place howling in my mind...until I stopped at the entrance to the basement.

The door was closed. The thick steel D shaped handle drew my focus.

I didn't want the study.

I wanted out.

And a plan filled in my mind.

Precision Storage...

The business card nagged at me. There was no way a man like London would have one without a good reason. I was betting that reason would lead me straight to Jack Castlemaine, or at least to *something*. I didn't need the card. No doubt it'd be gone anyway. The locks might not be in place in this house, but I was under no illusion that I was still a mouse in a tightly controlled cage.

I glanced toward the garage, then shifted my gaze to the entrance to the fully equipped gym, but my mind returned to that basement door. If London thought I was stupid enough to think the waiter wasn't also a prison guard, then he was about to get a shock. I headed for the gym but glanced into the garage to the gleaming Audi just waiting for me to take it for a spin.

I couldn't drive, I knew that. The three awkward lessons from my pretend father right before they dragged me to The Order told me that, but I'd give it a damn good shot.

Darkness waited for me in the gym. I stepped in, but didn't need to search for a light switch as they came to life overhead. "Huh." I stared at the place, expecting the room to be full of weights and treadmills. But it wasn't.

The room was black, black walls and black mats. The only bright things were the small white lights that illuminated the space. The entire room screamed *deadly*.

There was a boxing ring set up on one side. Various punching bags hung from the ceiling on the other side and in the middle was the strangest setup I'd ever seen. Mannequins. Armed mannequins and some kind of martial arts training blocks. A shiver tore along my spine as I neared the equipment. This was...unexpected.

A row of knives sat on a shelf against the wall. Behind a clear case, there were guns, *lots of guns*. My breath caught as I looked at the silencers and rifles that looked military. "Jesus," I whispered. Maybe these were the twins'? It sure looked like they'd be right at home here.

But the closer I came to the gleaming weapons that'd been honed to perfection, a whisper rose in the back of my mind. This didn't feel like them. No, it felt more like...

I swallowed hard and shook my head. No. These weren't London's. He wasn't a man stained with violence. A man like him paid people to do that kind of thing for him. *I wonder where he got the money?* The thought rose before I pushed it aside.

Focus, idiot.

I turned, scanned the room, and searched for something I could use, then I spied a thin steel bar toward the far end of the room and headed over. It was some kind of steel rod. I glanced over my shoulder to one of the weapons cabinets that was open. The lock was gone. I would bet the rod was meant to secure that. I gave a shrug. "Perfect."

The burn in my chest fueled me as I grabbed the steel rod and walked out, holding it discreetly at my side. I didn't allow myself to think this through, just focused on that black velvet case he'd walked out with. I bet he'd barely care if I was gone for a while anyway.

He'd be too busy on his goddamn date.

I strode to the basement door, pushed down on the lock, and shoved the door aside, peering into the darkness and the steep stairs as I tracked the faint sound of steps somewhere above. My heart was booming. Panic filled me for a second before I forced myself to step backwards, take a hard breath, and let out a shrill scream.

Steps thudded instantly.

Charging down the stairs.

"What is it?" the waiter roared as his eyes scanned the house.

I lifted one hand, the other keeping the steel rod against my side and pointed. "There's a fucking man there. I opened the door and he was staring up at me."

The waiter scowled, reached around to his back, and from under his shirt pulled out a gun. I fucking knew it.

"Stay here," he commanded and stepped in, taking the first stair with the gun aimed at the darkness.

I said nothing, just tried to swallow the booming of my heart as he disappeared.

Do it.

Wait.

No, don't wait...

DO IT NOW.

I strode forward, my hands shaking as I lifted the steel bar and pulled the basement door closed, then slid the bar through the handle and across the doorway.

"What the fuck!" the waiter shouted.

His steps thudded back up the stairs before he yanked the handle, but the door barely open an inch before it stopped.

"Open the door, Vivienne!"

I stepped backwards. "I don't think so."

He pressed his face to the crack, his eyes narrow with rage. "Open this door right fucking now."

I said nothing, just turned and raced for the garage, hit the door and snatched the keys from the hook. "Have me on the goddamn table, then leave for some bitch. I'll fucking show you exactly what your three million dollars bought you."

I pressed the button, unlocked the car, and climbed in, before staring at the stick shift. "Shit."

The engine roared to life as I stabbed the button. I reached up, pressed the remote for the garage door, then stomped on the clutch and wrenched the gearshift. A god-awful sound came as I jerked forward, lurching down the driveway in bone-snapping jolts until I tried the gears again, found one that didn't sound like it was screaming, and punched the accelerator, tearing away from the house.

SEVENTEEN

London
_____

"Yes, London, here," Ophelia murmured as the waiter slid the glass of Scotch along the bar toward me then discreetly left. She slid her dress up, her hand disappearing between her thighs as she lifted her foot to the barstool and hooked it on the rung. "I made sure I didn't wear panties just for this. Now, on your knees."

I could kill her.

I could fucking kill her and take out as many as I could.

Hale would be first.

Macoy Daniels next...

But would I get them all? What about all the others who didn't come to these things? The faceless bastards that jerked the strings. I tried to think it through, plan it out just like I used to in my life before.

Her fingers sank into her bare pussy and came away slick. "I'm waiting, London. Don't tell me you don't want me?"

The fucking contract.

The fucking contract.

I turned my head, grabbed the glass, and downed the contents in one gulp. My breaths were slow, aching slow. Hands steady. No matter what, I still had that steely state. One that I could use to kill any man in this room before they even knew I'd moved. So I could man up and get on my knees and eat pussy.

I swallowed, moved toward her, and slid my hand around to cup the back of her neck. But she didn't give in to me. Her spine was ramrod stuff. "What the fuck are you doing?"

I scowled. "Kissing you."

There was a cruel tug at the corner of her mouth. "I don't want you to kiss me, London. I want you to eat me. I want to ride that gorgeous fucking face of yours until I come. Now..."

Jesus.

Jesus...

My throat clenched. I tried to swallow the urge to retch and slowly sank to the floor. Wide brown eyes filled my head. My wildcat was all I focused on. Just think of her...just think of...*fuck you, London.* Her voice filled my head.

Fingers sank into my hair. "You're smiling, good."

In an instant, the pleasure faded along with my fantasy. I swallowed hard and ran my hand along her leg, closed my eyes and leaned close to kiss the inside of her thigh.

"What the *fuck*!" came the voice behind the bar.

"*London!*"

I jerked my head upwards at the roar.

"*LONDON!!*"

I shoved upwards as I caught movement in the corner of my eye. Stark blond hair and wild blue eyes that scanned the room and narrowed in on me before he jerked his gaze to Ophelia. A look of revulsion filled him as he swung the gun in his hand. A cold wash of panic filled me and forced me to my feet in an instant as Ophelia released her hold on her dress and ended the sickening view.

"What do we have here?" she murmured.

I saw the desperate need in my son's eyes as he leveled the weapon on her and for a second, I almost stepped aside so I didn't catch the spray, until it hit me...he wouldn't get out of this alive. One small shake of my head and I caught the movement behind him as Colt followed...with the heavy black body bag over his shoulder.

"Jesus fucking Christ," I muttered as I stepped forward and left Ophelia and her aching cunt behind.

My sons never slowed, just scanned the rooms and narrowed in on the low ruckus in the dining room, then headed that way. *Fuck!* I followed, knowing there was no way I could cut them off, and instead I caught sight of Colt as he carried the body through the dining room.

Heads snapped our way as conversation stilled. A pity my fucking sons didn't as Colt just stopped at the head of the table and heaved the body off his shoulder until it hit the dining room table with a sickening *THUD!*

Roars erupted from those sitting around Hale. The pompous pricks shoved up from their chairs and lunged backwards as glass shards and shattered fine china flew through the room.

"What the fuck is this?" Hale roared, his wide eyes fixed on me.

I stopped at the body lying across the table in front of him like a rotting fucking meal and I did the only thing I could...I gave the bastard what he wanted. Coldly. Calmly. I reached over, grabbed the thick zipper, and yanked, exposing the bloodless face of Creed Banks for all to see.

"Jesus fucking CHRIST!" Hale jerked his gaze from the body to me as his guests reeled in horror. *"What the fuck is this?"*

I wasn't just a skilled assassin at that moment. I was the protector. The guardian of those I loved and the orchestrator of controlled violence as I answered. "You wanted Banks, so here he is."

Hale's lips curled. My mind raced, tearing through every foul fucking thought that was running through his head. Don't look away...don't...look...away...

His seething stare pinned me to the spot. "Who?"

"Benjamin Rossi."

His scowl narrowed as he looked at the white, chalky skin of the corpse. From the corner of my eye, Ophelia stepped close, staring at the body. Hale narrowed in on her, and that hateful expression softened. "Get me that Rossi bastard," he demanded as he turned to me. "I want the sonofabitch on his fucking knees."

"Consider it done," I muttered as I reached into my pocket and pulled out the contract. It was a bold move doing this in front of an audience. But he left me no choice. "For your signature."

He glanced at the folded paper in my hand then met my stare. I tried to read those eyes, tried to pick his thoughts apart as he murmured. "I'll be in touch."

I gave a nod and turned to leave, but he stopped me. "And get this out."

I met Colt's gaze, but the son wasn't moving. His eyes were wide, the whites almost neon against the blue. But it was his pallor that filled me with fear. He was as pale as the body we'd just delivered in front of all these men.

I jerked my gaze to Carven, who looked from me to his brother, then he froze. "Out," I demanded with a jerk of my head before I turned and reached for the body myself, yanked the zipper closed, and heaved it up over my shoulder.

"Move," I growled, pushing against Colt to force the son out of the goddamn dining room and away from the one person I couldn't trust him to be around without mentally shattering into a thousand fucking pieces.

Carven shoved his brother, driving him backwards. Even though Colt could easily have taken his twin out, he let Carven propel him toward the door.

They all fucking stared, and if it had been just me, I wouldn't have given a fuck. But there was no way they were looking at what belonged to me. I met each of them with a savage glare of my own and strode from the room carrying the heavy weight of Creed Banks over my shoulder.

It wasn't the first body I'd ever carried and I was sure that by the time I had my little wildcat, it wouldn't be the last. But even as I hauled the heavy weight out to the sons' Explorer, I was so fucking grateful.

My phone gave a *hmm as it* vibrated in my pocket as Carven yanked the passenger door open and shoved his brother inside.

Hmm...

Hmm...

My phone kept vibrating as I yanked open the rear door and dropped the heavy weight to the floor of the car. "What the fuck is it?" I snarled as I pulled my phone out and stared at three frantic messages and two missed calls from Guild.

Ice slipped through my veins as I opened the first message and read: *She's gone.*

"What the *fuck?*" I scanned the rest of the frantic texts as I opened the app on my phone, finding the tracker on the display.

"What is it?" Carven stepped closer. "London..."

I jerked my gaze up as savage rage rolled through me. "Get rid of the body and take care of your brother," I snarled as I punched in a message. "You might not want to come home tonight." I turned away, stomped down the driveway, and left them behind. "I'm about to throttle that goddamn woman, as soon as I get my hands on her."

Headlights flared at the end of the driveway as they headed toward me.

I knew Gabriel would be close.

And for that I was thankful.

Tires crunched on stones as he swung the car and pulled up hard. But instead of climbing into the back seat of the sleek black Mercedes, I cut across the front of the car and opened the driver's door. He looked up at me, confused for a second, before he narrowed in on the rage in my eyes and murmured slowly. "I'm walking, aren't I?"

I clenched my jaw...unable to say a goddamn word.

EIGHTEEN

Vivienne
___

I WASN'T RUNNING AWAY. HE SHOULD BE GLAD OF THAT. But as the thought hit me, I realized how stupid this was. Of all the damn places in the world I could be running *to*, I chose a goddamn storage facility on the other side of the city, for no other reason but more information about my goddamn warden.

I gripped the steering wheel of the Audi and glanced at the GPS. For someone so fucking smart, he needed to make sure he cleared out his regular routes. The monotone drone urged me to take the exit. I did, grinding the sports car's gears as I went. "Leave me, motherfucker," I whispered, dividing my focus between the road and the illuminated map in front of me. "No way. I'm the one who is leaving *your* ass...and I'll take out your damn gearbox with me."

With each turn of the wheel, that tiny ache under my breast flared, reminding me he was going to track me down eventually. But how long would that take? Not tonight, I was sure of that.

No.

Tonight, he was busy with his goddamn date.

I clenched my jaw and jerked the wheel to turn into a darkened road in the middle of nowhere. I looked out the window at the glinting lights in the distance and realized that out here, I was on my own. But then again, I was used to that, wasn't I? I focused on the road but kept glancing at the blinking arrow beside me and tried to forget all about the clear blue eyes of my protector as he'd sat watching me while I slept and the soulless dark eyes of my captor. They could all go to hell for all I cared.

What I wanted was answers. Real answers, and deep down, I knew Ryth's dad would give them to me.

"Destination point on your left. Destination point on your left. Destin—"

"Okay." I reached over and pressed the button. "I got it."

There were no lights illuminating the storage yard, no vacancy or even a no vacancy sign out front. I leaned against the wheel after I'd tapped the brakes, peered at the expansive building, and shifted my gaze before I sighed. There was nothing but a gigantic goddamn fence barring my way. I didn't know what I'd been expecting, but it wasn't that. "Shit."

I slowed the Audi and jerked the wheel toward the driveway, slamming on the brakes and clutch at the same time as I prayed I wasn't about to launch myself through the gate...

Then again.

The idea hit me. In an instant, I tore my foot from the brake and instead, stomped the gas, making the car lunge forward. Steel glinted in the headlights. The engine roared before I hit the gate with a *crunch*. My head jerked forward. The impact snapped my seatbelt tight across me. But it was the howling of the car's engine that penetrated my shock.

I sucked in hard breaths and eased my foot off the gas as I stared at the dented front of the car. "Shit." Then I winced, released the seatbelt, and climbed out.

The impact wasn't as hard as I'd wanted. I was too slow and too close. I stared at the small gap in the gate at the front of the car, then shifted my gaze to the big crease in the hood. London was going to be *pissed*.

I scowled and stepped around the open car door. "Fuck London."

Then I shifted my gaze to the real reason I was here, the storage facility and what secrets it held inside. Even if it didn't lead me to Ryth's dad, it was going to give me something, I just knew it. A man like London didn't have a place like this without it being useful for something.

What better place to hide all his dark and dirty secrets? I stepped closer, looking at the nose of the Audi wedged against the gap in the gate. The faint howl of an engine drew my attention and in the distance, a car took the entrance to the long, darkened road *sideways*.

My stomach rolled.

My breath stilled.

Chills raced along my spine

"Oh shit."

I jerked my gaze to the narrow gap in the gate as the roar of that engine grew louder, and I lunged. My hand slipped against the dented hood of the Audi as I searched for purchase. I shoved again, drove my boot against the bumper, and scrambled up the fence.

My fingers burned as I grasped the chainlink and hauled myself upwards as tires howled and the car skidded sideways before coming to a stop behind the Audi.

"Goddammit!" London roared, inciting the panic even higher inside me. *"Vivienne, STOP!"*

I drove myself higher and reached upward to grasp the top of the fence. Pain lashed along my palm as my captor grabbed me and yanked, pulling me back down.

"Get off me!" I screamed as I kicked and fought.

The bite in my palm was *nothing* compared to the agony in my chest. Rage narrowed my vision. All I saw was that building behind the fence where I wanted to be, and his hands as they gripped my waist and pulled me away was a battle I wanted to win.

But I was no match for his pure brutal strength as he tore me from the fence and hauled me away on his shoulder. I twisted and bucked, driving my hands against his shoulder, then his chest as I began to fall. But he grabbed me and lowered me carefully to the ground, his dark eyes wild. "What the *fuck are you doing!*"

"What the fuck am *I* doing?" I screamed as I stumbled backwards until I hit the open door of the Audi. "I dunno, London. Maybe I want answers, *huh! Maybe I want the goddamn TRUTH!"*

He stilled, his chest rising and falling hard with savage breaths as he glanced at the building through the fence. There was a flicker of fear as he turned back to me. "And you thought a random storage yard in the middle of *fucking nowhere* would give you that?"

"Oh, *don't* fucking play me," I snarled as I took a step forward. Fear and anger were a Molotov cocktail inside me and I was staring at the match. "I know this is yours. I also know there's no way in hell you'd have a place like this without it being useful to you. Because that's your MO, right? You don't possess things you can't use." *Including me.*

It's the whole reason he'd gone out to fuck, wasn't it? Because he couldn't fuck me. I lowered my gaze to his crisp suit and froze at the bloody smear on his white shirt. "Anyway, it's not like you fucking care."

"I don't care?" he repeated, those dark eyes even more chilling. "You. *Obnoxious. Goddamn. Brat.*"

I flinched. *Obnoxious brat? Who the fuck was he cal—*

He closed the distance between us, grabbed me around the waist, and lifted me across the hood of his dented Audi. I shoved out my hand, catching myself as I landed. Pain stabbed my palm. I bit down on the agony.

Smack! His palm landed on my ass.

"I don't fucking CARE?"

SLAP!

I bucked and jerked as fire lashed my ass. Screams sounded in my head. Children's screams...*my screams* blended into them. Memories of being smacked just like this slammed into me. "*Stop!*" I writhed, trying desperately to get away.

Slap!

The blaze tore through my abdomen. "*London...STOP!*"

In the corner of my eye, I caught his hand as it froze in mid-air, as though in his blind rage he'd suddenly heard me. His breaths were savage as he slowly let me go. Without his hold, I slipped down until my feet hit the ground. My ass felt the fiery imprint of his hand as I stumbled backwards and away from the monster.

But he didn't look my way, just stood there staring down at the gleaming gray steel and, in a chilling voice, said, "Get your ass into the car, Vivienne. I'm taking you home."

I couldn't move. Couldn't run. Couldn't do anything but stare at the monster. Because at that moment, that's what London St. James was. A cold, heartless monster. He didn't care about me. The blazing burn on my backside told me that. He cared about his property and that's all I was to him. *His. Goddamn. Property.*

"Vivienne..." His voice was etched with desperation. "The car...*now.*"

I sucked in hard breaths and stepped away, putting as much distance between us as I could as I rounded the other side of the Audi and all but ran for the black Mercedes. My knees trembled and my hands shook as I clawed at the door handle and climbed in as the damn gate that had blocked my way slowly opened.

"Fuck you," I whimpered, wincing with pain as my ass touched the seat. *"Fuck you to hell."*

Tears came as I reached down and tenderly touched the sting. Outside the window, London climbed into the Audi and drove it through the gate toward the warehouse, where he parked it and climbed out. An ache bloomed in the back of my throat as the outline of him came through the darkness, growing clearer the closer he came.

Despite the blur of my tears, I yanked the seatbelt across me and snapped it in place as he cut around the front of the car and climbed in through the open door. I could only press myself against the door and glare at him. He scared me now, maybe more than anyone had scared me in my entire life. I'd battled the guards at The Order and kept my mouth shut the entire time I looked for a way out of that place. But I couldn't find a way out of this, could I?

I couldn't find a way out of him.

He yanked the door closed and latched his own seatbelt before shoving the car into gear. The honed blade of silence cut through the air as he pulled away from the warehouse and turned the car around.

"Don't look at me like that."

I tried to swallow the thickness in my throat and forced the words. "Like what, London? Like you just beat me on the front of your car?"

He flinched at the words, his eyes almost midnight black in the wash of the dashboard lights. "I didn't...*beat you.*"

My voice was so pathetically small. "My burning ass says otherwise."

He snapped his gaze toward me and his lips curled as he narrowed in on the slow tears sliding down my cheeks.

"*Fuck!*" He unleashed a snarl and slammed on the brakes.

I snapped forward as the car skidded sideways and came to a stop in the middle of the road. The rush of his breaths filled the space. He stared at his fists as they strangled the steering wheel. "Vivienne—" he started, and I just couldn't allow myself to hear another word.

I yanked the door handle and shoved, but fell out of the damn car. I didn't know where I was going. All I knew was that I couldn't stay there staring at him like that. He looked...*broken*... *desperate...in turmoil.* I couldn't afford to feel. Not for him. Not for any of them...

And here I was with tears burning just as hot on my cheeks as the handprint on my ass.

The driver's door opened behind me as I stumbled backwards and turned, scanning the darkness for a way out of this torment.

"Vivienne, *stop!*" he barked.

"Fuck *you!*"

"Vivienne..."

I stumbled, tripped, and fell, unable to see a damn thing through my tears. Still, I ran. The heavy thud of steps boomed behind me until I was grabbed from behind and hauled off my feet.

"You don't run from *me*," he raged as he pulled me against his chest. "Do you get that? *You don't run from me.*"

I hit him, pummeling his shoulders and the sides of his head with feeble blows. "Fuck you...*fuck you, London.*" But the fight was gone, leaving me washed out as I pushed and pleaded. "Let me go, London...*just let me go.*"

He carried me back to the car and pushed me against the hood of the still-running Mercedes. I whimpered at the impact but I had no time to wiggle or thrash as he slid his hands down my arms, captured my wrists, and pinned them above me as he growled. "You don't get to run from me, do you get that?"

I struggled against his hold, but he was too strong for me as his leg pushed in between my thighs...and tonight he was too dangerous. I didn't know what had happened to him, but I knew it was bad. I felt it in the cruelty of his grip and I heard it in the desperation in his tone.

He ground his body against me. "I shouldn't have done that. Shouldn't have hurt you like that. I'm not that man, Vivienne. I'm not that man."

Owned

"You *are.*" I shoved against him.

He stiffened, not fighting me. "I don't want to be. Not with you. I won't raise my hand again in anger. Not to you. But you don't get to run from me. Not now...not ever."

Heat burned and it wasn't just on my bruised ass against the car, it licked between my thighs, drawing me away from the pain. "No," I moaned as he thrust his hips, slowly grinding against me. "No."

"No?" That slow thrust came again, rubbing against that heat between my thighs. "Are you sure about that?"

I struggled, yanking against his vise-like grip around my wrists. "No, no. I don't want you."

He fucked me through our clothes, grinding his hard cock against my core. "You forget how wet I made you last night, Vivienne. You forget I can still fucking taste you."

I closed my eyes and released a moan.

"You think you don't fucking torment me?"

I thrashed my head from side to side even as my legs inched wider, giving him all the room he needed. "I don't want you."

He ground that hardness against my core. "Liar."

The burn in my ass was secondary to that unfulfilled ache between my thighs. His dangerous stare held me hostage until he lowered his head and kissed me. I closed my eyes, giving into those hard lips as they took what they wanted before he broke away.

He released my wrists, but they still stayed there, lying where the hood met the cold glass of the windshield as he sank to his knees.

"I fucking know you want me." He worked the button of my pants then tugged the zipper down. "So I'm about to prove you wrong."

My pants were yanked down. Those demanding fingers dug under the elastic of my panties before they were dragged to the side. "You don't want me, huh?" He slid his finger along my pussy, spreading me. "You're so fucking wet. Look at yourself."

I bit my lip.

"Do what I tell you," he snarled.

I had no choice but to obey, meeting that brutal stare.

"Open your goddamn legs for me."

Oh God...

My breaths were racing as I did what he wanted, shifting my stance until my pants pulled taut.

"Don't want me, Vivienne?" He slid his finger along my crease and pushed me. "You don't fucking want me?"

I moaned, exposed, lying against the front of his car in the middle of nowhere while he fingered my pussy. "You want me to fuck you?"

Heat bloomed. I bit my lip harder.

"Tell me...*do you want my cock here?*"

I shook my head. "No."

He pushed in deeper. "I'm breaking the fucking contract right now," he growled. "This is all they need to take you from me, you realize that? I'll kill them if they try. I'll murder whoever they send and they'll never find the bodies. All you have to do is say the word. Tell me, I'll break the contract even more. I'll spread you on this car right now and fuck you. I'll stretch you, wildcat. I'll fucking stretch this tight cunt until there won't be a goddamn second where you don't remember it. Tell me to do it. *Tell me right fucking now...*"

I tried to catch my breath, opened my eyes and lowered my gaze to him.

"Tell me," he forced the words through clenched teeth. "Tell me to fuck you and I will."

NINETEEN

Vivienne

"TELL ME TO FUCK YOU, AND I WILL," HE DEMANDED, thrusting his finger inside me as he looked up from between my legs. "I'll break the contract. I'll break every fucking thing."

Yes! I opened my mouth to moan the word just as he snapped his gaze to where headlights cut through the darkness.

"Fuck." He pushed upwards, dragging my pants with him.

I scrambled to yank my slacks up as I slid from the hood of the Mercedes as the nearing car slowly drove past. London covered me as I fumbled with the zipper and button, staring at the passing car before he motioned to the open passenger door. "Let's go home."

My cheeks burned as I hurried around the door and climbed back inside. London closed it behind me before he walked around and climbed in. But whatever had ignited between us seconds ago now simmered in awkward silence. I clenched my core, still feeling his fingers inside me as the storage yard disappeared in the rear-view mirror. We made our way back to the highway and headed for home.

Home.

That word didn't belong in my world. I had no home, no family, no matter what kind of sick impersonation London wanted to pretend this was. I was glad for the interruption. It had almost gone too far...for him and for me. I wasn't meant to have a family, I knew that now. Shame filled me as the Mercedes accelerated, swinging out around slower cars. Nothing was going to change for me, even after the contract was signed.

London would fuck me, then he'd leave for whatever woman he was courting. He'd already given me black to wear...so red was next, and the sick thing was, I'd let him.

I'd let him use me any way he wanted.

And I'd wait for more.

Because the truth was, I wanted him, far more than my heart could afford.

The weight of his gaze settled on me. Still, he said nothing as we pulled off the highway. By the time we turned into his driveway, I was desperate to get out. The garage door opened, letting him pull into the space where the Audi normally sat, and he killed the engine.

"Vivienne..." his voice was husky.

But I didn't wait, just climbed out. He followed, hit the button on the remote, and closed the garage door before we both strode into the house. I stalked toward the kitchen, and spied the waiter glaring at me from the far side of the kitchen as I passed.

"Lond—" he started, and my captor finished it.

Crack!

I jerked and spun, to see the waiter stumbling sideways and an enraged glare on London's face. He strode forward, grabbed the man by the shirt, and shoved him against the wall. "The next time you fail me will be the last fucking time you fail anyone. Do you understand me?"

Fear punched through me at the attack. But the waiter didn't fight back, nor did he show surprise. He just stood there as he met London's rage, and nodded slowly. "I take full responsibility."

He took responsibility?

"No." I shook my head and stepped forward. "I did it. It was all me."

London turned that brutal stare my way and in the steely glint, I saw it didn't matter what I said, or what I did. Only that the man London had trusted to protect me had failed...even if I was the cause. I inhaled hard and glanced back at the bodyguard, to see a slow trickle of blood from the corner of his mouth. I realized just how dangerous London St. James was to everyone around him...including his allies.

Panic filled me as I left them behind and raced up the stairs to my bedroom. Even as I closed the bedroom door, I knew it was pointless. My captor was deadly in more ways than one. A chill coursed along my spine, but as I dropped my head into my hands, I knew it was pointless.

I could still feel those hard lips on mine.

Still ached for his fingers.

Dangerous or not, I was falling for him and that thought was the most terrifying of all.

I was in love with my captor.

Through the window, lightning flickered in the distance.

A storm was coming. I could feel it bearing down on me and I wasn't talking about the jagged sparks that tore through the night. I waited, and leaned against the door as I listened for the heavy thud of his steps when he came to finish what he'd started. But they didn't come.

I pushed away from the door, then made my way into the bathroom, and glanced up at the camera before I undressed and wound my hair on top of my head. I stepped under the hot spray and showered, but all the time I cast nervous glances toward the camera. I was in over my head here...and I didn't know what to do.

By the time I stepped out and dried off, I could hear the close rumble of the oncoming storm. Lightning slashed through the sky outside and the faint patter of rain on the window did nothing to soothe that tight fist inside my chest. I made for the bed and climbed in, then pulled the comforter over my bent knees and up to my chin as I sat against the pillows and watched the neon flashes fill the room...and waited.

TWENTY

Carven

THE HOWL OF A SAW FADED IN THE BACKGROUND. I BARELY heard it as I stared at the photo of that vile fucking cunt on the wall of the warehouse. My mind was frozen, stuck on the fleeting image of the second London's gaze meeting mine when I'd burst into that fucking party.

The utter fucking relief in his eyes stayed with me and I couldn't shake it free.

Metal scraped on metal. The clang of shovels tried to invade before the heavy thud of footsteps pushed in and my brother grabbed my shoulder. I turned, met his gaze, and nodded. "I'm okay."

He scowled, and picked me apart with that cutting stare. I looked away and found anything else to focus on. He didn't want to be in my head, not tonight. Instead, I turned back to the wall of photos and details, narrowing in on the fucking bitch I wanted to kill above all. The vile, child-beating, soulless fucking bitch who was far too close to Haelstrom Hale for me to kill.

For now...

I stared at her picture, seeing again the look of sickening relief on London's face when he'd pushed up from his knees. He'd knelt in front of her. That alone made me want to drag a blade across her throat and watch her bleed out. No one made London kneel, not like that. Not unless he wanted to, and I knew there was no fucking way in hell he'd want to for her...

The daughter, now that was another female altogether.

She was different. I glanced at Colt as he closed up the now empty cold room and locked it. No, the daughter was...one of us. I headed for the door and followed my brother outside to the Explorer. In the distance, white light flashed in the sky, but I barely saw it. Instead, I climbed into the Explorer and started the engine.

The car door thudded beside me. I strangled the wheel, feeling fucking dangerous.

Those wide dark eyes of the man who protected us haunted me as I pulled out of the compound, stopping long enough to wait for the gate to close behind me. Rain smacked the windscreen. I hit the wipers, then pulled out.

Neon white ripped a jagged hole through the darkened sky in front of us.

I didn't even see it.

Instead, I sucked in hard breaths. My focus narrowed in on that rage trapped inside me. I needed an outlet. I needed...to fight. I drove my boot against the accelerator, pulled away from the compound, and headed west.

Silence filled my world.

Leaving me free to hunt.

Headlights bounced off the rain from the oncoming cars. I pushed through the streets as I headed to the outskirts of seedy suburbs where the law never came, turned into the familiar dead-end street, and slowed to a crawl. Fires burned in barrels, the flickering amber glow more than something to stave off the cold. Men stood around as they warmed their hands, watched us, and nodded as we crept past. One of them pulled a phone out of his pocket and typed out a message.

They'd know we were coming.

Good.

I slowed at the crumbling brick wall and waited for the black steel gate to slide open before I drove through. I parked, scanned the other cars that packed the yard, and killed the engine before I climbed out. Thunder snarled, the deep sound booming above us as I headed for the guy standing in the middle of the doorway.

Hands up.

The guy moved a wand over my body before he gave a nod and stepped aside. I strode in, still scanning the darkness of the abandoned warehouse, and cut through the demolition site in the middle of the building before I eased toward the back.

The guttural roars of men pulled me closer. Even from here I could smell the blood.

I stepped through the crumbling doorway to the fight room. Three rings were in play. One guy was taking a brutal fucking beating. His face was a fucking mess as he stumbled backwards and swung at his opponent, who just stepped out of the way, smiled, then swung, drove his fist upwards, and took the guy down.

Shouts followed and hands were thrown into the air as some of the spectators turned away in disgust.

They should.

The guy was a weak idiot.

I scanned the cars parked against the demolished external wall, narrowing in on one as I strode past. The Ares brothers were here. I scanned the rest of the cars for the Rossi's before I turned back to the four brothers that sat on the hood of their black Maserati. The oldest nodded as I neared. I didn't acknowledge him, which pissed the youngest brother off and it seemed like he wanted to make an example of me.

The young punk saw my lack of acknowledgement and slid from amongst his three older brothers and took a step toward me before he was stopped by Silas Ares, the oldest of the brothers. Anger sparked in the young brother's eyes as he turned to his brother. I caught the word *sons* muttered as thunder boomed overhead.

The punk stopped instantly and his eyes widened. He looked at me a little more cautiously then, staring as I walked past and headed toward Iron, who stood at the end of the row of parked cars.

He closed his eyes the moment he saw me. A hard inhale was followed by a long, slow release as I reached into my pocket, pulled out a thick wad of cash, and tossed it through the air toward him. A fat hand lashed out and snatched it mid-air before he stared at the bundle. "Carven."

"I want in."

Iron shook his head as he stared at the money, until some schmuck gave a low chuckle behind him. "You know we're supposed to pay you, right?" the idiot spoke, drawing my gaze.

Until Iron lashed out and smacked the six-foot idiot in the back of the head. "*Shut the fuck up.*"

I leveled my gaze on the asshole. "Iron..."

"Look, C. It's like this…" Iron started. "We don't want—"

I reached back into my pocket and pulled out another, smaller wad and handed it over as I still stared at the stupid cocksucker who now glared at me.

"Jesus," Iron muttered as he reached out and took the money. "It's going to be bad, isn't it?"

"You fight?" I asked the asshole.

The smile wasn't so cocky as he stared at the second fistful of cash. Slowly it dawned on him, I wasn't here to earn money…I was here to kill.

Boom!

Thunder cracked loudly right overhead. In the neon glow of the lightning, I saw the idiot shift his gaze behind me. "Jesus, man… you okay?"

And slowly it hit me…*harder than a fist full of brass knuckles.* I spun and found the wide, terrified stare of my brother. He wasn't just pale…he was white. Blood splatter looked neon against his bloodless cheek. "Jesus, Colt." I stumbled toward him. "Look at me…*Colt!*"

He didn't move, frozen, as he stared at that fading brilliant light. *FUCKING IDIOT!* I grabbed him and moved in front of him, trying desperately to catch his gaze. "Hey…*hey, look at me.*"

"What the fuck is wrong with him?"

I spun on the fucker, lunged to grab him by his shirt, and roared. "You *don't fucking look at him. YOU UNDERSTAND?'*

My roar was swallowed by the cheering of those who watched the fights…they didn't see…except for the Ares family. They watched, and I felt every fucking stare before I shoved the guy backwards and turned to Iron. "Thirty minutes...give me thirty fucking minutes."

The organizer looked at the money in his hand. "Not a minute more."

That'd be all I needed. I grabbed my brother by the arm and pushed him toward the doorway. I didn't look at the Mafia assholes as we passed. All I saw was Colt. I'd been so wrapped up in my rage, too fucking controlled by the image of London in my head, I'd forgotten all about the one fucking person who mattered above all.

"It's going to be okay," I reassured as I pushed him through the door and out of the building. "You hear me? It's going to be okay."

The rush of his panicked breaths was so fucking loud. I opened his car door and pushed him inside. He just let me, sitting there, frozen with fear. I yanked the seatbelt down and snapped it into place before I closed his door gently and ran for the driver's side. Carefully, I closed the door and hoped it muffled the sound a little.

Boom!

Thunder cracked overhead again, making my brother unleash a cry of terror. His fisted hands clenched even tighter. I cast a panicked glance his way and fucking prayed. "It's going to be okay. You hear me?" I started the engine and shoved the car into reverse.

I didn't give a fuck about anything other than getting Colt home. Stones kicked up behind the Explorer as I skidded sideways, almost ramming the gate as we tore out of the compound. I cast panicked glances at him and reached over to grab his arm as I drove like a madman. "I'm going to get you home and get you settled, okay?"

He said nothing, just flinched as lightning flashed above.

Thunder would follow.

Inside my head, I counted. But it wasn't my savage snarl I heard, it was a terrified scream of myself at ten years old. They'd beat him as I screamed. They'd cut him. They'd broken him. Their fists and belts were relentless as the lightning hit and the thunder crashed. He'd never truly escaped that place, had always known they'd come for him when the storm hit.

But not me, right?

Not me...because he'd taken my beatings.

"It's going to be okay," I murmured, pushing the four-wheel drive harder. "It's going to be okay."

I skidded as I turned into our street and all but mounted the curb as I pulled into the driveway. The garage door opened as I pulled in beside the black Mercedes. Where was the Audi? The thought hit me before I shove it aside. It didn't matter. Nothing mattered, only getting my brother upstairs to his room.

I climbed out and ran around to the passenger side as thunder hit again with a deafening *crack!*

Colt couldn't move.

He just stared, his fists clenched so tight the muscles of his arms strained.

"Come on...just follow me, just follow," I urged, pulling his arm.

"I'm here," London called behind me as he cut across the garage.

I stepped to the side and he pushed into the passenger's space and into my brother's view. "Hey, I'm right here, buddy. Come on, come back to me. I'm right here. I'm taking you upstairs, okay?"

He seemed to come around a little as he shifted that stare to London and slowly nodded. Together, we eased him out and across the garage. The lights were on. London was still dressed in his tux. I wanted to look for the daughter as we climbed the stairs and strode past her bedroom door, headed for our own. But I forced all thoughts of her aside. My only concern now was my brother.

"Easy now," London urged as he crossed the room to yank down the bedding.

"He needs to shower," I said as I glanced at the blood splatter on his cheek.

"Let's just get through tonight and we can worry about that in the morning."

I glanced at our guardian and saw the haunted look in his eyes as he met my stare then looked away. That savage rage seethed inside me. But I forced it aside and walked my brother to the single fucking bed he still used after all these years.

He'd tried to live a normal life, even sleeping in here alone. But night terrors and the haunted look I saw on his face every morning when we weren't together made me move my shit in from the room next door and back into his. But not even I could help on nights like tonight.

"Feet up, buddy," London urged as Colt lay down on the bed.

Seeing London care for my blood made that rage inside me burn even bolder. He was so careful, talking to him the entire time. "We're going to get you strapped in, okay?" He yanked Colt's boot off, then his sock, and started on the other. "We're going to get you strapped in nice and tight. You're not going to hurt us, okay?"

He dropped the boots and looked at me. "His jeans."

I nodded, unbuttoned my brother's jeans, and eased them down.

"You're not going to hurt us. You're not going to hurt yourself," London murmured as I yanked the jeans down his thick thighs and tight calves until I tugged them off, which just left him in his black t-shirt and boxers.

There was blood on his shirt and a darkened patch stuck against his chest. I wanted to at least change him, but I couldn't worry about that now. All I needed to worry about was strapping him in.

Rip!

The Velcro sounded at the same time as a deafening *boom!* cracked directly over us. Colt cried out and slammed his eyes closed. I lunged to grab the straps at the head of his bed and slipped them over his wrists. "You're going to be fine, buddy. You're going to be fine."

I secured the tether around his wrists over his head. His muscles were bulging, his blue eyes bulged wide. But he was holding it in somehow. I'd seen him at his worst, when he'd trashed the room as he tried to fight the demons of his past. He hit me once, knocked me the fuck out. He was the only person who I was cautious of. After that night, he'd made us strap him down.

London secured his legs in place, then rose to look down at my brother. "All strapped in now."

Boom!

Colt bucked with the sound, biting down to swallow his scream. I hated seeing him like this, hated the sight of those fucking straps and I hated that we had to use them even more. Colt closed his eyes and forced the word through clenched teeth. "Go."

"Go?" London glanced at me in question.

I knew instantly. "No, I'm staying." I muttered.

My brother opened his eyes and turned to me. "Go, you need to."

I inhaled hard. That savagery inside me still waited. He knew if I didn't let it out it'd only grow worse, until I did something stupid. London said nothing. He didn't need to. He knew, we all did. No one survived what we had without being royally fucked up.

"Go," Colt urged as he jerked those wild eyes my way. "Now."

The mere fact he spoke showed just how desperate he was. I gave a slow nod. "Okay. If you're sure you'll be okay here on your own."

He just glared, clenched his jaw, and gave a tiny nod.

"I'll check in while you're gone," London urged. "Do what you need to, son."

I glanced at my brother. "I'll be back as soon as I can."

TWENTY-ONE

Vivienne

BOOM!

I cried out, bit down on the comforter, and burrowed deeper under the bedding. But it didn't matter how hard I pressed the pillow against my ears, the terrifying sound still found its way inside my head. My breaths raced. My pulse was so fast I couldn't hear it anymore. But I felt it. The panicked thrumming speared agony through my chest.

White light ripped through the darkened sky, filling my room with the neon glare.

BOOM!

I cringed at the sound and lunged out of bed, then raced for my door, wrenched it open, and tore out onto the landing. The neon glare filled the house, increasing the panic inside. I scanned the floor, my breaths cleaving through my chest as I narrowed in on their bedroom door.

I didn't think, I just acted. I hurled myself toward that closed door and scrambled inside. It was dark, pitch black. The windows were covered by blackout curtains but in the fading white glow of the bolt, I caught the massive outline in the small bed.

I bit down on a cry as thunder rumbled again, rattling the windows. I scurried for the outline of my protector, yanked down the bedding, and climbed in beside him. He didn't move, just lay there. I didn't think he was awake. I prayed he wasn't as I just pushed against his hard body without saying a word.

Snarl...

The thunder resounded right over the house again.

I closed my eyes, wedged my arms against my body, and pressed against him. My breath blasted back at me as it bounced off his shoulder. I squeezed my eyes tighter and burrowed even harder against his warmth. The earthy scent of him invaded my nose. He smelled like dirt...and something else. I flinched with another loud rumble. Still he didn't move, not to shift in the bed, or shove me away. He was just...stiff.

Was he dead?

I opened my eyes and, in the faint flickering light, I saw him... and froze. His eyes were wide and filled with terror. I pushed upwards to look down at him. "Hey, are you...are you alive?"

Inch by inch, he turned that terrified stare toward me. Only then did I see his arms were over his head. Lightning flared again and illuminated the leather binding around his wrists.

The straps.

The straps I'd seen before on the bed.

I flinched and focused on them now. He wasn't just bound by the straps, he *gripped them*. His knuckles were white from the strain of his grasp. I jerked my gaze to his, and found those blue eyes blazing almost neon in the dimming light.

"I'm sorry," I whispered as I jerked at another thunder rumble.

But he said nothing, his wide stare still fixed with terror.

Boom!

I jerked again and drove harder against his body, this time wrapping my arms around him tightly. Terror made me push my face against his chest. Under the heavy rush of breaths, his heart was booming. The panicked sound made me feel a little less alone.

"I've never felt this terrified before," I whispered, then lifted my gaze to his. "Will you hold me?"

He said nothing, just stared at me, wide-eyed. Then slowly, I reached over him, holding his stare the entire time. *He'd had his fingers inside me.* That thought spurred me on. I used it to make me reach higher and pressed my breasts against his chest.

Tension arced between us. But it shifted, morphing from fear into something else, something desperate. My breaths slowed and became deeper as I brushed the leather shackle around his wrist.

"Don't," he forced through clenched teeth, stopping me cold. *"Want to hurt you."*

There was a moment of panic until I remembered him sitting against the wall, watching over me when I slept. I tugged on the shackle, then yanked the Velcro. "You won't."

His brow furrowed as his hand slipped free. I reached for the other. "Just one. Only one."

One was enough. I stared into his eyes and slowly nodded.

In the flickering light, hunger moved into his stare. His breaths eased, rising harder before falling and slowly he dragged his hand down until he reached around me. We said nothing, just stared into each other's eyes. The storm raged, but the thunder wasn't as loud as it was before. I settled against him, slid my arm across his chest, and slowly laid my head on his chest.

The panicked booming eased and the heavy thud of his heart lulled me. I closed my eyes as I listened to the sound and slowly slipped...

The steady beat stayed with me, fell quiet, then turned louder.

"No," I heard him say, but I couldn't surface.

I stayed in the darkness where the lightning didn't quite reach me and the thunder was his heartbeat, until I shifted and pressed against something hard. I opened my eyes as I slowly became aware we weren't alone.

I jerked my gaze to the foot of the bed and found the intense neon blue eyes of his twin brother as he stood there and stared at us. Only he wasn't the only one who stared. London stood next to him, those dark eyes wide and fixed on the two of us wedged in the tiny bed.

"London," I whispered. "What's going on?"

He licked his lips as he glanced at the male beside me. "I was about to ask you the same thing."

My thoughts were slow at first, before a low rumble in the sky above us brought it all crashing back. "The storm." I startled as Colt moved his big hand upwards and palmed my breast.

I froze with the touch, turning a panicked stare to my captor.

"He won't hurt you," London urged. But those fixed dark eyes told me otherwise.

"He's never..." Carven started. "He's never done that."

Never done that? I held his stare as Colt tugged my shirt upwards and exposed my breast. "Never done what?" I moaned as his thumb skimmed my nipple.

"Never touched a woman before."

Colt froze and his wide eyes searched mine. He'd never *touched a woman before?* I swallowed as I remembered his fingers inside me. He'd touched me. That was enough, wasn't it? He pulled his hand away and for a second, I thought it was all over, that whatever moment we'd had between us had passed, until he stretched up and worked the binding on his other wrist.

"Brother," Carven cautioned.

I shifted my gaze to them standing at the foot of the bed, and the memory of London punching Guild came roaring back. London's brow furrowed as Colt worked the other Velcro strap off his wrist and sat up. Even his ankles were tethered. But as his hands worked fast to tear the straps open, the energy in the room changed. Heat tore through me as Colt's blue eyes dragged mine back to him.

"Don't be scared," he murmured, his voice low and husky. "Won't hurt you."

He lowered his gaze to my breast. I could barely move, wedged in tight against him as I was in the cramped bed, but I lifted my arms when he tugged my shirt higher and off, leaving me in my soft pink boxers. His breaths were fast, almost as fast as last night, as he lowered his head and kissed my nipple.

"Jesus," Carven murmured.

Colt dropped my shirt to the floor and pushed up on his strong arms. I felt the weight of London's stare, but I didn't have time for fear as Colt lowered his head, kissed my nipple again, and reached between my legs. I closed my eyes, biting my lip as he dragged those thick fingers along my crease.

"Will you let him..." London started. "Will you let him fuck you, wildcat?"

I opened my eyes and swallowed hard as I sought London's gaze. "Do you want me to?"

Carven looked at London as Colt moved lower in the bed and dragged my boxers down.

"Yes," London answered.

Family...

The word raged in my captor's stare as I raised my hips and my boxers were slid off. Colt reached down, grabbed my knee, and lifted, parting my legs. A shiver of fear swept along my spine as I narrowed in on London's stare.

This is what he wanted, wasn't it? He wanted the sons to touch me like this. I watched London while Colt's fingers pushed inside me. But I winced and licked my lips.

"She's not ready," Carven muttered. "You have to make her wet."

Colt scowled and glanced at his brother.

"For fuck's sake," Carven snapped, and looked away for a moment before he turned back. With a snarl, he strode forward, grabbed his twin gently behind his neck, and pushed his head down. "Eat her."

I shook my head as heat welled in my cheeks. "He doesn't..."

"Yes," London answered coldly. "He does."

"You want to fuck, brother?" Carven's eyes blazed. "Then you do it properly. You don't get off until she gets off."

Panic filled Colt's eyes as they lifted to mine. I saw it, the doubt, he embarrassment. But then Carven pushed his brother's head back down. I flinched with his hard touch as Carven spread my pussy lips wide and dragged his finger along my nub. "This is her clit, you need to lick there, just like London did."

Oh God...

The heat moved in my cheeks. I started to pull away and close my legs until Carven jerked that savage glare to me. "Gone too far, wildcat. My brother wants you, and he's never wanted a woman in his goddamn life..."

He wanted to say more, but he didn't. Instead, he watched as Colt lowered his head. I turned away as that heat burned in my cheeks, and stared at the wall instead. This wasn't what I—

The slow slide of his tongue made me freeze.

"Now suck...*gently*," Carven instructed.

The tiny lick grew bolder, bringing back to life that spark of desire that had been dying inside me. My breaths deepened as he gently continued to suck.

"See how she's responding?" Carven murmured, his voice huskier. "Her breaths are deeper and her pussy is...now slide your finger in just a little, and keep doing that. They're so sensitive there, so..." Carven's strained breath caught as he watched his brother. "You need to see if she likes—"

"Oh...*God*," I moaned as Colt curled his finger and stroked as he gently sucked.

I lost track of his fingers and his mouth. Instead, I turned my head to see London's dark, consuming stare as he watched this play out. He wanted this, right? I lowered my hand and my fingers slid through Colt's hair as he unleashed a growl, lifted my leg higher, and opened me wider. London wanted them and me. Had he planned this all along? Maybe that's what he'd bought me for, with the plan to give me to these broken sons...

Heat bloomed as Colt sucked then dipped down to drag the tip of his tongue along my crease from my ass all the way up.

"Jesus." I tore my gaze from London to the massive male between my thighs.

He looked up at me, those clear blue eyes no longer terrified or unsure. I sucked in hard breaths and slid my fingers through his thick dark curls as he stared at me with amusement...and pride. Oh yes, there was pride.

"Don't get too cocky," I croaked as my body trembled under his touch.

He grinned with my words, then dipped his head to continue with satisfaction, only this time, his entire focus was on making me writhe. I cried out as the urgency grew bolder.

There were no more instructions given.

No more lessons.

No more waiting as Colt slid his hands under my ass, tilted my hips upward, and speared my pussy with his tongue. I cried out as I thrust against him and drove his mouth harder against me. I was going to...I was going to...

"Oh, *Jesus*..." I bucked as white sparks ignited behind my eyes.

He sucked and licked the warmth that flooded from me. The sensation only plunged me further into oblivion.

I barely heard Carven growl. "Fuck. Me," before Colt lifted his head and met my gaze.

But the smirk was gone, now there was only a desperate longing. I licked my lips and gave him a slow, careful nod. He was awkward once more, with a scowl before he stopped.

"Lie back," I urged. "Pull me on top of you."

He slid his hands from under my ass, grabbed me around the waist, and rolled. I was lifted on top of him. In that moment, there was only him and me. No one else mattered. That same panicked look returned in his eyes. He fixed his gaze to the ceiling, his heavy breaths consuming.

Agony plunged through my chest. I realized the temperature in the room had plunged to subzero. There wasn't a whisper, not a sound. I fixed my gaze on the powerful male underneath me and captured his hand which gripped my waist. "You made me feel so good." My voice trembled as I fixed on his wide, terrified stare. "But we're only going to do this if you want to, okay?"

His breath stopped, then slowly he looked down and met my eyes.

"That's it," I whispered as I slid his hand up my waist, then over my breast. "Look at me. Do you want to keep going?"

He was scared, but he nodded slowly.

It was all I needed. I made sure I moved slowly and held his stare the entire time as I inched his shirt upwards, before I froze. *Oh. My. Fucking. God.* My gaze skimmed across the mess of scars that had savaged his body. But then I forced myself to keep going and didn't once let him see that I saw him as anything other than perfect.

"I'd say keep talking to me, but I don't think that's an option here," I whispered as I moved his hand from my breast to the back of my neck and slowly dipped down. "So I'm going to let you guide me, okay?"

I met his stare and made sure he understood, then left his hand on my neck as I brushed my lips across his nipple and the jagged scar that savaged his dusky flesh. Jesus, he'd been savaged.

The sons had it worse.

London's words pushed in before I drove them away. I didn't need those words in my head. That would all come later. Right now, it was about us, about finding what felt good for him. I needed a starting point, that's all...

"I'm going to touch your cock, okay?" I whispered as I met his stare. "I want you to grip me if you want me to stop."

I lowered my gaze, kept my fingers light, and traveled down his hard chest to his stomach, then slowly made my way lower. The heat of his brother's stare burned as I skimmed the thick, hard length and gently closed my fingers around him. My silent lover flinched, but his grip never pulled me away as I tugged down the waistband of his boxers.

Instead of pulling me away, he rose up, grabbed me under my armpits, and lifted me so that I straddled him. The motion couldn't be clearer. *Do it now.*

"We can go slower next time," I whispered. "If you want there to be a next time."

The hunger in his eyes told me all I needed to know. I reached down and cupped his cock again. He was big...*really big.* I looked down, dreading to see a mangled mess of scars just like his chest. But there wasn't, there was just perfection. The thick vein pulsed under my grip as I stroked, lifted my body higher, and angled him at my entrance.

"You're so fucking perfect," I whispered.

One slow slide of that slick head and I felt the resistance. Pressure burned. Colt scowled as a flare of panic moved deep in his eyes, but he didn't know what it meant. So I whispered, "That's it. Keep going."

He closed his eyes for a second as he drove his cock into the sting. I winced and relief swept through me as I focused on his concentration. I didn't want him to see me as I bit down on my lip and pushed him deeper inside.

The pain grew intense and built and built, until it broke through and made me gasp with the rush. My pulse boomed but I didn't dare look down, didn't want them to know this moment was just as important for me as it was for Colt.

I focused on him as a look of peace washed across his face and he slowly thrust and drove his hips upwards. Flickers of memories pushed in as I rose and dropped back down. It was London I thought of and somehow, he sensed it, as he stood behind me.

"Ride him, wildcat," he urged, his voice thick with desire. "Take what you need."

Heat burned in my cheeks. I ground my hips as I let London's voice roll through me. I didn't need to push his words from my head, or the memory of what he'd done on the table and on the hood of his car. I could have them both. London in my head and Colt under me. My breaths quickened as the realization hit me.

There was no need to choose.

Colt's hands gripped me as he pulled and pushed while he drove his hips up from the bed and that crease cut deeper between his eyes.

"Look at me," I whispered, my breaths urgent. "Look into my eyes. Give yourself to me...*give yourself*."

He unleashed a low, savage moan as his cock twitched. Warmth followed, and filled me as he held me in place. I didn't need to take what I needed... because *this* was it. My heart thundered as a deep ache bloomed. It was this...him...*them*. All of it.

A slow smile tugged at the corners of Colt's lips.

"How was that?" I asked as I nervously searched his gaze.

That smile only grew wider as he dragged his thumb across my nipple, then gently rolled it between his fingers and pulled a low moan from me. "You don't want to do that," I murmured as my body clenched, still feeling the burn of my first time. "Not unless you want to go again."

There was a low chuff of delight before he circled that tight nub once more and I understood that was his exact intention.

*Oh fuck...*I'd unleashed a goddamn animal.

TWENTY-TWO

London

Carven turned from watching his brother and strode through the bedroom door, leaving the low moans behind. But I couldn't move. I'd thought watching her with Colt might ease that hunger inside me...

But I was wrong.

I wanted Vivienne even more.

I stared, mesmerized as she dropped her head back and slid her fingers through Colt's hair. The way she touched him...the way she talked to him, made that longing ache inside me even stronger. My body responded and deepened my breaths. My cock hardened as I watched him enter her again.

She'd started out as a means to an end, a way for me to get to King. But over the years of my watching her, she'd become more. My obsession. My need.

Colt gripped her around the waist and turned in the tiny bed, gently throwing her onto her back. I wasn't the only one falling for this kitten. She howled even louder than the darkness, her needs more tempestuous than any storm. Even if she did drive me fucking wild with fear.

I left them as Colt lowered his head and gently nipped the flesh at her collarbone, which made her yelp and laugh. That sound stayed with me as I made my way to my bedroom. Even with the doors closed and the snarl of thunder from the lingering storm above us, I still heard them.

I knew I always would.

Thunder growled above as I worked my tie and tore it off. I reached for the buttons on my shirt and jerked it free then froze. *I thought I'd lost her...*

That ache grew until it beat bloody fists inside my chest. My shoulders sagged as that fear rolled through me. In those blinding moments as I'd raced for the storage yard, I thought she'd somehow been able to get inside. A tremor coursed through me. If she'd been able to get to Jack Castlemaine, then he'd...*what?*

Tell her how dangerous I was? I clenched my fist, which still ached from my blow to Guild's cheek.

I was pretty sure she knew that already.

I kicked off my shoes as I made my way into the bathroom. I turned the faucets for the shower and lifted my gaze to where the sons' bedroom was. That ache grew as I shoved my boxers down and stepped into the heat of the water. Faint memories of Ophelia tried to push in, but they didn't have a chance, not where Vivienne was concerned.

I dropped my head, let the fine spray hit against my shoulders, and reached down to grip my cock. I was hard, maybe harder than I'd ever been. She made me that way, like I was headed to my fucking grave and I didn't care. Because Vivienne wasn't just a means to an end. She was my result, my salvation. If the last hour watching her and Colt told me anything, it was that she was the balm for our souls.

Because I might be too far gone, but the sons weren't.

I braced a hand against the cold tiles and stroked my length, working my cock.

She is ours...

I squeezed my eyes tight and replayed the image of her splayed out on the hood of my car. I would've fucked her, would've broken the contract in a thousand different ways, and I wouldn't have cared about the consequences. At that moment, I would've taken all of us and run.

My balls tightened as the feel of her pussy returned. Christ, it had just been my finger and my tongue. But the sensations of her lingered. I closed my eyes, dropped my head, and unleashed a moan as I came.

Hard breaths filled my ears.

It wasn't enough.

It wasn't anywhere near enough.

But until the contract was signed, I had to stay away.

Colt would take care of her. There was no doubt of that.

I straightened and finished washing before I turned the water off, and stepped out then dried myself and headed for bed.

Sleep didn't come, not for a long damn time. Instead, I thought about her upstairs in the son's bed and stared up at the ceiling until my eyes burned. Eventually the darkness came and when it did, it brought with it Ophelia's face, haunting me like I deserved.

I CLIMBED out of the Mercedes and pressed the code into the keypad at the storage yard, then watched the buckled gate wobble when it opened.

"Fuck." I stared at the damage, then lifted my gaze to my goddamn Audi where I'd parked it late last night. But there were more reasons than one for me being here. I climbed back into the Mercedes and drove it in, then parked next to the beat-up sports car and climbed out.

There wasn't as much damage as I'd expected. I pulled out my phone and made a call to a friend who would come collect it and take it to the Audi dealership. The damn car was less than six months old and here I was buying another. Because the woman was unpredictable at best.

I headed for the door, punched in the code, and walked through, glancing at the other doors as I went.

"London." A male voice filtered out. "Talk to me. Tell me what you want to let me out of here. You know I'd never tell them about Killion."

I stopped and stood in the middle of the hallway.

"Tell me what you want," he begged.

I scowled and glanced at the door beside me. Kill him or use him, that was always the question. But one for another day. So I kept going and just left the heavy thud of my footsteps behind.

"Let me out of here!" he screamed as I entered another code and opened the door.

Silence greeted me when I stepped inside Jack Castlemaine's room. There was no yelling, no pleading, just the kind of silence that felt empty. I scanned the gloom and found him sitting cross-legged against the wall, his eyes closed and his breathing steady.

As I neared, he opened his eyes, and for a second, I saw a flicker of the dark depths he held inside. But then the glimpse was gone and he inhaled deeply before speaking. "Don't tell me, you want information on King."

I stopped in front of him. "He hasn't reached out to me."

Jack rose slowly and stretched his arms over his head. "I'd be surprised if he did."

I scowled. "You would?"

He settled that careful focus on me. "King isn't the kind of man who asks for permission. He's the kind of man who takes when you least expect it."

But this wasn't just about information now. This was about controlling all the threats. There was no way I'd let any man come for her, even if he was her biological father. "How did he find out, do you know that, at least?"

Jack turned to me and scowled as he slowly shook his head. "He never told me. He just said that one day he'd find them both and he'd get them back somehow."

"And you were okay with that?"

"What choice did I have? Her mother made it very clear to me that Ryth was never mine."

"And still you risked your life to save her."

That hit a nerve and that steely glare shone once more. "Blood or not, Ryth is my daughter. She always has been and always will be. There is nothing I won't do to ensure she's safe."

I reached into my pocket, took out my phone, and hit the icon.

On the other end, the phone rang and rang and rang...until it was answered.

I held the cell out and listened to them as they had their fleeting moment of happiness before I pressed the icon and ended the call. There was a flare of happiness behind the pain in his eyes before he smothered it with steely control.

I didn't like hurting him. But he'd pissed me off. No one was going to come for Vivienne, not without me knowing. My phone gave a *beep* as I slipped it into my pocket. I pulled it back out and looked at the screen.

> Ashwood: You've been requested to bring
> Vivienne Evans to The Order for processing.

For processing? I stared at the words.

"What is it?"

"They're signing the contract," I whispered before I even knew I'd spoken.

Blood rushed to my cheeks as elation took hold.

"You're playing a very dangerous game," Jack murmured. "I don't think you realize how deep you're in here."

I lifted my gaze to him and it all hit me, the desire, the excitement, and the danger as I answered. "Oh, I know, believe me."

I left him behind as I made my way out of the storage yard to head for home. The sooner I took her back to that hell, the sooner she was finally free. I only hoped after what had happened last night, she'd hold it together...and lie.

For both our sakes.

TWENTY-THREE

Colt

————

THE LOW HISS OF THE SHOWER FROM ACROSS THE HALL caught my attention. My brother was in there and he'd been in there for a while now, avoiding me, and I didn't blame him one bit. Heat raced to my cheeks...*this is her clit, you need to lick there,* his words pushed in, making the burn even hotter. I should go to him and try to explain what had fucking happened.

But I couldn't move, because I didn't understand it myself.

I could only sit here on the side of my bed and stare at the marks the leather straps had left on my wrists....

Straps I'd needed not to hurt them. Straps she'd undone.

Jesus...

My breaths carved deeper as I tried to piece together the seconds when my bedroom door had flown open and a damn wildcat had hurled herself into my bed. I clenched my fists. I'd been so fucking scared of moving, terrified that one flinch, one whisper, would send me over the edge.

Then she was there. Her need, her panic, resounded louder than any roar of thunder and burned brighter than any neon glow. In her desperation, my own terror fell away. I couldn't battle the demons in my nightmares—*I had to battle hers.*

Her body had trembled as she all but climbed under my damn skin. Maybe she already had? I didn't know, but sitting here, I could still feel her, her lips on my body, her hands on mine. Those dark brown eyes were so fucking soul-destroying when she looked at me like that, like she wanted to...*like she wanted to...love me.*

My own heart boomed, sending pangs through my chest. Christ, I...*Christ, I wanted to...I wanted to...*

Touch her.

I licked my lips.

Smell her.

I turned my head, reached for my bunched-up pillow, and caught the corner of the crumpled sheet. I tugged it out of the way, and froze...

There was blood...

Bright blood.

I jerked my gaze to my hands, then my bare chest, and rose from the bed. There was no sting, no pain, not that I felt much anyway. I ran my hands down my body and turned back to the bright drops and crimson smear. It was low down in the bed, right where she...*right where she lay...*

A wounded sound ripped from the center of my chest. I snapped my head upwards and heard the quiet in the bathroom. I didn't think, I just acted, tore the sheet free and plunged across the hall. The door flew open with a *bang!* My brother was there, towel-drying his stark white hair.

"What the fuck is it this time?" he snarled, not looking my way. "You need me to point out your cock too?"

I grabbed his arm and wrenched him around as I gave him a savage glare. His lips curled, baring his teeth. "Brother, you're pushing it way too—"

I punched the sheet into his chest. But it wasn't the bedding that stopped him. It was me, my terror, my fear as I roared. *"What have I done?"*

He scowled, then slowly looked down at the bright crimson blotches.

My breaths consumed me as I stared at my brother with desperation.

His eyes widened. I wanted his fists and his fury. I wanted his beating...because this time, I deserved it. This time I'd...*I'd...I'd beat myself.* I clenched my jaw, tightened my fist, and swung for my own face. *YOU BROKE HER, YOU BASTARD!*

But before the blow landed, my brother's hand lashed out and grabbed my wrist, and he spoke carefully as he stared at the drops of her blood. "You didn't do anything. I mean, you did... but you didn't hurt her, not the way you think."

I scowled and stared at him before I wrenched my hand away.

He looked into my eyes and saw the panic. "You know how... how you never." He licked his lips. "How you'd never had a woman before?"

My chest rose and fell and my jaw clenched. *Say it...say I ruined her. Say I fucking deserve all the beatings. I deserve all—*

"Well, she hadn't had a man, either."

I *froze.*

Then I shook my head.

No, I'd heard her that night when she'd touched herself.

I touched her when she was on the table with London.

"You fingered her cunt, but she'd never had cock. She was a virgin, brother, and she gave her virginity to you."

I rocked backwards.

She gave her...

I grabbed my brother's chin and wrenched him closer to force his stare to mine. *She gave her virginity to me?* I searched for the truth and found a flare of...*jealousy? Anger?* I couldn't think straight. Everything was a mess. *I* was a damn mess.

But Carven held my stare. "You should feel fucking honored." He yanked his chin free. "Now get the fuck out and leave me in peace."

I lowered the bloodstained sheet from against his chest as my heart thundered and my head spun. She'd given her virginity to *me?* She'd given it to me. I didn't ruin her. I didn't...I lowered my gaze and took a step backwards before I slowly turned to the open door.

"You might want to go to her." I turned back to him. There was no anger in his eyes now, just a hunger I'd never seen before. He dragged his fingers through his hair and exhaled. "That is what a man who's been given something like that should do. You're that man, Colt. Do you understand me? *You are that man.* She'll be freaking out, afraid we'll tell. We can't tell, brother. You understand that, right? We can *never* tell."

We can never tell.

I lowered my gaze to the sheet and slowly nodded.

"Then go to her and make her realize that this *stays* with us."

With a loud swallow, he turned away, his voice hardening. "And close the door behind you."

TWENTY-FOUR

Vivienne

_____

OH, SHIT...OH, SHIT...OH, SHIT. I GRIPPED THE SINK AND rocked forward. I hadn't meant for that to happen, hadn't meant for it to go that far. I'd fucked it all up. I'd...*fucked...up.* My core throbbed and pulsed, swollen and aching. *Needing like I'd never needed before.* It was this house and these men. It was London...

London had caused this.

London, and now Colt.

Their fucking mouths, their tongues in my...

"Idiot," I whimpered as that desire bloomed like a deadly flower once more.

Goddammit.

I closed my eyes. This will ruin them. This will fucking destroy—

A touch dragged along my arm and made me wrench my eyes open to find movement beside me. I unleashed a scream, stumbled backwards, and slammed into the wall. My head impacted with a *crack!* But he was there, filling up my bathroom, all magnetizing blue eyes and thick, dark curly hair.

Horror flared in his eyes as he lunged, grabbed me by my arm, and yanked me forward. I slammed into the brick wall that was his chest and was pinned there as he probed with those big fingers along the back of my head and my shoulder.

"I'm okay," I muttered, and pulled back. "I'm okay." He just stood there, watching me as I shook my head. "You don't have to worry about me. You don't have to..."

Then I saw what was in his hand.

A sheet.

With tiny blotches of bright red blood.

I turned away instantly as my cheeks burned, and stared at the wall. My throat thickened and pinpricks of pain flared through my head. Then there was that warm touch again as he slid his hand along my arm and reached up, captured my chin, and turned my gaze toward him.

Heat burned in my cheeks. I just wanted to crawl into a hole as I forced the words. "It's not a big deal."

There was a scowl. Pain flared in his eyes as he slowly shook his head and quietly murmured. "It is to me."

My heart thundered. Too loud. Too fast. The bloody sheet was in his clenched grip. It all meant too much to me at that moment. Him. Them. *Everything.*

"Our," he murmured. "Secret."

Our secret? What did that mean?

He took a step forward and slid his hand around the back of my neck and tilted my gaze to his. *Our secret.* Those blue eyes raged. I knew then...I knew he was more than my guardian in the night, he was now my lover...he was *mine.*

He lowered his head, closed his eyes, and kissed me.

I'd never felt something so pure, so tender, so...*real.*

When he pulled back, he brushed his thumb along my cheek. I stared up at him as I felt the thunder of hooves in my chest and whispered. "Oh shit."

There was a curl at the corner of his mouth. He knew. He knew because he felt it too. A slow nod, and he dropped his hand, then the silent asshole turned around and left me standing like I'd just been blindsided by a blow I hadn't seen coming.

One that was as silent as the night.

And just as fucking deadly.

My bedroom door closed with a thud as he left me to stand there and try to remember how to breathe. He wasn't going to tell. I stepped back, then glanced at my empty bedroom and the closed door before I undressed and stepped into the shower.

I'd just had sex...

I'd just had...sex.

It hadn't been how I'd thought it would be. The pain and the sting I'd expected. The panic, even I'd known that would come. But him...he wasn't what I'd expected at all, nor the way the rush stayed with me even now, or the way I could still feel him, his terror, his pain...his utter devotion.

I washed and scrubbed, then stepped out and dried myself, but when I walked into my bedroom, London was there. I froze as I watched him stride out of the walk-in closet carrying a pair of black slacks and a red top. I stared at the color, then lifted my gaze to his. Red. He'd never asked me to wear red.

"Get dressed" he murmured. "We've been summoned back to The Order."

Cold plunged all the way deep inside me and tore away the moment of happiness. "The Order...no."

He straightened, then lifted that stony stare my way. "You do this, and they sign the contract. You become...mine."

Become his?

My heart thundered, slammed by happiness, fear, desire, and above all, uncertainty.

He took a step toward me, but there was no kindness in his eyes. Just the same cruel hardness he'd had last night. "If you don't do this, they will come and take you back for good."

"But you paid..."

"It's an interim contract, Vivienne. This summons is...a good thing. If you want that after what's just happened."

I searched his gaze. "This is what you want?"

He didn't answer, just took a step backwards and went to the door. "I'll be downstairs waiting."

I'll be downstairs? He hadn't answered, but I still heard the *thud* he left behind as I glared at the clothes waiting for me. *Red.* He wanted me to wear red. My hands shook as I stepped closer and grabbed the soft satin top, knowing exactly what that meant.

If he wanted me to wear it, then I would. After all, that's what he'd paid for, right?

I dressed in the clothes he wanted and slipped on the shoes he'd bought. I brushed my hair and put on light makeup, the ones he'd chosen for me, and made my way downstairs.

He didn't look my way as he waited in the kitchen. But Colt was there in the doorway to the dining room, which drew my gaze to that glass-topped table. I swallowed hard and looked away, but I saw the tortured stare of my silent protector. He looked tortured and terrified all at once. But he didn't make a move to stop me. He held my stare for a second and gave a careful nod when I walked past him as I followed London out to the car.

No words were spoken when I climbed into the Mercedes, pulled the seatbelt across, and latched it. He just started the engine, put the car into gear, and drove. I didn't see the streets or the cars. I didn't see a damn thing as we left our home behind and drove through the city streets.

By the time we were out the other side of the traffic and headed toward the towering trees in the distance, I could have cut the air with a knife. My thoughts turned to this morning and my pulse raced. I clenched my jaw and looked out the window.

London finally spoke. "I don't need to remind you how important this is."

I jerked my gaze to his, to see that same cold stare fixed on the road in front of us. "Important for you or for me?"

He swung that careful gaze my way, but he didn't answer. Something had changed between us and it wasn't even this morning. It had started last night at the warehouse. Was he starting to think he'd chosen the wrong woman from The Order? Maybe being here might give him an opportunity to find a Plan Fucking B.

I turned away, saw the towering steel fence of The Order, and tightened my grip on the seatbelt. The closer we got, the colder London became. My heart leaped into the back of my throat as we pulled up at the guard hut outside the gates and all of a sudden, I had the urge to run.

My hand went to the door handle, but London reached out and placed his hand on my thigh.

"Thank you," he spoke to the guard and hit the button to shut the window.

He didn't move his hand as he drove through the gates and headed toward the building. The warmth of his touch seemed to permeate my panic. But when he turned the wheel into the parking area in front of the building, he pulled his hand back. "They can't know. You get that, right?" he murmured as he stared straight ahead. "They can't know, or they'll take you away from me."

Take you away from me.

The world felt far too small. The car doors pressed in, crushing me. I couldn't breathe, couldn't think, couldn't do anything but feel the terror wash through me. He was so cold to me. Did that mean he was just as scared? I searched that unflinching stare before he broke the connection and climbed out. "They'll be watching our every move," he murmured.

Heat lashed my cheeks as it hit me. I followed, closed the door behind me, and went toward the pit of Hell itself. How should I act here? What should I say? I didn't need to worry, as London met me behind the car, gripped the back of my arm, and steered me toward the front door as it opened and The Principal stepped out.

"Say nothing unless spoken to," his whisper reached me as we neared the stairs. "And whatever you do, *do...not...react.*"

My stomach rolled as The Principal headed toward us. He didn't look at me, barely even noticed I was there. His sole focus was on London.

"St. James."

"Cruz," London answered coldly. "How long will this take?"

The answer was a twitch at the corner of his mouth as he stepped to the side and motioned for the open door. "Let's find out, shall we?"

My steps stuttered as I stared into the empty foyer. My heart smashed against my chest as that urge to run for my fucking life became overwhelming...until a brush came at the back of my arm. The touch was so slight, no one else could see it.

But I'd felt it.

The slow slide of his thumb let me know I wasn't here alone. As The Principal turned and headed for the door, London met my gaze. *I'm right here,* those unflinching dark eyes whispered. I saw in that second, he was just as scared.

Because if this went wrong, then there was no coming back from this...

For me...

And them.

TWENTY-FIVE

London

I BRUSHED MY THUMB CAREFULLY ALONG THE BACK OF HER arm, hoping like hell she understood what I couldn't say out loud. She didn't look my way as we stepped through the doors of The Order, nor did she flinch. So I was taking that as a good sign.

Our footsteps resounded along the stark white hallway as we headed to the double doors that would take us deeper into this nest. The nest...that's what the sons called it and the name was fitting.

Festering, slithering, vile fucking creatures dwelled within these walls.

I should know, I pretended to be one of them.

A careful glance Vivienne's way and I saw the color drain from her face as Riven opened the door and motioned for her to enter. *Just keep it together for a little while longer, wildcat.* I urged her in my head. *Then we'll leave this place and never come back.*

Images of her and Colt from this morning slipped into my head. As much as I wanted to relive those moments, I pushed them aside. I couldn't afford to think about her like that, not here, not now. I couldn't let them see this as anything more than a transaction.

They had my money.

All I needed was a signature and we'd be done.

One fucking signature and I'd have her out of here.

And King's daughter would be mine.

No, she'd be ours.

The thought filled me. I reached into my jacket and pulled out the contract. Riven flinched as he stared at the folded paper in my hand, then looked away. I didn't like that. No, I didn't like that at all. But before I could push him, the heavy thud of footsteps drew his gaze.

There was that flinch again. Only this time, it came with a curl of his lip. "Ashwood," his voice was tense. "You were supposed to be on patrol."

I glanced toward Hale's new head of security as he headed our way. At six-foot-seven, he was a mountain of raw menace. I guessed Hale wasn't taking any chances after his last commander was found dead in a ditch not far from the building on the same night I'd taken Vivienne. Whatever had come Tig's way, he'd deserved it. But this...*Ashwood*, didn't look at me, just focused on Vivienne. "Mr. Hale asked me to take charge of the transition."

Did he just?

That curl in Riven's lip twisted tighter. There was something happening here, some kind of shift in power I hadn't seen before. But I saw it now and I didn't like it one fucking bit.

"The interview is normally led—" Riven started.

"The word *normal* doesn't apply here anymore." Ashwood stepped to the side, and didn't bother to look away from Vivienne. "Inside, Vivienne."

I didn't like the way he stared at her, didn't like the way he used her fucking name, either. It was more than jealousy that burned inside me as she glanced my way, desperation blooming in her eyes.

I'd come because I knew the players, because I knew exactly where I stood where Riven and his brothers were concerned. But this piece of shit...he was a whole other story. All I could do was nod and fucking watch her follow him into that room.

Fuck that. I went right behind her. "I'll be sitting in as well."

I didn't give them a chance to refuse and headed for the corner of the interrogation room, not bothering to take a seat. The brute took a seat beside her as I crossed my arms and leaned against the wall.

Riven barely had a chance to close the door before it was opened again and his brother, Kane, stepped through. A careful glance at his brother, and he stepped aside. "It seems we're to take a back seat with this."

"What the fuck," Riven muttered as movement came behind his brother...

And my blood ran cold.

Ophelia stepped into the room. I barely saw the asshole who followed her. I pushed off the wall as she settled that glinting gaze on me. Her red lips curled and her kohl-lined eyes widened at the sight of me. "London," she purred, heading my way. "So soon we meet, my love."

"Ophelia." It was all I could manage.

I didn't dare look at Vivienne, but I still caught the movement as she glanced over her shoulder and watched Ophelia slide her hand around the back of my neck and pull my lips down to hers.

Get on your knees...

Those sickening words echoed as her cold lips widened. I broke away and glanced at Vivienne instead. But she'd seen. She'd fucking seen, and the pain in her eyes cut straight to my heart.

"What are you doing here?" My voice was cold as I turned back to the woman I'd gladly hand over to my sons and watch them tear her apart.

"When I heard one of my girls was being transferred to my lover, I had to come and complete it myself."

Heat bloomed in my cheeks. "I'm not your lover."

She gave a small chuckle and walked around the head of the long conference table to take a seat opposite my wildcat.

"Vivienne," she murmured with a fake smile.

But the curl of her lips was anything but disarming. Vivienne didn't flinch, just held the woman's stare as Ophelia looked her over. "She is quite pretty, London, in a *street rat* kind of way. I can see why you're keen to get your dick wet with this one."

My stomach clenched.

My breaths deepened.

Vivienne blanched.

"Unless that's already happened?" Ophelia prodded.

"You know it hasn't," I answered. "The conditions of the contract..."

"Yes," Ophelia murmured, then glanced at the other male who'd come in with her and gave a nod.

He moved fast as he lifted his hand and strode toward Vivienne. Only then did I see the needle.

"What the fuck?" Vivienne shoved up as he grabbed her arm and yanked.

But Ashwood was right beside her, holding her steady.

"What the fuck is this?" I snapped, watching with horror as the needle plunged into her vein.

"Just a little Pentothal," Ophelia replied, unable to look away as Vivienne lashed out, bucked from Ashwood's hold, and shoved backwards in a rush.

Her chair tipped and fell, hitting the floor with a *crash* as Vivienne backed up to the wall. "You injected me with *what?*"

"Truth serum," Ophelia explained as she coldly lifted her gaze to mine. "Short-acting, so it'll wear off soon."

"You bitch." I stepped closer, braced my hands on the desk, and met her stare. "You didn't fucking trust me?"

There was nothing but malice in her tone. "Trust has nothing to do with this."

I'd never wanted to kill someone so much in my entire fucking life. I sucked in a hard breath, knowing there was no way out of this for me...or for Vivienne.

"Sit," Ophelia ordered Vivienne as she motioned to the upended chair.

"Fuck *you*," my wildcat hissed, her words a little slurred already as she started to feel the effects of the barbiturate.

"Suit yourself." Ophelia turned to Ashwood and gave a nod.

He moved instantly...but so did I as I stepped backwards into his way.

I met the bastard's stare, knowing full well I was making all the wrong fucking moves here and I had no way out. There was no Carven to stop this, no Colt to fight to the death. There was just me and *her*. I licked my lips, hating I had to do this, and spoke. "Vivienne, take a seat."

She said nothing, but I didn't need words to feel her betrayal. The catch in her breath said it all.

She slowly stepped forward, wobbling a little as I reached for her upturned chair. I wanted her sitting, not for those bastards, but because I was worried she'd damn well fall and hurt herself.

That venomous stare from across the table followed every movement as I lifted her chair and stepped aside. Vivienne sat, unable to look away as Ophelia reached for the neckline of her blouse and fingered the teardrop diamond necklace I'd given her the night before.

Vivienne stared at the jewel hanging over the bitch's manicured fingernail, but her look gave nothing away.

"Tell me," Ophelia started. "Has London fucked you?"

Vivienne flinched and jerked her gaze upwards, breaking out in a shiver as the barbiturate took hold. I clenched my jaw and concentrated on maintaining my neutral expression. *Please, baby...please, just keep it together.* Questioning was one thing, but this...this was setting me the fuck up.

As Ophelia smiled I, knew that had been her plan all along.

"N-no," Vivienne stuttered as her teeth chattered.

"No?" Ophelia continued, narrowing in on her. "So you're telling me, this man, London St. James, hasn't put his cock inside you?"

Vivienne straightened her spine. "I said, *no*."

"His tongue?"

"No."

There was a twitch in the corner of Ophelia's eye as she leaned closer and snarled. "His...fingers?"

"*No.*"

I'd seen men fight the drug, and seen them as they weakened, as well.

But I'd never seen anyone beat it...until now.

Sweat broke out along Vivienne's forehead and the color washed from her skin, leaving her a sickly shade of yellow. Still, she held on, even if it was making her sick.

"You've got your answer," I snarled. "That's enough."

My fucking pulse boomed and filled my head with the deafening sound.

"You seem to be a little uncomfortable, Vivienne," Ophelia murmured, her gaze narrowing as my wildcat shifted in her seat. "Tell me, are you a virgin?"

Vivienne dropped her head and her hands trembled, white-knuckled as she clenched her fists. "N-n-no."

The word was so small I barely heard it.

Heat rushed to my cheeks as hard as I tried to keep the images at bay as they rushed forward. Vivienne on top...the tip of Colt's cock sliding in.

"What was that?"

Vivienne jerked as though she'd been slapped. "I said, *no.*"

"So, if you're not a virgin, who took it?"

The rush of deep breaths filled the room. I didn't know if they were mine or hers. I hadn't broken the contract...*I hadn't broken the contract.* But knowing this bitch, if she knew the sons had had a taste, she'd ruin our family out of fucking spite.

"Myshfseh."

"*What?*" Ophelia snapped. "Speak *clearly, what are you, retarded?*"

That word *seethed* inside me. I'd heard it snarled too many times about my son.

"*I SAID, MYSELF!*'" Vivienne screamed, her eyes wide and wild, her long hair just as untamed. I saw the moment she reacted, as she shoved upwards and lunged forward. "*NOW GET THE FUCK AWAY FROM ME!*"

Ashwood went for her...and I went for him, stepping in his way once more, and shook my head. "Uh-uh."

He didn't like it, narrowing those gray-blue eyes at me. "That's the second time you've been in my way, St. James."

I gave a smirk. "Believe me, there won't be a third."

His gaze stayed on me and for a second, there was a flicker of uncertainty before he jerked he looked to Ophelia, who just sat there, staring at Vivienne.

"You are a filthy fucking whore, aren't you?" Ophelia growled as she rose from her seat and glared at Riven. "We're done here."

She slowly rounded the table, stopped in front of me, and met my stare. "I see your streak is two for two unsatisfied women. I'll expect you at my house within the week, and you'll pick up where you left off...*on your goddamn knees.*"

I stared at the table as she left, until my vision blurred. The *thud* of the door sounded, leaving Riven, Kane, and my rage behind.

My breath was a rock inside my chest, trapped, but I couldn't let it free as Vivienne slowly straightened and turned around.

There was already color coming back into her cheeks and a strength in her walk as she took a step, closed the distance between us...and slapped me *hard*.

My head snapped to the side with the blow as the air ripped from my lungs. The sting was brutal, searing and hot, but I didn't reach for it. I slowly turned my head felt the weight of the Principal's gaze, and knew the moment would haunt me.

"I think the interrogation is over," Riven spoke carefully.

I didn't have the focus to hand him the contract.

All I could do was stare into the depths of her hate.

And know...we'd crossed the line.

"I think it's best if you leave," he finished.

I gave a nod, transfixed by the curl of her top lip. "Vivienne," I said so fucking carefully. "Let's go home."

TWENTY-SIX

Vivienne

I SHIVERED AS WE DROVE. MY TEETH GNASHED AND chattering until I clenched my jaw even tighter. The drug still lingered, and tasted like metal on the back of my tongue. God, I'd felt sick in that room, so sick I'd been afraid I was going to...*tell them everything.* My thoughts had been hazy, my words were a blur. But now they were sharpening, bringing to light what had happened in that room.

Has London fucked you?

Oh shit...

Oh...shit.

Fear took hold, cold, dark, and swallowed me down. What had I said? What the fuck had I said? I wanted to glance at London. I wanted to see the truth in his eyes, but in the wake of the dread came something else...something that tasted like jealousy and anger.

That bitch...that fucking bitch...

She was the one he'd dressed up for, right? *She* was the one he'd fucked. I closed my eyes as he drove into the garage and parked.

*She was the one he'd given the necklace to...*and she'd wanted me to know it as she fingered the chain and ran the diamond pendant across her collarbone.

Revulsion burned inside me. It wasn't even that the woman was fucking hideous. On the outside she may have been stunning, but inside...inside she was festering and foul. She'd triggered something inside me, something that was terrifying, something that filled me with fear, just like the storm from last night.

She's quite pretty in a street rat kind of way...I can see why you're keen to get your dick wet with this one...

Dick wet...

Dick...wet...

"Viv—"

I didn't give him a chance, just climbed out of the car and slammed the door as hard as I fucking could. The *BANG* resounded in the garage and in my ears, and I *didn't fucking care.* I'd have slammed it harder if I could've. No, I'd tear it from its hinges and hurl it across the garage.

From the corner of my eye, London stormed around the front of the car and bore down on me like an avalanche.

"VIVIENNE!" he roared, but I didn't wait.

I ran for the house, my steps frantic. Whatever had been building between us from the first encounter at The Order was now unleashing with terrifying consequences. The arid tang of the drug welled in the back of my throat and brought tears to my eyes. But they weren't of anguish or pain...because I didn't care.

I wasn't bought for three goddamn million dollars to care. I was bought so he could get his dick wet.

A wounded sound tore from the back of my throat as I kept running. I couldn't think...couldn't breathe. All I could feel was the consuming agony in my chest and the aching throb between my thighs. Because the truth was, I wanted him so much it fucking hurt and that was the cruelest thing of all.

I tore past the kitchen, with London close behind. Guild was there, and looked up as we passed. His lip was still swollen and raw from London's rage yesterday as he tore his gaze from me to his employer. "Mr. St. James..."

"GET THE FUCK OUT!" London bellowed. *"NOW!"*

I spun, my heart hammering with the sound, and stumbled backwards. Lethal hunger rolled from my captor as he narrowed his gaze in on me. The red mark from my hand was evident now, blazing and a bit swollen, but he didn't touch it, he didn't act like he felt it at all. Guild didn't speak again, just went to the door and left as silently as possible.

Because there was a shark hunting....

And he was fixed on my blood.

"Do not react, not until the drug is completely out of your system," he snarled as he stalked closer. "Before we do or say something we'll later regret."

"You mean something like fuck you, why don't you go back to that whore at The Order you seem to like so much...*lover?*"

He flinched as though I'd slapped him. For a second, I saw him pale before he steeled himself. "Vivienne...do not push this."

He used me like a whore, then he wanted to treat me like a child? *"Fuck. You. You. Piece. Of. Shit."*

He froze and his brow furrowed, then his top lip curled just before he lunged. His cruel hand went around my throat and his fingers gripped under my jaw as he pulled me close. Here was the monster I knew, the vile bastard who used and controlled and played everyone...including me.

"You think I'm a piece of shit?"

"No," I didn't look away. "I know it."

He lowered his head and pulled me against his chest. Through his shirt I could feel the racing of his heart as he murmured. "You're right, I am a vile piece of goddamn shit. I'm a murderer, a betrayer, and many, *many* things that would make your blood run cold. And I don't care that you know the real me. Do you want to know why? Because we're far beyond that now, Vivienne. We're well past the point of no return." He stopped for a second and drew in a deep breath, his words more dangerous than ever before. "I tried to do the right thing here, tried to give you a way out of my desires. But I see it's too late for that now. It's far too *fucking late.* You're under my skin, wildcat. You're so far under my fucking skin I can't do a damn thing without thinking about you. *So I don't want you to push me here. It'll be better for the both of us if you don't fight. I want you to go to the basement...and I want you to go there* now."

The basement?

The basement?

Because he wanted me on that machine, right? He wanted me splayed open and exposed for him. My face burned, and I couldn't swallow. I shoved against his chest as I met that predatory stare. "*Make. Me.*"

He froze for a second and his hold eased, just enough for me to slide out. Sounds came from above. The thud of footsteps moved down the stairs and stopped on the landing as they listened. They knew this was...*bad.*

"Vivienne..." London started, staring at the floor.

The way he said my name sent chills down my spine. I swallowed hard and took a step backwards, suddenly rethinking and cursing my temper. The movement drew his gaze. Those dark, malevolent eyes seized me before he said. "Get back here...*now.*"

Get back here? *No...no...no.*

The way he looked at me with that dark, ravening glare told me to do the opposite. So, I did the only thing I could...I turned...*and ran.*

I hurled myself toward the stairs. My steps were slow because my knees still trembled, but I gave it all I had left. The pounding of my steps was soon drowned out by the thunder of his.

Panic filled me as I gripped the banister and wrenched myself upwards.

"Get back here, Vivienne...*I said...get—*" he grabbed my shoulder but his fingers tangled in my hair, tugging the strands until I tore free with a cry and hurled myself upwards.

"*Back...here...NOW!*"

I didn't know if he wanted to hurt me or fuck me. I wasn't about to take the chance. My fight from seconds ago turned into flight. I threw myself onto the landing, turned to watch him, and stumbled backwards. He advanced slowly with harsh breaths and that steely, unflinching stare. His long legs closed the distance and forced me backwards.

"I did warn you." He kept coming, that glare slowly taking in my body. "I tried to give you a way out of this, kitten...but you kept pushing me. You kept..."

Movement came behind me. A scream tore free as I turned and slammed into Colt. But the male didn't protect me...not this time. He lifted those intense blue eyes to London as he advanced, and something passed between them. I realized that this had always been inevitable for me. Then the quiet son stepped back and stood against the wall.

What the fuck?

The action spoke volumes. I was on my own here. No one was going to help me. No one was going to save me. Not from the man who wanted me to call him *daddy*. I jerked my gaze back to London, my voice trembling. "You j-just stay the f-fuck away from me."

"I think it's a little too late for that, wildcat," he snarled, those long legs eating the distance between us.

I tore my gaze from him to Carven, who was further down the hallway, his stark white hair a beacon in the gloom. Maybe he'd help. I stepped backwards and turned at the last moment, to see the son's lips curl with a smirk. "No help here, female."

"*Ugh!*" I snarled and spun around, then lifted my fists, ready to fight. "You want to do this, London? Then let's fucking *do*—"

I didn't get to finish as London unleashed a guttural growl and lunged toward me. I swung, which caused him to chuckle as he ducked the blow easily and grasped me around the waist.

"*Put me down!*" I thrashed in his arms.

"I warned you," he snapped as he threw me over his shoulder and headed back along the hall. "I tried to keep you from this side of me...tried to keep you safe. But you pushed me, female. You pushed and pushed with your fucking eyes and your goddamn taste. You crawled under my skin and haunt my mind. You force me to want you. You force me to give into my fucking desires, so from this moment on, you've got no one to blame but yourself."

"Blame? *Blame for what?*" I beat his back and tried to swing for the side of his head, then my body jolted as he stepped down the stairs. "Blame FOR WHAT?"

"For me taking you to the basement and fucking you with the machine."

I froze with my heart in my throat until he stepped off the stairs. The foyer was a blur as we headed for the kitchen and stopped at the basement door.

"Wait." I shoved his shoulder as I listened to the tiny beeps when he entered the code.

"I tried to warn you, Vivienne," he muttered as he yanked open the basement door. "There's no more waiting, not for this, not anymore."

TWENTY-SEVEN

Vivienne

"Put me down!" I kicked and raged as he reached up and pushed my head down to keep me from smacking it on the ceiling. "*LONDON!*" I fought his hold and almost shook free as we hit the bottom stair.

Smack!

His hand landed on my ass. I bucked with the sting, hating him...*no, I fucking loathed him.* Teeth clenched, I unleashed a snarl. But the heat between my thighs told me otherwise. Even my blows were pathetic as they smacked against his shoulders. "London..." I moaned. "London, *stop.*"

My mind refused to give in, even as he stepped into that room. I still tried to hold onto that anger, to use it to find a way out of this.

"I tried to warn you, Vivienne." He gripped my hips, yanked me off his shoulder, and caught me as I fell. "But you defy me at every fucking opportunity. You give me no choice but to show you."

My feet landed on the floor and speared shockwaves through my ankles. I glared up at him. "Show me *what?*"

He held me until I found my balance while he drew in heavy breaths. "What it means to be owned. Now take off your clothes."

I flinched. "What?"

There was a coldness about him now, one that made me tremble.

"Your clothes, Vivienne." He pinned me with that glare. "I won't ask again. Next time, I'll tear them off."

Pulse.

My core clenched and my breaths raced. I swallowed hard and started to shake my head.

"The clothes I *provided.*" he growled. "The clothes I carefully chose for you."

My pulse skipped. The fabric brushed my skin as I shifted. He...*he chose them?* No...I wanted to argue, but in my heart, I knew it was the truth. Deep down, I'd known he controlled everything when it came to me, from what I wore, to where I went, and now, how I was fucked.

"The clothes I want back," he continued as he lowered his gaze to take in every inch of my body. "Now."

I stood there, unable to move, until I slowly lifted my shaking fingers to the buttons. One by one, I fumbled them open. But he didn't look away, just held my stare as though the depths of my being were created for his amusement...and his pleasure.

I dropped my blouse to the floor, swallowed, stepped out of my shoes, and reached for the zipper of my slacks. When they crumpled at my feet, he moved around my side to the bench, grabbed something, and returned.

"This room is for us and us alone, do you understand that?" His predatory stare watched my every flinch. "While we are in here, there are rules. Rules I..." he drew in a hard breath that caused my own breath to stutter. "Want."

His fingers grazed the middle of my back and sent shivers along my spine as he unclasped my bra took it off, and let it fall to the floor. "In this room, you are to call me daddy. Is that clear?"

Daddy? A surge of desire mingled with the rage, I clenched my jaw. If he thought I was giving in, then he was very much mistaken.

"At least nod so I know you understand me," he snarled.

Nod? Ha! I lifted my hand and flipped him the bird. How's *that* for understanding?

A savage snarl resounded against my ear. *"Keep...it...up."*

My pussy clenched at the words.

"There needs to be a safeword," he continued. "You understand what that is, right?"

Safeword? *What* goddamn safeword? "You forget this is what you paid for, right?" I muttered as heat rose in my cheeks. "I'm here to serve, whether I want to or not."

I flinched as his hand landed on the back of my neck. His breath was hot against my ear. "No, that doesn't happen here. I don't give a fuck what they trained you to do in that place. But that doesn't happen when you're with..."

Me?

Family?

That's what he wanted to say, right?

"Here, that shit doesn't happen here. So, we'll keep it simple. 'Green' means you feel safe and secure. 'Yellow,' you want to pause and discuss...and 'red'..." He kneaded the back of my neck. "Red stops everything. Red gives you the power here, Vivienne. You say that word and I'll take these off." He lifted the cuffs in his hand. "And I'll take you out of here. There are no repercussions. Just me taking care of you, do you understand?"

I swallowed hard.

"Do you—"

I gave a slow nod as he grazed his thumb along my neck. "Good...that's a good girl."

He stepped around to stand in front of me. "Hands."

I closed my eyes, unable to move.

"Don't make me ask again."

My pulse raced as my breaths grew panicked...*flightless*. I lifted my gaze to the door behind him.

No...the word whispered in my mind, but it didn't reach my lips.

"No?" He leaned close to murmur against my ear. "You disobey me, you disobey your daddy?"

I jerked at the words. *But you're not my Dadd*—his scowl deepened, and the sight of that made me freeze.

"No..."

"No, *what?*"

"No, Daddy," I whispered, my voice barely audible.

There was still the contract...the one he'd already broken, the one he'd break again. But not right now, not today. Steel links clinked as he lifted the cuffs. I clenched my fists and lifted my hands as I met his eyes. No, today was about him being in control.

"You made a fool out of me today."

Air punched deep into my lungs.

"You know my standing with The Order, yet you reacted." Steel jaws ratcheted around my wrists. "You slapped me in front of those I need to keep in the dark about us. You drew their attention, and now I have to fix that...*right after I fix you.*"

Fear plunged deep at the words.

He wouldn't hurt me, that I knew. He wouldn't leave so much as a mark. But still the panic rose as he grasped my hands and stood there for a moment. "Do you want this?"

I froze. *No. Yes. I don't know...I...*

"Tell me now."

I met that hard stare and gave a small nod.

He lowered his gaze to my clasped hands, then reached up and gently tweaked my nipple. I jumped, and gave a small cry. Faint silver strands shone amongst the black of his hair as he moved. The sight of that roused something desperate in me. I felt our difference like a lick to my core. It was all I saw, all I felt. It was the way he looked, the way he scolded...the way he touched. My body responded instantly, heat blooming.

"Words, Vivienne."

I stared into the black pools of his eyes and knew fighting him was useless. "Y-yes, *Daddy*." My tone softened and turned deeper, mirroring my breathless urgency.

He turned, reached up, and hit the light switch to dim the room. Even with the lights turned down so low, I could see it. Big and shrouded, it loomed at the end of the bench. I clenched my jaw and closed my eyes. My body was on fire.

"In front of The Principal," he continued as he sank to his knees in front of me and gripped the sides of my panties. My pussy clenched with the slow drag as he rolled them down my thighs. "Others heard, as well."

They were gone in an instant, tossed to the side as he went on. "That *cannot* be tolerated. You've made me have to spill their blood to clean it up. I hope you're aware of that." He leaned close and whispered against my ear. "You're going to make me dangerous. Because I'm telling you right now, I'll kill any other man who even looks at you. Every fucking one. You belong to us, Vivienne...*and you belong to me.*"

I closed my eyes as his words hit home. "That's what you bought me for."

He gave a low, throaty growl. "That and *so much more.*"

My body trembled at the threat. He would kill for me. He'd clean up my mess, then he'd bring me back down here to take it out on my body. "Get on the bed, Vivienne...you've been a very *bad* girl."

My knees trembled as I opened my eyes, but I forced myself to move.

Steel-buckled straps hung down from the leather bench, but I didn't care about them. My focus was on that *thing* at the end, its hard edges and the glint of cold steel. My core pulsed as I sank onto the leather bench.

"Lie back, arms over your head."

I did as he instructed. There was no use fighting now, I'd only be fighting myself. My hands were secured, pulled taut, then given a little slack, though not enough for me to jerk free.

"Knees up...and wide."

I clenched and lifted. Leather slapped around my ankles and spread me a little more.

"Such a pretty little cunt."

His hand slid up the inside of my thigh, reached my slit, and pulled me open. "So fucking pretty."

Then he moved around to the other side to secure my other ankle. I lay there, knees to my chest, Feet wide apart. I lifted my head as he rounded the foot of the bed and stood next to that thing.

"You understand this is your punishment?"

I couldn't do anything but nod as my cheeks burned.

Steel shone as he moved to the front of the machine, snapped open a case, and pulled something out. Steel and smooth, the end snapped on to the hungry mechanical beast. He gripped the remote and the whirr of the motor was instant as the arm lifted.

I let out a whimper as that thick end came toward me.

"I punish you because you need to learn your place." He stepped closer. "You are my ward, Vivienne. *I own you.*"

The head of that cold dildo slid against my pussy, pressed against my entrance, then stopped, pressing in just a little. I bit my lip as I fought a whimper and the urge to bear down. I shifted until my arms snapped taut. My slit had barely opened around the smooth head. But it wasn't enough, not anywhere near enough. "Please..."

"Please?"

The head backed out.

I slammed my eyes closed. "Please."

Pressure pushed against me again, right where I needed it. It slid in, just enough, but then it pulled out again. I opened my eyes and turned my head to look not at that *thing* that sat at the foot of the bed, but at him...at the man who held the remote in his hand.

God, his eyes were so dark, endless dark like he'd swallowed all the light in my world. I ached for that darkness...*I craved it.* "*Daddy.*"

The corners of his lips twitched at the word. I knew he liked it. The motor whirred as it drove the cock deeper inside me.

"Good girl," he whispered.

I held his gaze as the cold dildo pushed in and drove deeper, all at his direction. Black pools...that's what I sank into. Black. Endless. Pools. My pulse raced. A current surged through me, making me moan and buck *hard.*

"More, kitten?"

I nodded as I desperately fought the whimpers.

The machine fucked me harder, until all I could hear was that whirr. The dildo pistoned in and out of me. Then he did break my gaze as he leaned over, slid his finger along the bottom of my crease, and came away slick and wet.

"Close, so close." He placed his finger between his lips and sucked hard. The sound mingled with the wet, sucking sounds my body made.

I didn't care at that moment, didn't care what fucked me...I didn't care *who* fucked me. I was past the point of no return, barreling headfirst into oblivion.

"Who owns you, Vivienne?"

I clenched my eyes as the peak rose higher and higher inside me as he leaned down, his voice like gravel in my ear. *"I said...who owns you?"*

I turned my head as the desperate need to buck and claw and fuck roared inside me. I tried to hold on, tried to keep the desire from sweeping me away. But I was fighting a losing battle as I finally gave in...

TWENTY-EIGHT

London

"*WHO...OWNS...YOU?*" I DEMANDED AS I WATCHED HER EYES flutter and her body bloom.

"I...*ah...*" Her pussy clenched around the shiny dildo as she neared her climax.

"No, you don't, wildcat," I clucked as I pressed the button and slid the toy from her pussy. Still, her perfect pink lips gaped and her body clenched. "No coming until I say so."

Anger flared in her eyes and she bared her teeth. *"Please."*

My cock twitched at her pathetic plea. *That's it, kitten, show me your claws.* I was already fucking hard from chasing her through the goddamn house and her spite only made me harder. Did she honestly think she could escape me? Did she think the sons would step in like white fucking knights and save her pretty fucking ass?

She didn't get it...

But she would.

Fuck yes, she would.

She belonged to all *of us.*

We'd all take turns with her.

And protect what was ours.

I lowered my gaze from the challenge in her eyes to the weapon poised outside that perfect cunt. I pressed the button, easing the tip inside...in and out...*in and out*...toying with her. "Please doesn't answer the question, now does it? And you don't want to make me ask again, do you, Vivienne?"

She unleashed a moan and dropped her head. Her words were a mumble.

I leaned close. "What? I can't hear you."

I reached between her legs as that gleaming head teased her entrance, and brushed her clit. She whimpered as my callused thumb grazed her tender flesh, then lingered. Press...release... press...release. I watched her body quiver.

"What have I told you about mumbling?" I shifted my gaze from her pussy to her eyes. "Use your fucking words, Vivienne..." Press. Release. "*Use. Your. Words.*"

Her low moans were torturous.

My cock twitched. It took all my strength not to shove the machine aside and bring her to a screaming release right then. I bit my lip and turned back to that tight trembling nub as it turned plump under my touch. Fuck, I ached to be inside her. My tongue, my fingers, my cock. The woman was driving me mad. But not before I made her a goddamn mess.

"You will learn to use your words, or this room will become your penance. You don't want that, do you, Vivienne?"

Her pussy clenched and slick shone. She was so fucking wet. I jerked my gaze to her eyes. Christ, she liked it when I was firm with her. She liked it when I was the one in control. I dragged my teeth across my lip, transfixed by the wildness in her eyes as she yanked on the steel bonds and arched her back as she tried to drive her body down.

"You can say the word anytime you want, wildcat. You can say red and we will stop right now, if that's what you want? Say red, Vivienne...*say red.*"

I pressed the button, slowly sliding the dildo all the way inside. Her breath caught, eyes fluttered. "Oh, fuck...*oh, fuck.*" She whimpered as I slid it free. "Green...green...*green green green greeeennn.*"

"That's fucking right." I watched it fuck her, watched how she pulled her legs wider, desperate for that ache to be sated. The whirr of the motor filled the room until she grunted, so close. Then I slowed the machine.

"Look at how wet you are." I pulled her pussy lips open and watched the dildo come away slick. "Such a good little pussy... such a..." I pressed the button and drove the sleek thing back inside as she writhed. "Perfect fucking cunt. Look at that." I swallowed hard, my breaths heavy as I slid my fingers through her come. "Look at the mess you made."

That guttural groan had to have fucking hurt. Her wide eyes were fixed on the movement as I slipped them into my mouth, and that pretty fucking hole clenched tight.

"That's the way, kitten, clamp down...clamp all the fucking way down." I leaned closer to slide my fingers back along the warmth until I hovered at her core. "You did so well keeping our secret today, wildcat." I slid two fingers inside and felt her greedy pussy clench. "So fucking well. I'm so proud of you, so fucking proud." She bit down on her lip at the praise. "Now, I want you to be a good fucking girl and tell me who owns you."

Her head thrashed from side to side.

Fighting it...

Fighting me.

The muscles of her jaw flared as her lips curled and bared her teeth. Fuck, she was glorious. Defiant, savage. I pressed the button sliding the dildo into her. "Tell me, wildcat, or I'll keep you strapped here until you do."

Hate flared as her eyes widened. "I fucking hate you."

My breaths deepened as I swallowed. "I know." I looked down and saw her cum coating my fingers. "I can see how much."

I'd thought I could control it. I thought I was...the one in charge. But her panting breaths got to me, and the desperate need in her eyes drove me over the edge.

I leaned over, moved that thing from her, and licked her quivering pussy. Warmth coated my tongue as I swallowed. "I can taste it, too. You're etched in my memory now, kitten, branded on my goddamn soul."

She whimpered, her body pulsing as I broke the contract for the second time and pushed my fingers inside. "That's it." I slid them deeper, feeling her clench. "That's a good girl. That's a real, fucking good girl. You fuck these goddamn fingers."

The chains of the cuffs snapped taut as she tried to drive her body downward. I snapped my gaze to the strain. She was so fucking desperate, so goddamn riled. "Tell me. Use your goddamn words and tell me what I want to know."

"No," she whimpered.

But she was so close...

So goddamn close.

In and out. In...and out. I fucked her with my fingers and pushed the button, watching the glistening head push her apart.

She moaned, her hips bucking, desperate to fuck.

I watched her to make sure she didn't pull too hard on the cuffs, then pulled the machine out and stopping it as I licked her from ass to clit.

She might not feel it now, but I was betting tomorrow this perfect cunt was going to be tender. "Tell me," I insisted again as she thrust her hips against my mouth. *"Tell...me..."*

I caught her ass and held her body against my mouth as I sucked her twitching clit.

"You do...you...oh, Jesus...you own me, London. You own me." She opened her eyes to look down and warmth spilled around my fingers as her pussy clenched. "You do, London. *Oh, fuck, you dooo."*

I lowered my head, not giving a fuck that I made a goddamn mess of my shirt, and opened my mouth wide as I licked her salty sweetness, then swallowed. "That's fucking right," I growled against her body. "So next time you feel like testing me, you'll want to remember that."

Her ass unclenched as her legs relaxed as much as they could, spent. I gave one last lick of that fluttering core before I rose and swiped my mouth with the back of my hand as I looked down at her glistening pussy. I wanted more, so much fucking more. I wanted everything when it came to her.

It took all my strength to press the button to pull the machine back and switch it off. I'd come down later to clean and stow away the attachments for next time. Because I was damn sure there would *be* a next time. Our wildcat had enjoyed it as much as I had.

I grabbed the key for the handcuffs and moved to unlock her hands. Her hands dropped to the leather with a smack, causing me to slide my arms under her body and lift her.

Limp in my arms, she slid her arms around my neck and curled into me as I carried her to the door. Fuck, I'd never felt so goddamn good in all my miserable life.

I leaned close, stabbed the code into the keypad, and carried her out. My steps resounded in the darkness as I made my way back upstairs and through the open door to the foyer. Colt was waiting on the landing as I climbed the main stairs. Concern flared in his eyes as he looked at her. I gave him a careful nod to let him know our kitten was well fucking spent and okay before carried her to a place I'd never had a woman before...my bedroom.

"You've been such a good girl letting me play with you," I murmured as I pushed on the handle then carried her inside to my bed. "I'm going to take care of you. I'm going to hold you so you can sleep. When you wake up, I'm going to shower you and feed you."

Love you...

Fuck, my pulse was a goddamn train in my chest.

My voice was husky as I forced myself to continue. "I'm going to give you everything you want and more..." I looked down at her as I pulled the bedding down and placed her gently on her side. "I'm going to give you me."

TWENTY-NINE

Vivienne

DARKNESS CLAIMED ME. I SANK AND ROSE WITH THE EBB and flow. Hard breaths echoed in my ears and warmth pressed against my back, lulling me into the deepest slumber I'd ever had in my entire life. One where I was safe...and protected.

Kitten...

I rose with the murmur. Soft, deep snores pulled me to the surface. A hard breath and I inhaled the familiar scent of male. One that made me turn toward it. Strong arms were wrapped tightly, pulling me in close. I cracked open my eyes, to see a murky silhouette beside me. Dark eyes looked back at me, illuminated by the spill of silver moonlight.

I knew him instantly.

His name resounded in my soul.

London...

He pushed up to kiss the top of my shoulder. "Sleep, pet," he murmured, his voice husky with exhaustion. "Your body needs it."

I obeyed him, closed my eyes, and sank once more, to fall headfirst into a place I'd never been before, a place where I was no longer alone. Only, when I surfaced again, clarity came with it.

Before I'd had a chance to steel myself, it hit me all at once.

The drug.

The Order.

I opened my eyes and found him watching me...and caught my breath.

The slap.

Something else hovered on the horizon of my mind, something fueled by rage.

"Easy now," he murmured.

My pulse spiked as I jerked fully back to the present, and one memory drowned out all the rest. Heat rose in my cheeks as an empty feeling bloomed in the pit of my stomach. *The basement...oh god, the*—my body tightened—*the machine.*

My body clenched and an ache followed. But it was a good ache, a throbbing ache. My attention was drawn to the sensation and an acute surge of desire followed. My body knew what it wanted, and it wanted him.

His brow furrowed. "Are you sore?"

I swallowed and shook my head.

Instantly, the corners of his mouth curled and the sight of that did unholy things to me. My chest fluttered and heat rose in my cheeks, but I forced annoyance. "I say something funny to you?"

There was something erotically dangerous in his eyes as the smile faded. "No, kitten, not at all." An awkwardness took its place as he searched my gaze and murmured, "Can I...can I kiss you?"

My pulse stuttered, then surged. He'd fucked me, tasted me, had me naked with my legs spread open on the dining room table in front of him, and yet the thought of him kissing me made me feel so very...vulnerable as it danced around an emotion I wasn't ready to handle.

Still, I found myself nodding, and I watched as a spark of excitement erupted in that dominating stare when he lifted his hand. The back of his curled fingers grazed my jaw before he leaned closer. His hard lips brushed mine before they slowly opened. Slowly, so achingly slowly, he took my mouth. Softly at first, he kissed the corners of my mouth, then he gently bit my lower lip until, with a cup of my cheek, he took more.

A low moan rumbled in his chest and spilled into my mouth. I groaned at the vibration and my body instantly responded, until I grabbed his strong shoulders and pulled him against me.

I should be angry with him.

The words rose in my mind just before he pushed me backwards and his weight pressed me into the plush bedding. He broke the kiss and his breaths were heavy as he looked down at me. "We can't go any further. You understand that, right, kitten? Not until that damn contract is signed."

I licked my lips, hating him and needing him all at the same time, and slowly nodded.

That soft smile came again. "But I can look after you. How about a shower and some food? You must be starving, because I know I am."

My belly tensed and snarled as he rolled off me. He chuckled softly as he stood from the bed. My gaze moved down his body, to his firm, hard chest, where on one side a small mass of silver scars in an ugly rose bloomed. I knew what it was, the aftereffect of a gunshot. *Who the hell are you?* My eyes drifted lower. I felt the heaviness of his stare, but he didn't move, just let my gaze wander until I found the tented front of his dark blue boxers and looked away.

"You want to look, kitten, then look." He turned to me, then his fingers slid under the waistband and pushed them low enough to let his thick cock spring upwards. The head was blushed, and his balls were tight. I swallowed hard and stared as that ache between my thighs grew hotter.

"I know you've been in here before," he commented. "You messed up my bed and rifled through my things. Did you touch yourself here, on my sheets?"

I jerked my gaze to his, scowled, and shook my head.

He took a step toward me and his hand dropped to his length. "Will you do it now?" He licked his lips. "Will you show me what you like?"

Show him what I like?

My mind went to the night I'd refused to wear his clothes and, instead, had pushed him to distraction, the kind of distraction he wanted now. I didn't nod, just slid my hand down my bare body and under the sheet. He swallowed as he watched the movement, then reached out and tugged the sheet from my body to expose my lower half.

"Open your legs, wildcat. Let me see."

Desire moved through me as I parted my thighs.

His fingers sank into the ache. I bit my lip and closed my eyes.

"You are sore, aren't you?"

I opened my eyes to look at him. "Yes."

He shifted his hand around his cock. "Show me."

The sting was beautiful as I parted my lips and ran a finger around my tender clit.

"Fuck," he moaned, his breaths heavy as he released his cock and rounded the bed to stand over me. "So red, so swollen. Will you let me lick it better?"

I trembled as I sank my fingers in deep. *Yes,* my body whimpered. *God, yes.* But with the words came another memory from yesterday...the memory of my anger...and the sight of that fucking *bitch.*

I can see why you want to get your dick wet, London...

The words echoed through me as I stared at his engorged cock. His fist closed around the girth and drew the smooth skin all the way to the head before he stroked it back down to the base. He wanted to get it wet, alright, deep in my pussy...before he left me to ram it into *hers.*

Jealousy carved through the illusion and reminded me of the kind of man I was dealing with. One that couldn't be trusted, especially not with my emotions. "No," I forced the word as anger flashed inside me. "You can't."

Anger flared in his gaze, cutting me. In his anger, I found myself once more. I wasn't going to fall for this man. I wasn't going to yield, not for that beautiful mouth or those deft fingers. Not even when he took me downstairs and spread my legs wide.

He'd get his money's worth from my body, of that, I was sure.

But there was no fucking way he was getting my heart.

Instead of giving in to him, I gave in to myself and slid my fingers through the swollen ache. "I can still feel it," I whispered. "Still feel your mouth, your fingers."

"Careful, kitten," he warned as he licked his lips. "My resolve only goes so far."

"I know exactly how far it goes," I whispered as I widened my legs and pushed two fingers in deep. "All the fucking way, right, London? *All the fucking way inside...me.* Oh, that's right. That's the machine you use to fuck me, because you can't do it yourself."

Hard breaths came as he lowered his hand to that rigid cock again. My eyes darted down with the movement, to watch the tiny eye at the head weep with a single tear. "You want it in my mouth, don't you?" I moaned, as I slid a finger around my inflamed clit. "You want me to choke on your cock, isn't that what you said to me? That I'll choke on your cock and like it?"

Hard breaths.

A curl of his lips.

Rage burned.

There you go. That's the monster I know.

That's the *good...little...monster...*I worked my clit, then slipped my fingers into my pussy before pulling away, my fingers wet and sticky, then I rolled from the bed and winced as my feet hit the floor.

"Where the fuck are you going?" he snarled as I headed for the bedroom door, naked.

I grabbed the handle, and turned as I opened the door. "Going to find someone for the job. I'm sure you won't care, either way. Don't you have a date with Ophelia to get ready for? Maybe you can get *your dick wet with her?*"

A terrifying snarl ripped from him and darkness shifted in the room. He was a blur of menace as he tore the door from my grasp and slammed it closed with a *BANG!*

I didn't dare lift my gaze, didn't dare meet that stare. But I felt the *rage* roll off him in terrifying waves as he leaned close. "You want to watch yourself, kitten. Jealousy isn't becoming on you."

"Then maybe I need to find something else to come on me?" I murmured as I slowly lifted my gaze to his. "I think Colt would be only too happy to help me out with that."

He went utterly still...

And dark.

Darker than I'd ever seen anyone enraged before.

And I'd seen plenty at The Order.

I grasped the door handle again. This time, he didn't try to stop me. Instead, he slowly lowered his hand and let me open the door and walk out of his bedroom.

Hard, frantic breaths consumed me as white sparks ignited behind my eyes. It took all my willpower not to run up the stairs, but I managed it by climbing the stairs one by one until I headed for my bedroom.

The moment I was inside, I closed the door and leaned back against it. My knees trembled so hard, they finally gave out and I slid all the way down until my ass hit the floor.

Oh fuck...oh fuck...oh fuck...

I rocked forward and closed my eyes.

Because the truth was, I was already falling for the monster.

And there wasn't a damn thing I could do to stop it.

"I fucking hate you," I whispered as I opened my eyes and lifted my gaze. "I fucking *hate you*."

THIRTY

Carven

"PUT ME DOWN!" WILDCAT SCREAMED. *"LONDON!"*

The sound was swallowed by the thud of fading steps.

My brother's brow furrowed as he took a step toward the basement door, until I blocked his way.

"Uh uh," I shook my head and met that threatening glare. "This is inevitable, you know that."

Anger shifted to concern in his eyes. The flare of his jaw told me more than words ever could, and for the first time in our life together, I didn't know what to say. So in the end, I turned back to what I knew, what kept us moving and soothed the rage. "We need to get going. You up for this?"

He just stared at the closed basement door as we listened to her screams fade until they suddenly ended as the room door closed with a faint thunk.

"Hey." I softly slapped his cheek, drawing his focus. *"I said, are you up for this?"*

He jerked those blue eyes toward me. His hard breath told me he wasn't, but he nodded, because that's what he did...he went wherever I went and he battled the demons for me—the faint whirr of a motor drifted up to us—and right now, I wanted out of here.

I headed for the garage. Three heartbeats later, he followed as I climbed into the Explorer and started the engine. The door closed with a *thud* and a heavy silence filled the space as we left. I caught the shift of his gaze to the side mirror and knew instantly what he was thinking.

"He won't hurt her," I assured him as I shifted gears. "The man is..." *Obsessed,* I wanted to say, but even that was too small a word for what London was with that female.

Consumed.

Controlled, maybe?

Owned. That was closer to the mark.

Pathetic and pointless, if you asked me.

A tremor cut across my chest as I glanced at my brother. I shifted my gaze to the rear-view mirror, but it wasn't to the house. It was to the quiet street behind us. One that was normally busy mid-afternoon, before I turned the corner and I realized I didn't have to say anything at all. Because he wasn't fucking listening to a word I said.

"Fine." I grumbled. "I'll just talk to myself."

His deep blue eyes found me, broodier and darker than ever before, saying everything and nothing at the same time. I met that glare, then turned back to the road and for the millionth fucking time, that nagging thought slipped into my head. Were they the eyes of our mother? Or were they, at this moment, staring from the faceless man who'd sired us?

I'd always imagined Colt's blue eyes were hers, careful, deep, with one look you just knew they were home. I lifted my gaze to the rear-view mirror and found the neon fucking blue I couldn't hide even if I'd wanted to. But there was no life in them. They were dead, empty. I knew in my heart they were *his*...whoever the fuck he was.

One day I was going to hunt him down.

And make him relive all those special moments that were given to us.

In that place called fucking *Hell*.

I drove to the warehouse, pulled up at the gate, and climbed out. That nagging feeling brushed the back of my neck as I punched in the code, then spun around. I swept the empty streets as I waited. I was jumpy...too fucking jumpy. My thoughts rioted around London, that fucking bitch from The Order...and the female at home, one my brother seemed to be falling in love with.

I climbed back into the car and parked near the warehouse. It was too early for the job we had to do and planning was crucial. The last thing we wanted was another fucking surprise. By the time evening had faded and night had fully moved in, we'd cleaned and oiled every firearm, honed every blade, and we were ready.

The familiar bite of steel pressed against my back when I climbed into the Explorer. Colt had changed out of the dark blue t-shirt he liked to wear at home to the long-sleeved black vest he wore on jobs like this. He pressed the button on the door and left it to close behind him as he carried the duffel bag to the car stowed it on the floor.

Night was our playground.

Night was when we liked to hunt and there was no better prey than the fat fuck who thought he was untouchable. Tonight, he was about to get a lesson on just how touchable he was. I drove out of the gates and searched for whatever was causing that nagging feeling that someone was watching me, then headed for the highway that'd take us where we needed to be.

King occupied my thoughts. This was beyond a hunt now, beyond obsession. Beyond needing to find the motherfucker to unleash him at the one festering fuck behind this. It was because...I couldn't find him at all.

I hated it...

No, hate was too easy.

I was consumed, unable to rest, unable to slow.

King.

King.

King...

I winced, forced the constant drone to the back of my mind, and tried to focus.

"You good for this?" I asked as I watched the road. "The last thing we want is for that fuck to get the drop on us again."

A glance his way, and he nodded. I looked at his side, where the bandages were taped over the deep lacerations. "Good." I turned back to the road and headed to the south side of the city. "'Cause that motherfucker needs to pay."

I shifted gears and pulled onto the highway as my mind returned to the female. The panic. The excitement. The fucking pure adrenaline that made those big brown eyes wide. I swallowed hard as my pulse kicked up and a hunger pushed in. I wanted to be there in that room, wanted to watch London strap her to that bench, and most of all, I wanted to watch her come.

My cock twitched.

I clenched my ass tight.

No. I wouldn't think about her. Not like that...*not again.*

No matter how hard I battled the thought, she still lingered. Her fucking hair. Her fucking body—I glanced at Colt—the way she was with him. It fucking got to me. By the time I slowed the four-wheel drive and pulled over in the quiet residential street, I was controlled, ready to exact some revenge.

I reached around into the back of the vehicle and pulled out a black duffel bag before I lifted my gaze to the back window and stilled. Colt glanced at the mirror. I felt the scowl. "Wait here," I muttered and climbed out of the car without making a sound.

Darkness filled the windows behind us. I scanned the street for movement to please that instinct inside me. *King...King... King...*I turned and made my way back to where Colt quietly opened his door and climbed out.

A shake of my head said, *nothing, it's all good.* But that didn't stop me from searching the parked cars and the houses before I took the item my brother gave me and slipped it over my head.

The balaclava pressed against my face and sucked in when I breathed.

I caught a glimpse in the tinted window, and my blue eyes were haunting against the faceless image. The sight would stay with them forever. Good, because I wanted it to. The Hellfire Rebel bastard was lucky I wore one at all.

Colt tugged his balaclava down and glanced my way before he nodded. With the duffel bag slung over my shoulder, I headed for the house. My steps thudded, and with each impact I grew colder, and colder, and colder. Until I became the thing The Order had created...

Until I became *a son*.

I reached into the duffel bag, pulled out a plastic snap-lock container, reached inside, and yanked out two steaks. A soft whistle and the deep snarls of the two German Shepherds came, right as I tossed the meat over the gate and retreated.

Ten minutes, that's all it took for the dogs to consume the steaks and sink to the ground. I unlocked the gate, but before I had a chance to enter, Colt had already pushed past me to kneel beside the sleeping beasts and feel for the rise and fall of their chests.

He didn't like it when animals were involved.

Not. One. Fucking. Bit.

His dark blue eyes flashed with anger when he looked up at me.

I held that stare, grasped the gun from the waistband of my pants, then reached into the bag for my silencer. "Don't bitch at me. If the ugly fuck would've given us the information when we went to him, we wouldn't be here. So, if you're gonna be pissed at anyone, be pissed at him."

My brother rose and swung his glare toward the house. Fuck, I didn't like doing this shit. But the fucker hadn't given us any choice. I headed for the sliding glass door and pulled out the pick. Five seconds, and the lock was open, as was the door.

We were silent when we entered.

The soft scrape of a boot sounded, then there was nothing at all.

We passed the kitchen and made our way to the hall. The photos on the real estate website had been perfect for tonight. We knew the layout, knew the location...even knew it had been upgraded to an expanded, double-lined garage for all those noisy motorcycles.

Colt stopped at the cracked-open bedroom door. Soft yellow light filled the space, fluttering and dancing with stars from the bedside lamp. Colt moved into the bedroom quietly and stood over the small form curled in the middle of the bed before he reached down with a gun in one hand and gently tugged the comforter high, draping it over the boy's head.

I swallowed hard and turned away when my brother looked at me. I couldn't see the pain in his eyes, couldn't acknowledge the desperation. No. That's wasn't going to get the job done. We left, and Colt closed the kid's bedroom door all the way with barely more than a whisper before we both moved to the bedroom at the end of the hall.

The one where deep, guttural snores and the stench of tobacco and sweat spilled out. My gut clenched as I gripped the edge of the door and opened it wide.

I glanced at the piece of shit, but it was the wife lying beside him I focused on. She lay closest to the door, one arm hanging down from the bed as she perched precariously on the edge, while that bastard...that bed-hogging, brother-glassing, secret-fucking-keeping hunk of turd lay, legs spread, in the middle of the king-sized bed.

The sight of that pissed me the fuck off. I glanced at the wife, then at him as I rounded the bed and stood on the side next to him.

Cold steel pressed against his temple, but the bastard didn't wake. I gave a soft shove, pushing the silencer against his head. He. Didn't. Move. Colt's eyes blazed with anger when I met his gaze. I gave a shrug, *what the fuck do you want me to do, shoot him?*

Even under the mask, I knew he snarled.

Goddamn, fat...*fuck*. I gripped the gun, clenched my jaw, and punched the silencer in a place I knew I'd get a reaction—right against his balls.

His eyes flew open instantly. His gaze shifted to me in the gloom. There was a flare of anger and he opened his mouth to roar, right before I shook my head and nodded to the other side of the bed. The President of the Hellfire Rebels followed the motion, to find Colt next to his wife, gun in hand.

Fear filled his eyes. He knew instantly.

Knew who we were.

Knew why we'd come and he also knew the repercussions if he didn't get his ass out of bed. A mammoth draw of a breath and he nodded. I withdrew the gun and instead aimed at his head as I stepped back.

"David?" The soft murmur came.

"It's alright, angel, just getting some ice cream."

She rolled from the edge and toward the middle now that there was room. "Put the lid on it this time."

Soft steps, soundless. We made our way out of the bedroom, me with my gun pointed at him and my brother held back near his sleeping wife. She didn't wake, didn't know, just snuggled into her half of the comforter as we left her behind.

"Garage," I said softly behind him in the hall.

Colt quietly closed the bedroom door and followed us to the semi-detached garage and stepped in. The overhead lights blinked on, filling the space with a blinding glare that bounced off the gleam of the three Harleys parked in the middle.

"Look, if you want—"

He didn't have a chance to finish before I walked up and pistol-whipped the bastard right across the face.

He was big...but not that big. The blow knocked him sideways, but he stayed upright as he jerked a savage glare my way...so I did it again, only this time, harder. His knees buckled and he hit the concrete floor beside the bikes.

I stepped closer and pointed the silencer at the floor beside him. "You scream, and they are both dead, do you understand me?" He didn't look up, didn't even flinch as Colt found a chair and dragged it closer, "Now, we're going to try this again...and this time, you're going to give me the information I want."

He started to shake his head, then stopped and lifted a hate-filled gaze to me. "You're asking about the wrong fucking guy. King is a goddamn ghost."

I reached for the edge of the balaclava and dragged it off my face, smiling. "Let's just see about that."

Colt did the same and revealed his face as he stepped forward. I saw fear in the bastard's stare—real fear. Maybe he knew what was about to happen?

I WIPED sweat and blood from my brow and sucked in hard breaths as I stared at the bastard who'd passed out for the third time tonight. "Hey. Wake the fuck up, we're not done yet."

His face was bloody, and both eyes were swollen almost shut. Blood and saliva dribbled from his mouth and he was missing three fingers from his hands taped behind him. One of which was currently shoved up his nose.

"Maybe he's telling the truth?" I glanced at Colt, who was just as winded as I was.

He gripped the bloody bolt cutters, then glared at the cocky bastard who wasn't feeling so cocky anymore. A high-pitched whine came from the door. Colt strode over, opened it, and let both Shepherds in. They moved to their master and sniffed the blood, before my brother sank to his knees and held out his hands.

They went to him like he was their best friend, letting him rub their ears and give them all the love and affection they wanted. A low moan came from the President of the Hellfire Rebels. "I don't know him," he moaned. "No one does. Please...please, no more."

I stepped closer, swiped my bloody hand on the back of my pants, and lifted the silencer to press it against his head. "I believe you."

There was a sudden draw of breath and a low moan before I caught movement in the corner of my eye. Colt shook his head. I met his stare with mine and looked pointedly at his side. One jerk of his head toward the house, and I knew...*he had a family*.

But the bastard should've thought about that before he'd decided to glass the fuck out of mine.

We've done enough. Those blue eyes urged. *Let him live.*

Let him live?

Let him fucking live?

But we hadn't gotten what we'd come for. I clenched the patterned grip of my gun and turned back, finding the pained stare through the tiny slits of the bastard's swollen eyelids.

"We're done here," the president urged. "We're done."

I knew what he meant.

He wouldn't come after us if we let him go.

Hate fueled me as I stepped closer. "My brother has decided to let you live. But if I even think...even for one second, feel your ugly, hot, fetid breath down the back of my neck, you know what will happen."

He gave a slow nod, one that dislodged the thick finger and it fell into his lap.

"King?"

The man swallowed hard. That fear shone in his eyes. "I... don't...know...where...he...lives," he repeated for the hundredth time tonight. "All the correspondence we had was over the phone, even his voice was muted by one of those synthesizers. No one's ever met him. We just did the jobs he requested and took his money. I swear to you on my son's life."

I pressed my gun hard against his head. "You don't do that. You don't bargain or promise something like that away. He keeps his fucking existence. He keeps it and he grows up none the wiser. Get out of the fucking game, David...and keep your family safe."

He just gave a slow nod as I turned and headed for the door as we left the garage.

"Hey. You gonna leave me here?" the bastard called.

"Yes," I muttered, listening to the crunch as one of the Shepherds found one of his fingers. "I am."

I made my way out as I detached the silencer, and Colt followed a few steps behind with the bag full of our things. It was just one more goddamn night of disappointment. I was too pissed off to feel a kick of panic as I stepped through the open gate and neared the thick brush.

But I heard it...

Heard it in the snap of a branch as some asshole moved just enough for me to see him and murmured, "Now, what do we have here?"

I jerked my gaze around to see a crisp black shirt and a steely fucking glare as Colt closed the goddamn gate behind us, then turned and froze.

"I fucking know you?" I snarled.

The walking deadman just smiled. "No...but I know you."

THIRTY-ONE

Colt

_____

THE GLINT OF STEEL SHONE FROM THE TREES AS MY brother turned his head. "You know me, hunh?"

I stiffened at the way he said the words. But my focus was fixed on the muzzle of the gun as some asshole stepped from the bushes. "Yeah." He cut a glance my way. "I know all about you."

There was a twitch at my brother's lips. That was *never* a good thing. "Looks like you're in charge then, *champ.*"

A groan came from the garage behind us, drawing the focus of the asshole with the gun. Only then did he really look at us, the balaclava in my hand, the black duffel bag in the other. The blood splatter still wet on my face. But he didn't flinch at the sight. No, if anything he became even more wary. His brow creased as he drove the gun into Carven's shoulder and growled. "Move."

I clenched my jaw and stepped forward, which earned me a cutting glare from Carven. A tiny shake of his head and I stopped. *King?* Carven gave a shrug. He didn't know who this asshole was. Until we did, then we'd play along.

Carven strode for the street and glanced at the four-wheel drive further along the street. "You've been the one following us, right?"

The guy said nothing as we strode toward our Explorer. "In," the asshole snarled. "You." He glared my way. "Drive. One wrong move and I'll put a bullet in your brain, got me?"

My brother went fucking still. "You don't want to do that," he said carefully. "He's shit at roundabouts."

The asshole pushed in closer to snarl. "Not today he isn't."

But it was the way the deadman moved, the way he held his gun, close to his chest, finger on the trigger. He was military of some kind.

"Fine," Carven muttered as he rounded the car to the driver's side. "Don't say I didn't warn you."

Carven was too calm, too controlled. I didn't like it. He opened the back door. "After you."

The moment the guy glanced inside, my brother moved with savage ferocity, grabbed the big bastard around the throat, and moved behind him faster than I could track. The guy jerked and fought for a second, but my brother was so fucking strong as he pressed his arm like a steel bar across the guy's throat.

"Easy now," he murmured as he lifted his gaze to me.

The guy didn't put up much of a fight. Pity. I held Carven's stare as all two hundred and some pounds of the fucker slumped in his arms. He let the guy fall through the open door before he heaved his feet in after him and closed it behind him.

We both stared at the dark form on the back seat. That had been a surprise. Carven glanced my way. "The warehouse."

I nodded, but I didn't move when he stepped toward the driver's door.

He stopped and turned my way. "What?"

I met my brother's stare. "I am not shit at roundabouts."

There was a chuckle. "Brother, you are *so* fucking shit at roundabouts. You just can't pick a goddamn lane, swerving all over the fucking place like you're tryin'a do your goddamn makeup."

I scowled, then stalked to the passenger side. "You know, sometimes you can be a real dick."

He flashed me a grin. "Yet you fucking love me."

I climbed in and tossed the duffel bag onto the back seat, where it landed on the asshole's head with a *thud*. It was that love for him that beat inside me, that love that was its own entity altogether, breathing and living. That love where I existed. I glanced over my shoulder as I pulled the door closed and tugged my seatbelt over. It was lucky Carven had acted. Lucky *he* was the one who'd had control, because I would've torn the fucker apart.

Carven cut a glance my way as he started the engine and pulled out. His bright blue eyes seized mine. He knew I would have. I'd kill anyone who touched my brother. Thoughts of *her* pushed in and my heart thudded loudly as we accelerated and headed for the warehouse. She beat inside me just as loudly now. A different tone, but still heavy and resounding. And I'd kill anyone who touched her, too.

She was mine.

I sat with the sound of that and she filled my mind. Her wild hair, her cutting anger. The way she'd run to me for safety when London had hunted her through the house. But it was the way she'd winced when I'd driven my cock all the way inside her that burned brighter than everything else. I hadn't realized what that had meant then, but I realized it now. Heat flushed my cheeks and that thunder in my chest grew louder. I knew *exactly* what it meant...and I wanted more.

We pulled into the entrance of the warehouse. I glanced at the still form behind me as Carven climbed out and entered the code. The guy was still alive. How long that was...was up to him. We drove inside and parked alongside the building. Carven climbed out and unlocked the door while I heaved the heavy fucker out and across my shoulders, and walked inside.

My brother already had the chair waiting in the middle of the space. I dropped him hard and let him flop forward. Anger flared in my brother's stare as he caught the fucker and shoved him back. The tape was next, wrapped around his wrists as he gave a low moan and started to come to.

"There he is." Carven bent into his line of sight. "Had a little nap, but you're okay now."

Carven pushed his head upwards and watched as life roared back into the motherfucker's eyes. He bucked and fought, then jerked his gaze from Carven to me.

"You know about us." Carven lifted the large knife in his hands. "Tell me...what exactly do you know?"

There was a flicker of fear as the sudden realization hit home. This guy had thought he had the upper hand, had thought he could get a jump on us and that we'd...*what*...come quietly?

"Let me fucking go," he demanded.

Carven played with the honed tip of the blade. "Not until you tell us why the fuck you're following us?"

There was a moment of rage before he glanced from Carven to me. "Fuck you."

"Uh oh, brother." Carven looked my way. "I think we have one of those assholes, you know, the ones who know all about being interrogated."

He dragged the tip of the blade down his cheek. The asshole didn't react, just held his stare with a look of defiance, right before Carven clenched his grip and drove the knife down, plunging it into his thigh all the way up to the hilt.

The guy bucked and reared, howling his agony until Carven slammed his hand across his mouth. His eyes were wild with rage. "You know all about us, right? Tell me, I wonder if in all your fucking *knowing*, did you find out we were *a son?*"

My stomach clenched as I watched the realization hit home.

A son...

If he knew anything, then he'd know exactly what that meant.

Born from a ghost. Raised in an orphanage. Tortured mentally and physically until it either broke us or created a monster... monsters just like us. Monsters London had saved.

The asshole shook his head as his eyes widened.

"So, I'm going to ask you one last time," Carven growled as he pressed his hand harder over the guy's mouth. "Who the fuck are you and why are you following us?" He slipped his hand free.

"Daniels..." The name spilled out instantly.

Carven glanced my way. "What about him?"

"He knows St. James was blackmailing Killion. He also knows that he was the one going to meet Killion that night. He's going to expose him to the rest of The Order and he's going to destroy him."

Fear punched through me as my brother went utterly still, then quietly said. "Is that so?" He reached down, grasped the handle of the knife, and wrenched it free as the deadman howled in agony once more.

Because he was a dead man...there was no doubt about it.

When the screams and the death threats ended, the asshole just glared at us.

"Now. You're going to tell us exactly what it is that Mr. Macoy Daniels knows..."

"Fuck you," the asshole groaned as sweat beaded on his brow. "You're going to kill me anyway."

"Oh, that's without a doubt. You were dead the moment you shoved a gun in my side and tried to make me sit in a car with my brother behind the wheel. The only question is...how long will it take. Will we kill you slowly as we draw it out for days, or do we kill you fast and end the agony?"

He looked up at my brother and desperation glinted in his eyes as his lips curled. He said nothing for a second, until defeat moved in and caused him to nod.

"That's what I figured," Carven muttered as he reached around for his gun. "Now talk."

By the time the guy was done, my brother was deathly quiet as he stood over him.

Daniel's didn't know everything...

But he knew enough.

Enough to cause problems and get London killed.

"That's all." The guy shuddered and turned pale.

Blood had soaked through his pants and now trickled down his leg to pool on the floor under his boot.

"Just fucking leave me," he muttered. "I'll walk away. You'll never hear from me again."

Carven rose and lifted his gun.

"W-aait," he stuttered. "I'll tell you everything you want to know about Daniels."

Carven just smiled and shook his head. "There isn't a thing you can tell us we don't already know," he sighed, then pulled the trigger and ended the guy with a *bang!*

The deadman slumped forward, restrained by his bound hands.

"Fuck!" Carven snarled. *"FUCK!"*

This was bad. This was *really fucking bad.*

My brother reached for his phone, pulled it out, and stabbed the icon. "Yeah, it's me." He eyed the dead man. "We've got a problem, London. A really big fucking problem—"

THIRTY-TWO

London

CHRISTMAS MUSIC CHIMED FROM THE SPEAKERS overhead. I was stuck on the sound, unable to understand why they were playing, or what kind of song it was. I ended the call and slipped my phone back into my jacket pocket, still hearing Carven's words.

Hale knows...if he doesn't know everything, then he knows enough. We're fucked here. Let me take them out tonight. We'll kill as many as we can before they scatter. Hale first, then that cunt...

Then that cunt.

"Mr. St. James?"

I lifted my gaze and found a confused woman staring at me. "Yes?"

"Is there anything I can show you, sir?" she asked, smiling carefully. But there was nothing flirtatious, just professional.

I took in her smoothed back blonde hair and perfect bun, then the pearl cashmere top with the sleek blood red skirt.

"Were you after something similar to the pendant necklace you purchased last week?"

I flinch at the reminder, unable to remember why the hell I was even here. I shook my head. "No, thank you."

Her smile faltered, confused as was I. I turned for the door, but caught a glint from the corner of my eye and stopped. Not one sparkle...a mess of them, which gleamed even brighter as I stepped toward the display. The saleswoman moved around the other side of the counter. "This is brand new. In fact, I've only just set it out for display. It's stunning, isn't it?"

I stared, mesmerized, as she reached under the hardened glass and grasped the white velvet cushion it perched on.

"It's meant to go around the ankle."

I jerked my gaze upwards and met her stare. "Is it?"

Christ, all I could see was those fucking leather straps against her olive skin, her knees pushed to her chest, and her legs spread wide. *I fucking hate you.* Her words rang inside my head.

I licked my lips and reached out to finger the band.

"One hundred and seventeen radiant-cut gems, mounted in sleek eighteen-carat gold, with exceptional color and clarity, wouldn't you agree?"

You use a machine to fuck me because you can't do it yourself...

My pulse sped as my desire came alive.

Even in her fucking hate, I wanted her more than I'd wanted any other woman in my life. I stared at the anklet, imagining it against her skin. "I'll take it."

There was a flare of surprise. "I haven't even told you the price, Mr. St. James."

"It doesn't matter." I slipped the black Amex from my billfold and slid it across the counter. "Have it ready immediately."

She nodded and reached for the card. I wanted it to be expensive. I wanted it to fucking *sting*. She rang up the purchase and handed the card back with a confused smile.

An anklet...

Yes, that's what I wanted.

I didn't look at anything else, just stepped to the rear of the store as an older couple came in, and glanced around. The husband met my stare until he looked away. You could see a lot in a man's stare. The awkwardness wasn't so much a sign that they had something to hide, more like they instantly knew what kind of man you were and they wanted as far away from you as possible.

I crossed my arms and watched them hem and haw with one of the other assistants at a simple gold necklace until the blonde came back with the sleek black velvet box. My gut clenched instantly as I took it and slipped it into my jacket before I left, and that Christmas music haunted me all the way to the car.

I'd barely slipped in behind the wheel when my phone vibrated. I glanced at the caller ID, then swallowed hard and answered it instantly. "Hale."

"Are you in the city?"

He knew I was. "Yes."

"Good, join me for lunch at the club."

I winced. "I'm not really—"

"It's not a request."

A chill swept down my spine and a sinking feeling took hold. "Then I'll be there in twenty."

279

This is really bad, London. Really fucking bad. Carven's fear filled me as I stabbed the button and started the Mercedes. My breaths were heavy, my mind racing. Shit was falling through my fingers. The ends of all my lies were untethered and flapping in the wind.

They were long enough to choke me.

Long enough to choke us all.

I headed for the club, my mind stuck on the two options: kill those we could and lose the rest, or figure a way out of this. Both opportunities would take the kind of precarious precision that made me nervous. I pulled into the parking lot and killed the engine.

The velvet box dug into my chest. I reached in, pulled it out, and slipped it into the glove compartment. The last thing I wanted was the box ruined by my blood...if it came to that. I grabbed the door handle and climbed out. Christ, I hoped it didn't. I liked living at the moment, as long as I had the wildcat in my bed.

The CCTV cameras tracked my movement as I headed for the rear door of the club and entered the code. Once inside, there was only darkness. Just how they liked it.

My steps resounded in the hallway, until I stepped out to the closed-off private area and headed for the low drone of voices. Three men sat around the low table, legs crossed in immaculate suits, drinking top-shelf Scotch and smoking cigars.

A trembling, naked form knelt on the floor at the edge of the room, her head down, red welt marks bright against soft, tender flesh. Her hands were braced on her thighs, her quaking elbows locked in tight. I skimmed her and quickly looked away, that savage part of me sinking fast. This was no time to get angry. No time to pull my gun and put a bullet in each piece of fucking shit in this room...

But that was all I wanted to do.

Instead, I sank down behind that stony exterior and met each beady fucking stare as I neared the table. "Gentlemen."

It wasn't lost on me that Hale rarely went without a tight squad of ass-licking vile scumbags.

"St. James," Lions murmured as he eye-fucked me.

I ignored the stare and instead focused on Hale, who sat at the head of the table, legs crossed, belt undone. I smothered a wince, now knowing the reason for the broken female too scared to fucking move. "Nice day for business."

"Isn't it?" He watched me, then motioned to the empty seat to his right. "Please."

Fuck no. That was the last thing I wanted, yet I found myself nodding as I pulled the seat out a little further than necessary and sat. Anything to be away from him. The conversation died away and it became awkward. But I knew awkward was exactly what Hale liked. He spent the lull watching every shift of your body and catching every look of fear. So I turned my head and met that empty stare. "You said something about information?"

He waited for a heartbeat, then slid his phone across the table. "Apparently there's been a recording from The Order that's been leaked, an important recording. Let me play it for you."

I steeled myself, but it was useless as he pressed the button and Ryth Castlemaine's screams echoed in the room around me. I knew the recording, had heard it hundreds of times. I forced myself to wince when she called for her stepbrothers to save her, and when the recording had finished, the silence was heavy.

"Ryth Castlemaine," I murmured. "I can't place the male voice, though."

There was a curl of Hale's lips. "It's Killion."

I nodded. "That makes sense."

"But what *doesn't* make sense is why a recording like that would be taken from The Order and sent to a private IP address. One we now have."

Thanks to Daniels.

"That's not all. There has been a private investigation being conducted and during that investigation, we were able to locate CCTV footage of a street camera not far from Killion's house. I'd like you to take a look." He swiped the screen to open up the black and white video footage of a car pulled over to the side of the road.

As he pressed play, I watched Ryth Castlemaine as she retched and heaved next to the car as her brothers stood around her.

Fuck!

"I take it you know who that is."

I gave a slow nod.

"Information has come to light that Killion was being blackmailed and that night he was meant to meet with the man who was extorting money to keep this from getting out."

Lions rose from the table, adjusted his belt, and moved toward the kneeling woman. She let out a whimper and jerked backwards as he neared, gripped a fistful of her hair, and forced her to her feet. The movement drew Hale's gaze, hunger burned in his stare as Lions dragged the woman over.

But she didn't fight, just stumbled under the heavy grip until she stood near us, weeping.

282

"She's beautiful, isn't she?" Hale murmured.

I clenched my jaw, but didn't turn from his gaze. "Yes."

"She reminds me of your bitch, what's her name again?"

My blood ran cold. "Vivienne."

Hale nodded slowly. "That's right, *Vivienne*. I heard she was a bit of a..." He glanced at the others. "What was the term that was used? *Ah, yes*...wildcat." He met my gaze. "This one was a '*wildcat*' too. But I've tamed the wildness out of her. Maybe I could help with yours?"

My gut clenched, my heart *boomed*.

The others at the table had no idea what was happening here. But I did...I knew *exactly* the game Hale played. I kept my tone careful, controlled as I held the bastard's stare. "It's been a while since you were involved in a daughter's education, considering how well the last one played out. Where did we hide the body on that one again? I'm sure Riven and his brothers are still reeling from the aftereffects."

His eyes glinted. "Well, you know what they say, old friend. If you want something done right..."

Hard breaths filled the space before he shifted his gaze back to the woman. "You can fuck this one, if you want? Since I seem to have forgotten the signed contract that's sitting on my desk. I do know you weren't able to finish your time with Ophelia and I'm sure by now you're...*hungry.*"

My stomach rolled as I forced the words. "No...thank you."

In a blur of movement, Hale lunged forward to slam his palm on the table in front of me. He leaned a bit closer, his tone full of menace. "You'd better not be playing me, London. You and I both know how that will end."

I forced myself to meet that stare, to keep the thunder in my chest constrained. "I'll get you the information you need, Hale."

Those pitiless eyes bored into mine before Hale gave a slow nod and pulled back. Instead, he turned his attention to Lions...and the low, terrified moans from the woman under his hand. "I'll be waiting."

I met each stare as I rose...except for hers.

Because to look into those terrified eyes would bring me undone.

Think of the big picture.

Think of King.

I left that place, careful to make sure each step was slow and precise under the weight of Hale's stare. It wasn't until I'd pulled out of the parking lot and headed toward home that I jerked the car to the side of the road. Acid rose in the back of my throat as I threw the door open. I barely managed to lunge out of the car before I was sick.

And the entire time my stomach heaved and rolled, all I thought about was Vivienne...and getting her out of The Order. Because the wolves weren't circling anymore. No, this was the hunt...and we were in the thick of it.

THIRTY-THREE

Vivienne
_____

I HATED HIM.

I really fucking hated him.

I closed my eyes and pressed my head back against my bedroom door. I really...*really* fucking hated him. The more I tried to hold onto that rage, the louder my pulse became until it drowned out the snarl in my head.

Fuck this.

I opened my eyes, pushed up from the floor, and headed for the bathroom, hating how I wanted to walk back to him. No...not walk. *I wanted to crawl.* I wanted to kneel for him, to let him take me back down to the basement and strap me down.

I wanted to look up at him while his breath was hard and heavy and that glint in his eyes ignited. I wanted him, any way he'd take me. Hard. Slow. Soft and tender. *Sleep, pet...your body needs it.*

A moan resounded in the back of my throat as I stepped into the bathroom and reached for the shower faucets. The hiss of the water filled the space. I waited for the heat and stepped in.

Flashes filled my head, snatches of desire so blinding I couldn't have fought them even if I'd wanted to. And I didn't want to.

I needed to feel them.

Needed to relive them.

I needed to remember.

Just how dangerous that man was...

I washed and scrubbed, probing between my legs to feel the ache. *Will you let me lick it better?*

"No," I whispered. "I won't."

I turned off the water and stepped out, shivering with the cold, and didn't bother to look at the cameras. I didn't care anymore. Not about the tracker in my breast or the fact he watched my every move. There wasn't a thing he could see that he hadn't already scrutinized.

I dried and dressed, then made my way to the door. My belly rumbled and burned. I was starving and after this morning, I knew there was no tray coming. Because he was the one who'd made them, just like he was the one who'd brought my clothes. I brushed the soft lavender sweater and opened my bedroom door.

The place was quiet...really quiet.

I glanced at the closed door to the sons' bedroom and wondered, were they home? I took a step, sensed the emptiness, and stopped. No, I didn't think they were. That left just...*him.*

I turned and headed for the stairs. I wanted to avoid that broody, seductive stare at all costs and hurried past the landing on his floor. My belly gave a howl the moment I stepped into the foyer, driving me to the kitchen. My gaze immediately went to the basement door that was now closed.

"Can I help you with anything?"

I let out a yelp as I slammed my hand against my chest and spun, to find Guild behind me. "Jesus, you scared the shit out of me."

"Sorry." He held my stare. "Do you need anything?"

I glanced at the refrigerator. "Yeah, I'm hungry."

"I'll fix you something?"

"No," I shook my head. "I can look after myself."

He gave a shrug. "Suit yourself."

He wasn't exactly a waiter, was he? I glanced at the swollen corner of his lip. He didn't act like one and London sure as hell didn't treat him like one. I glanced at the hallway that led to the study.

"He's not here."

I flinched and pulled open the refrigerator to peer into the blindingly white compartment. "I wasn't even thinking that."

He crossed his arms and leaned back against the counter as he watched me pull out cheese, tomatoes, and butter, and search for meat. "Sure, you weren't. Ham is in the meat refrigerator."

I glanced over my shoulder. "And where the hell is that?"

He gave a long, hard sigh, pushed off the counter, and strode toward me to pull out a sliding compartment at my side. Cold air billowed out white as he reached in and pulled out a sealed slab of ham. I just watched him as he set to work, placed it on the counter, and grabbed a knife from a cutting block. "Sandwich, or on a plate?"

"Sandwich, please."

A simple nod and he gathered the rest of the ingredients from my hands, then opened the fridge once more and plucked a bottle of mayo from the door with a, "Trust me."

I couldn't do anything as he moved with precision. "The lip looks painful."

"It's nothing."

"No, it's not. London has a..."

Guild jerked his gaze to mine. "He is one of the most honorable men I've ever met."

Laughter escaped me. "Honorable? Are we talking about the same man? Tall, broody, moody, demanding."

Guild gave a sigh and placed the knife down on the block, then reached up and unbuttoned his shirt. Heat rushed to my cheeks. I jerked my gaze to the doorway. "Wait, I ah..."

"This was a knife attack in Berlin," he started, drawing my focus. "They came for me in the middle of the night. It was just lucky that London was staying with me at the time."

"They...*came for you?*"

He nodded. "It was a stealth attack, retaliation for taking out the head of a Russian Mafia operation."

The blood drained from my face. "The *Russian Mafia?*" I glanced at the deep slash across his shoulder and neck. "Who the fuck are you?"

He smiled and shook his head. "The better question is...*what* am I...or *was*. Because I've left that life behind, as has London. Well, he's trying to, at least. The rest is not my story to tell."

I stepped a little closer as he buttoned his shirt and set to work, cut slices of fresh bread, layered it with a smear of mayo and razor thin ribbons of ham, then topped that with tomatoes and cheese and slid the cut sandwich my way.

"Not everything is as it seems," he murmured as he gave me a nod.

I moved in, grabbed half of the sandwich, and bit down, then watched while Guild packed the things away and gave me a nod. "I'll be around if you need anything."

I wanted to ask him more about London, but I had a feeling it wouldn't get me anywhere. Everyone was so damn protective of the man. I glanced toward the basement door and savaged the sandwich.

I still hated him.

That wouldn't change.

By the time the sandwich was gone, I was bored walking around. There was no car for me to steal and I'd already invaded his study enough to piss him off. Maybe I could hack his accounts...or read his emails? Or maybe I could—

The rumble of the garage door sounded, drawing my attention. An engine growled, louder than the Mercedes or the Audi. *The sons*...a surge of nerves moved in as the sound died and the slams of car doors followed.

I stepped backwards, embarrassed. I was sure by now they knew what had gone on last night. As the sound of the closing garage door drifted and the heavy thud of steps followed, I felt that anger rise once more.

London had betrayed me, but he'd also forced me to feel things I didn't want to.

Things I ached for.

And the more I felt that need of belonging, the more painful his infidelity became.

Carven strode in and flashed me a glare, his lips curled. His stark white hair was a mess. "What the fuck are you looking at?" he snapped as Colt followed him inside.

A surge of desire cut through me. I stepped around the counter, but stopped as Colt looked away, his cheeks reddening. I tried to swallow the sting. "What's going on?"

"Like you give a shit," Carven snarled as he headed for the foyer. "Why don't you go bury your head in the sand a little deeper, or, I dunno...wreck another fucking car, because London sure as hell needs that on top of saving your ass."

Colt just followed, without a sound or a look.

I didn't know which hurt more, the comment or the shun. It didn't matter, they were like pouring gasoline on an out-of-control fire. I stepped into the doorway. "You know what, *fuck you and fuck London, too!*"

Carven froze with his hand on the banister.

"I didn't fucking ask to be abducted! I *never* goddamn asked to be led on and lied to, either. So you and your brother can take your bratty moodiness and *shove it far up your ass.*"

The son swung his gaze to me. His electric blue eyes were flared with rage. "You *never asked?*"

Colt pushed him toward the stairs, shaking his head at his brother. But there was no stopping this, no leashing his fury as he sidestepped his brother and charged across the foyer. But Colt wasn't having it and lunged in front of him with a shake of his head, to block the doorway. "Carven, no."

"No?" his brother barked, glaring at him. "*NO?*"

He turned that rage my way, then took a breath and stepped backwards. "You know what? *Fuck this shit...and fuck you!*" He stabbed the air in my direction. "Fucking *brat.*"

"Fucking *brat?*" I yelled as I flew toward him, until Colt stopped me with his hand on my chest. *"Fuck YOU! You have no idea what I've been through!"*

Even Colt flinched at my scream. His hand fell as he turned and slammed into Carven as he came for me. It was brother against brother, both deadly, both savage as they grappled each other... on different sides when it came to me.

"I don't think so, brother." Carven spun, sidestepped him in the kind of fluid motion that couldn't be believed, and in an instant had grabbed my arm.

"Get the fuck *off me!*" I bucked and swung, fighting him even though I knew it was useless.

He bent, not even dodging my blows, and lifted me over his shoulder. "What *you went through, huh! What YOU FUCKING WENT THROUGH!*"

I bounced and jolted, kicked and reared to meet Colt's stare as he leaped up the stairs after us. There was fear in his wide eyes as he grabbed his brother's arm and yanked. "Carven, she's not ready!"

But Carven wasn't stopping. He just wrenched his arm away, shaking me like a rag doll in the process, and kept taking the stairs two at a time until he stepped out onto London's landing. At first, I thought he was going to take me to London's bedroom, and there was no fucking way *in hell* I was doing that with him.

But he strode past and instead stopped at a door next to London's bedroom. Tiny beeps came as he entered a code and shoved the door wide. I swung to look behind me as Carven carried me inside. Colt closed the door behind him and plunged us into darkness before a tiny *click* came and soft light illuminated the room.

Strands of my hair flew in my face as I fell when Carven released me. I gasped a shrill scream, clawed the air, and found Colt instead.

"Carven!" Colt roared as he grabbed me before I hit the floor.

But his brother was already headed behind a large desk that sat against the wall. In an instant, a bank of screens came to life. Black and white images filled them. I sucked in hard breaths as I gripped Colt and stared. "You fucking asshole."

"Yeah?" Carven snarled. "I might be an asshole, but at least I'm not naive."

I took a step, wanting to lunge for him, but he pushed a chair my way. "Sit."

I didn't move as he stabbed buttons on a monitor that turned from the black and white footage of my bedroom to a computer screen. Then he entered access codes.

"Carven...don't do this."

"She needs to know," he growled as he stared at the screen where he'd accessed what looked like audio files then snarled, clicked out, and searched again. "Here...here it is. Here is everything you hate about him."

"Brother." Colt took a step forward.

But Carven just straightened and glared at the empty seat, then strode across the room, grabbed me by my arm, and dragged me to the chair. "I said, *sit!*"

I fought when he forced me down, until he pushed his face close to mine. "I'm not London, wildcat, and I'm sure as *hell* not my brother. So push me, and you might just find yourself taped to the fucking thing for a very...*very* long time."

I glared at him, but my hands fell to my sides. *Fuck you,* I wanted to snarl into his stupid face. But he turned away, leaving me to glare at his ear instead, and clicked a button which filled the room with sound.

Heavy breaths echoed from the speakers. A woman's breaths, hard, heavy, out of breath, but underneath those was a low, quiet moan, so quiet I almost missed it. It came again, only this time it was a boy's plea. "Not...my brother."

Colt stiffened beside me.

Carven hung his head.

"I will beat you, you foul, little *beast.*" The panting woman snarled so close that the speaker vibrated with the guttural threat. "I will *ruinnnn you!*"

But in the background came screams. Male screams. Screams that suddenly ended.

I flinched as a *boom* came. My mind raced, then placed it. It was the sound of a door flying open, followed by the heavy thud of advancing steps.

"Get the fuck away from them, Ophelia."

I flinched as she hissed. "Come near me and I'll have you killed. I'll have all of them killed, is that what you want? I'll start with them, the ones you seem to care so much about."

"No—" that tiny sound came again...

And in front of me, the desk started to shake. I turned to Colt, who gripped the edge, trembling with rage.

"Not my brother," that broken little voice moaned. "Not...*Carven.*"

For a second, I couldn't breathe, couldn't think. I could only exist in the torment.

"Step away from them," London urged, the sound of his voice louder. "Step away from the sons."

"You won't make it out of here. Hale will know. He'll hunt you down out of spite, you know that."

I swallowed my heart back down. My mind howled for me to run, to get out of there. This was too real...too...

There were scratches on the door.

I closed my eyes as London spoke again. "Then tell me what you want. Whatever it is, I'll pay it."

"I don't *need your money!*"

"Then *WHAT DO YOU WANT!*"

"You."

I jerked as though I'd been slapped, and my blood turned out ice. "No." The word escaped.

"You want these *pathetic things?*"

Thud.

And a soft moan followed.

Carven jerked his head toward Colt, those blue eyes burning like never before.

I knew what was happening then. I knew it and still my mind rejected the truth. *Because...because...*

The desk shuddered and shook, the far edge crashing against the wall. I reached out with a trembling hand and touched his arm. He jerked at the contact and recoiled, his enraged stare finding mine.

"That's what I want," Ophelia demanded as I rose from the seat. "I want to fuck you. I want to own you. I want you on your goddamn knees for me when I demand it."

There was silence from London.

It was louder than a scream.

I touched Colt's arm once more. He shook his head, his body trembling with fury. "I'm right here," I murmured. "I'm right here."

He turned toward me and, in a rush, dragged me into his arms. I was swallowed by him, by the hardness of his body.

"Then it's a deal," London declared. "But I take them now and you will *not* speak their names or look at them *ever* again."

"Fine," Ophelia snapped through the speakers as Colt turned his head to find me.

"I'm right here." I slid my hand through his hair, my stomach churning with the truth.

Tears sprang to my eyes as the thud of steps sounded from the speakers.

"Easy now," London soothed. "I've got you. Hold on to me."

"Hold on to me," I echoed, and Colt gripped me tighter as he towered over me. "Hold on to me."

I rose upwards as far as I could go. My heart was in charge now, it called the shots. My body had no choice but to obey as I kissed him. His mouth was rigid, and refused to move. But I kissed him again, only this time more softly. Memories of London's mouth rushed in. I followed the same path and kissed the corners of his mouth as, through the speakers, a little boy whimpered in pain.

"Easy now, Colt, right? I got you, Colt."

"M-my...br-brother."

"We're not leaving your brother, not a chance. You're with me now, son...*you're with me.*"

Tears came to my eyes as I gripped the back of his neck and pulled him closer. His mouth opened and he kissed me back with such ferocity that it took my breath away. His hands went around my waist and he lifted me until my legs went around him.

A low moan echoed in my ears. We moved, rocking and tipping until he slumped in the chair and my legs fell. He cupped my breasts as he looked up at me. In my head, all I saw was all those scars. He'd been beaten and tortured at the hands of that vile fucking bitch. The bitch who used London's body as payment for their freedom.

"Like I said, wildcat," Carven murmured behind me. "Naive."

I turned my head as Colt tore at my shirt, dragged it high, and yanked down the cup of my bra. I rose, leaving his mouth to find my nipple, as I met his brother's vibrant stare.

"He sold himself to her for our freedom..." Carven murmured, not once looking away. "Just like he's selling himself to her for yours."

Buttons of my shirt tore free to scatter across the floor. I closed my eyes and unleashed a moan as my shirt was ripped in the frenzy, but it wasn't a sound of pleasure. It was of pain. *He was fucking her* for my freedom. *He was...he was...he was—*

Colt fumbled with the buttons on my pants and pulled as he lifted me to shove my pants down low. I swallowed hard while I let him do what he wanted. His fingers plunged into my slit and rubbed me where I was sore. A snarl and he lifted me like I weighed nothing. I raised one leg to shove my pants down and tore one leg free, then the other. But my pain was nothing. My anger was *nothing*. Because my heart howled the truth.

The clink of a buckle, then the slide of a zipper.

He rammed his cock all the way inside.

I dropped my head back with a cry.

Pain. Pleasure. Desperation. I needed the ache. I needed to feel him. "Fuck me," I gasped and opened my eyes, to see the agony in his eyes. "Fuck *me, Colt.*"

His lips curled and bared his teeth. He held on to me, gripped my hips, and drove my body down, impaling me to the hilt. He fucked me, hard and savage, with fury and anguish in his eyes.

Warmth pressed against my back. For a moment, I didn't feel it. All I felt was the frenzy and the madness of Colt. But the heat moved, slid up my spine to brush my hair aside. Warmth that grew bolder, until there was more, and as his brother ground his cock inside me, desperate to find oblivion in the warmth and comfort of my body, Carven lowered his head, pressed his forehead to my shoulder, and found his.

"That's it, wildcat. Now you know the lengths we will go to protect what's ours...*now you fucking know.*"

THIRTY-FOUR

London

I SWIPED THE BURN OF ACID FROM MY LIPS WITH THE BACK of my hand and stared at the mess on the asphalt in front of me. *I've tamed the wildness out of her. Maybe I could help with yours?* Hale's threat resounded in my head. I pushed upwards as thoughts of getting my hands bloody surfaced. These hands. I stared at the shake and dragged my fingers through my hair.

My past was calling me back to its darkness, where men like Hale had paid me for murder. Only this time, the hit would be him. I'd take him out right now if I knew he was the beginning and the end of it all. But I knew without a doubt he wasn't...he was just one in a slithering, writhing nest.

If I cut the head off one...they'd all scatter.

"Fuck." I lifted my gaze from the glistening splatter next to my car and slumped back behind the wheel.

The car door closed with a thud and for a second, I was lost in the moment, unable to move, until *she* pushed in. My pain in the ass, insubordinate wildcat. One who was determined to send me to an early grave...or give me a goddamn ulcer. I winced and rubbed my breastbone before I grabbed my phone.

298

I'd bet right now she was trashing my goddamn study...*again*.

The phone unlocked with a press of my thumb and I opened the camera, flicking through screens one by one. She wasn't in the study, nor was she in her bedroom...*shit*. I flicked to the garage and found Carven's Explorer, then switched back to the internal cameras to search their room, but found it empty.

My stomach clenched as I hit the icon for my bedroom...then to the monitor room next to it.

Movement drew my focus. From high up in the corner, I watched as she fucked Colt on the chair in the middle of the room. His hand was fisted in her hair, his other gripped her waist as she writhed and ground against him. I leaned close and expanded the view. Fuck, she was glorious. Untamed. Unbroken. It's what called me to her. Her olive skin looked darker in the wash of the monitors' glow.

As I watched, Carven took a step forward and placed his hand in the middle of her back. A surge of love filled me with the movement. My broken son was warming to her, just like I'd known he would. He bent down and placed his forehead against her shoulder as she arched her back while she rode his brother. She was for them. She was for me. King's daughter...and our way out.

One hard breath and my thoughts turned darker. I pressed the icon to end the view and pulled up another app instead. Red dots flickered. I moved in, and found Ryth's location in an instant. If it came down to handing over her and her brothers in exchange for Vivienne's safety, I'd do it in a heartbeat.

But that wasn't my choice to make...

I'd make it their father's decision and force King out of hiding to do it.

Then I'd use him to take out every one of those vile fuckers once and for all.

I closed down the view and started the engine. My hands no longer shook, but I didn't head home. Not yet. Not with Hale's threat still ringing in my ears. I needed a drink and somewhere quiet, somewhere I could think and try to find a way out of this. One which wouldn't get my family killed...or me in Ophelia's bed.

I headed east and pulled up outside the discreet bar in the heart of the city. Black steel, exposed brick, and moody amber lighting pulled me in. I stepped inside, motioned for a waiter, and headed for the plush leather chairs at the back. I barely saw anyone else as I unbuttoned my jacket and sat.

"Your best whiskey," I ordered when the waiter came. "A bottle."

His eyes widened, but one nod and he disappeared.

I've tamed the wildness out of her...

I swallowed hard and shifted my gaze, trying to focus on anything else.

Maybe I could help with yours?

It didn't matter where I looked, to the two women drinking cocktails at the bar, or the guy who'd strode in behind me and taken a seat not far from them, or the asshole who sat in the shadows and stared at me. I winced when I realized it was tempered black glass and that asshole was me.

One of the women sitting with her friend glanced my way and smiled. I didn't respond and looked away as she rose, left her friend behind, and made her way over. *Go away,* I urged. *I'm not in the mood to be nice.*

"Hi," she said boldly. "I see you're on your own. Are you waiting for someone?"

"No."

She didn't flinch at the bite in my tone, but stepped closer to run a painted red nail along my hand and over my Rolex. "I can wait with you, if you like."

I lifted my gaze to meet hers. They were all the same, weren't they? *Except for her...my wildcat.* "No. Now, if you'll excuse me."

I pulled my arm away and ignored her long enough for tension to fill the air.

"Fine," she muttered as she turned. "Your loss."

"I doubt that very much," I murmured as she left.

Maybe I could help with yours?

"Sir," the waiter said nervously as he stepped around the retreating woman and neared. "I'm sorry, but I'm going to need—"

I reached into my jacket, plucked my billfold free, and slid out my Amx. "The bottle...now."

He hurried away and returned moments later with a newly opened bottle and a set of glasses. I only needed one. I poured and drank. The first glass barely warmed me. By the third, that foul fucking promise had slowed in my head. By the fifth glass, my mind was swimming.

Laughter cracked out from somewhere to my right. I lifted my gaze and saw unfamiliar faces, glad that the woman and her friend had gone. But how long had I been here?

"Can I get you a glass of water, sir?"

I turned to the waiter, but he wasn't the awkward guy from before. I shook my head and reached for my glass...but it was empty. So I grasped the bottle instead. That, too...empty. "What time is it?"

"It's a little after nine."

I glanced at the door, and saw darkness outside. "Nine?"

"Yes, sir. You've been here for a while now. Can I call you an Uber?"

I met his gaze, scowling. "No, thank you."

I grabbed my phone instead. My fingers fumbled the damn thing until I pressed my thumb against the screen and unlocked it. *Contacts...where the fuck is he...there.* I pressed the icon.

"Mr. St. James."

"Lucas, I ah..." I mumbled.

His words sharpened. "Can I pick up, sir?"

"Yeah, I don't think I should be driving. I'm at..." I searched for the name. "Marquis Bar."

"I know the place. I'll be there in thirty minutes."

I gave a nod. "Thank you." And hung up the call.

It took me almost the same time to visit the bathroom, wash and dry my hands, and make my way outside. The moment I stepped out, the cold night air hit me and made me shudder. Flames danced through the glass from the fireplace inside. I hadn't noticed the cold until now, just like I hadn't noticed the Christmas songs piping through the speakers in the stores.

Because that wasn't my world, was it? My world was darkness, death...*and her.*

Headlights blinded me for a second before the familiar dark blue Range Rover pulled up alongside the curb. Lucas left the engine running and climbed out to open the back door for me.

"Thank you," I murmured, my words slurring a little as I started to climb in, and froze. *"Wait."*

Lucas just looked at me as I stepped back out. Clarity hit me colder than any fall breeze. I reached into my pocket, grabbed my keys, and hit the button before I opened the passenger side door and pushed the button on the glove compartment.

I couldn't forget this. I stared at the black velvet box before I tucked it into my jacket, closed up and locked the car, then made my way back to where Lucas waited. The car doors were closed and we were moving before I knew it. Oncoming headlights blurred and made me look away.

"I put chilled water in the compartment next to you."

I glanced at Lucas and nodded before I reached for the bottle. My head swam a little, maybe drinking a bottle was a bit too much? Ice cold plunged down my throat as I drank. I closed my eyes and let the sway of the vehicle lull me until I felt the familiar turns and opened my eyes.

I've tamed the wildness out of her...

My grip tightened around the container and sloshed the water against the sides. No matter how many glasses of Scotch I consumed, that sick fuck had a way of crawling under my skin. I lifted my gaze as Lucas pulled up outside the house and hit the button to open the garage door.

I didn't wait for him, just yanked the handle and spilled out of the car. The driver's door shoved open and Lucas was there to grab my arm. "Easy, now. Do you want me to help you inside?"

I met his stare, shook my head, and straightened while I carefully gripped the velvet box in my hand. "No, I got this."

Cold night air carved through my chest with a deep breath and with it came the slap I needed. "Night, Lucas, and thanks. Go home to your family."

Family...

I lifted my gaze to the windows on the third floor of my home. My family waited up there...*my...my...stubborn...irritating, goddamn perfect fucking wildcat.* I licked my lips and stumbled forward.

"I'll have the Mercedes delivered here in the morning," Lucas called after me.

I gave him a wave and kept walking as I hit the button for the garage door as I passed. The rumble resounded behind me as I made my way through the house and up the stairs.

I worked the buttons of my jacket, pulled it free, and draped it over the landing to my floor, then climbed until I stumbled for her room.

I didn't knock, didn't waver, just turned the handle and pushed open the door, to find her lying in bed, knees up, reading something. Her eyes widened as I lifted my hand to brace myself on the doorframe.

"London?" She shoved upwards as a look of concern flared in those mesmerizing brown eyes.

Why the fuck did she have to be so goddamn beautiful? It would've been easier if she wasn't...if she wasn't so—defiant.

I unleashed a snarl, shoved from the doorway, and strode toward her...

THIRTY-FIVE

Vivienne

_____

"London?" I shoved upwards and stared at him as he leaned against the door. "Is everything okay?"

There was something dangerous in his eyes. Something..._unholy_ as he pushed off the doorframe and stumbled forward, gripping something in his hand.

I glanced down, to see that black velvet box. _I can see why you want to get your dick wet with this one..._

That bitch's words pushed in, but they were drowned out by the low snarl that rumbled in his chest as he stopped at the foot of the bed.

"You defy me," he mumbled. "Every goddamn time."

I glanced at the doorway, then turned back to him. Fear pushed in and I licked my lips. "Has something...happened?"

Had he somehow seen me and Colt? Was that why he looked so...angry? Heat tore through my veins as he leaned over and yanked the bedding off to look down at me. He scowled as he took in the caramel lace camisole and French panties. There was a catch in his breath before he met my gaze. Need echoed in his stare. I hadn't ever seen him so...vulnerable.

"The harder you push me, the more I want you." He dragged his fingers through his hair, leaving it tousled and untamed.

Desire rocked me to my core. The more I knew about him, the deeper that ache moved, until it throbbed between my legs.

He licked his lips as his gaze traveled down my body and lingered at my feet. "Do you trust me?"

My breaths deepened, but I didn't need to think. "Yes."

He moved, but kept those dark eyes fixed on me as he grasped my ankle. My ass slipped against the expensive sheets as he pulled me toward him down the bed. I could do nothing as he placed my foot flat against his chest and lifted the box.

"London..." I started, hating the sight of it.

If he thought I was going to wear that fucking necklace after that vile fucking bi—

He opened the case and reached inside. Something glinted from his fingers, reflected from the bedside lamp as he plucked the small chain free and dropped the case on the end of the bed. I met his gaze and froze. God, I'd been *so* wrong about him, so incredibly fucking wrong. I saw it now...I saw...*him*.

So cold. So unreadable. So fucking brutal...and yet, he wasn't. Not to those he loved.

Because when this man loved...*he loved fiercely*.

He licked his lips as he lowered his gaze. Those large fingers worked at the tiny clasp before he draped it around my ankle and clipped it closed. I stared at the shimmer, my heart beating a thousand miles an hour as I realized what it was.

They were diamonds.

A lot of goddamn diamonds.

A pang tore across my chest.

I jerked my gaze to his as I opened my mouth to tell him, *no... that this was way too expensive. I didn't want this. I wasn't comfortable with th—*

The graze of his curled fingers stopped me. He looked down, brushed across the gems, and continued along my ankle. "You fight me," he murmured. "You...answer back. You make me so —" his chest rose with a heavy breath before it fell. "Fucking horny."

I froze at the sensation of his fingers as he moved up my calf and grasped the back of my knee.

"I fucking want you, and I don't care about the contract...not anymore." He gripped my other knee and yanked me hard until I stopped at the edge of the mattress.

All darkness. That's what he was as he towered over me. All *raw, unforgiving power.*

He leaned forward, placed a knee between my legs, and rubbed against my core. "They can't have you." He ran his hands up the sides of my body and swept under my arms. "Because you're mine."

The pressure built between my legs as he grasped my wrists and pulled them over my head. "I saw you today. I sat in the car and watched you fuck Colton in my monitor room."

I stared up into those endless dark pits as he ground against my clit and eased. "You fucked him well, wildcat." Desire unfurled as he drove against me once more. "So fucking well."

He dropped his body and pressed his chest against mine to growl in my ear. "You think I can't have any woman I want? I could, easy." His voice turned guttural. "I could've had a woman tonight. Fucked her in the bar. Probably had her friend join in too."

White-hot rage ripped through me as I jerked my gaze to his. The stench of Scotch on his breath told me the truth. "Did you?"

Desperation creased his brow. "No. I barely even looked at them. They...*they disgusted me.*"

I want to fuck you. Those vile words surfaced, no wonder he'd loathed them, they must sound just like her, always wanting, always craving. *I want to own you...I want you on your*—

That burning anger cast white spots behind my eyes. "Do I disgust you too?"

He searched my stare and for a second, I was terrified he'd see the same desire in me. That confused look grew bolder while he shook his head.

"No." The moment suspended in silence, until he gently rocked forward and rubbed his knee against my clit. "You don't disgust me in the slightest. You...Vivienne, have the completely opposite effect."

My blood hummed in my veins at his words.

"You, female," he bent to whisper against my ear. "Drive me to distraction."

"Good," I snarled, somehow knowing that is what he needed... what he craved. He didn't want a woman using him and he sure as fuck didn't want a woman propositioning him.

No, London St. James was a predator.

Only he chose his kill...

And his mate.

Goosebumps raced across my skin as that pressure came between my legs, rocking and easing...rocking...and easing, until he pulled away and released my hands. "Keep them where they are."

I was helpless to do anything but obey as he gripped the edges of my panties and slid them down. Lace rolled and slid down my thighs until he cast them aside and slid those big hands to my waist, captured the bottom of the camisole, and dragged it upwards. Soft lace grazed my nipples and made me catch my breath.

"Mine," he whispered as he looked down while my nipples tightened into peaks. I closed my eyes at the heat of his breath. "*Ours.*"

Warmth closed around my nipple as he licked it. The sensation raced all the way to my clit, where it buzzed and throbbed.

"Ours to fuck, to own...to do whatever the hell you'll allow us to do."

Allow them? My breaths came far too fast as a moan tore free, until he pulled away. I opened my eyes to find his. "What will you allow us to do, kitten?"

His words were a challenge and a promise all rolled into one. "Anything," I answered. *"Everything."*

The slow, seductive curl of his lips made my heart flutter. "That's my good pet."

I grew wet at the name. "Call me that again."

"Pet." He lowered his head and murmured the word against my nipple. *"Pet."*

My body tightened and hummed as he gently sucked, then moved down my body and kissed the bottom of my ribs, then the dip of my belly and the edge of my hip. "My good little pet,

309

aren't you?" He lifted his gaze to mine as he moved between my legs. "My pet, who lets me take her down to the basement and fuck her with my machine."

He parted my legs with a push against my thigh and slid his finger along my crease. "You're wet thinking about it, aren't you?"

I could only nod.

"Strapped up, helpless and exposed. I'll have the remote, kitten. I'll fuck you how you need to be fucked." His fingers came again, slid deeper this time and parted me just a little until they lingered at my entrance.

He pushed in until I moaned.

My eyes fluttered.

My breath was trapped somewhere between the thundering of my heart and the warmth of his mouth.

"Do you want me to take you back down there?" He pushed in a little further. "Strap you up. Take turns fucking you with the machine and me. A cock in every hole. How about that, kitten? Does that sound good to you?"

I bit my lip and nodded.

"Colt in your mouth, the machine in your tight ass, and me ramming home in this perfect fucking pussy." He pulled his fingers free and lowered his head to lick my wetness. "Fuck, you taste good. Better than the finest fucking Scotch."

I moaned and looked down as he licked me. He held that connection, then opened his mouth and sucked on my clit, driving my hips up from the bed. "Such a greedy little pussy." The low vibration of his voice only drove me closer to the edge.

Until he pulled away and rose. My desire glistened on his lips as he worked the buttons of his shirt, those dark eyes fixed on me. Memories of this morning pushed in...*you can look...*

I wanted to do more than look. I pushed upwards. He stopped and held my gaze.

"I want to do more than look, London," I murmured. "I want to...touch you."

Pain. Disgust. *Trust.*

They all collided in those dark eyes until he gave a slow nod and let me place my hand against his hard chest. Thud. Thud. Thud. His pulse pounded, while inside my head was a kaleidoscope of voices. *London saved my life. London rescued me. London...London...London...*I closed my eyes and leaned forward to kiss his chest.

He cupped the base of my neck and speared his fingers through the strands until he grasped a fistful of my hair and gently pulled me away. "Wildcat..."

"Fuck me," I whispered. "Any way you want to. I don't care about the contract anymore. I just want you inside me."

My words were torture. Sparks ignited in his stare until he leaned down and kissed me. No, not kissed...*he consumed me.* Hard lips took my mouth and bruised my lips against my teeth until they throbbed when he pulled back. He released my hair, tugged his shirt off, then worked his belt open.

"Same rules apply up here, kitten. You remember the safewords, right?"

I licked my pulsing lips and nodded as he pushed down his pants.

"Say them, kitten. Just like before."

His boots were kicked off, then his pants, socks, and boxers were shed, leaving him naked. I forced myself to concentrate. "Ges for yeen...I mean, yes for green." I licked my lips, mesmerized as he picked up his shirt and twisted the arms.

"Keep going," he demanded.

"Yellow for we need to talk about it, and red for stop."

He nodded. "Good. As long as you remember." He held up his shirt. "Now, hands."

I didn't need to be asked twice. This moment had been a threat between us and now it was a hunger more savage than anything else I'd ever experienced. He used his twisted shirt as a tether and wound it around my wrists. In one fluid motion, he drove me backwards, then advanced like a predator to push me against the bed. He was all I could see. His darkness. His power...his beautiful, strong body.

I tugged on the binding, desperate to touch him.

"Uh unh," he clucked as he stretched my arms high with one hand while he reached for his cock with the other. "I warned you before, kitten. I told you exactly what was going to happen between us. Now...you're not going to be able to give the safe word just now. So, for this special moment, two fingers raised will suffice. Do you understand me?"

My mind was reeling as I tried to keep up.

"Use your goddamn words, Vivienne."

"Yes." I met his gaze. "Yes, I understand."

A slow nod, and he rose above me. Still, I lifted my head, kissed his nipple as it passed, and brushed my lips against the faint silver scar that carved across his side. Was that from a knife? My pulse hammered. Fuck, this man was dangerous. He was so very...*very fucking dangerous.*

All that power. I kissed his stomach and looked down, to find his thick cock hard in his fist coming toward me. My core clenched at the sight. My mouth opened, and hard breaths blasted back at me from his hips. I closed my eyes, absorbed by the feel of the strain of my arms over my head and that smooth, firm touch against my mouth.

He was in control.

Always in control.

I opened my mouth as his cock slipped against my skin and pushed in.

"Fuck," he grunted as he drove in deeper and forced my mouth to go wider until the corners stretched.

My pussy clenched and tightened as he slowly thrust and pulled out. I opened my eyes, looked up at him, and watched as his world was narrowed down to this moment.

"Don't you make me fall for you, kitten," he murmured as he thrust again, and watched as he pushed in.

I opened wider and swirled my tongue around the edge before I sucked hard.

"Jesus fucking *Christ*," he groaned.

Salvia pooled in my mouth. I swallowed with my mouth stretched wide and my tongue found a thick vein that kicked as I sucked. He unleashed a moan with the sensation, so I did it again and again, driving my head down until I couldn't take any more.

One day you'll choke on my goddamn cock and you'll love it.

Fuck, I was desperate for him, ached for him. I licked and sucked until, with a groan, he pulled away and released my hands. Hard breaths claimed me as my mouth burned at the edges.

He tugged the shirt off and cast it across the room until it hit the floor.

"Don't care about the contract, huh?" He slipped his fingers inside me. "Then I guess we'd better make this worthwhile."

I opened my thighs as he sank between my legs. One hard jolt and he was inside, stretching me until I could take no more.

"Such a tight pussy," he moaned as he eased out before he drove back in. His body moved in sleek, powerful thrusts. "Such a beautiful, tight pussy. That's all mine." Those dark eyes pinned me where I lay. "All fucking mine."

My body stretched and clamped down, until he pulled out and slowly pushed back in. He rose up on strong arms and looked down between us. "Jesus," he groaned. "Look down, kitten. Look at us."

I followed his gaze to where we joined as his cock thrust inside once more and drove all the way inside.

"Gonna get my money's worth from you, wildcat," he murmured as he lifted those dark, unfathomable eyes to mine. "I'll take every dollar from this perfect cunt."

I moaned at his words and drove my body down. "Yes. God, yes."

He held my stare as he rose above me like a god. His arms were a cage around me as he worked his cock all the way inside, claiming me, owning me the only way he knew how. The pressure built and my pussy clenched tight. I loved the way he rubbed me.

"That's it, kitten," he grunted as he thrust harder. "That's fucking it."

I closed my eyes as every cell of my being focused on the sensation as he thrust and thrust and *thrust*.

"Oh." I bucked as sparks collided behind my eyes and ignited over and over again.

A second later, he unleashed a growl and thrust deep, held all the way inside...and spilled.

Warmth flooded me before he eased down beside me on the bed and exhaled hard. "Jesus."

My mind floated. My body fluttered.

For a second, I hung suspended in oblivion until slowly, London turned toward me. "You okay?"

I met his stare and nodded...

Knowing in that instant everything would change now.

THIRTY-SIX

London
<hr>

I SURFACED, INHALED A LONG, SLOW BREATH...AND FELT like I'd been hit by a truck. Flickers of memories filtered in.

The bar...the bottle.

Her.

I cracked open my eyes to find a fist shoved against my cheek. Vivienne was asleep beside me. Arms raised over her head, her wild hair was a fan on the lavender Egyptian cotton sheets. All breathtaking and serene, her eyes closed, those full lips parted. The faint freckles across her nose made my throat clench. I blinked and forced myself to focus. Christ, she was beautiful.

My heart gave a *boom* at the sight. My breath got trapped somewhere in my chest, held down by that floating feeling. *No, not floating...goddamn falling.*

Don't you make me fall for you, kitten. My own prophecy came roaring back to bite me in the ass.

Fucking fall?

Who the hell was I kidding?

I tore my gaze away and slipped quietly from the bed. The first peeks of sunlight filtered through her window. I scanned the mess at my feet, grabbed my trousers, boxers, and shoes and quietly left the room. Heat rushed to my cheeks the moment I stepped outside her door and I glanced toward the sons' room as I made my way down to my floor naked.

Colt pushed into my mind as I slipped into my room. I cast my clothes on the neatly made bed and dropped my boots beside it. The son was falling for her, if he hadn't already plunged headfirst into the same goddamn abyss I stared at.

I strode into the bathroom, hit the faucets, and stepped under the spray. But not Colt, not yet. I closed my eyes as the hot water pummeled me, and remembered the footage from the monitor room, where Carven had pressed his forehead against her shoulder as she fucked his brother.

Carven was feeling something for her, which gave me hope. If anything happened to me, he'd protect her. I washed, then leaned backwards and let the soap sluice away. He'd protect her. Right now, that's all I cared about.

My thoughts turned to Hale's threats.

I've tamed the wildness out of her...maybe I could help with yours?

Hate shivered inside me as I ended the spray and stepped out. I'd kill the bastard before I let him put his hands on her, then I'd kill them all, every single vile person associated with that place. I dried and dressed in navy blue pants and a white shirt and deep blue tie before I headed downstairs.

Guild lifted his gaze as I headed into the kitchen. I glanced at his damn lip, then looked away.

"London..." he started before I lifted a hand to cut him off.

"Don't." I shook my head as I rounded the counter. "I was out of line. I'm sorry. Forgive me."

His eyes widened with a look of surprise. "Who are you and what have you done with my friend?"

I gave a chuckle, but it died just as quick, leaving me to reach out a hand. "I promise."

"Then I accept." He took my hand in his. "And I'll promise not to let the damn woman get a jump on me. She's one...*one*...*"

"I know." I nodded as he released my hold. "Believe me, I know."

"How about a coffee?" Guild asked, turning to the machine that took up real estate on my kitchen counter. "Triple shot, strong enough to wake up the dead?"

"Coffee sounds good," I answered, then stilled.

He sensed it instantly, stopped, and turned around to meet my gaze. "What is it?"

"Harper and the team, are they still around?"

"Harper? Yeah, they're around. Why?"

A plan had been brewing in the back of my mind, a dangerous plan with a predator on one side and the Devil himself on the other. One I hadn't wanted to entertain, yet here I was...

"London," he said quietly. "Careful there, brother."

I gave a nod, then glanced at the coffee machine. The last thing I wanted was to step back into the past. It was dangerous enough escaping the last time.

"Believe me, I am," I answered carefully, then turned and made my way to the study

Being careful was all I thought about. But that wouldn't get me out of the damn corner I found myself in. No, this wasn't a time for careful moves. This was a time to be bold, to be forceful, and make the kind of play that could start a war. As long as that war wasn't aimed at us.

I strode into the study and closed the door behind me. Hale knew about the recording now and he also knew Killion had been waiting for his blackmailer to show. But what he didn't know was that there had been no blackmail, not really. All there'd been was vengeance of the most brutal kind.

Vengeance I'd help orchestrate to get Ryth and her stepbrothers where I needed them to be.

And that was owing their lives to me.

I pulled out my phone as I rounded my desk and pressed a number I didn't think I'd ever call again. The call wasn't answered. Instead, it went to a voicemail. "I'm calling about my midnight black Chevy Impala," I spoke carefully. "You can call me back at...."

I gave my number and hung up, then booted up my computer and logged in. No more than five seconds later, my phone rang again and a deep familiar drawl came. "The Impala is gone."

"The Impala needs a little work done to it."

Silence. Then. "What kind of work?"

"Some scratches and dents, nothing major."

"Then, I'll give you a number you can call."

I memorized the number he gave before he hung up. The number was to a secure line. Untraceable. Undetected, created by the best of the best. I should know, I'd worked with them for over ten years. They were as careful as you could get. But I didn't call right away. Instead, I stared across the study and weighed up all the options I had. If there was another way out of this, I'd take it. But there wasn't, I knew that, and if I failed to act, then this would all have been for nothing.

"For the greater good," I murmured, picked up my phone, and entered the number I'd been given.

"London," Harper Renolt answered carefully. "I didn't think I'd ever hear from you again."

"I didn't think I'd have to call again."

"Yet, here we are."

"Yeah, here we are."

The study door opened, drawing my gaze, then it froze as Vivienne walked in carrying two small cups of steaming coffee. I froze at the sight of her wearing my shirt...my crumpled shirt from last night that now hung mid-thigh on her.

*Hands...*my voice resounded.

The memory came roaring back, the arms of my shirt wound around her wrists. Her hands held high...just like they'd had been when I woke up. Had she been dreaming of us? My cock came alive instantly with the thought as I dragged my gaze over the same damn shirt she wore now. *Jesus.*

"You there?" Harper muttered.

"Yeah," I answered, my gaze trailing down her long, bare thighs as she strode around the desk toward me. "I'm here. I need you to adjust some records, swap out one IP address for another."

"Reroute specialist information. Do you have the details?"

"Yes," I murmured as Vivienne placed a coffee cup on the desk in front of me, her gaze fixed on mine. "Dates and times."

"Sounds easy enough. When do you need it?"

She perched her ass on the desk in front of me and casually lifted her foot and placed it on my seat between my thighs, her toes brushing my cock. "Yesterday," I answered, as I met her gaze.

Her hair was tied up in a messy bun and strands had escaped to float to her shoulders. She looked at me so goddamn innocently as she sipped her coffee while her toes curled and massaged my cock. Jesus, the woman was insanity in its most erotically stunning form.

"And this IP you're wanting me to switch to is someone dangerous?"

"Very," I murmured as she continued to stroke and rub.

"Number?"

I forced my gaze away from her and reached over to punch in the details on the keyboard which brought up Benjamin Rossi's personal IP address. I gave the number to Harper as I licked my lips and turned back to her, knowing full well I was staring at the vixen while I orchestrated a war between Haeletrom Hale and the Stidda Mafia.

I could've been jotting down a grocery list for all I cared... because all I saw was her.

"Fuck, you know who this is, right?" Harper snarled.

"I do."

"And you're prepared for the fallout of this?"

Vivienne licked the rim of her cup, chased the bead of coffee, and stared at me as she kneaded my cock, until I couldn't take it a second longer. I lashed out, grasped her ankle, and lifted her foot.

"Exactly how deep are you in here, brother?" Harper questioned and for a second, I forgot he was even there.

I lowered my head and kissed the inside of her knee, but was careful to keep the phone to my ear. "So deep I can't see the light."

I gripped her ankle and stroked the diamonds before I moved higher and pushed my shirt out of the way.

"I don't have a choice," I murmured, which confessed more than I wanted to, and froze when I found the black-strapped, crotchless panties. The corner of her mouth curled as I lifted my gaze to hers. She knew what she was doing...

Fuck.

"Then I'll get this set up and contact you for details. Does this mean you're back in?" Harper asked on the other end of the line.

But I had already lowered my head and pushed her backwards with the phone still in my grasp.

"London?" The faint sound of his voice tried to push in as I curled my hand under her knee and parted her thighs.

She smelled like us...

She smelled like us.

I closed my eyes and inhaled the deep, musky scent. Hunger took over. I wasn't a man making moves anymore. I was a man too far gone to care, a man pushed past the point of no return. A touch came at my temple, making me open my eyes as she spread her fingers through my hair and cupped the back of my neck.

No words were spoken.

But the desire in her eyes said all there was to say.

It was useless to fight this...

Because no matter how hard I tried, I knew I'd never win.

It was always going to be her. *Always* going to be this.

With a growl, I lowered my head and kissed the soft flesh inside her thigh, then moved upwards to lick her slit. The woman never missed a beat, just cupped my head and tilted backwards, the coffee cup still in her other hand.

"London?" Harper's voice barely reached my ears.

But her moan pushed in as I sucked her clit. That sound was all I fixed on, all I wanted. I wanted that sound. I *craved* that sound. I curled my arm tighter under her knee and pulled her ass toward me, forcing her back even more. A *clink* came when she placed her cup on the desk as I released her leg, let it fall, and slid my finger down her slit.

"It's about time you wore the clothes I bought you, woman."

"And it's about time you made it worth my while." She lifted her head, meeting my gaze.

"You smell like us," I groaned. "Taste like us, too."

"Us," she whispered, and the word rocked me. "I like the sound of that. Are you just going to stop, London?"

I scowled.

"Use your words," she reprimanded, and a gleam of amusement shone in her eyes.

"I'll show you goddamn words," I growled, and lowered my head to lick her. "How about *Jesus Christ?*"

"Gotta earn that," she moaned as I slipped my fingers inside and fucked her. *"Oh, fuck yes, you gotta earn that."*

It was my turn to smile.

THIRTY-SEVEN

Vivienne

LONDON LET OUT A DEEP, THROATY CHUCKLE AS HE lowered his head and licked my slit, leaving me trembling. I released a sigh and slid my fingers through his hair as he moved higher and drew my clit into his mouth. "Oh *fuck*." My body jerked and shuddered, and my legs widened on their own. "Oh, *Jesus*."

A moan resounded in the back of his throat. The vibration hummed against that sensitive nub as those powerful arms tightened under my knees and he pulled me close, until I hovered at the edge. "You think you can come in here and distract me like that," he whispered as he lifted his gaze to mine. "You think you can—"

"Yes," I answered breathlessly. "I do."

There was a twitch at the corner of his mouth. "Goddamn brat. Let's just see about that, shall we?" He slid his finger along my slit and pushed in. "Do I look like I'm messing around here, Vivienne?"

His brazen fingers stoked the heat. I couldn't focus as my body clenched around his touch.

"Well?" he challenged, his gaze fixed on mine as he slowly thrust. "Look down, kitten. Do I look like a man who can be tested?"

I dropped my focus to where his fingers disappeared and shook my head. "No."

"No, what?" he growled.

"No, *Daddy*," I whimpered.

"That's what I fucking thought." He looked down, then slid two fingers inside. "You're going to learn to obey me, Vivienne. *Fuck me, but you're going to learn.*"

My orgasm barreled down on me like a storm. My pussy clenched as the rush swept through me. I was so close...*so close*... *so*—. I closed my eyes and whimpered, fixed on that sensation before he slipped his fingers out and left me trembling as I hovered on the edge of release.

I jerked open my eyes as anger flared. "Why the fuck are you stopping?"

He moved fast and stepped backwards, his fingers shiny and slick. With a jerk of his head, he motioned to the floor. "On your knees, wildcat."

Jesus, my entire body trembled and my legs barely worked as I slid from the desk, took a step, and sank to the floor. I was so desperate I would've done anything.

"Only good girls get to come." He fisted my hair as I knelt. "Are you going to be good for me?"

My pussy clenched as I looked up and nodded. Those dark eyes bored into mine.

"Good." He opened his belt, worked his button, and shoved his zipper low. "Show me how fucking good you are."

I reached for him as his cock sprang free. Fuck, if being on my hands and knees didn't make this hotter. My core clenched as I gripped the base of his cock and opened my mouth.

"That's it, pet. Open wide."

Smooth skin slipped across my lips. He fisted my hair and splayed his fingers wide to cup my head, then thrust deeper. My breath caught and pressure built in my chest as he pushed in deeper, then slid out.

"Such a greedy girl, aren't you?"

I opened wider, desperate for more.

He gently pulled me away by my hair, which caused his glistening cock to spring from my mouth. "Two fingers, kitten."

"Yes, *yes, two fucking fingers,*" I snarled. "Please, just let me suck your cock."

He smiled down at me. "Fuck, I love it when you beg like that. Better get used to it, wildcat. Now open that pretty mouth of yours."

I did, panting and desperate. I slid my hands along the back of his powerful thighs as he pushed my head down. *This...this is what I wanted.* I was so wet, hovering on the verge of climax as he thrust all the way in and cut off my air.

"Through your nose, pet." He held my head gently then released me and slid out. Saliva dripped from the head of his cock as I sucked in hard breaths.

"You're going to be the end of me," he murmured, looking down. "Desk, wildcat, don't make me ask you twice.

I'd never moved so fast in my life. My knees trembled as I scurried for the desk and turned.

"Uh unh," he corrected. "Turn around, Vivienne."

He was a locomotive as he grasped me around my waist, twisted me around with a hand on the back of my neck, and forced my cheek to the desk.

"That's my good pet," he growled and slid his finger along my slit all the way to my ass. *"That's my good...fucking...pet."*

With a brutal thrust, he drove all the way inside, making me buck with the force. My breath punched out with a whimper as I dragged my hands on the desk, trying to find something to hold on to.

But London was ferocious and gave me no time to steady myself, just left my hands to flail across the desk and scatter files and pens to the floor.

He unleashed a savage snarl. "Fuck!" *Thrust.* "Those." *Thrust.* "Files." *Thrust.* "Were." *Thrust.* "In...alphabetical order."

His cock drove into my pussy with punishing blows.

And left me in a quivering, moaning mess.

I clawed for the edge of his desk as my orgasm crashed down and swept me away. I thrust my hips backwards. I was just a throbbing, needy mess. "Harder," I moaned as my pussy clenched..."*Fuck me harder.*"

With a guttural growl, he thrust all the way inside and stilled as warmth spread. He eased his hold around my neck and his thumb slid away as he growled through shuddering breaths. "I'm going to ruin you, you get that, right?"

My breaths were too fast, my throat too dry. I swallowed once, then twice, as I lay there on his desk, unable to find the strength to rise, and gasped, "I can't fucking wait."

His cum was warm and slick, cooling on the inside of my thighs as he pulled out. Then my belly decided it was time to snarl and howl as I slowly pushed upwards on shaking arms and turned to meet his gaze.

God, he was devastating. "Seeing as how I fucked you," he muttered. "I may as well feed you, too."

"Yes, please...*Daddy,*" I whispered.

There was a quirk at the corner of his mouth as faint sounds came from outside the study. London gave me a glance. "I like you...wearing my shirt."

"Good," I responded. "You better get used to it. I plan on making a mess of everything of yours."

That quirk only grew bolder. I realized two things, how drop-dead gorgeous he was when he smiled, and how seldom he did it. The man had lived in darkness for so long, he didn't know how to be anything else.

I slipped from the desk as he tucked himself back into his pants and adjusted his belt. The moment I slipped from the desk to stand, I felt him, sticky and wet, coating the insides of my thighs. I turned and headed for the study door, and felt London close behind. I needed a shower...desperately, and food.

But before I could open it, he placed one hand on the door and the other on the doorjamb and boxed me in. "Careful here, wildcat," he warned as I turned and met his gaze. "Never forget what I am."

I inhaled deeply and slowly nodded.

There was a heartbeat before he slid his hand away so I could open the door and leave. But as I made my way through the kitchen and headed for the stairs once more, it hit me. Had London just warned me about *himself?*

He did...

Hell if I knew why. My cheeks grew hot as I went to my room, stepped inside, and headed straight to my bathroom. My bed was still a mess, my underwear discarded on the floor. I'd gone downstairs to rattle him more than anything and ended up getting nailed on his desk.

Warm slickness spread between my thighs. I tugged his shirt off and stepped into the shower. By the time I was done, I stepped out, my hair washed and my body smelling of the deep, seductive wash he'd bought for me. Because there wasn't a damn thing about me that London didn't control.

Careful there, wildcat. His warning resounded as I pulled on a tight black skirt, sheer stockings, and a long-sleeved blood-red cashmere sweater and went back downstairs. Muffled voices came from the kitchen and the smell of food cooking hit me the moment I reached the foyer. Growls and snarls of bickering males filled the kitchen.

"You're going to burn it," London insisted.

"Who the fuck is cooking this?" Carven snapped as I stepped into the room, to find Colt sitting on a stool on the other side of the kitchen counter, watching the theatrics.

"You don't listen to me." London shook his head. "No, that's not how you flip a damn omelet."

Carven cut him a savage glare, then froze as his gaze shifted to me, took in my breasts in the sweater, and turned away.

"What's going on?" I took the seat next to Colt as he stabbed a sausage from the plate in front of him.

"Carven is murdering your breakfast and London is about to murder him," Colt muttered, chewing.

"I'm not murdering anything," Carven protested and stepped backwards as I leaned over and plucked a sausage from the spare plate in the middle of the bench.

Colt froze mid-chew and glared my way as I bit down on the sausage. "Mmm, these are good."

"That was *my* breakfast," Carven said carefully and watched as I took another bite.

I gave a shrug and popped the last of the sausage in my mouth as all three males watched me with ravening stares. "I was hungry," I muttered, and leaned across the counter again to pluck a second sausage from the plate.

"Carven" London warned, watching as I grinned and bit down.

"That's it!" Carven lunged.

But I slipped from the stool in an instant, unleashed a squeal, and raced around the end of the counter as the lethal son rushed me. I grabbed London, yanked him sideways, then pushed him with all I had. I caught the smirk before he careened into Carven.

I just threw my head back and laughed, shoved the last of his sausage into my mouth, and raced for the stairs. I didn't make it three steps before I was hit by a tsunami and driven sideways before I fell. But I didn't hit the stairs. No, Carven grabbed me just in time. Still, he pushed me against the stairs, gripped my mouth with cruel hands, and squeezed until my mouth opened.

"Mine," he snarled savagely while he stared into my eyes and pushed his fingers into my mouth.

I bit down and clamped tight around his fingers. There was a curl of his lip as those blue eyes bored into mine. Slowly I opened and gave him enough leeway to pull the half-chewed meat from my mouth and place it into his. He slowly straightened, chewed, and swallowed as he looked down to where my skirt had ridden high in the scuffle and exposed the lace tops of my stockings.

But the dangerous son didn't step away. Instead, he pushed the inside of my knee hard, throwing my leg wide. "Eat what's mine again, wildcat, and I might just take it out on this sweet body." He licked his lips as he stared between my thighs. "Only I won't be sweet like my brother...and unlike your playtime with London, there won't be any fucking safewords. I'll smother your mouth and fuck you until you scream. You won't like that..." he lifted his gaze and took a step backwards. "No, you won't like it at all."

He turned around and headed back to the kitchen as I murmured. "How do you know?"

He stopped, then turned his head to see me over his shoulder. "Because no woman ever has."

THIRTY-EIGHT

Vivienne
___

THE DAYS TURNED...STRANGE, QUIET ALMOST. IF QUIET WAS a loaded gun aimed at each of our heads. The guys hovered around the house, which weirded Guild out. There were more than a few altercations with the sons as they got in his way, until the assassin/butler started barking. *"'Out of the kitchen...out!"*

I found myself hanging around downstairs, taking over the unused living room and making myself at home on the plush sofa. The massive flat screen TV still had the plastic wrap attached to the front. The plastic was the first to go. Popcorn, thick socks, and an oversized hoodie I stole from Colt, and I settled into a sense of familiarity.

Being inside, staying quiet.

Living my life through movies and TV shows.

That's all I'd had before I was dragged to The Order and fuck, if I wasn't more than happy to have it once again. Anything, as long as I didn't have to go back to that Hell.

It still didn't mean I didn't long for a normal life. One like others lived. I watched with more than a little envy as London and the sons argued with each other and left, leaving me alone with Guild for short stretches at a time.

Carven pushed London for action, snapping at him like a tethered predator. He didn't like all this waiting around. But the last thing London wanted to do was to react without thinking, without planning.

While I...stayed inside. I stood at the window of the living room while Holidate played on the screen behind me one afternoon and watched as the icy wind howled outside and whipped bare branches in its fury. Until the heady smell of popcorn wafted from the kitchen.

"What are you watching?" Colt asked as he carried in a massive bowl that was so full it almost overflowed.

I tore my gaze from outside to see the son striding into the living room. His deep blue eyes met mine as he sank down on the other side of the sofa.

"Holidate," I answered.

"A Christmas movie?" He glanced at the TV, his brow rising.

"Yeah," I answered with a scowl. "I kinda...love them."

That made him smile. "That's...cute."

"Cute, huh?" I crossed my arms and met his stare.

He was still awkward with me, staying away even though I could feel the weight of his stare haunt me every second we were close.

"What's fucking cute?" Carven snarled as he strode in to lean over the back of the sofa and grab a fistful of popcorn.

"Viv loves Christmas movies," Colt answered, his gaze fixed on me.

"Christ, I hate them." Carven rounded the arm to plonk down in the middle of the sofa. "I hate everything about this time of year. I hate this fucking waiting more."

The move earned him a glare from his brother. "Viv was sitting there."

His brother gave a shrug, muttering. "There's more than enough room."

I scowled. It wasn't the first time he'd pushed in between us. I didn't know if it was territorial about his brother, or if he actually wanted to be close.

"I wouldn't know," I muttered as London's snarl grew louder when he strode from the study.

He was pissed off about some IP address. I sat next to Carven and turned to press my back against the armrest. As soon as I did, Carven reached down, grasped my feet, and dragged them up to his lap. Colt watched his brother from the corner of his eye, frozen mid-handful of popcorn to his mouth.

"Wouldn't know *what?*" London snapped, in a foul goddamn mood.

That only pissed me off. I jerked my gaze to his. "Christmas, that's *what.*" The man could be pissy as hell when he wanted to be.

He stilled, glanced at the sons, then at the movie playing on the TV. The air turned charged. Truths unspoken sparked and hummed in the air. "But you knew that, right?" I looked carefully. "They didn't beat me, but they sure as hell may as well have. I never had a normal life, never had anything."

The sons looked at me.

London stepped closer, gripped the back of the sofa with one hand, and leaned in to glare at me. "You're alive, aren't you?"

"That's one way to put it." I glared back.

"Believe me, it's safer for you to be inside."

I looked away, ignoring him. "So you keep saying. I guess I'll just live my entire fucking life strapped to the goddamn machine in your basement, shall I?"

"Keep her inside," Carven snarled under his breath. "Keep us *all* in-fucking-side."

London's jaw clenched, but he didn't look at Carven. He kept that seething glare fixed on me. Still, I stared at the screen, not watching a goddamn thing until, under his breath, he muttered. "Fine. You want Christmas, then I'll give you fucking Christmas."

Hope surged inside me. I almost snapped my neck in two as I jerked my gaze to his. "You will?"

Those dark eyes simmered with cold, chilling fury as he gave a slow, careful nod and lifted his gaze to the TV, where Sloane was making her way through an overcrowded mall. "The South Diamond Mall is having their first late night sales leading up to Christmas." He turned to me. "And you're going."

I dragged my feet from Carven's lap and slowly rose from the sofa. "Don't fucking play me, London. This isn't funny."

He slowly straightened. There wasn't anything remotely amusing in his stare. "I wasn't trying to be funny. I forget how... cruel your life was." He nodded toward the TV. "So, if going to a goddamn mall is going to make you happy, then we'll take you."

"Fuck no, count me the hell out," Carven muttered, which earned him a glare from London. "Unless that's code for taking Hale out, then I'm all in. Hell, I'll even take Viv here, get the daughter's hands a little bloody."

London cut him a seething stare. "If one goes to the mall, then we *all* go."

While the son growled and glowered, I grinned and clenched my fists and forced my happiness through clenched teeth. "Holy shit...holy shit, a real fucking mall." I stumbled backwards as the three of them stared at me. "I have to get ready...I have to find something to wear."

"It's a mall," Carven snapped.

"You have all afternoon," London added.

"I don't care," I barked as I laughed and spun, then rushed for the stairs. *"I'M GOING TO THE MALL!"*

"Jesus..." London muttered behind me. "What the hell have we gotten ourselves into?"

"You mean, *you*," Carven corrected. "What have *you* gotten yourself into? Because there is no way in hell—"

Someone snarled.

Another cursed.

I left them all behind as I hurried to my room, my mind spinning. But the moment I stepped inside my room, I froze. *A mall...like a real, damn mall.* Fear gripped me. The kind of fear that grew talons in my mind. Maybe this was all too much. Yeah, I licked my lips...I think it was way too soon. I spun around, ready to head back down and tell London I'd changed my mind.

But I didn't get the chance...because Colt was there, standing in the doorway with a tortured look in his eyes.

"Colt," I took a step closer. "You okay?"

He strode in like a silent predator, grasped the back of my neck, and kissed me. I closed my eyes and gave in to him. His body trembled. I didn't know if it was in fear or hunger.

I pressed my hand against his chest, then broke away to stare into his eyes. "Hey, what is it?" He scowled, then shook his head. But he wasn't getting away from me so easily. "Talk to me."

He went still, then lifted his gaze. "There's a storm coming," he said, those blue eyes like the deepest depths of the ocean. "I can feel it."

I shook my head. "It's just winter."

"It's more than that." He searched my gaze. "It's...I can't put my finger on it."

I licked my lips as I watched the muscles of his jaw flare with the tension. "I'm glad you're here. I kinda need your help." I took a step backwards and reached for the belt around my waist. "I have no idea what to wear."

I grabbed Colt's hoodie around my hips and removed it in one smooth move.

His gaze widened, then fixed on the black lace bra and matching panties. I realized he hadn't ever actually seen me. Even when we'd fucked, it had been hurried and we were mostly clothed. I dropped the dress on the foot of the bed and took a step closer. "You can touch me if you want?"

He shook his head quickly.

"No?"

"No," he muttered as he stared at my breasts, and the vein running up his neck fluttered and beat faster than a rabbit fleeing for its life.

He lifted his hand and for a second, I thought he was going to touch me. But then he stilled, clenched his fist, and pulled away. So I helped him, gently grabbed his big hand and lifted it to my breast. "You won't hurt me."

He swallowed hard, his voice husky. "How do you know?"

"Because I know." I ground his hand against me, then reached up to slide down the strap of my bra. "Tell me to stop and I will."

"I don't...I don't know how to touch something so perfect."

I froze, and my heart thundered as I met those beautiful blue eyes.

"These hands are made for violence, not...this."

My breast bounced free from the cup as I let his hand go and reached around, unhooked the clasps, and let the garment fall. "You think you don't deserve this?"

"Not *think*," he answered as he still stared at my body. "I *know* I don't."

I slid my fingers under the elastic of my panties and dragged them down until I stood naked in front of him. "If you don't deserve to touch, then I don't deserve to be touched. Is that what you want?"

His throat worked as he swallowed hard and shook his head.

"So, touch me," I whispered. "Touch whatever you want."

He met my stare. "Anything?"

I gave a slow nod. "Anything."

So he did the one thing I didn't expect, he lifted his hand and brushed his thumb along my cheek. My breath caught with the contact. Something so tender, so careful and yet this feeling grew between us until it swept me away. He took a step closer, towering over me. His thumb grazed my cheek so gently it was barely there.

Slowly, he lowered his head.

This man who'd hardly known affection.

Was so utterly tender with me.

I closed my eyes as he kissed me. His fingers ran along my jaw as he tilted my chin higher. Slow, gentle, the kiss deepened until my heart pounded and my thoughts vanished. There was just this...just *us*, until finally he broke away.

It took me a moment to come back down. I floated with the feel of his mouth and slowly opened my eyes. "Holy shit."

There was a flicker of satisfaction in the deep depths of his stare. The kiss only made him bolder, as he lowered his focus and dropped his hand from my jaw to brush the outside of my breast. A shiver raced in the wake of his touch.

"You sure you haven't done this before," I whispered.

But he didn't answer. His focus was fixed on his hand as he gently cupped the swell, ran his thumb across my nipple, then lowered his head. I caught the tremble of his fingers a second before the warmth of his mouth took my mind away. It'd been days since the study. Even though I was getting used to living with these three men, I still felt awkward.

They came to me when they wanted me, yet there was still a disconnect.

One I didn't know how to navigate.

But this...this didn't feel awkward or strained. I lifted my hand to cup the back of his head as he gently sucked my nipple, then kissed the sensitive flesh, and moved to my other breast.

"God, you're so soft," he murmured. "Like satin."

"And you're so beautiful," I whispered.

He lifted his head. "I just...want to be near you, like all the time. I don't know how to do that without..."

Something in my chest fluttered. "Without feeling vulnerable?"

He gave a slow nod.

"Then that makes two of us."

He arched his brow. "Really?"

I gave him a slow smile. "Really. This is definitely not the kind of feelings I imagined myself having."

"With London?"

"Yes, with London, and with you." A dull pang filled my chest as I looked at the door.

"Carven isn't like me. He's..."

"Different," I nodded. "I get it."

"But he's changing. I don't understand how. If it was anyone else, he probably would've—"

"Killed them in their sleep?" I offered.

He gave a smile, and nodded. "Probably."

"Yay for still being alive." I smiled, then gave a sigh. "So, are you going to help me figure out an outfit for shopping, or what?"

He grinned, turned, and sat on the end of my bed. "Absolutely."

I laughed, lowered my head, and without thinking, kissed him. A surge of adrenaline coursed through my veins, and I lifted my head and met his gaze. That happiness lingered and for the first time in my life, I dared to hope.

I stepped back and headed for my closet. "I always dreamed of one of those moments in the movies where they dance under the falling snow dressed in something white and red." Then I froze, realizing what I'd said.

White.

I wanted to wear white.

My breaths came faster and a sense of panic rushed in.

"I think white is beautiful," Colt murmured, breaking my trance. "But I like you in black more. It makes you look..."

I closed my eyes. White. Red. Black. *White. Red. Black. White...red...*

"Stunning," he finished in the doorway of my closet.

I opened my eyes to find him right there. Those damn blue eyes saw too much. He knew. I don't know how, but he just...*knew.*

"So maybe it doesn't matter what color you wear underneath?" He shifted his gaze to the glass topped drawers of my lingerie. "Like the pink. I like pink."

My breaths were still too fast as I whispered, "You do?"

"Yeah." He angled his big frame around me to move deeper into the closet and pulled out the soft, pastel pink set. "This one."

I swallowed and forced myself to move and took the panties with a trembling hand when he held them out. He saw it and kept going. "So, it's going to be cold. You'll want warmth."

I strode closer as he stared at the rack of expensive clothes and wrapped my arms around him, hugging him from behind. He slid his hands over mine pressed against the middle of his chest. We stayed like that for a while, until the shudders eased and I felt more like myself again.

A.K ROSE & ATLAS ROSE

Then I slowly pulled my pink underwear on and reached for a pair of black designer jeans.

"Wise choice," he approved.

I slid them on, selected a V-neck sweater, and pulled it on. "Hair up or down?"

He turned. "Down. Always down, wildcat."

I smiled. "Down it is." I grabbed tall black boots and cushioned socks, then strode back to sit on the bed as he stopped at the doorway and leaned against the frame with his arms crossed.

"Is that what you're wearing?" I nodded at his black cargos and t-shirt.

He gave a grin. "I was, but I guess I'd better at least change my shirt."

For me. That's why. Not for any other reason.

He straightened and strode across the room, headed for the door. I watched him leave, then laced up my boots before I stood. Clear lip gloss and a little bronzer, then I dragged my fingers through my hair and headed for the doorway, but stopped short in the middle of my room.

"How's this?" he murmured.

For a second, I couldn't breathe. Colt had not only changed his shirt, but he'd traded the black cargos for gorgeous black jeans that fit him perfectly. A black turtleneck made the deep blue of his eyes mesmerizing.

"Holy shit," I whispered.

But Colt was the one who bit his lip and lowered his gaze to take in the deep V of my sweater and the high boots.

His sly smile told me all there was to know.

As much as he affected me, it seemed I affected him just the same.

––––––––

"I'M LETTING you know this is under protest," Carven snarled as he pulled open the passenger side door of the Mercedes.

"Noted." London held open the back door for me as his phone gave a chime.

There was a pinched expression on his face as he reached into his jacket, pulled out his phone, swiped the screen, and answered. "This better be good news." The moment his eyes narrowed I knew it wasn't. He turned away and strode across the garage. "You told me it was done, now there's a problem?" There was a second of silence. "What do you mean you can't hack their system? Now?"

He glanced my way and my heart sank. We weren't going...

I tried to keep the look of disappointment from my face.

But London saw every twitch.

"Can't this wait? Yeah...yeah, I need this done. Okay, I'll be right there. But I need this done as fast as possible."

He ended the call and I stepped away from the open door. "It's fine."

"What's *fine*, Vivienne?"

I shook my head. "We don't have to go tonight."

"Oh, you're going, I made a commitment." He looked at Carven. "Stay with her. I'll be there as soon as I can."

There was a hard sigh before the son jerked his head toward the Explorer. "Looks like it's just us, wildcat. But I swear to God, I'm not carrying your damn bags."

"I will." Colt gave me a wink.

His brother shot him a glare and took in the black turtleneck and jeans. "I don't even know who you are anymore."

I gave a shrug, closed the door, and strode toward London, then rose up on my toes to kiss him on the cheek. "It's fine."

He gripped my shoulders and stared into my eyes, the act sudden and awkward. Obviously, we could fuck, but this level of intimacy felt strange. "Just stay close to your brothers and whatever you do, don't take Carven's pissy attitude to heart."

"I don't plan on it," I murmured as I slowly stepped away, until I rounded the back of the Mercedes, then turned and lunged for the Explorer. *"I call shotgun!"*

"What?" Colt barked. *"FUCK!"*

THIRTY-NINE

London
_____

I watched the Explorer drive away before climbing into the Mercedes alone. The hard *thud* of the car door filled my ears as I leaned forward and stabbed the button to start the engine. Three goddamn days it'd been since I'd contacted Harper to hack Rossi's routers and change the records at The Order.

The latter proved relatively easy...but changing the Stidda's metadata was proving to be a goddamn nightmare. Harper and his team were the best of the goddamn best. So the fact that it was taking so goddamn long to hack their IP addresses was starting to piss me the fuck off.

Three fucking days.

And I felt every goddamn second like a blade against the back of my neck.

Still Hale had been quiet.

That was concerning, to say the least.

I shoved the car into gear and pulled out of the garage, left home behind, and headed for the quiet, secure block of offices four suburbs away. Vivienne's smile was etched into my brain, making me strangle the goddamn wheel and drive the car faster. This was the last goddamn thing I wanted to be doing.

I wanted to be with her, to see the smile on her face as she stepped into her first damn mall in her favorite time of the year. I wanted to be the one to spoil her, to show her all the goddamn things she'd missed out on. I wanted to be the one who gave that to her...*me,* not the sons.

Jesus.

Listen to yourself.

I ground my jaw so hard it cracked and pushed the Mercedes harder. Maybe I could deal with whatever this was and be back at the mall before they even had a chance to make their way inside. I turned the wheel, pulled into the quiet subdivision, and pulled up at the tall black gates, then lowered the window and hit the intercom.

"Yeah?"

I scowled. "What do you mean, *yeah?*" I snarled. "I taught you better than that, Davies. Now open the goddamn gate."

A buzzer sounded before the gate rolled open and I drove through. "Yeah? What kind of greeting is that? I swear to God, these damn kids."

The moment I said the words I stopped. *Kids.* Like Vivienne was a kid? I pulled into the parking lot, killed the engine, and climbed out. Nineteen was hardly a damn kid. A damn brat for sure, but not a kid. My heart pounded as I thought about her... what we'd done in the basement and the study.

Fuck if I didn't want more.

Like a whole lot more.

I was falling for her. I knew that. I *hated* that. Still, I couldn't stop it.

Her smile. Her laughter. Her fucking body. My heart pounded as I stepped up to the door, lifted my face to the camera, and scowled. *Buzz.* The door opened instantly, leaving me to walk along the barely lit corridor and climb the stairs.

I smelled them before I heard them. The pungent scent of freshly brewed coffee mingled with the heady scent of three men who hadn't showered in days. I winced and stepped inside to a mess of strewn coffee cups, open pizza boxes, and discarded jackets and ties.

"Fuck!" The bark came from one of the desks closer to the window.

I looked over and saw Harper shoving back from the desk with a look of pissed off frustration on his face, one he directed my way as I headed toward him.

"I don't wanna hear it, London," he growled as he shook his head and practically flung himself toward the desk once more. "I mean, *who the fuck is this guy?'*

"No one, just the Stidda Mafia boss."

"No." Harper shook his head. "I mean, *who is* this *fucking guy?"*

I stepped closer to look at the scrolling DOS prompts, and saw a name repeated. *The Ghost. The Ghost. The Ghost. The Ghost.*

"Never heard of him," I muttered. "Some kind of hacker?"

"Hacker, my ass. This dude is *good,* like *really* fucking good." He attacked the keyboard and punched in commands that I barely understood. "The thing is, this guy isn't even there. It's a secure network...one I can't seem to fucking *gettt throughhhh!"*

His face was a mask of determination, illuminated by the screen as he worked.

"We got him!" a scream came from the back of the room.

Harper jerked his gaze toward the sound.

"We got IN!" Brett bellowed once more. *"Holy fuck, we got in!"*

Harper's screen changed in an instant, revealing some kind of mainframe.

"Holy fuck" he muttered, his fingers flying furiously across the keyboard.

"Are you changing it?" I stepped closer.

"BRETT!" Harper roared. *"YOU READY?"*

"Whenever you are, old man!"

"Give you 'old man'," Harper mumbled as he punched in a list of commands and stabbed enter. *"And we have it. We goddamn HAVE it."*

He had a second of happiness, or pure exhausted relief, before his entire screen went black.

"What the fuck? *WHAT THE FUCK?"* he barked.

"It's okay!" Brett growled, drawing my gaze. "I'm still in. Holy shit, this defense is fucking good. Like, seriously...goddamn good! It's done. Rossi's has been changed and now I'm just... changing this in The Order's mainframe nowwww."

The room went still.

I could almost hear a pin drop, then, "Three motherfucking days." Harper lifted his gaze to mine. In the eerie glow as his monitor came back to life, I saw his blood-shot eyes. *"Three... mother fucking days it's taken all three of us to get through their system."*

"But you're through." I checked.

Harper glanced across the darkened room to Brett. "Yeah, we're through."

Then it hit me, just what we'd done. No, what *I'd* done. I'd not only given Hale a false lead away from us, but I'd thrown Benjamin Rossi under the bus to do it. But there was no way around it, no other way to get Hale away from my family.

A wave of relief hit me. I might've made a goddamn enemy of one of the most powerful Mafia bosses in the state, but he was nothing compared to the disease Haelstrom was. I'd take guns and violence any day. Anything to keep the sons safe. Now Hale had no choice but to sign the contract. A ghost of a smile tugged at the corners of my mouth.

"Well done," I praised. "Well fucking done. I'll pay you double."

"Fuck double," Harper snapped. "We want you back. *They* want you back."

"They don't want me back, Harper." I shook my head. "Besides, I'm done with that life."

He pushed away from the desk, rose, and scratched his balls. "Are you through?"

I narrowed my gaze. "What does that mean?"

He jerked his head toward the monitor. "You're still a hunter, London. No matter how hard you try to hide it."

Flashes of memories invaded my mind. The sons. The Order. Ryth and her stepbrothers running for their lives...and at the end was her...*Vivienne*. "No. Not a hunter. Not anymore. I truly appreciate your effort, you and your team will be well compensated."

I gave him a nod and turned to leave.

"If you're not a hunter, then what are you?" Harper called out as I made my way between the desks and past the mountain of pizza boxes and discarded coffee cups.

"What are you, London?"

The words haunted me as I made my way out of the building. What was I? Not a good guy, that was for sure. I grabbed my phone from my pocket the moment I stepped outside and punched in the number I had stored.

"Rossi, who's this?"

"Benjamin, this is London St. James. We met briefly when I—"

The response was anything but friendly. "I know who you are, St. James. What do you want?"

He was cold, careful. He had good reason to be. "Right now, I'm giving you a heads-up you're about to come under considerable heat."

"From who?"

"Haelstrom Hale," I answered.

There was silence, then a low chuckle. "If he thinks for a fucking second coming after me is going to get him his fiancée back, then the sick sonofabitch is in for a rude shock." Then his voice turned threatening. "I'd *love* for the bastard to come after me...give me a fucking excuse."

My stomach tightened and that tight smile tugged at my mouth once more.

"We aren't friends, St. James. So why are you really calling?"

"Call it a nagging conscience," I answered as I stared into the night.

There was a shift on the other end of the line. "That will only get you in trouble."

"Or killed."

"Or killed," he agreed. "*Or* rewatching the same recording of a certain bloodbath a hundred times over, trying to figure out how the hell a daughter and her stepbrothers were simply handed vengeance on a silver platter. If only they knew, right?"

"Knew what?" I answered, my tone cold.

He knew nothing. If he did, we wouldn't be having this conversation, not here...and not like this.

No, knowing the reputation of the Stidda leader, I'd be gagged, with my hands bound and a gun to my head.

"If they'd only known how close he was. Maybe if she'd searched the house instead of her brothers..."

What the fuck did that mean?

I wanted to push the Rossi leader for answers. But we weren't friends, and I'd done exactly what I'd wanted...taken the heat off my family and placed it on someone who wanted to go to war with Hale.

And I'd let him.

I hit the Mercedes' remote button and unlocked the door. If I hurried, maybe I'd find Vivienne and the sons before they make it to the Wonderland display. She'd love that...

Beep.

I yanked open the door, contemplating ignoring it.

Beep.

"Fuck." I lifted my phone, caught the name on the message, and my stomach sank.

Ophelia…

I swiped my thumb across the screen and opened the first message. It was a picture….

Of Carven's four-wheel drive, parked behind the warehouse where Hale had sent his men to get Ryth.

The same warehouse we'd defended with savagery.

My heart thundered as I opened the next message. There was no way she should have that footage, no way that she should even know what we'd done that day…*if she did—*

I didn't want to think about the consequences.

> Ophelia:
>
> You owe me a visit, London. This time, my apartment in Westrock. This way there'll be no interruptions. So, I'll expect you in twenty minutes…otherwise Hale will get the entire thing.

Hale will get the entire thing?

I swallowed hard and opened the picture once more, seeing the date and the time and clearly the warehouse with Hale's men in the background. I closed my eyes and braced my hand on the open door. How much more?

How much fucking more?

Revulsion made my stomach roll.

This way there'll be no interruptions.

She meant Carven.

This time there was no way to save me.

This time I had to go through with sleeping with her.

352

For Vivienne...

And my sons.

I lifted my phone, pressed the icon, and waited for it to be answered. "Carven," I said carefully. "There's been a change of plans."

FORTY

Carven

_____

LOOK AT HIM...

I stared at my brother as he carried her damn *Tooti Frooti Bumble* bags. He'd had to force her into the candy store after she'd stood outside staring at the damn thing for twenty minutes. If I had to hear, *'It's just like Holidate'* one more damn time, I was going to throw up.

No, it wasn't like fucking *Holidate*.

It was worse.

A piercing child's squeal ripped through the air. I winced at the sound and was smacked from behind, driven facefirst into the glass window of a lingerie store. *Dong.* My head hit the window and rage seethed just under the surface, making me jerk a savage glare toward the woman wrestling three goddamn terrors in an attempt to pass through the crowd.

A low threatening sound rumbled in the back of my throat and spilled outwards. Under the roar of the shoppers, she heard it, cast a panicked glance my way, drove her creatures forward, and disappeared.

Fuck, I hate Christmas. I searched the crowd and found my brother, glaring at me over his shoulder as they walked.

Fine...

I shoved away from the wall and kept moving until I saw where she was heading. "Oh fuck no."

A snarl resounded in the back of my throat as she headed for the towering Winter Wonderland display that took up the entire span of the massive shopping center.

An ugly red sleigh was wedged between two massive Christmas trees smothered in three inches of fake snow, the kind of snow that spewed out of a machine in the corner of the exhibit. Kids squealed as parents were frantically trying to look everywhere at once. Still the white shit floated in the air. It was a goddamn nightmare.

My phone vibrated in my pocket as I pushed faster through the crowd. "Colt, *tell her no fucking way!*" I roared, as I pulled my phone out. "*Colt! COLT!*"

But my goddamn brother kept walking as Vivienne rushed forward with an ugly ass grin on her face.

No...

Fuck no.

I glared at the caller ID: *London,* and answered. "I swear, I'm about to end them both."

"Carven," He started, and the cold, careful tone made me freeze. Someone smacked into my shoulder as they passed, but I barely saw them as London kept talking. "There's been a change of plans."

A change of plans.

The way he said it sent a chill down my spine. I lifted my gaze to Colt and Vivienne as she laughed and lined up with the herd of shouting kids to gain entry as I murmured. "What kind of change?"

"I'm heading into the city."

"*Why?*"

"There's...there's a goddamn picture. I don't know how she got it. I don't even know how much information she has. But Ophelia has a fucking picture. She has this."

Beep.

I pulled my phone away and hit the message on the screen to pull up a picture of my vehicle. *My goddamn vehicle outside the warehouse where we'd saved Ryth and her fucking stepbrothers.* I lifted the phone. "How the fuck did she get that?"

"I have no idea."

Then it hit me. "She sent it to you and not Hale."

Silence, then. "Yes."

I ground my jaw, lifting my gaze to my brother as the line moved closer to the towering display. "She's blackmailing you..."

"Yes."

I shook my head. "You can't—"

"I have no choice, son. I can't take the risk she has more. It could...*ruin us.*"

I closed my eyes and felt my world sway. The shrill screams of kids pushed in...

Ruin us...

Ruin...us.

Ruin me, he meant.

"I'll be back when I can."

My gut clenched with the words. *"London, no."* But it didn't matter how hard I pleaded, because he'd ended the call.

Rage filled me as I found Colt staring at me with a look of concern. It was like he knew, like he always knew. That invisible tether that bound me to him hummed with a charge. Then slowly, my vision widened and the glimpses of black moved in.

Crack!

I jerked my gaze toward the sound at the same time my brother did.

Crack!

Crack!

CRACK!

Screams started, turning deafening as mothers and children ran for their lives. Colt was already moving as the gunmen pushed their way through, tearing the Winter Wonderland display apart in an attempt to get to her...

To her...

I jerked my gaze toward the woman in the center of it all.

The woman who couldn't see a damn thing around that ugly fucking sleigh.

"VIVIENNE!" I screamed, and lunged.

But the frenzied crowd slammed against me, driving me backwards. Black peppered my view and between the gaps of frantic shoppers I caught the sight of more of the bastards heading their way.

"Get the fuck out of the way!" I roared, shoving people aside.

I reached back for my gun and was bumped sideways. I wrestled my weapon free and drew it up as one of the attackers went for my brother. The *fuck you do.*

I raised the muzzle, took aim, and sidestepped a kid before I squeezed the trigger.

Crack!

The shot went to the side and slammed into one of the Christmas trees. I took aim again as shoppers continued running away and squeezed off a shot as Vivienne screamed.

Crack!

The bullet hit true that time and slammed into my brother's attacker as he drove the butt of his gun at Colt's head. But I didn't have time to shoot again as one of the assholes grabbed Vivienne from behind and lifted her feet off the floor.

Colt roared as he threw his attacker to the side, only to be surrounded by more of them. He took the blows and lifted his hands to protect his face as he lashed out, clocking one in the jaw.

I shoved forward, raised my gun, took aim, and was slammed from the side. More of those motherfuckers came out of nowhere. One tore a screaming kid from its mother and threw the damn thing at me.

Flailing hands and legs and a wide-open mouth. I grabbed the screaming missile with one hand, dropped him to the floor, then rounded the kid and pistol-whipped the fucker across the face.

A calmness washed over me. Quiet. Controlled. The panicked roar of the crowd dulled. There was only blood now. Only violence. *Only this.*

The square jaw of the bastard in front of me snapped sideways, but I didn't give him a second to recover. I lunged forward, driving my fist and the barrel of the gun upwards...but a voice pushed in.

Her voice.

Her screams.

Her fighting.

"Get the fuck off me!"

I sank deeper into that cold, hard rage, where there was nothing but revenge, and drove the patterned steel of my weapon into his nose. Again, and again, and *again.* Even as he stumbled backwards, I advanced.

Blood shot out of the attacker's nose as his buddy lifted his gun. But I was expecting it. *I hoped for it.* I swung my fist and pulled the trigger. *Crack!* And the side of his head disappeared in a spray of red.

I turned back as the first guy wiped at his nose.

Fear bloomed in his eyes.

He saw me now.

Saw what I was.

What they'd *made me become.*

And it terrified him.

I lunged and pushed him backwards into the scattering crowd so fast his feet couldn't keep up. He swung, but his blow was pathetic and too fucking wide. I ducked, then rushed forward, grabbed him around the throat, and shoved.

His arms windmilled as he fell backwards and hit the floor with a sickening *thud.* Chaos descended around us. All I saw were boots and legs and black. *Black. Black like mercenaries.* I risked a glance upwards, to see my brother fighting two of them, before I looked at Vivienne...but she was gone.

There were no screams for me to track now, no thrashing fists as she fought. I scanned the crowd as I lunged after the bastard, grabbing him as he lay on the floor and gripped the bastard's throat as more of his team invaded, one shoving the panicked shoppers aside to get to my brother.

I didn't think anymore, just lifted the gun. *Crack.*

The gunman's head snapped backwards as blood sprayed. But I was already scanning the crowd, until I saw her. One bastard held her shoulders, his hand over her mouth. Another carried her legs, his body between her thighs as she bucked and thrashed, reaching over her head to claw the other fucker's face. The last guy followed them through the service. She fought...

Still, it was three on one.

I shoved against the bastard on the ground, driving myself upwards as Vivienne disappeared through the door, and tripped.

"Where the fuck do you think you're going?" the bleeding scumbag croaked underneath me.

I swung my hand upwards, taking aim. But he was on me in an instant, shoving against the ground to drag me back down as I slipped in that fake fucking snow.

My face hit with a *crack!* Pain stabbed through my cheek, making my eyes water. Still, through the blur, I saw rage as he swung his fist. The animal in me snapped. I went for his face, driving my thumbs into his eyes until they bulged.

"You have idea who you're messing with." Slick coated my nails and flowed over my knuckles. "But you will."

I didn't stop, twisting with all I had until I heard a gut-clenching *pop*.

Then it was over...and so was he.

His body dropped to the floor.

I didn't waste a second as I shoved upwards, using all the strength I had, and leveled the gun on my brother's attackers. But they were gone. I scanned the crowd, then looked down. No, not gone. Dead.

Three of them lay on the ground, one with his head at an angle that wasn't conductive to life, the two others motionless. I tore my gaze away and rushed forward, headed for the open service door, praying I wasn't going to find my brother lying in a puddle of his own blood at the bottom of the goddam stairs.

Move!

I drove myself forward...*and prayed.*

FORTY-ONE

Vivienne

_No!_

_NO!_

I bucked and clawed, my screams muffled against the grip over my mouth as they carried me through an open side door and into a stairwell. They were going to take me..._they were going to take me..._

Cold plunged through my belly. I clawed the hand over my mouth, opened wide, and bit down.

"Oww!" Reflex made my attacker yank his hand away. His blood welled neon bright from the bite mark as he grabbed my throat and clenched. _"Bite me again, bitch, and I'll throw you down those fucking stairs."_

I didn't care.

I knew what waited for me...

The Order.

The Order...

"COLT!" I roared as they hit the first stair, the thud of their boots mingling with the boom of my heart.

"*Get her to the fucking car!*" came the command from the one who held my knees. I twisted, kicking with all I had. "*COLT!*"

I clawed and thrashed, managed to tear one foot free, then lashed out and kicked the bastard right in the middle of the chest. He stumbled backwards, dropping one leg and then the other. Concrete rushed toward me until I hit the edge of the stairs hard. Agony tore through my cheek, but I shoved upwards and ran.

The stairs blurred.

My heart hammered.

I made it up one...two stairs before I was grabbed again and lifted. Arms like steel bands clamped around my waist as they dragged me backwards. "COLLLTTTT!" I screamed as I stared up at that open door.

"*Downstairs!*" one barked.

I couldn't fight, couldn't get free. The white walls of the stairwell were a blur as we descended one floor then another...

"Castlemaine," the one who'd dragged me backwards growled in my ear. "We know they have him. Where the fuck is he?"

My thoughts froze. My mind was a mess...*Castlemaine?*

Jack.

Jack.

Was this why they'd taken me?

I drive my heels backwards, catching my attacker in the shin. He let out a grunt of agony, his hold slipped, leaving me to crash to the floor. Still, he had hold of me. My boots scraped against the concrete as I stumbled. I stopped fighting, my thoughts frantic. *Protect London...*

"Answer me, *bitch. Where the fuck is he?*"

I twisted around and stared into the bastard's eyes. "*Fuck you!*"

He released one arm from his hold on me, clenched his fist, and drove it into my belly.

Oof...

Agony made me double forward over his arm.

I tried to breathe, tried to keep from throwing up. But the washed-out white world spun and stars ignited behind my eyes. But then the service door behind me was thrust open and slammed into my abductor.

The bastard stumbled sideways as a man barged out, driving a loaded cart into the stairwell, then caught sight of the men...and me. "What the fuck?"

It was all I needed. The bright lights of the shopping mall called. I kicked free and lunged, scrambled around the trolley, and tore away from them.

"*FUCK!*" my attacker screamed. "*Get her...GET HER!*"

The rush of the crowd swept around me. The *boom* of a gunshot rang out on the stairs. I didn't stop, couldn't stop. *Colt. Carven. Hide. Colt. Carven. Hide.* I spun around, to find an open door to a clothing store on my right as the terrifying screams of my attackers came from the stairwell behind me.

"*Get the fuck back here!*"

My hair was yanked backwards, drawing terrified stares from the shoppers all around me. There was already a frenzy from the gunshots and, as I stumbled, I caught sight of that red sleigh on the floor above.

"I'm not fucking done with you," my attacker snarled.

"How the fuck do we get out of here?" the assailant behind me roared at the shop assistant.

She stared at us with a terrified expression as I kicked and bucked, tearing at his hand fisted in my hair. *"Help me!"* I begged her.

But she didn't come to my aid, just lifted a shaking hand and pointed to the back of the store with a terrified look on her face. Black invaded the stark white of the store as more of my attackers rushed in.

"MOVE!" one roared as he charged forward with a panicked look on his face.

Then through the frantic rush came Colt, moving with long, purposeful strides. There was no blue in his eyes now, just a swirling sea of obsidian wrath. He didn't flinch, didn't even look at anyone else, just the asshole in front of him, before he lunged forward.

The sickening *snap* of bone made me freeze. The shoppers stumbled backwards, pressing their backs hard against the wall as Colt unleashed, one blow after another driving his fist upwards, until the asshole's head snapped backwards with a gut-wrenching *crunch*.

I'd never seen anyone so...*mechanical*. So cold. So...*dangerous*.

The asshole crumpled to the ground, those wide, unblinking eyes fixed on nothing.

"Easy, now." The biggest attacker lifted his gun and took aim as he muttered, "We just want the bitch, that's all."

The seconds slowed as time stretched. All I could see was the curl of his finger around the trigger and the flare of fear in his eyes as he stepped between Colt and me. It was the wrong thing to do.

"Tell me where the fuck Castlemaine is?" my attacker snarled against my ear.

They were scared now.

They should be.

Still the gunman's finger cinched tighter. "Stop," he warned Colt. *"Are you fucking deaf, I said—"*

I didn't think, just reacted, lunged forward until my hair snapped taut and grabbed a handful of folded clothes, then hurled them through the air as the gun fired with a *crack!*

Pink and black and blue fluttered through the air. My heart stopped until I saw movement as Colt charged forward.

Chaos erupted.

Brutal.

Frightening *chaos.*

Colt drove the gunman backwards along the hallway toward the back of the store until they crashed through the door of the dressing room. I spun around and lashed out, punching my attacker in the face. "Let me *fucking go!"*

But it was the chilling *crash* that made me freeze.

One that sounded like breaking glass.

My heart boomed and my blood froze. My attacker's hold slipped, allowing me to scurry forward. But I wasn't the only one. Black figures charged for the dressing room as grunts and roars sounded in that small space.

Mirror shards crunched under my boots as my attacker grabbed me again and hauled me backwards. But there was another who moved in behind Colt, leaving two on one, and the brutal thuds of fists on flesh sounded, chilling me to the bone. They were going to kill him...*they were going to kill him!*

I spun, the clawed and kicked with all I had, until a bloodcurdling *snap* sounded...and the dressing room became terrifyingly quiet.

No...

No.

NO!

I punched and tore at my attacker's hold until it slipped and I was able to jerk free. The tiny door of the dressing room was all I saw. My boots slipped on glass slivers, and I crashed to the floor. Colt was all I saw. Colt lying on the floor, covered in glass...Colt *not moving.*

White hot rage ripped through me. I jerked my gaze to those bastards. *I'll kill them. I'LL FUCKING KILL THEMMMM!*

My body shuddered with adrenaline, shattering something inside me.

"See how fucking tough you are now." One of the attackers dragged back his foot and took aim at Colt's face.

"NO!" I lunged, slammed into his back, and unleashed that savagery inside me, clawing his face like the animal I was.

My nails buckled with the force. Bloody streaks slashed across his cheek in their wake. My attacker stumbled sideways and knocked into the other piece of shit with a roar.

Shrieks of terror pushed in, the sound shrill and *feral.* Until I realized they came from me. I tasted blood as I slapped and punched, until the bastard grabbed me, tore me free, and threw me across the room.

I slammed into the wall and bounced, to land hard on the floor next to Colt. Still they came, stepping forward, drawing their guns. Fear punched through my rage.

I didn't care about myself at that moment. I plunged headfirst into a tsunami, ready to kill with the desperate need to protect.

I threw my arms out wide as I curled my body over his. A biting sting slashed across my palm as I felt and grasped a long, mirrored shard. I didn't care. Not about me...

Only him...

ONLY HIM.

"Get the fuck away!" I slashed the air toward them. *"GET THE FUCK AWAY FROM HIM!"*

And from the corner of my eye...death came for them.

Death with piercing blue eyes and an unquenchable thirst for violence.

Crack!

CRACK!

CRACK!

Blood red mist sprayed in the tiny space as the heads of the three gunmen exploded. Warmth splattered my face. I couldn't move, couldn't think. All I saw was those piercing blue eyes as Carven looked down at me, then at his brother.

"Get back." I still slashed the air. I didn't know how to stop. *"Get back. Get back. Get back."*

Still, Carven didn't hurt me.

He didn't step closer.

Just sucked in hard, consuming breaths and murmured, "It's me, wildcat...it's me."

A groan came from underneath me. Low, guttural, it drew my gaze. My arm stopped slashing. I looked down into those obsidian depths and they looked back at me.

"I'll come for you," Colt whispered. "I'll always come for you."

Agony slashed across my chest. The sting was more brutal than any glass shard. He shifted his gaze, first to his brother, then the gunmen at his feet. "Who the fuck were they?"

"I have no idea," Carven answered, staring at the way I hunkered over Colt. "But we have to go...*now.*"

"I don't think I can move," I whispered.

Colt grasped me around the waist and eased himself upwards. Shards of glass fell as he pushed to stand, then looked at the jagged weapon in my hand, one coated with blood. He was so careful as he unfurled my fingers before he cast the shard aside.

"Here." Carven stepped away and disappeared for a second before he returned with a red scarf.

One his brother wrapped around my hand.

"Let's get you home," Colt murmured.

But Carven didn't move.

I felt the chill.

The fear.

The agony.

Colt turned his gaze toward his brother. "What is it?"

"London called a second before the attack." He glanced at me and my heart sank. "Ophelia's blackmailing him, threatening to go to Hale with a picture of my car at the warehouse where we saved Ryth Castlemaine and her brothers. He has no choice, wildcat. He's on his way to see her now."

FORTY-TWO

Vivienne

"HE'S GOING TO OPHELIA?" MY WORDS WERE A WHISPER.

I closed my eyes as the dressing room swayed.

It hurt...

Jesus, it hurt.

I clenched my hand and drove the sharp sting across my palm deeper. Still, it was nothing compared to the jealousy that savaged my chest. The memory of that bitch roared to the surface. She was all I could see, her ugly fucking smirk and the way she looked at him with that predatory stare and fingered the fucking necklace London had bought her.

He'd bought it for her.

Because they were fucking.

Just like right now they were fucking.

Not fucking...more like rape.

The thought of that stopped me cold. An icy white rage burned in me. She had forced London, pushed him into a corner where

371

the only way out was to please her. He would...*I knew he would.* He'd do it because he had no other choice. My stomach clenched. *I was going to be sick.*

"Wildcat."

I flinched at the name and opened my eyes, to find the deep, dark blue of his eyes.

"Do you trust me?" Colt stared at me.

Screams from outside registered as I gave a slow nod. "Yes."

Movement drew my gaze. Carven stepped back into the dressing room, glanced at his brother, and nodded. "We need to move."

"It's going to get dangerous out there. So I'm gonna need you to stay close to me," Colt urged as he tied the scarf tightly around my hand. "Can you do that?'

I gave a careful nod as he grasped my other hand and pulled me out of the dressing room.

I tried not to look at the dead bodies or the terrified shoppers as they fled the store. The blood was neon red, flaring with the punishing blows in my head. I tore my gaze from the sight of those dead men. It felt like forever since I'd been dragged inside that store. All that chaos, all that pain.

My cheek throbbed, and I winced. But I pushed the pain away and focused on running as we tore along the hallway that connected the backs of the stores.

"What the fuck is going on?" a guy barked as we hurried past.

We didn't answer, just pushed through another service door and into a panicked crowd. Carven slowed and we followed, careful to keep our gazes low, and moved with the frantic rush of the shoppers.

I was shoved, and stumbled. But Colt was there, he held me steady and pulled me hard against him as Carven closed in. I was wedged between the sons, two men who smelled like gunpowder and blood.

"Get the fuck out of the way," he growled as we barged through until finally, we were outside.

My hearing was just a dull, muffled roar when we spilled out. Carven broke away, lengthened his stride, then pushed into a run to disappear between parked cars.

"It's okay." Colt drew my gaze as I searched for him. "He's just getting the car."

Headlights flared, blinding me as other cars passed. I scanned each one, searching for the four-wheel drive. But I didn't need to. Colt pulled me forward as the Explorer pulled up hard in front of us.

Horns blared as Colt opened the back door and calmly waited until I'd climbed in before he closed it and climbed in the passenger seat himself. Then we were pulling away from the horde of revving engines and honking horns. Carven worked the gears and swung the four-wheel drive around tight turns until we pulled out into a quiet back street.

One that seemed empty.

The packed frenzy of the bumper-to-bumper line we'd left behind spilled out further down from us. But we were free. *Jesus...we were free.* I closed my eyes as the engine of the four-wheel drive roared as it pulled us away from the mall.

The mall I'd wanted to attend.

I released a low moan and rocked forward.

"Wildcat?" Colt called, his voice filled with concern.

"It's all my fault," I shook my head. "This all happened... because of me."

I should never have left the house. Should never have asked to go...should never...should never.

Carven unleashed a snarl, spun the wheel, and pulled over hard. I grasped the door handle and held on as the car jerked to a stop.

"Let me tell you something, wildcat." Carven turned his head to seize me with an icy stare. "Listen up, 'cause I'll only say this once. It's thoughts like that which will break you. You want to be a victim? Then keep acting like one. But if you want to be one of us, then *we act. You* are a by-product of what they created...a *daughter.*" He turned back and shoved the car into gear. "Just like we're goddamn sons."

I sucked in hard breaths as he pulled the four-wheel drive back out onto the street. His words weren't soft. If I wanted soothing, I wouldn't get it from Carven. But he *would* give me the truth.

"You wanting to go to a fucking mall had nothing to do with being attacked, wildcat," he growled as he scanned the area. "And *everything* to do with those motherfuckers who want to control you."

"They asked about Jack...Jack Castlemaine," I whispered.

Carven slammed on the brakes, which threw me forward until the seat belt snapped taut. A low, savage snarl came from Colt, but his twin barely gave him a second glance. "They what?"

"They wanted Jack, Ryth too, if they could get her."

Carven shot Colt a glare and his scowl moved deeper with the careful nod of his head. "Fuck." Carven punched the accelerator and drove even harder as we wound our way through the streets, and only then did I realize that nothing looked familiar. "Where are we going?"

"Well, it seems like now's a good time to figure it out, wildcat. Are you prey or a predator?" he muttered as he turned into a darkened street and pulled up in front of a massive black gate outside what looked like a two-story warehouse.

He pushed the button to wind down the window and pressed his thumb onto a keypad. The gate instantly rolled open and he pulled in quickly. I barely had time to catch my breath, let alone think, as he nosed the car into a set of large doors and climbed out, leaving the engine running.

Colt followed but turned to open my door. I winced at the thud in my head as we followed Carven to a heavy steel door and watched as he punched in a six-digit code and unlocked the door. He glanced over his shoulder to me before he stepped through and disappeared into the darkness.

Goosebumps raced across my skin as Colt glanced at me, then he disappeared after Carven. That careful look said it all. They were trusting me, allowing me into a place no one else went, other than London, of course.

Lights flickered and danced overhead before the space brightened a little. I stopped and stared. This...this was no warehouse. Dark moody lights flicked on to illuminate a sleek black Camaro parked in one bay and at the back was an open weapons room.

Black metal and glass glinted. I stared at the guns. "Holy shit."

Carven moved forward, grabbed a gasoline can, and carried it to the door. "I have a plan," he muttered, and turned back.

I tried to listen, but really, I was staring at what looked like rocket launchers.

"I can't just walk in and interrupt them this time," he continued. "That vile fucking *thing* has made it so they're alone. So, if we can't interrupt them, then we need someone who will...and a damn good reason." He glanced at his brother. "That's if you're with us, wildcat."

"To do what?" I murmured as I stared at a wall filled with names, a wall that called me forward.

Names. Pictures. Information. It was all there. All listed in a circle of filth...and in the middle was a name. *Weylyn King.*

King...

"To burn the bitch's house down," Carven answered, and threw something through the air at me.

I caught it on instinct and stared down at a balaclava.

My head throbbed.

My scalp burned.

My stomach clenched with the sickening tang of blood in the back of my throat...

Still, I stared at the woolen mask in my hand as I realized this was all too real.

The Order.

King.

And *her.*

"Yes." I lifted my gaze. "I'm with you."

One careful nod and Carven grabbed a small flashlight from the bench. "Then you need to keep up, got it?"

I took the flashlight and tucked it into my pocket. "Got it."

He lowered his gaze to my low-cut top. "You'll need something warm. Brother," he muttered. "Want to help her out with that?"

Colt strode toward a hanging rack in the middle of the room, right next to what looked like...a massive cold room or freezer. What on earth did they need something like that for? I shivered, staring as Colt grabbed a black t-shirt and a jacket from the rack and turned back to me. I tugged my blouse over my head and shivered with the cold as I pulled on the shirt Colt handed me.

The heat of their gazes danced across my breasts. Colt I was used to, but the way Carven looked at me now was ravenous. The prospect of his desire both excited and terrified me all at once. I glanced his way, then tugged down the shirt and pulled on the jacket, zipping it up tight as I shivered.

He cared.

It hit me as Carven glanced at Colt, then jerked his head toward the gas can and muttered, "Let's go."

He could be snarly and moody all he wanted, but something was changing between us, and he felt it. I moved fast and headed for the Explorer as Carven climbed behind the wheel and Colt stowed the gas in the back.

I clenched my painful fist as I used it to push myself inside before I pulled the door closed behind me. Still, I couldn't take my eyes off the son as I tugged the seatbelt into place.

"Keep looking at me like that, wildcat, and I might just do something about it," Carven warned as he backed out and headed for the gate.

Colt glanced at his brother, then shifted to look over his shoulder at me.

A twitch came in the corner of his mouth, like he knew.

One tiny wink and he turned back.

Our headlights carved through the dark, and that dark only grew deeper as we left the faint city lights behind. The road turned quiet. I caught glimpses of large, imposing houses set far back from the street.

But it was eerie out here, the kind of place where you didn't want to be caught stranded in case you ran into—blue eyes met mine in the rear-view mirror. Carven's stare was cold, hungry, dangerous—*him. In case you ran into someone like him.*

He glanced back in the rear-view mirror with the piercing stare of a killer, because that's exactly what he was. Then he reached and killed the lights

I stared out through the tinted windows and caught sight of a driveway behind a wrought iron fence before we passed. A second later, we pulled over onto the shoulder of the road, nosed between two tall ash trees, and parked.

The throbbing pulse in my head eased as I climbed out and shivered with the cold. The rear door of the car was quiet as it opened, and the interior light stayed dark. We were soundless as Colt dragged out the can of gasoline and eased the door closed.

Silver glinted in the moonlight and drew my gaze as Carven handed me a gun. "If you're with us, then you need to protect yourself."

I stared at the weapon, then lifted my gaze to his. He grabbed my hand and pressed the grip against my good palm. Jesus, my heart hammered. Still, I closed my fingers around the gun.

"Point and shoot, wildcat. Only if you need to."

"But you won't need to," Colt murmured as he strode forward. "No one's gonna touch you ever again, I'll make damn sure of that."

They tugged on their balaclavas, with nothing visible but those piercing blue eyes. I quickly followed, the wool warming my face instantly as I shoved my hair out of sight.

"Stay low and move fast," Carven's words were muffled as he strode toward the fence line in the distance.

In an instant, that panicked night I'd escaped The Order came rushing back. It was a night just like this, full of terror. But the memory was soon swallowed by that wall of faces back at the sons' place.

Faces of those of The Order.

I glanced at Colt at my side. I'd lived with these men long enough to know they were targeting each name, finding ways to infiltrate and destroy The Order from the inside. The idea would once have shocked me. Now I knew the truth...better than they wanted to admit.

Those I lived with were bad, dangerous, honest men.

The kind who risked their lives for those they loved.

Now, that seemed to include me...

That thought filled me as Carven bent for a moment, then yanked the fence upwards to widen the gap for us. Colt dropped to the ground and scurried through, then turned to help me as he pulled the gasoline can through.

Then we were hunched over, running. Carven moved ahead, a gun in one hand as he lifted his other with two fingers skyward and motioned toward the front of the mansion we ran toward.

Not *a* mansion...

Her mansion.

One bought with the blood and terror of all those beaten children, ones like Colt. He ran beside me, his stony gaze fixed on the dark windows up ahead. Carven rushed forward. The pounding in my head struck with every brutal step. I tried my best to keep up.

But damn, they were fast.

I sucked the wool against my face with every hard breath as we headed for the rear of the house. The *crack* of glass breaking sounded far too loud in the night. I searched for the two guards I'd seen before, but they were nowhere to be found. A thin wooden side door was opened from the inner courtyard. My heart lunged as Carven stepped out and motioned us forward.

Then we were inside.

Just to walk on those floors felt like a betrayal.

Part of me didn't want to see the lavish lifestyle her vile ways had afforded her.

But it was the faint smell of gasoline that kept me from falling apart. I had to remember what we were doing here...and why.

London.

Carven glanced our way, then motioned forward. I don't know how he knew where to go, but we found ourselves in an expansive, gloomy room. I scanned the walls, finding murky outlines hanging on the walls.

Click.

The sound came behind me. I spun, to find a narrow glare aimed at the wall.

"What the fuck are you doing?" Carven hissed.

But Colt didn't answer, and this time it wasn't because he chose not to speak. He couldn't. Because he was staring at a painting on the wall, his blue eyes impossibly wide. I moved closer and shifted my gaze to the blackened mess on the canvas.

It was a boy crouched down, with his hands raised up in surrender. But it was the deep blue eyes that gripped me. The only color on the smeared blackened sheet, a deep blue that almost looked like...

I lifted my gaze to Colt, then slowly shifted to the rest of the pieces that lined the wall.

Lost Boys.

The brass plaque in the middle of the wall made me gag. *Lost Boys...Lost Boys...Lost...Boys...*

Those terrified whimpers came rushing back through the depths of my pain. The tortured sounds from that recording. I knew what this was now. What this *all was*. It was *them*.

Carven.

Colt.

She'd never stop. She'd never. *Fucking. Stop.*

Not until she owned them. Not until she had what was...

Mine.

I sucked in that frigid night air. Still, it burned against that seething icy rage I held inside. I unleashed a roar and lunged forward to tear that ugly, fucking *thing* from the wall.

I was uncontrollable as I slammed it against the wall, then flung it down to the floor, where the frame shattered.

"Vivienne," Colt called my name.

But I was too far gone already. I couldn't have stopped even if I'd wanted to...*and I didn't want to*. My fingers roared with agony after I'd torn apart the gunman's face as I'd tried to save Colt. But I didn't care as I ripped the drawing from the broken frame.

I didn't care about the pain.

Or the blood.

The pungent stench of gasoline bloomed. Carven was a darkened specter as he strode around the edges of the room and splashed as many of those foul fucking images as he could.

When he ran out of gasoline...I was there. I tore them from the wall and hurled them into the middle of the room as Carven flicked a lighter and held the flame to the puddle of gasoline on the floor. Still Colt stared at that space on the wall. Agony filled me at the sight.

The need to protect followed. I cast the ugly fucking thing in my hand toward the growing flames and grabbed Colt's hand. "Hey...I'm right here."

He didn't move.

Carven jerked his gaze our way as he lowered the empty gas can.

"Colt, my hand..." I whispered. "It hurts."

I knew if there was anything to bring him back, it'd be my pain. He blinked, pushed that empty stare aside, and glanced at the red scarf wrapped around my palm.

"We need to get out of here," Carven urged as he glanced around.

At that instant, the shrill sound of the fire alarm blared as the flames reached higher.

"Now, Colt!" Carven roared as he strode toward the hallway.

Colt grabbed my hand and dragged me with him. I risked a last look over my shoulder at the hungry orange flames as they reached for the ceiling. *Burn, motherfucker, burn...*

We tore back along the darkened hallway and out that courtyard door as shouts came from the guards. There was no stopping now, not until this was done.

The *crack* of shattering glass came behind us as we scurried through the cut fence.

By the time the guards rushed through the house, it was far too late.

Those hungry flames had consumed the room and filled the night with a glorious glow. I stumbled backwards, pulled by Colt. We raced for the car, threw the empty gas can inside, and clambered in.

The engine started with a roar. The wheels spun and kicked up pebbles as we lurched back onto the road and tore away. I couldn't catch my breath as I leaned over and grabbed my knees. Colt reached around and slid his hand along my arm.

I clung to him as Carven turned the headlights on and we raced through the night.

But that panicked fear was still there.

The kind of fear that was choking as thoughts of London pushed in.

I prayed this wasn't for nothing.

And that we weren't too late...

Please, London, hold on.

FORTY-THREE

London

AMBER SWIRLED, THE EDGES TRANSLUCENT AGAINST THE
sides of the glass. There was no ice in my drink. Not because I
didn't like the cold, but because I didn't want the dilution...not
tonight. No, right now I needed the alcohol as strong as I could
get it.

I licked my lips, then upended the glass down my throat to
chase the last remaining drop with my tongue, and stared at the
sparkling city lights down below. There was a soft sigh behind
me, followed by movement as Ophelia rose from the sofa in her
expensive penthouse apartment in the middle of the city. I
fought a wince, then turned for the half-empty bottle.

I planned on getting wasted tonight.

So fucking wasted I wouldn't feel a thing.

And hopefully tomorrow I won't remember this night.

"You didn't eat the meal I had prepared." She moved closer and
I tried not to notice her in the windows' reflection. But it was
like trying not to watch a viper slithering closer. "Yet you seem
to have a thirst," she finished.

She stopped at my side and reached to grab my jaw. Her nails dug cruelly deep as she forced my gaze to hers. "You think I don't see you're different?" She searched my stare. "How you're so...*cold.*"

I tore away from her hold, pushing my rage as far down as I could. "You blackmail me, forced me here. What the fuck did you expect, *flowers?*"

Her nostrils flared.

Her blood red lips clamped tight.

Her long black silk dress shifted as she slowly placed her hands on her hips. I didn't need to look to know she was bare underneath. Ophelia had orchestrated this moment down to the second. There was nothing she didn't plan, including the waiting bed in the middle of the open-plan apartment.

"*This* is what we are, London," she urged. "This is what we've *always been.* This is what we've always been, I do for you and... you do me."

My stomach clenched. I looked away, to the sparkling lights far below.

"Yin and yang." She dragged those red painted nails along my arm. "One person helping another, or have you forgotten your alliances now that you have that fresh young pussy under your roof?"

Anger flared, making me turn to her. "Don't speak like that about her."

Ophelia grew still, those hateful fucking eyes glinting. But underneath, she was cold, and growing colder by the second. "Still, you're here," she murmured. "And we have an agreement, don't we, London?"

The fucking Scotch wasn't strong enough, not anywhere near. Not for this.

I reached up and yanked my tie loose with one hand.

Get this over with. Get this fucking done...and I can get out of here. I can get back to...

Vivienne...

I swallowed hard to drive that bitter tang back down my throat and placed the glass on the edge of the dining table. Ophelia watched me greedily, then reached over her shoulder and tugged the tie of her dress free, to let it fall around her feet in one movement.

"You're going to fuck me, aren't you, London?" Her predatory stare drifted down my body. "You're going to unleash all that anger on my body and I'm going to enjoy every second of it."

I stepped closer to the table, grabbed the bottle, and poured before I lifted the glass to my lips. She flinched at the act. But I wasn't here to stroke her vile fucking ego. I was here to do my duty. It was that duty I focused on as I swallowed the Scotch and placed the glass back down on the table.

"You want me to fuck you." I grabbed her and spun her around, forcing her forward until she had no choice but to brace her hands on the table. "I'll fuck you...*my way.*"

She shoved backwards, trying to turn back around. "*No.* I want—"

I grabbed her arm and yanked her hard against me. Pain flared in her eyes. But I was beyond caring now, beyond controlling that savage side of my nature. "You don't get to fucking *want* anything when it comes to me, *get it?*"

I shoved her away as the hate gathered inside me like a vengeful storm.

I could kill her.

It'd be better than...*this.*

But her death would only bring me more problems, and right now, I had enough on my plate. I was still dealing with the last fucking bloodbath. I needed a way out of this. A way I could control. I drew in a hard breath, leashing that rage...until she lashed out.

Slap!

My head snapped to the side.

She was on me in an instant, clawing the back of my neck to pull me down. Those cold, flat lips pressed against mine before she forced her tongue into my mouth. I unleashed a hiss and shoved her *hard.*

She stumbled backwards, then her ankle buckled and she fell and hit the floor with a *thud.*

Oh shit...

She pushed her hand against the floor, driving her torso upwards, then lay there. There was a savage glare in her eyes when she looked up at me, an unhinged look of wrath. I'd pushed her too hard and driven a wedge between her desire and my need to control her.

"Is this what you do with your *whore?*" she snarled as she pushed up from the floor and stumbled for a second, until she stepped closer. "You like to manhandle her? Do you take her to the basement, London?"

I froze as my blood ran cold. "How do you know about that?"

She gave a blood-chilling smile. "I know about everything, London." Somewhere in the apartment, her phone started to ring. "I know about the contract, as well. The contract where the ink has been dried for a very... *very long time.* But you won't like it...no, you won't like it at all."

What the fuck? I glanced toward that insistent ring, but inside, I was reeling. I clenched my jaw, desperate to force her to tell what she knew. I needed that fucking contract. Vivienne's life depended on it. Hale had said it was signed. He wouldn't *dare* betray me.

"So, this is how this is going to play out. You will fuck me. You'll fuck me for as long as I tell you to and you'll *keep* fucking me whenever I demand it, do you understand?" She jerked her glare away as her phone rang and rang *and rang.*

With a snarl of frustration, she strode toward her phone and snatched it from the counter. "I thought I said I wasn't to be disturbed?" she snapped, then froze. Her brow furrowed before her eyes widened. "What the fuck did you say?"

I licked my lips as I watched fear give way to rage. "And my art? *What the fuck do you mean, you don't know the extent? WHAT THE FUCK DO I PAY YOU FOR?*"

Her scream resounded through the apartment. Before my eyes, she transformed.

No longer desperate for me...

In fact, she didn't look at me at all.

Instead, she hurried toward the bed and shifted her phone to her other ear while she pulled on panties and a bra. "Do not do a thing until I get there. I'll call Howie now. You do nothing, do you hear me?"

He must've heard her.

Because she hung up the call and tossed the phone onto the bed while she hurriedly finished dressing.

"I take it our dinner is canceled?" I sneered.

"I can see you're heartbroken," she snapped, then cast a cutting glare my way. "Don't make the mistake of thinking this is over, London, because I can assure you it's not."

She yanked up the zipper of her dress and snatched her phone from the bed before she hurried to grab her long coat and bag near the door. "I'll be in touch, and you have a lot to make up for."

But I scowled, as an eerie feeling crawled along my spine. The call and me being here wasn't a coincidence, it couldn't be. "I'm sure," I answered.

In a heartbeat she was gone, leaving the *slam* of the door behind.

I stood there in silence for a second, until it hit me.

She was gone...

She was gone.

I closed my eyes and rocked backwards, before I froze.

What the fuck had they done?

I wrenched open my eyes. I knew it was bad. It had to be.

That meant they were in trouble.

I drained my glass, placed it on the table, and headed for the door, not even bothering to pull on my jacket. I couldn't feel a damn thing anyway, nothing but the panic inside. Cold cut through my cotton shirt, sobering me fast. I headed for the elevator and made my way downstairs, to the parking lot.

I was pulling out in the Mercedes before I knew it, my thoughts fixed on that call and the growing fear for those I loved. I needed to get home...*I needed to get home.* "What the hell did you do?"

FORTY-FOUR

Vivienne

My teeth clacked, sending shockwaves through my skull. Carven tore his gaze from the traffic and his wide blue eyes found mine. "We're almost there, wildcat," he soothed. "Hold on."

Heat blasted from the vent in the back seat, drying my eyes. But that clacking of my teeth was all I could hear. *Clack... clack...clack.*

Sounding just like gunshots.

In the mall.

And the store...

And the cracking glass in that dressing room.

I wrapped my arms tighter around my middle as I stared at Carven's stark white hair, still wet from the rushed shower at the compound. We'd disposed of the gasoline can there and the smoke-stained clothes, so I had to change back into the V-cut top I'd worn at the beginning of the night.

Before it had all gone to hell.

Red and blue lights still flashed inside my head. I couldn't shake the image, no matter how hard I tried.

Red and blue from the fire trucks we'd passed as we raced from the mansion. But they were way too late. I closed my eyes. They were *way too late*. I clenched my jaw, trying to stop the violent clacking sound.

Carven said I was coming down from the high.

Of rage.

And adrenaline.

But still, in the dark depths of my mind, all I could see was that drawing.

That *son* with big blue eyes, his hands raised over his head in an act of submission.

Submission that bitch caused.

I opened my eyes to glance at Colt, silent in the front seat. Not just any son...*mine*.

The car turned hard and the headlights splashed against familiar houses. We barely slowed as we hit the driveway, the gate still open. I jolted as the seatbelt snapped tight as Carven braked hard, then slowed as the garage door rose. I searched the grounds, but found no one else. There were no guards to protect the house tonight *and no witnesses*.

I jolted forward as the Explorer slammed to a stop and the doors were thrown open. Colt slowly climbed out, his movements strange and mechanical. He hadn't said a word since we'd run from that house and this was more than someone deep in his own thoughts. This was someone in pain.

My fingers trembled as I yanked the door handle and climbed out.

"Colt," I called. But he had already reached the entrance to the house.

The garage door closed with a rumble. I started after him and hoped Carven would follow quickly. Guild wasn't anywhere to be seen and for that I was thankful. I caught sight of my reflection in the kitchen window. I didn't recognize myself with that pale, washed-out complexion, and the wide, unblinking eyes.

I followed Colt up the stairs, with Carven right behind me.

"You need to shower," Carven muttered. "Scrub everything well, especially your hair."

I nodded as my teeth continued to chatter. But I couldn't take my eyes off the curled shoulders of the son in front of me. "C-Colt," I called out again as he stepped onto the third-floor landing. "P-please *stop...*"

He halted just outside my door. But Carven didn't, just strode past to throw open my bedroom door before he looked at his brother. There was panic in his gaze, real panic. He licked his lips, glanced my way, and turned back. "Brother, you might need to help her."

I knew what he was doing.

He was using me.

And I wanted to be used.

"I feel l-like I'm coming apart," I whispered. "I can't stop shaking."

Colt slowly turned his head toward me. I could see, even in the deep ocean-blue, that he saw me. He was fighting, fighting to surface through his memories and pain.

"Colt," I whispered. "I need you."

Anguish filled his gaze.

I stepped closer until I grasped his hand and pressed it against my breast. "I need you so much."

There was a flicker, a deeper draw of breath. "I need to feel something more than this...*panic*."

Carven unleashed a low moan and looked away. "I told you before, brother, this is what a good man does. You take care of your woman. You give her what she needs."

I held Colt's stare. "So, take care of me."

The squeal of tires ripped through the night and drew our attention. I turned my head with the sons as that shrill sound ended and the faint *thud* of a car door followed.

Seconds.

That's all it took before the front door crashed open, then slammed shut with a *boom!*

I couldn't move, frozen by the resounding thuds on the stairs as they came closer. Then he was there, all unforgiving darkness as he strode toward me. His face was a mask of barely controlled rage. He turned that unmerciful glare to the sons, first to Carven, then to Colt, before he turned back to me.

He was angry...

No, he was savage.

All because of what we'd done.

"N-no one will k-know," I tried to reassure him as I dropped Colt's hand and stepped in front of them, protecting them as I shook my head. "London...*no one will ever know it was us.*"

He unleashed a growl and closed the distance to grab me around the waist and lift me.

"You smell like smoke." He searched my eyes as I wrapped my legs around his waist, then carried me into the bedroom.

Carven and Colt followed, but hung back as he lowered my feet to the floor in front of the bed and continued. "And fear and pain."

I looked up at him as he loomed over me. Those dangerous eyes stole my thoughts. Still, I whispered, "We had to do it."

He reached up, cupped my jaw, searched my face, and scowled. "You think I'm angry about that?" He shifted his stare to mine. "You could've been hurt. They attacked you a that goddamn mall. They tried to take you. Fuck, when Guild called I thought my entire world was gone. I thought *you* were gone."

"But I'm not," I soothed.

He tugged the bottom of my top. "Arms, Vivienne. Let me look at you. Let me see what they did to you."

I did as he commanded and lifted my arms over my head, just like I always did as he commanded.

Lie on the table.

Spread your legs...that's a good girl.

My breath hitched with the rush of fabric across my face. The stench of smoke filled my nose, then it was gone.

"My little arsonist." He dropped my top and reached around to unhook my bra. "You saved me tonight, *all of you saved me tonight.*" He met my stare. "I don't want you to do that ever again." He gently grasped my jaw as his eyes bored into mine. "Do you understand me?"

I sucked in hard breaths as pain flared deep.

"You could've been cornered," he murmured. "You could've been killed."

"We'd never let that happen," Carven protested.

London looked at him. "Do you think I'd risk that? You think I'd risk any of you?" He flanked my side, stopping at my back. "You're *my* fucking family. You're...you're all I have."

Desperation surged with the words.

All I have.

I'd never had this...this connection, this savage need to belong. But it raged inside me now, churning and howling like a beast. My gaze was fixed on Colt's as London worked the button of my pants, then dragged my zipper down.

I needed him. I needed him so fucking much. My breath caught as he reached up, grasped my jaw, and turned my mouth to his. The kiss was demanding and strong. I gave into the force and melted into that demanding hunger.

My slacks dropped to my feet.

London broke the kiss and left my lips throbbing as he turned to Colt.

The son's gaze was riveted on the way London touched me and he blushed bright red as London skimmed my belly and cupped my breasts. My nipples reacted instantly, tightening as he thumbed the sensitive flesh.

"The thought of having to do that with *her* tonight sickened me," London murmured against my ear. "I don't want to do that ever again." He lowered his hand, his fingers delving under the elastic of my panties. "I want this...*only this.*"

I shuddered as he found my clit.

"No more Order. No more training." He reached lower and slid his finger inside. "It's only us from this moment on. Do you understand me?"

I shuddered as his deft fingers stroked me while I stared into Colt's eyes. "Yes."

But my silent protector glanced at his brother, then murmured. "I made her...bleed."

London let out a tortured moan. "You gave yourself to us," he growled, his breath hot against my ear as he bent and pushed my legs wider before he reached back down and slid two fingers inside. "Is that what you did, Vivienne?'

"Y-yes."

"Yes, what?"

"Yes, Daddy," I obeyed.

London lifted his gaze and found Colt's stare fixed on the movement of his fingers. "That's my good pet." Slick sounds came from my body as he thrust his fingers deep inside, stoking that ache. "Fuck, I love fingering your cunt, look how wet you are for me. Always fucking needy, aren't you, pet? *Always a needy, fucking girl.*"

His breaths were heavy, and slow thrusts from behind drove his hard cock against my ass. One hand grasped my throat while he drove two fingers deep inside me. I released a moan as I thrust against his fingers. "You needy, pet?"

I trembled as London ran his fingers down each side of my clit to massage my orgasm closer. I reached up and grasped the back of London's neck. "Uh huh."

"Words, Vivienne."

"Yes," I moaned, panting. My senses were overwhelmed, then they crashed from the high, only to be swept away once more. "Yes, I'm fucking needy. Is that what you want to hear? Yes, *I'm fucking needy.* I want to fuck...I want to be fucked. I want..."

"Say it." London dropped his head to growl against my ear. "Say what you want."

"I want to be owned."

His deep chuckle sent shivers along my spine. "That's my good girl. It feels good to say it, doesn't it? *Say it again.*"

"I. Want. To. Be. Owned."

"That's a good girl," he snarled, his movements faster and more desperate, driven home with hard gasps in my ear.

"I'll go," Colt murmured, his voice raspy as he tore his gaze from the sight and turned.

"No," London breathed against my neck. "Don't."

He pulled his hand out of my panties, then slowly dragged them down and knelt as they fell to the floor. "She wants you and you want her. I want you to want her." He rose behind me, unbuckling his belt as he stood, and kicked off his shoes. "I want you both to want her. This can be just for us. *She can be just for us.* We can take turns, we'll share her."

Colt turned back to us, those dark blue eyes filled with so much hope. London unbuttoned his shirt, staring at the son. "Let her touch you...let her love you." His shirt dropped to the floor beside me.

He reached up, gently grasped my jaw, and turned my gaze to his. "Is that what you want, pet? You want to be owned by us?"

His consuming stare raged with hunger. He searched my stare, his breaths heavy. I'd never seen him so raw, so...*primal.* So real. "Yes," I answered. "Yes, I want that."

London shifted his gaze to Colt. "You have your request, Colt. Stay, or go, but know this stays within our family. There is no sharing her, not with anyone else. Do you understand?"

Colt scowled as though the thought of sharing had never crossed his mind...until now.

Then he looked from London to me and slowly licked his lips.

My pulse kicked as Colt took a step, then another, and stopped in front of me. London released my jaw so I could look up at the son. Still, London didn't stop as he dragged his hand down to cup my breast.

I stood suspended in desire, craving Colt's touch, even as London's fingers grazed my nipple. The son lowered his gaze to watch as London touched, then kissed the side of my neck.

"Make up your mind," he urged behind me. "I'm about to fuck her, either way."

Desire surged inside me at his words.

Colt didn't speak...he didn't need to. My silent protector was all about action as he grasped his shirt and dragged it over his head in one fluid motion. Those callused fingers were so gentle as he brushed my cheek. So tender, so controlled. I turned and kissed his thumb as London reached back down and slid his fingers through my slick and inside me again.

I shuddered and moaned at the breach of my defense.

Slowly, Colt leaned down and kissed me.

I closed my eyes at the brush of his lips.

Warmth against my neck.

Fingers slipping deep inside.

I slid my hands over Colt's hard chest, and felt his racing pulse. "I want this," I whispered against his mouth. "I want you, *all of you.*"

Carven hadn't moved. I knew he wouldn't, but still, he didn't leave. No, he stood against the wall and watched.

Oh *God.*

Shudders tore through me at a stroke of my clit. I dropped my hands to the button of Colt's pants. "I need you." I stared into Colt's eyes. "Please, Colt, I need you."

"Listen to her, begging." London reached around, grasped the inside of my thigh, and parted my legs. "I fucking love it when she does that. Beg, pet. Beg him to fuck you," he growled as he reached up to grasp my jaw once more. "Beg him to slide his cock in your mouth."

"I...I need," I started, searching that bottomless stare.

"Please, pet," London reprimanded as he searched my eyes. "Always start with please."

My cheeks burned red, but I was helpless to do anything other than obey him. "*Please,*" I whimpered. "Please."

"That's a good girl." London turned my face to Colt's. "Now beg."

"*Please,*" I gasped to Colt as London slipped his fingers out. One sudden surge, and he drove his cock inside. My breath caught with shock. My pussy stretched as I whimpered. "*Oh fuck...oh fuck. Please, Colt! Plleaassseee.*"

"That's the way," London moaned. "What daddy wants, daddy gets."

My pussy stretched a bit further with the invasion. He was big... so fucking big. I opened my legs wider, desperate for more.

"Look down," he grunted as he pulled out, only to thrust right back in. "So fucking *tight. Jesus Christ, you're so tight.*"

My body trembled, my knees shuddered and shook. London placed his hand on the middle of my back and urged me to bend over. Colt had already opened the button of his pants and pushed his zipper low. There was just this now, just *us*. I reached out and grasped Colt's thigh as London drove into me from behind and jolted me forward with a guttural growl.

I opened my mouth, desperate for Colt's cock. Warmth slid along my tongue as I closed my eyes. He was so gentle, so fucking gentle, with feather-light brushes as he ran his fingers through my hair while London unleashed all that desperate need on my pussy.

Brutal.

Soft.

My core clenched as I worked that slick head along my tongue. Colt shuddered and gently grasped my jaw as he drove deeper into my mouth.

"That's the way, son," London urged. "Fuck that pretty mouth of hers."

I couldn't stop the impacts...or that wave as it built inside me.

Colt released a groan and cut off my air as he thrust his cock into my mouth all the way to the base. My body clenched and pulsed around London as Colt drove harder and faster, turning that big, sweet male into someone demanding...and savage. A moan tore free. *Oh, God...oh, God...*I clamped tighter as my body spilled over and sparks ignited.

"Look. Up. At. Him," London growled.

I opened my eyes as my climax peaked. Colt's deep blue eyes were riveted to mine. I opened my mouth wider as London gave one last hard grunt. My body trembled as he gripped my hips and kept himself buried deep as he came inside me.

Hard. Breaths. Short. Sharp. Whimpers. They were all I had.

Colt's brow creased and his eyelids fluttered closed as he gripped my jaw, not once hurting me, and drove his cock in deep to flood the back of my throat with warmth. I swallowed, again... and again, then gripped the base of his cock and licked him clean.

"That's the way, pet," London praised as he slid from my pussy. "Get it all...don't waste a single drop."

I swallowed and swallowed, and caught the last drop with my tongue as Colt released my jaw. He sucked in deep breaths, his gaze fixed on mine as I straightened.

"You want her, you fuck her," London urged, as he glanced from Colt to Carven. "But anything rougher needs to be discussed with all of us, understand?"

Surprise surged in me as Carven gave a slow nod.

Did that mean...he was thinking about it?

He watched me, then his gaze went to my thighs.

"Now, I have...things to do." London bent down and grasped his clothes. "I take it you can entertain yourselves...this time without fire?"

Carven jerked a glare his way, but then the corners of his lips twitched as London stepped around, gripped the back of my neck, and gently kissed me. "Vivienne," he murmured as he searched my eyes. "You know where to find me."

Then he lowered his hand...and left the room.

Leaving me behind with my knees shaking and the tang of smoke and come in my mouth.

"I guess it's time for that shower," Carven muttered as he gave a slow nod. "Wildcat." Then he followed London out.

"Do you want me to stay?" Colt asked.

I nodded. "I...don't want to be alone."

With a ghost of a smile, he headed for the bathroom, then stopped and held out his hand. That aching need to belong blazed inside me once more. I knew that this wasn't normal...but then, what love was?

The hiss of the water sounded as Colt hit the faucets and adjusted the temperature, then he turned to me as he shed the rest of his clothes. I melted into his arms and lowered my forehead to his chest.

"Holy fuck," I whispered as he ran those big hands down my back, and in a rush, it all came to the surface.

Losing them.

Losing me.

Finding us...

The real us.

The one I'd been craving my entire life and had found...*finally.*

And as the hot water beat down on my shoulders and his arms closed around me, I dropped my walls and cried.

FORTY-FIVE

London
___

I SLOWED OUTSIDE HER BEDROOM TO LISTEN FOR A SECOND before I headed for the stairs. I'd give anything to be able to stay with her, to find every goddamn scrape and fucking bruise those bastards had inflicted. I wanted to be the kind of man who kissed those wounds better and whispered promises to keep her safe.

But I wasn't that man. I wasn't *anywhere* near that kind of man.

I was a man of vengeance.

A man of wrath.

I didn't speak much because violence spoke for me...and that never whispered...it only screamed, and begged, and pleaded. No amount of pleading would help them now, *whoever the fuck they were.*

I searched my pockets, pulled my phone out, and typed out a message. *Where are you at with the footage?* And hit send.

From the moment Guild called, I'd been in overdrive. I wanted those bastards identified...and tracked back to the dead man who'd gone after her. Because if he wasn't a dead man already, he soon would be.

The bedroom door opened behind me.

"Meet me downstairs," I murmured without turning around.

"London, listen—" Carven started.

I cut him a glare. He *fucking knew better*. Carven's blue eyes narrowed before he gave a slow nod. I left him and made my way down to my room naked. I wanted a blow-by-fucking-blow account of everything that had happened tonight. The mere fact they were alive and safe with me left me little solace. I wanted fucking blood...

My bare feet thudded softly on the stairs. My mind was a damn mess as it bounced between conversations and violence. *If only they'd known how close he was.* Benjamin Rossi's words resounded as I stepped into my bedroom.

Beep.

If only they'd known...

I grabbed my phone as I tossed my clothes on the foot of the bed and opened the messages.

> Guild: The footage is problematic but I'm working on it, and the men are now at the house. I'm on my way there now.

I swallowed the flare of anger. Carven knew better than to pull the goddamn detail away. But the son didn't trust lightly, especially where I was concerned.

I replied:

> Send it as soon as you can. I'll be awake.

I cast my phone onto the bed and strode for the shower. The hiss of the water filled the bathroom as my mind wandered. None of this was fucking coincidental. The fact it happened so soon after my call to Benjamin Rossi wasn't coincidental. It couldn't be. But would the Stidda leader come after Vivienne? I didn't think so.

My gut told me that wasn't his...*style*.

If not the Mafia, then who the fuck was it?

I stepped into the heat, wincing until the fine needles of water numbed my skin. *If only they'd known...if only.* I grabbed the soap and lathered. Still, I couldn't shake his damn words, or the fucking lies Ophelia had sprouted.

I braced my hand against the wall. *Fucking think, figure it the fuck out.* I needed to stay a step ahead of all of them. The lies. The fucking diversions.

I know about the contract as well. That bitch's voice echoed. *The contract where the ink has been dried for a very long time. But you won't like it...no, you won't like it at all.*

But Hale said he'd only just signed the contract, so why the lies? What advantage could that give them?

None.

Signed now or earlier, it didn't matter. I didn't care either way. I opened my eyes and dropped my hand from the wall. As long as Vivienne was mine. I turned the water off and stepped out, grabbing a towel.

My thoughts turned to Rossi's words about Ryth. *Maybe if she'd searched the house instead of her brothers...*

I found my own reflection. *Searched the house...had he meant Killlion's house?*

Rossi's voice kept coming. *If only they'd known how close he was...*

The house...

I draped the towel around my shoulders as I strode into the bedroom and pulled on boxers and a pair of gray sweatpants before I padded barefoot into the monitor room. The monitor flicked on. I grabbed the chair from the middle of the room and sat as I pulled up the details.

I'd watched the footage a thousand times, reliving the moments when Killion's home had been invaded by Ryth and her brothers. There wasn't a damn thing I'd missed...but still.

My senses sharpened, aware of movement as the door quietly opened and Carven stepped in. The son moved like a damn ghost, one just as lethal as he was silent.

"I fucked up," he started. It was the closest thing he'd come to an apology.

But I wasn't there to make him feel better or soothe his damn nerves.

I was there to keep him alive, to keep him safe. *To keep all of them safe.*

He stopped behind me as I ran the footage again, rewinding from when Killion met his gruesome death. Tobias moved backwards in slow motion. Blood splatter disappeared as the stepbrother lowered his gun, then looked down at Ryth. She straddled the piece of shit and drew the knife back out of Killion's thigh.

The man was dead, even without the bullet to the brain, destined to bleed out in minutes from a severed femoral artery. But Tobias had killed him instead, protecting her. Robbing her, more like it. Still, the piece of shit had it coming after what he'd done.

I could still hear her screams from that recording, still hear her begging for her fucking stepbrothers to save her. I'd heard screams like that far too often.

"What are you looking for?"

"I don't know," I murmured as I fast-forwarded past the aftermath to when they'd searched the house. "But something."

Maybe if she'd searched the house instead of her brothers.

I followed her brothers as they made their way through the darkened rooms. Caleb moved deeper through the house and stopped in the study, where he'd found the stack of money intended for me, or so Killion had thought. I was blackmailing the bastard, but it wasn't his money I wanted, it was his damn life.

I'd given Ryth and her brothers vengeance, and they'd given me their allegiance and moved me one step closer to King. Because that's what this came down to—

"What's that?" Carven muttered. I jerked my gaze up as he leaned closer to the screen, scowling. "Rewind it."

I wound it back.

"There," he motioned. "There's a light."

"Impossible." I leaned closer. I'd watched this footage more times than I could count. I knew the moment Caleb shoved the money in the bag and left. So there was no way—

A glint shone in the darkness of the study, and caught my focus. It was so damn fast, one blink and you'd miss it.

"What do you think that is?" Carven asked.

I rewound and watched it again as Rossi's fucking words repeated in my head. *If only they'd known how close he was.*

How close he was...

How close he...

"King," I whispered as a chill raced along my spine. "It has to be."

I rewound the footage, caught that glint, and slowed the replay down.

"That's a cell phone," Carven added. "If it was King, then he was *right there.*"

"And if he used his phone, then maybe..." I grabbed mine, thumbed through my contacts, and pressed a number.

Harper's voice was a slur. "You're really riding my ass with this, aren't you?"

"I need something else. You still have access to the IP addresses from that night?"

"Yeah," his voice sharpened.

"And you accounted for all those you found?"

"All but one. It's no longer active."

My pulse sped. "But it was active prior to that night?"

"For about a week. A burner SIM, no doubt."

"Can you track that IP, send me the locations of the pings?"

"Yeah, now?"

"Now."

There was a rustle of bedding and a groan. "Okay, give me five."

"I owe you," I muttered, my mind racing.

"London. You don't owe me shit. But thanks for the sentiment. Watch your inbox," he answered, and hung up the call.

Five minutes. I could almost time it. *As discussed*...the message landed in my inbox. Carven crowded me as I opened up the text document. There it was...the IP address. My pulse sped. *King's IP*. It was the closest we had come to finding him.

Now we had...

"Punch in the locations."

I entered the GPS coordinates one by one. There weren't that many to go through, not many at all.

"Look, that one's repeated. There and there and there," Carven pointed.

I narrowed in on the location on the map, then switched to satellite view.

"We have him," the son whispered. "We fucking *have* him."

"Don't get carried away," I reminded, but damn, it was hard not to get swept away with excitement.

The coordinates tracked it down to a place downtown. Trees shrouded the view, but still I caught the edge of a building tucked away before I rose. "I'll get dressed."

He met my gaze, excitement in his eyes. "I'm coming with you."

I hurried back to the bedroom, pulled on black cargos and a black long-sleeved shirt, and zipped up my combat boots. Déjà vu hit me hard as I punched in the coordinates. In an instant, I was back there in that other life, where I'd killed people for money. Only this time, I didn't want to kill him.

I wanted to use him.

To force him to destroy The Order and everyone in it.

Now that I had his daughters, he'd have no choice but to do what I wanted. I controlled King and I controlled the game. The thought both exhilarated and filled me with fear. I glanced at the movement outside my bedroom door.

But there wasn't one set of boots...there were two.

I grabbed my bag and headed out, to find both sons waiting for me on the landing. I scowled and glanced at Colt. "I figured you'd stay with her."

"She's asleep," Carven answered for him like it was the most natural thing in the world. Which it was, he'd been answering for his brother almost his entire life.

I didn't like leaving her...but every second we wasted was one second too long, and we'd waited far too long as it was. I grabbed my phone and punched a quick message to Guild: *We're out. Vivienne is asleep. We'll be back as soon as we can.*

Then I gave them a nod before we made our way downstairs and piled into the Explorer, with Carven behind the wheel. *If only they'd known how close he was.* If it was King, then he'd been watching them the entire time. How the fuck had he known?

I glanced at the clock in the dashboard...it was later than I'd thought, nearly the early hours of the morning. What if King was there when we got there? Would he put up a fight? "I don't need to remind you how important it is to take him alive?"

Carven cut me a glare. "No, you don't."

I gave a nod, then turned my thoughts back to the capture. He'd fight. I know he'd fight. He might even hurt us. "I want you to hang back when we get there. I go in first, got it?"

I didn't wait for them to answer. They'd expect it anyway, thinking I wanted the first sighting for myself, the hunter spotting his target. But it was more to do with the man being unpredictable...and cunning as hell.

We turned once more. I glanced at the coordinates and the tiny dot heading toward it.

This was it...

This...was...it.

I drew my gun and held it close to my chest as my other hand went to the door handle. Towering trees rose up ahead and shrouded the apartment complex. One that was deemed to be under construction, only there was no fence or barrier I could see. Carven braked, pulling up hard but quiet.

I was out of the four-wheel drive before I knew it as I fell back into that cold, careful hunger, my boots soundless on the ground. The sons were close behind, two, three steps. It was all I needed as I scanned the area, found external stairs, and motioned forward.

Gravel crunched under my steps as I rushed upward.

If only they'd known how close he was.

My breaths were heavy as I climbed, my focus on the debris at my feet.

I flicked on a flashlight, then back off. There was a slight track... worn, leading upwards.

I climbed, headed to the next floor...the track was still there. I climbed once more, all the way to the third floor, where it ended. I glanced behind me to my sons and motioned silently forward. Carven gave a nod, the black Glock pressed against his chest.

I moved along the landing of the third floor as I searched for a way in, and caught sight of a blinking red light.

There.

My heart thundered as I grabbed my bag and pulled out the soft explosive. The sons hung back as I worked fast to set the charge and move backwards, turned, then pressed the icon on my phone.

Bang!

The charge exploded and we rushed in. Laser beams cut diagonally low across the floor. I swung my gaze. I'd expected nothing less. I dragged out the second charge as I scanned the hallway and stopped at the black steel door.

Fuck.

I didn't think the charge would be strong enough, but I couldn't risk it any louder. Panic rose as I pressed the charge against the lock, the sons moving back, guns raised, their focus fixed on that door. Hungry, so fucking hungry. I moved back, then pressed the icon.

BANG!

The sound was deafening in the narrow space, but he already knew we were coming. For King, it was far too late. I rushed forward, bore down on the handle, and drove my shoulder against the door...then stumbled inward as it gave way.

Into the gloom...

Of the dull light coming from a bank of monitors on the wall. Only one was switched on...my face filled the screen. I scanned the apartment, searching for movement, and tried to take it all in. The darkness, the surveillance information. Walls of information. It took up most of the apartment, leaving a bed and a sleek, expensive kitchen to take up the rest of the space, with what must be a bathroom off to the side.

This wasn't an apartment. This was a lair, one filled with the kind of sophisticated equipment even I couldn't get my hands on.

"Jesus," Carven muttered. "What the fuck."

"What the fuck, indeed," I murmured as I stepped closer to the wall of monitors.

The apartment was empty. The energy was stale. But I was drawn to the bank of monitors.

Click.

The sound came from behind me. I glanced over my shoulder and scowled as Carven hit another switch. In an instant, the wall became a digital instrument filled with names, details, locations. Five faces ran down the side, details digitally revolved.

"Jesus motherfucking Christ," Carven whispered, staring.

Haelstrom Hale.

Killion.

Ophelia.

Macoy Daniels.

Me...me?

I stared at my name, date of birth, social security information, list of addresses. I gave a chuff, then froze, even my fucking training was there. *Jesus*...then, underneath that, *Threat Level High.*

Threat level high? My pulse raced at the words as Carven touched the screen. *He had no idea.* In an instant it changed, bringing up Ophelia's face to fill the screen. More information loaded and all her filthy fucking secrets from the long list of addresses to the company she kept. *Daniels*...his name in red.

In red.

I moved closer to the screen. "Bring up Daniels."

"London, this shit is insane," Carven muttered as he pressed on fucking *everything*.

"Daniels," I urged as I stepped closer.

Chills raced along my spine as Carven hit Daniels' name and that ugly, smug, fucking face filled the screen. A warning flashed...drawing my gaze. *Contract initiated.*

Contract initiated? There was a paperclip icon next to it.

I know about the contract, as well. Ophelia's fucking voice crept in. *The contract where the ink has been dried for a very long time. But you won't like it...no, you won't like it at all.*

I swallowed hard, forgetting where I stood, forgetting everything else. "Pull up that link."

Carven tapped the wall, bringing up the attachment, and in a heartbeat, a page opened.

Permanent right to possess/use:

I scanned the document and dropped to the names listed...

The property: Vivienne Evans.

Owned by Macoy Daniels.

Owned by Macoy Daniels? Owned...by Macoy Daniels. The apartment spun, the neon text on the screen blurred.

"London..." Colt moaned, his gaze fixed on the details, before he turned that terrified stare to mine.

The contract where the ink has been dried for a very long time. But you won't like it...no, you won't like it at all.

I jerked my gaze to the date...the date that was weeks old on the same day I took her from The Order. Hale's signature was next to Macoy's.

He'd sold her...

Even after he took my fucking money and looked me in the eye, promised me she was mine.

The *sonofafucking BITCH sold her.*

"No...no...no...no...no..." Colt forced the words through clenched teeth. His jaw just as tight as his fists until the son whispered, *"I'm going to kill him."* He turned away from the display and strode to the door. *"I'm going to FUCKING kill him."*

Lights flashed on the screen....

I fixed on that as cold rage ripped through me, plunging all the way into the pit of my stomach. It had all been him, the cars following me, the attack on the mall tonight. The moment Carven called Guild and told him about what they did, it all changed.

"London," Carven called as he jerked his gaze to mine. There was terror there...real fucking terror...from both of them.

On that display a red light blinked, moving through GPS tracked streets. *Daniels* the tracker flashed.

He wasn't just being monitored...he was moving.

"That's our street," Carven whispered as he stumbled backwards and spun. *"London, that's our fucking street!"*

Their wide, panic-stricken eyes were all I saw as it hit me.

He was coming for her...

HE WAS COMING FOR HER...

I whirled and lunged for the doorway as panic drove needles through my veins and I roared, *"NO!"*

FORTY-SIX

Vivienne

_____

CRACK.

I moaned, then rolled over in bed.

Crack!

The faint, annoying sound invaded.

CRACK!

My pulse thundered as I opened my eyes. The frantic thrumming in my ears turned my breaths shallow. I stared around my dark bedroom, hating how the memories pushed in. Vivid, brutal memories. The mall...the attack...Colt. I winced as my head throbbed. I could still feel the grip on my hair, still feel the terror as they'd dragged me down that stairwell. But I was here...I was safe. I was with...

Them.

I was with them.

My pussy clenched, and I felt that delicious ache. I closed my eyes and forced the fear aside. I wasn't there now. I was here, safe in my bed and my home.

Jesus, I can't believe that happened between us.

London.

Colt.

Carven watching.

I licked my lips. My body warmed at the memory, stole me away from the fear, and turned it instead to desire. *"Oh fuck,"* I whispered and reached under the comforter to cup my breast.

Crack!

The sound invaded again. I snapped open my eyes and shoved upwards. That wasn't a dream. No, that was *real*.

"THE FUCK!" a roar came from downstairs.

I moved fast, scrambled out of the bed, and raced for the door. A pang tore across my chest and clenched my throat as fear pushed in, but I shoved that aside. London, Colt, and Carven were out there...

I yanked open the bedroom door to the sound of raised voices. A quick glance to the darkened hallway, and I stepped out onto the landing.

"Colt?" I called.

Boom! The impact rocked through the house. I gripped the banister and froze as the front door shuddered and shook.

"London?" Guild's voice roared out. *"You need to get here!"*

He's not here?

HE'S NOT HERE?

Boom!

I cried out with the sound, panic taking me over once more. But I forced myself to move and hurried down the stairs as the front door shook. Guild had his gun aimed at the door as a man's shrill, pain-filled scream came from outside. I knew instantly who they were from. They were the men assigned to protect us, the men London had patrolling the grounds. The men now being slaughtered one by one.

"I can't hold them back!" Guild roared as he turned around until his panicked gaze found mine.

I knew instantly...

The men from the mall had come for me.

All I saw was the gun in Guild's hand and the front door of the house as it shuddered again.

BOOM!

Wood splintered and barely hung on as I scurried across the foyer and Guild wrenched his gaze to mine, his wide eyes full of panic. "The basement, Vivienne," he ordered. *"Get to the basement NOW!"*

I didn't stop, didn't think, I just ran. My bare feet skidded on the slick floor as another *BOOM* came and, with it, the sound as the fractured door gave in.

"Please...please...please..." I whimpered as I punched in the code with trembling fingers.

"You *are* NOT TAKING HER!" Guild roared.

Crack!

The sickening sound of a gunshot rang out. Terror plunged through me as the tiny red light on the lock turned from red to green. But the heavy thud of boots sounded, and as I yanked the handle to open the basement door, my world was invaded by the terrifying face of a familiar male....

Ashwood.

His dark eyes glinted and his lips curled with a demented smile. "Where the fuck do you think you're going?" he called out as he surged toward me.

I yanked the handle of the door, wrenched it open, and lunged for the darkness, until a merciless grip grabbed my hair and dragged me backwards.

"Let me go!" I screamed, kicking and fighting as he hauled me into the air.

The Order...they were taking me back to The Order!

I clawed and swung. My vision blurred under the tears as I was dragged backwards. All I saw was the open door of the basement slipping away as Ashwood flung me over his shoulder and carried me toward the front door. *"I WON'T GO BACK THERE! I WON'T FUCKING GO BACK THERE!"*

Cold night air swept over me. All I saw were dead bodies lying around the house, their faces blurring as the thud of steps and the throaty sound of a car's idling engine pushed in. I was yanked, and fell down Ashwood's body until my feet hit the ground.

My knees buckled with the impact and dropped me all the way to the asphalt. But I didn't stop. I punched my hand against the hard surface and drove myself upwards. All I saw was the streetlights and the night as I lunged.

"Bring her back here," a man's voice sounded.

The heavy thud of steps sounded in an instant as I was grabbed once more. I screamed and kicked and howled as he dragged me back to that waiting car. *"LONDON! LOOONNNDDDDOOOONNNN!"*

WHACK!

My head snapped to the side and my body followed.

Stars ignited behind my eyes as Ashwood dragged me back to that waiting car, the door now open. The blurry face of the man who waited for me turned sharper. Through the haze of agony, memories pushed in. The corridors of The Order, the smirk he'd given London. They were enemies. I'd known that then...just as I knew that now.

Daniels. That's what London had called him.

"I'm not going back there," I moaned, forcing the words out. *"I'd rather fucking die!"*

"No," he answered coldly. "You're not."

His words stopped me cold. Through the blur of tears, I saw the paper in his hand as he shoved it into my face.

"You're coming home with me instead." He lashed out, grasped my throat, and clenched tight. "Now be a good whore and get in the fucking car."

No...

No!

NO!

Ashwood grabbed me, then drove me through the open door and inside the car. There was no fighting now. No kicking and screaming as Daniels pushed in behind me and the door closed with a bang.

"I'm going to enjoy the fuck out of you." Daniels drove me forward until my face smashed against the seat. His hands mauled my breasts through the satin pajamas London had bought me as he groaned against my ear. *"London won't want you at all...by the time I'm done."*

Wait...want a hot as hell bonus scene between Viv and London? I wrote one just for you. Click here to grab it!

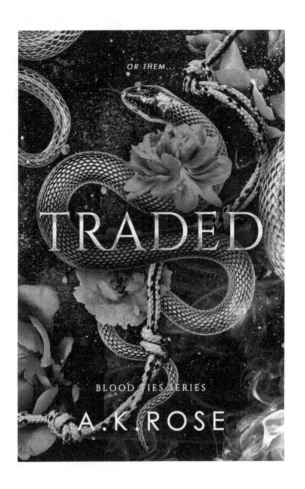

Preorder Traded here

I've been lied to, used...and played.

The Order took something from me...

My property.

Vivienne.

Releasing March 31st.